THE SILENT TERROR OF CHU-SHENG

SHADOW OF CHU-SHENG

YELLOW MAGIC

The **DANCING TUATARA PRESS** Books from **RAMBLE HOUSE**

CLASSICS OF HORROR

CLASSICS OF SCIENCE FICTION AND FANTASY

DAY KEENE IN THE DETECTIVE PULPS

THE SILENT TERROR OF CHU-SHENG

SHADOW OF CHU-SHENG

YELLOW MAGIC

EUGENE THOMAS

Introduced by

John Pelan

RAMBLE HOUSE

2014

Introduction © 2014 by John Pelan

Cover Art © 2014 Gavin O'Keefe

Shadow of Chu-Sheng — Originally Published by Sears 1933

To Otis Sheridan

Yellow Magic — Originally Published by Sears 1934

To Nez and The Three Christines

This edition © Ramble House Publishers 2014

ISBN 13: 978-1-60543-779-8

Edited by Fender Tucker

Dancing Tuatara Press #46

THE SILENT TERROR OF CHU-SHENG

TABLE OF CONTENTS

THE SILENT TERROR — THE MENACE OF CHU-SHENG

Ever since M.P. Shiel published his novel of the sinister Dr. Yen How (*The Empress of the Earth* or *The Yellow Danger*) in 1898, authors have been utilizing the Asian mastermind as the lead villain in their thrillers. Obviously, the best-known is Sax Rohmers' Dr. Fu Manchu, but there are dozens of examples of this type of novel, usually labeled derisively as "Yellow Peril".

When done poorly, (as was often the case) the result is racist drivel; when done well, some truly memorable characters and stories have been the result. We've actually come up with over a dozen volumes that we feel merit your attention and that will be added to the mix of weird menace, supernatural thrillers, and fantastic mysteries that you've come to expect from Dancing Tuatara Press.

Shiel considered both versions of his novel (the magazine serial is a full third longer than the book version!) to be mediocre hackwork, and I'd have to agree. Despite being formulaic, the Fu Manchu tales by Rohmer were vastly superior and hold up quite well today, nearly one hundred years after their initial publication. In fact, the main criticism of the Fu Manchu series has always been that Nayland Smith and Dr. Petrie (his opponents), are pretty colorless by comparison and completely overshadowed by "the Devil Doctor".

The first really noteworthy character to follow Fu Manchu was A.E. Apple's Mr. Chang. Mr. Chang's adventures comprised seven novels in the pages of *Detective Fiction Weekly* and make for an interesting counterpoint to the Fu Manchu tales. Whereas Fu Manchu is the mastermind orchestrating events behind the scenes with hundreds of henchmen to do his bidding, Mr. Chang is all too happy to carry out most of the dirty work himself.

By the mid-1920s, the genre was in full swing, with a veritable host of Asiatic fiends stalking the streets of Western cities, usually London or New York. San Francisco, with its huge Chinese population, is pretty much ignored.

By the 1930s, the genre had exploded to the point that characters such as Wu Fang and Dr. Yen Sin were given their own magazines, and *Operator #5* featured the most massive Asian invasion since Shiel's day with the long-running saga of "The Purple Invasion", which contained thirteen novel-length installments.

It's in the midst of this boom period that Eugene Thomas came to the fore with his novels of the deaf-mute villain, Chu-Sheng. Thomas is best remembered today for an entertaining bit of Theosophist nonsense, *The Brotherhood of Mt. Shasta.* This is unfortunate, as not only the present two novels, but also *Death Rides the Dragon* and *The Dancing Dead,* are truly excellent books that deserve to be much better known today.

A good part of the reason for the obscurity of Thomas' work is that while his publisher (Sears) was very good at selling home goods via catalog, marketing a line of fiction was not really their strong suit. We have no way of knowing what the print-runs were on Eugene Thomas' thrillers, but I suspect that the numbers were not large and none of the four titles were reprinted.

What sets Eugene Thomas apart from many of his contemporaries is not plotting, though he is an exceptional plotter, nor is it pacing, though you'll find that both novels are compelling page-turners; no, rather it is the ability to make the character of Chu-Sheng come to life. It's difficult enough to make a villain believable since thousands of writers forget the cardinal rule of creating a believable villain, and that is *that the character must not consider him/herself to be a villain!* The fact remains that every evil-doer, no matter how crazed, believes that their course of action is not only justified, but that any other course would be impossible. Thomas pulls this off with Chu-Sheng, making him far more than the sort of cardboard caricature that so often features in pulp-era thrillers. What's more, he gives us a fully three-dimensional character who doesn't get to speak a single word of dialogue!

John Pelan
Midnight House
Gallup, New Mexico

SHADOW OF CHU-SHENG

Chapter One

ONE STREET in Washington, not a stone's throw from one of the
buildings that had once been occupied by the Bonus Army, is the
curio shop of Ly Hoi. It is directly opposite a little park where
men, believing in destiny, sit on benches to wait for it. The dust-
encrusted windows of the shop hold a collection of ginger jars,
covered with wicker work, bright paper packages of tea, bits of
spurious carved ivory and embroidery of dubious ancestry.

A wide door leads to the cool interior which smells of dried fish
and sandalwood, old books and stale incense. The shop is hardly
more than thirty feet long, and is covered from floor to ceiling
with shelving holding discarded loot of the Orient.

The activities of a merchant were but the least of Ly Hoi's
businesses. He was, more than he was a merchant, a clearing
house for most unusual activities.

Oriental servants of the nation's capital flocked to the little
shop. Among the Negroes he had the reputation of a cunjur man
who got results for the charms and potions he sold. He translated
letters, wrote letters, lent money, was not above a transaction in
articles that might have been acquired in devious ways and—
among a certain clientele—had the reputation of having in stock
many things difficult to purchase across the counter of a department store. Such things, for instance, as a knife and the hand to
wield it from behind on a dark street; poisons . . . the slower the
poison, the higher the price. He seemed always to have at his finger-tips a most intimate knowledge of life in official circles of the
capital. And what he did not know, he would undertake to find out
for you . . . for a consideration. Nobody knew much about him.
The secret service had used him once or twice in obtaining information concerning foreign legations that had been hard to come at,
and although they kept an eye on him, left him pretty much alone.

On this particular day he sat alone on a high stool in the rear of his shop casting accounts. The sharp click-click of his abacus was the only sound to disturb the quiet of his shop.

The noise of the door opening caused him to lift his slanting black eyes to encounter those of a white man who stood in the doorway, fanning himself with a straw hat and looking upon Ly Hoi's abacus with a slightly cynical smile.

He was handsome, as these foreign devils go, observed Ly. A man whose emotions were as well disciplined as his muscles. The eyes smiled with the assurance of one who knows much and is aware of his wisdom. Rather reckless grey eyes that held in their depths a glint of steel. His skin was tanned as if from much exposure to a hot sun.

Ly Hoi slipped from his stool and came forward.

"You're Ly Hoi, the merchant?"

The man spoke in fluent Cantonese, but there was in his arrogant, staccato syllables a false intonation. He was, Ly Hoi decided, hardly an American. A European, possibly. Or a Slav. Or perhaps from one of those numerous little countries on the fringe of the Near East.

"I am Ly Hoi," he returned in English.

For answer the man brushed by him and walked toward the rear of the store. Stopped at the high desk where Ly Hoi had been sitting. The Chinese pattered after him in his felt-soled slippers.

"Are you alone?" the man asked, again in Cantonese. And again there was in his voice that note of unconscious arrogance.

This time Ly Hoi replied in the same dialect, a germ of suspicion beginning to multiply in his brain. What did this foreigner want?

"Not entirely," he answered. "My unworthy family reside in the rear of the shop."

The man made a quick gesture that brushed them aside as being beside the moment.

"There is no one else?"

"No one."

For one of the rare occasions in his life, Ly Hoi felt frightened. Why, he did not know. But the eyes that bored so steadily into his own did not match the young, bronzed face. They reminded him of the lidless, unwinking stare of a cobra. He answered in the affirmative.

"You have been recommended to me," the man said, "as one whose tongue is not hinged in the middle."

"There is no profit," Ly Hoi retorted, "in a loose tongue."

"Good," the other responded. He reached in an inside pocket and withdrew a fat wallet. Opening it, he withdrew slowly a hundred-dollar note and laid it upon the desk before him.

"The War Department to-day will issue orders to Captain Robert Nicholson to proceed to the Panama Canal Zone and report to the Commanding General for assignment. I want, not later than to-night, a copy of those orders, with the proper signature, and as complete a history of Captain Nicholson's service history as the files of the War Department can give. Can you do it?"

A hundred dollars! Ly Hoi's commercial instincts, never asleep, became more alert . . . but the War Department. Why did this stranger want these papers?

"Nay," he said, his suspicion and prudence outbalancing his desire for money. "I have had trouble with the police before. Even a camel will not drink twice of bitter waters."

The man laughed shortly.

"Not high enough, eh?"

The tones carried a cold undercurrent that made Ly Hoi uneasy. "All right. Two hundred dollars."

Ly Hoi's imagination took wings. But still his native caution held him to earth. It might be a trap.

"I cannot do it," he declared firmly. "It is against the law. And I do not risk prison."

For answer the man extended his hand, palm upward. The movement exposed to view a ring of hammered Chinese gold, thick and wide. Set in it was a yellow translucent stone about an inch square. And within the stone was the shape of a spider—its hairy, fuzzy legs spread out fanwise from its body. The head had the effect of reaching forward through the yellow stone, as if upon the verge of a leap. The black spider had not been cut upon the jewel. It was within it, as a fly is imprisoned within amber.

Ly Hoi's face went livid at sight of the ring.

"The Slayer of Souls. The mark of the Tongueless One," breathed Ly.

"It is the mark of the Tongueless One," agreed the other grimly.

"What is your will?" inquired Ly Hoi humbly.

"Those things that have already been told to you."

"It is an order," the Chinese said simply. He hesitated a moment and then asked. "Is it permitted that this unworthy one know to what use these papers are to be put? There may be other papers that this unworthy one can obtain that would be of assistance."

The stranger surveyed him a moment in grim silence. His hand dropped to the top of the desk, as if in a casual gesture, so that the ring was in full view. Ly's gaze flickered from the impassive face of the man to the ring and back again. A faint semblance of a smile was painted upon his yellow face for a moment.

"You need not fear," he said briefly. "I obey the Tongueless One."

The stranger smiled in turn. But it was a smile that held no mirth.

"I have no fear of betrayal," he said, equally brief. "Men do not betray the Tongueless One. I wish these papers because I take upon myself the identity of this Captain Nicholson."

"And the Captain himself—?" Ly left the question hanging in midair between them. The stranger finished it for him.

"Will not be in a position to protest," he said.

"May this unworthy one suggest," the Chinese laid, "that it would be simpler to use the original papers. They could be obtained. There are many dark streets in Washington."

The stranger shook his head impatiently.

"Impossible. The originals bear his signature, and his fingerprint to guard against just such a contingency arising. The orders that I carry must bear *my* fingerprint."

At almost the same moment that Ly Hoi was talking with the grey-eyed stranger in his shop on E Street, the subject of the discussion, Captain Robert Nicholson, was facing the Secretary of War across the latter's desk in the War Department.

The Secretary was speaking.

"On the face of it, Captain Nicholson, your transfer from Fort Hamilton to the Canal Zone is a routine matter . . . merely one of those shifts in post that take place dozens of times in an officer's career. That is what I want your friends, your associates, even your superior officers to think."

He paused a moment.

"But such, actually, is not the case."

He paused and drummed on the table top for a moment.

"You were born in China, I believe?"

"Yes. Hanoi province," Nicholson responded. "My father was a medical missionary there."

"Forgotten your Chinese?"

Nicholson smiled.

Always, the wonder of the East had waked a gypsy spirit in him. The magic and the mystery of China had possessed him since a boy. He knew its music . . . that blended discord and harmony. He knew its thousand smells, half fragrant, half repulsive, wholly enervating. But more than anything else, he had always been conscious of an unknown life underlying it all . . . of the throbbing of emotions he could not understand; of whispered suggestions hinting the existence of unmapped country; of marvels closely hidden, yet marking their presence, as it were, by means of a cryptogram to which he might find the key; of an atmosphere of mysteries that fired his imagination. More than once in the fantastic purple of a Chinese night he had felt himself standing on the brink of some discovery, his ears strained to catch the murmured sound that perhaps might be the master word of a great enigma. His brows puckered by the effort of peering so eagerly into the luminous darkness, in which, as behind a veil, figures, dim, secret and wonderful seemed to move.

That was why he smiled as he answered simply:

"I spoke Chinese before I spoke English."

The Secretary nodded.

"As I have intimated," he said slowly, "this transfer is not an ordinary matter. You have been selected for a special mission because of certain notations upon your service record, made by my predecessor. This mission may develop into nothing at all, or"—he paused a moment and then added with emphasis—"may decide the fate of the nation."

Nicholson's jaw tightened. A tiny spark of light appeared in his eyes. He said in unemotional, grave inquiry:

"Yes, sir?"

The Secretary opened his desk drawer and abstracted a clipping; handed it to Nicholson.

"Read that," he said curtly.

The Secretary studied the officer as the latter read. Nicholson was a person of inscrutable age, with skin brown as sandalwood, and crinkled at the corners of his grey eyes. And his face, his impatient, almost hard mouth, proclaimed him a man not easily cajoled or coerced. A good man for the task in hand, the Secretary told himself, a driver of men, exacting, relentless in his judgment of himself as of any other person.

Nicholson read the newspaper clipping carefully. It was from the New York *Herald Tribune.*

Mystery Ships Dog
U.S. Fleet At War Trials

One Unregistered Tanker, Flying No Flag,
Follows Vessels to Battle Grounds
By The United Press

SAN PEDRO, Calif., Oct. 21.—Mysterious ships have been trailing the United States battle fleet to sea in recent months—possibly with the intent of spying on maneuvers, it was learned today.

Naval officers, who refused to be quoted, said a number of oil tankers flying a foreign flag had "blundered" upon the scene of maneuvers. Unable to escape the prying eyes, naval headquarters announce maneuvers for a certain date, and then go through their exercises a day in advance.

One "mystery ship" in particular has followed the fleet to the battle grounds off San Clemente Island. It resembles a tanker, flies no flag, and is not registered at any Pacific Coast port, officers said. It never has been known to venture within the twelve-mile limit of United States ports.

Navy officers at first believed the presence of the tankers at the scene of maneuvers was accidental. But so often have these appearances occurred that fleet officers have become worried.

Scores of tankers flying a foreign flag take on crude oil cargoes at San Pedro each week. Although shipping records do not show that any unusual number of them sail when the battle fleet steams out of port. They invariably appear upon the scene a few hours later.

When Nicholson had finished, he looked up at the Secretary.

"That, Captain," the Secretary said, "is one of the reasons for your hasty transfer to the Canal Zone." He paused, and then asked abruptly. "Have you ever heard of a Chinese who calls himself Chu-Sheng?"

"The name is not an uncommon one," Nicholson said reflectively. "The family is an important one in certain districts of China."

"The man to whom I refer," the Secretary said, "is known as The Tongueless One, because he is a deaf-mute."

Nicholson hesitated for the merest fraction of a second. Into his brain flashed the thought that he should tell the Secretary what he knew of this man who called himself The Tongueless One. Already his lips shaped the opening phrase, when, instantaneously, an abstruse something in his soul surged up and submerged the opening word of his sentence in a deliberate decision.

Instead he said slowly:

"I have heard of the Tongueless One. Everyone in China, from coolie to mandarin, has heard of the legend, I believe."

"What is this legend?" the Secretary asked.

"He is reputed," Nicholson said, choosing his words carefully, "to live in a black pagoda as old as the hills of Chi'jen among which it stands, overlooking the city of Kara Khoja, the age old meeting place of the silk roads of the East and the West."

He hesitated a moment. "Kara Khoja is the heart of what is sometimes referred to as Black China, because it was from here, ancient Chinese records tell, that most of the sorcerers of the old dynasties came, and the legend has it that the Tongueless One is a descendant of some of the greatest of China's magicians. Certainly, the coolies fear the name of The Tongueless One and attribute magical powers to him. But I have never met anyone who could say, for a fact, that such a person existed."

The Secretary drummed on the desk top for a moment, his eyes looking out through the window toward the cool green reaches of the White House grounds next door.

"The Tongueless One," he finally said slowly, "is a living man . . . an exceedingly clever and cunning man. It is his power you will have to fight."

Nicholson repressed a desire to smile. He did not know then how the commonplace can intensify the terrible.

The Secretary caught something of the thought in Nicholson's mind.

"Do not underrate your opponent," he begged. "If only a part of the things that have been told to me are true, he is one of the most dangerous men alive to-day. And this man is in the Canal Zone at the present time. From certain information that has come to us, we believe that this dogging of the fleet, during maneuvers, is the forerunner of something far more dangerous and sinister that will have its inception in the Canal Zone with Chu-Sheng as the motivating force behind it."

There was a puzzled expression upon Nicholson's face.

"You think, then, that China . . ."

The Secretary cut the sentence short.

"No, Captain. Not China. Another Oriental power. Weeks ago we received information from our G-z agents in the Far East that two ships, ostensibly oil tankers, were undergoing mysterious alterations in naval yards of this power. They were so closely guarded that any attempt to reach them met with failure. These ships are, we believe, the same as those referred to in the clipping. Of late, radio operators on the fleet have been picking up messages in code, originating from a plant much more powerful than any on the fleet. Direction finders indicate that they originate on these tankers. The code has defied the efforts of our experts to break it down, but a certain symbol is recurrent in most of them. And this symbol, we are authentically informed, refers to Chu-Sheng.

"There, Captain, are the reasons for your transfer to the Zone. And you will not find your task an easy one." A somber note came into his voice. "One of the best men in the Army intelligence service has been assigned to the job of keeping tabs upon Chu-Sheng in Panama. A week ago he disappeared. Vanished utterly. So do not make the mistake of underestimating your opponent.

"In order to simplify matters and to provide you with as much free time as possible, I suggested to the Commanding General, in the orders assigning you to the Canal Zone, that you be assigned as officer in charge of the control room. An exceedingly important post in time of war, it is merely a routine assignment in time of peace, since all wires leading from it are disconnected. However, the post will keep you in constant touch with the General, which may prove of importance."

He rose and extended his hand.

"Good luck, Captain. And will you see the Assistant Secretary as you go out. He will give you your travel orders, and a folder containing all the information on Chu-Sheng that the department has been able to gather. Incidentally, you will go by plane. We are sending down three planes, with stops at Brownsville and Managua for fuel."

Chapter Two

PATRICIA FENTON'S hotel in Panama was a three-story structure set opposite a little plaza filled with palm and almond trees, with the languorous fragrance of frangipani, tainted by a breath from the mud flats left by the outgoing tide, creeping in to the interior dusk of her room.

She had disembarked at Balboa, the Pacific terminus of the Panama Canal, shortly before noon, and instead of going to the big rambling hotel in the American section, run by the Canal government, had followed her brother's recommendation and registered at the Casa Central.

Now, after a leisurely bath, the sun was nearing the tops of the palm trees in the plaza when she defended the stairs that led to the patio, with its rust-red tiles, warm and mellow in the afternoon sun.

She stood for a moment against the foot of the stairs, her slim young figure silhouetted against the dimness of the cloistered arches that surrounded the patio. She stood there only a moment. But it was long enough for Lieutenant Daniel Martin's roving eye to rest upon her.

"Boy, howdy!" he murmured to himself. "What a break for somebody."

For which he was not to be blamed. Pat was lovely enough to trouble hearts much less susceptible than his. Her black hair was a lacquered sheen, closely sleeked down to her small, delicately moulded head. Beneath her sweeping lashes, her eyes seemed as black as her hair, but when she smiled, there were golden glints in them; often a man found himself remembering those flecks of gold when he should have been remembering other things.

Then she moved further into the room and the indrawn breath whistled sharply through Dan Martin's teeth as he recognized her. He knocked over two chairs and almost upset a waiter in his haste to reach her side.

For Dan Martin had known Pat nearly all his life. They had played together as children and, although he had always been mercilessly impertinent and overbearing in his manner toward her, he had always held her in secret awe on account of her two years superiority in age and her subsequent vaster experience.

"Hot diggety!" he cried. "Pat Fenton. I wouldn't have believed dreams could come out so absolutely true."

"Dan," Patricia cried in astonishment. "Dan Martin. Why, you look positively grown up in that white uniform with that gold bar on your shoulder."

"Say, just because I'm two years younger than you is no reason for you to act like Noah's grandmother. Wimmen have even been known to marry younger men . . . and liked it."

Her eyes were suddenly warm with laughter.

"You don't say?" she said in mock surprise. "Am I to take that as a proposal?"

"Sure," he grinned, "any time. I'm a full-fledged second louie now, entitled by Act of Congress to be a gentleman and raise a family. Come on and sit down and have a drink while we discuss the wedding date. I'm down here on the Zone on my first tour of duty . . . aide to the Commanding General. But what in the world are you doing here, and when did you get in, and why, and how long will you be here, and will you have dinner with me to-night . . . and lunch tomorrow, too?" he added, after catching his breath.

Pat laughed as she slid into a chair.

"This morning . . . to meet my brother . . . I don't know . . . and yes . . . and maybe," she said, ticking off her answers on her fingers and matching his breathless tone. "Now that you've finished, haven't you got a nice long questionnaire you'd like me to fill out?"

"You have to be a fast worker in this man's army," he commented.

"I didn't know," she countered critically, "that anyone had ever accused you of slackness in that respect."

There was a grin on his freckled face.

"That's woman's inhumanity to man for you," he said, looking at her quizzically. "Right on the button, as usual. But after you've been here a little longer, you'll know why a fellow has to work fast in the Zone. Gosh, Pat, I had no idea until I came to Panama that so many women live so long." He turned to her with a smile. "Gee, it's swell to see you again! Lemme see: to-morrow afternoon we can take the launch over to Tobogo Island—that's out in Panama Bay, you know—and have a picnic lunch on the beach by moonlight. And then the day after I think I can wangle a couple of horses out of the quartermaster, and I'll show you some of the trails through the hills. And then the next day . . ."

He stopped with an injured expression, as she burst into a peal of laughter.

"Dan, will you never grow up?" she queried. Then she went on: "Did it ever occur to you to ask if I already had engagements?"

Even that didn't subdue him. He grinned.

"Well," he said hopefully, "you haven't, have you?"

"No," she admitted, "but you forget I've a brother arriving on one of the battleships and I'll have to save a little time for him."

"Aw, for pete's sake," he pleaded, "you've got a heart as cold as charity. You'll have your brother all the rest of your life. What's he doing with the fleet, anyhow? You haven't got any brother in the Navy."

She shook her glossy head.

"He's not. He's a major in the Coast Artillery reserve. But he's been doing a tour in the office of the Chief of Coast Artillery, and they detailed him to the fleet to study the effect of coast artillery fire on aircraft during the maneuvers."

She opened her bag and glanced immediately into a mirror. Pat, it developed, carried her lips and part of her lovely complexion in her handbag. She refinished her face.

"Classy bag," Dan commented, eyeing the modernistic design on it critically.

"It is good looking, isn't it?" she said, passing it to him. "I got it in Hayti."

Dan took the bag, not noticing that it was not closed and turned it over. A snapshot and the usual jumble of articles that a woman carries in her handbag fell out upon the table.

"Sorry," he said apologetically, "clumsy as usual."

"Oh, that's all right," she said. But there was a suspicious haste with which she snatched up the picture and returned it to the bag before gathering up the other articles.

"Is that," he drawled with his gay impudence, his impish eyes dancing, "by any chance my handsome likeness that you're carrying around with you? You don't mean you've been carrying the torch for me all these years?"

"You saw it," she countered. "It's a snapshot I've been carrying around for a long time for no good reason at all."

He took a long pull at the straw in his drink.

"Let's see, it's been about two years since I saw you last. Panama is sure the last place I expected to find you in, after that summer at Montauk Point. I thought you'd be married by now, after the way you raved about that John Somebody or Other the day I spent with you." He stopped and looked around at her. "Say, I'll bet that's his picture you're carrying around."

"And what if it is?" she queried.

"And you the hard-boiled gal," he said, "carrying around a picture for two years to look at every night before you go to bed."

"Summer flirtations never mean anything," she said. "I'd forgotten John ages ago. So, you see . . ." She ended in a shrug.

Dan, smiling, drew out cigarettes; passed them. He lighted hers, then his own, and flicked the match to the tiled floor. The smoke coiled about her head, leaving her face 'unobscured' to glow in the foggy blue as vivid, he told himself, as a flame burning through gauze.

"What's the matter?" he demanded with the impertinence which young people seem to expect from their own kind. "Did he give you the gate?"

She was silent for the fraction of a moment, her eyes fixed upon the mellow façade of the cathedral rising above the green of the plaza. Then she said evenly:

"Don't be silly. I haven't heard from him since that summer."

"You did like him, though, didn't you?" he probed.

"Of course I did . . . then. But that's ancient history. Tell me about yourself. Any love affairs?"

"Scads of 'em," he said shamelessly. "Dames fall for me like sinkers in coffee. I have to fend 'em off with my sword."

Pat laughed.

"You're such a fool, Dan," she said good naturedly. "But such a lovable fool."

"Ah," he retorted, "therein lies my fatal charm. What, I asks you, is more irresistible to a dumb dame than a lovable fool? The two go together like ham and eggs. My only trouble is in finding one dumb enough. But when I do . . . boy, what a pair we'll make."

"And you tell me that after your proposal of marriage? Boy, take your ring and go home. Just wait till the fleet gets in and I'll turn my big brother loose on you. By the way, when does the fleet get in?"

"That," he drawled, "is a military secret for which, in theory, I could face a firing squad for revealing. We simulate war conditions in the annual maneuvers, you know, and no one is supposed to know when the fleet arrives."

"I'll promise not to betray the secret to the enemy," she said, dimpling.

"Well, what reward if I betray my country's secrets?"

"My gratitude."

"Pretty empty reward, if you ask me. Anyhow, the fleet gets in to-night or early to-morrow."

"And when does the attack on the Canal take place?"

"End of the week, most likely. They'll all make the transit of the Canal. Then some of them will be assigned as defending fleet, and the rest of the ships will put out to sea and return as the hostile fleet . . . and capture the Canal, most likely, as they do every year."

Then he looked at her with dismay in his eyes.

"Sweet sister," he exclaimed. "Now I've gone and done it."

"Done what?" Pat wanted to know.

"Invited you to have dinner with me when I'm dining with the General and his wife. Seeing the old girl over there reminded me of it. Maybe I can wiggle out of it. I've got to go over and pay my respects, anyhow. You won't mind my leaving you a moment, will you?"

"Of course not," she said. "But it's quite all right about the dinner."

Her eyes followed his progress across the patio to a table on the far side of the room where a woman with a voice like a cultivated foghorn argued with a waiter. Then, not wishing to be caught staring, she turned her head away . . . and her heart gave a little bound.

Almost in arm's length stood a tall man, in whose pongee suit the sunlight seemed to take refuge and give it a golden sheen. His grey eyes were flickering about, searching for a waiter.

She called softly: "John."

The man's eyes flitted across her without recognition. His eyes widened a trifle   only that, but there was the impression of a steel spring tightening.

Thinking that he had not recognized her, she got to her feet.

"John," she said, and her eyes looked deep and hurt, "don't you remember me?"

The man looked at her squarely. His voice, when he spoke, was quietly pleasant.

"I'm afraid," he said courteously, "that you've made a mistake."

Then her ears caught, in a swift, slurring undertone, the words: "You've never seen me before."

She looked at him in utter bewilderment, something reaching out and touching her soul with the chill of an indescribable uneasiness.

"Why . . . why . . ." she stammered, at a loss for words.

Again that swift whisper evidently meant for her ears alone.

"For God's sake, Pat, play the game. You've never seen me before."

Then he raised his voice and his courteous tone carried to tables nearby.

"Sorry, I'm not the man you took me for," and, with a slight bow, he turned toward the little lobby of the hotel.

Her eyes followed him for a moment, then, with an abrupt gesture, she summoned a waiter. A folded bill was pressed into the man's hand.

"That man . . . the tall one in the pongee suit . . . just leaving the patio. Find out his name from the desk."

She sat quietly until the waiter returned with the name written on a slip of paper.

"Robert Nicholson, Captain, U.S.A.," she read, and for a moment she was possessed by an illusion that the figure that had been standing before her was not real, but a reflection upon a flawed mirror.

She stared out across the plaza in unseeing, meaningless scrutiny. Because she knew that the snapshot in her bag was that of the man who had just left the patio. And the name he had written across the back of the picture that day two years before was not Robert Nicholson, but John Sobieski.

Chapter Three

IN THE DOORWAY of the Casa Central, the man who had registered as Nicholson paused for a moment and looked out over the sunlit square before him.

He was feeling with full force that uncomfortable sensation of being watched that had harassed him ever since he had left Washington. A curiously prickly, cold feeling deep under the skin; an odd sort of tingling pressure. It was a queer sort of sensitivity that he had in common with most men who spend much of their time in the open. It was a throwback to some primitive sixth sense, since most savages and animals have it.

Never once had he been able to localize the sensation. It seemed to trickle in on him from all sides. He scanned the street. Three carametas were drawn up along the curb in front of the hotel. They were empty, save for dozing drivers. He studied the loiterers in the square opposite. There was no sign in them of watchers.

Yet eyes were upon him. He knew it.

And inwardly he was filled with a sense of panic. Patricia Fenton. The last person in the world he had expected to meet in Panama. And one of the few persons in the world who could penetrate his masquerade. What if one of the unseen watchers had witnessed that meeting. At the thought, he clamped his teeth tighter; drew a deep breath. He was under no illusions as to the game he played, and there was in his mind a very clearcut picture of the penalty that would be exacted should he slip. With this to aid him, he conjured up a series of quite surprisingly unpleasant pictures, for he had a strong imagination and was no man's fool. Also, he was guiltless of that madness which drives men to charge stupidly at impossibilities, as Don Quixote flung himself against the windmills. He must watch his step. And at all hazards he must keep out of the way of Patricia Fenton. She was, he told himself as he halted a moment to permit a car to pass, undoubtedly on a pleasure cruise, and if he registered at another hotel until he was assigned quarters, and avoided the usual tourist haunts, the danger would pass. It was unlikely she would move in Army circles.

Queer, he thought, how just the glimpse of her, the sound of her voice, had brought to a sharp focus pictures that he had tried to forget. He could see . . . and he shook his head determinedly and the picture faded. But it left him with a dull ache in his heart.

Overhead the molten sun poured down fierce rays; underfoot dancing heat waves rose from the pavement. In the palpable haze thus produced, men and vehicles moved back and forth like puppets behind a gauzy curtain, remote, ineffectual. Nicholson looked unnaturally tall and white in the glare, an individual marked for observation as he sifted through the traffic.

The street down which he walked was a torrid dusty world—a world swarming with life. Perspiring white men, Canal employees in white linen, khaki clad soldiers, Negroes from half the islands of the West Indies, Latins of every shade from pure-blooded Spaniards to café au lait, an occasional Chinese and Hindoo in occidental clothes, rubbed elbows in passing. And everywhere babies, naked black and brown babies with swollen stomachs, sleeping on doorsteps, rolling in the gutter, miraculously missed by horses' hoofs in the narrow, cobble-paved street. An occasional prostitute openly plying her lure from a doorway. But there was about it all a sense of order, of cleanliness, and activity that was not native to the tropics.

"The American touch," he told himself with a tinge of irony. "Well regulated and organized . . . even to the vice."

Three or four squares away the vista of walls melted suddenly into the desolate beauty of the bay, green as melted jade and filigreed with sunlight. Glancing at the street name on the corner of the building, the man called Nicholson turned down another narrow street, hardly more than an alley, climbed a flight of worn stone steps and was on the top of the sea wall.

He shot a glance behind him. That shadowy tracker of whose presence he had been conscious ever since he landed from the plane, had not materialized. But he understood. He was at the threshold of his destination. There was no further need for a watcher to keep tabs upon him . . . for the present. But his face was thoughtful. What sort of reception would he get? He had slipped back there at Washington. Just a tiny slip. But it was the little things that sometimes tripped a man up. And he could not afford to trip.

Far below him the tide chuckled and laughed against the huge stones. A line of green marked the furtherside of the bay, above which rose the lonely ruins of the cathedral of ancient Panama, destroyed by Morgan, the pirate. The air was heavy, damp, filled with the odor of growing things. The terrific fecundity of tropical life was heavy about him.

Boats were anchored almost beneath the sea wall. The water was fifteen . . . twenty feet deep there now. A few hours more and there would be only a stretch of coral reef and mud flats where the boats floated. Here and there a man fished from a *cayacua*, hollowed from a single log. In an angle of the sea wall a beggar, hardly more than a pile of rags, slept. A lazy life; a strange tropical world, riddled with carelessness, neglect, decay, so different from the streets he had just passed through.

The top of the sea wall was some twenty-five feet wide, and rising from its inner edge, hard by the stairs, was the wall of a house. It was no new structure, this. Built of the same quarried stone that composed the moss grown sea wall, it seemed a part of the ancient structure whose enormous cost had caused King Philip to strain his eyes from the window of his Madrid palace in an attempt to see it. The idea being, that anything that had cost so much must surely be large enough to be visible halfway across the world.

Nicholson came to a stop before an iron grille that stood across an arched opening in the middle of the blank wall of the forbidding looking house.

The passage behind the grille opened into a patio where the purple and scarlet of bougainvillea spilled over columns supporting a balcony, and snow white egrets posed on the edge of a pool built of opalescent pearl shell.

There was no one in sight. The man hesitated for the fraction of a moment.

No matter what the certainty of a coming ordeal a man may carry in his soul, he cannot help a certain shrinking when he knows his foot is on the threshold of it.

Then he stepped forward and rattled the grille loudly. After a moment a grass-sandaled Panamanian, flat of face and incurious of eye, shuffled up.

"Señor Mendoza?" the man called Nicholson queried.

The native replied in Spanish, and when Nicholson signified that he did not understand, he melted into the dim recesses of the patio again, leaving the visitor standing outside the grille.

Minutes passed and Nicholson was wondering if he should rattle the grille again, when the servant reappeared, this time with a boy of about 17 years in tow. This latter spoke English.

To him Nicholson repeated his request for Señor Mendoza.

Murmuring a conventional Spanish phrase the boy unlocked the grille, and conducted Nicholson across the patio where the afternoon sun picked out the pattern of dull red and ivory in the ancient Spanish tiles and intensified the colors of the hibiscus blossoms growing in great burnt-orange pottery urns. An opening . . . more of a slit than a door in the four-foot thick walls . . . proved the entrance to a windowless room where the boy signified the visitor was to wait. A lamp with shades of thinnest pearl shell glowed on carved Spanish furniture, on a long polished table of native mahogany, on old portraits looking out of heavy gold frames.

Nicholson turned suddenly at a slight sound behind him. A man stood in a doorway leading to an inner room . . . a tall, gaunt, slightly stooped man with a face reminiscent of a vulture.

"You wished to see me," he asked in almost accentless English. "I am Diego Mendoza."

"Permit me," Nicholson said courteously, and handed the man a card.

Mendoza glanced at it.

"Won't you be seated?" he asked, indicating one of the high-backed chairs. Nicholson smiled inwardly as he noticed that the chair the Spaniard indicated stood in the pool of mellow light cast by the pearl shaded lamp. "May I offer some refreshment, yes? A glass of wine?"

"Thank you, no," Nicholson said. He dropped his hand to the table top. The Spaniard's eyes flickered for a fraction of a second to the ring, with its setting of translucent yellow stone in which cold depths a black spider was held suspended. There was no expression on his face. "As a matter of fact, my visit is rather an impertinence."

"So?" came from the Spaniard whose face formed a bronze oval above the dead white of his linens. Just the one word. Throwing the entire burden onto Nicholson's shoulders.

"I was informed in Washington," Nicholson went on slowly, "that your house is an exceedingly interesting one."

"You are most kind," Mendoza said. "Will you smoke?" He extended a mahogany box. "It *is* an old house. The only house of the ancient days that remains intact in Panama. One of my ancestors built it when Morgan, the pirate, burned old Panama four hundred years ago, and the city was removed to its present site. Save for necessary repairs and the addition of a few modern comforts, it has not been touched since."

Nicholson, in the act of lighting a cigarette, glimpsed a smile on the long, narrow face. Even after the match expired and they were in semi-dusk again, two pale ghosts at the very frontier of the stars, he imagined he could still see that smile. Rather mocking. Rather haunting. A sensation, faintly cold, spread over him.

"I wondered," he said slowly, "if you would think me presuming if I were to ask to be shown over the house?"

There was a thin film of dust over the polished surface of the table. Idly his hand went out, his forefinger traced a line or two in the dust. A numeral. Two numerals. The figure 92.

Then he glanced apologetically at his host.

"I've heard that the Mendoza collection of Chinese art is marvelous . . . probably the best outside of a museum in the world. Would it be possible for me to see it?"

For a moment the Spaniard sat quite still and stared at Nicholson out of his black, opaque eyes. Something naked reached out and touched the latter's soul, leaving the chill of an indescribable uneasiness. Then Mendoza dragged his hand across the table top, obliterating the figures, and rose.

"If you will follow me," he said silkily, "I think I can promise you something quite marvelous in the way of Chinese art. It is not ordinarily open to the public. But in your case I think we can make an exception. Your credentials seem to be quite satisfactory."

As the iron grille at the entrance to the Casa Mendoza had swung to behind the man called Robert Nicholson, a bundle of rags lying in a corner of the sea wall parapet stirred and resolved itself into a man . . . a Chinese with the broad, flat face of one from the borderland of China where the blood of Tibet mingles with that of the sons of Han.

Slowly the figure got to its feet and limped off down the broad sea wall, past Chiriqui prison, where the dungeons are flooded at high tide, and down a flight of steps, opposite the French consulate, several hundred yards further along.

Then, when he reached a narrow winding alleyway whose depths were turned into bitter, blotched duskiness by the overhanging houses, despite the stabbing rays of the afternoon sun, he broke into a shuffling run. Through a network of narrow streets he kept up the run, through lanes where the poor, unwashed and diseased of the tropic's motley races seemed to live together in friendship and evil odors. He kept up the run until he reached the façade of a house almost as old as that of the Casa Mendoza . . . a simple place; thick, weather-beaten walls, solid, eternally calm; great weather-beaten doors, tall enough for a man on horseback. As if his coming had been foreseen, the great doors swung open noiselessly on well-oiled hinges; then swung to behind him.

A word or two in the guttural Mongol of the Gobi, of Inner Mongolia . . . the tongue of the red-faced clansmen who once buried China under a bloody avalanche . . . passed between the new arrival and the gatekeeper.

The new arrival trotted up the stairs that led to the balcony of the patio and scratched gently on a massive door of wood let into the stone wall at their head. In answer the door swung open.

Through the casement on the opposite side of the room, sunlight poured, like water released from a floodgate, sluicing a great inlaid chair where sat a Chinese . . . a tall man with a square, expressionless, yellow face. In the stabbing rays of the sun through the open window casement, a hint of sadness showed in his hooded eyes. He was clothed in a robe of vivid orange.

Advancing toward him, the newcomer made a low obeisance and the man in the chair raised his hand in a gesture of benediction.

"One enters the house of the Tongueless One, O Excellency."

"Who is this one?"

"A foreign devil of the Americans who speaks not the tongue of the gatekeeper. His name he gave as Captain Nicholson. But he wears no uniform."

For a moment there was silence in the room as the man in the chair gazed out through the window to where the Gulf of Panama spread out like a purple map, contoured with rich gleams; the west was peach-red, behind the fortified islands at the Pacific entrance to the Canal.

Then he said quietly, speaking with that air of absolute authority that only years of use of it can give:

"Return to your watch on the house of the Tongueless One. If the man Nicholson comes out, follow him. Report to me his movements; those to whom he speaks. If he has not come out by midnight, then return here for further orders."

The man bowed deeply.

"It is an order, O Excellency."

He made his exit backwards and closed the door behind him. For a long moment the eyes of the man in the chair were fixed on a l'ien box on the table beside him, a box that had once contained the rice paste and carmine and kohl of an empress, as if his thoughts were using the bronze top as a focus for concentration.

Then he picked up a padded stick and struck the bronze gong on the low table. Before the rich, deep-throated sound sank into an echo, a Chinese appeared at another door.

"It is an appointed time," he said in clipped accents. "Bid the brethren gather in the Room of the Gods."

Meanwhile, far out at sea, the sun melted in a furnace of smoky gold across the water where the main battle fleet of the United States Navy steamed toward Panama.

Chapter Four

YOUNG DAN REGARDED PAT with mock gravity on his return to the table.

"Beware of the Greeks bearing gifts," he said portentously.

Pat cocked an eye at him inquisitively. She had not yet recovered from the shock of the encounter of a few minutes before.

"I never," she returned in as close an approximation of his tone as she could summon, "look a gift horse in the face."

"I come," he announced, "as a herald bearing tidings; as an ambassador upon a delicate mission."

"Advance, ambassador, and give the countersign," she laughed.

"Do you, by any chance," he queried, "admit the ownership of a brother named Leslie Fenton?"

"Guilty," she said promptly. "Is it to be a firing squad at sunrise, or merely life imprisonment?"

"Worse, much worse," he said. "In fact, I see no way of escaping the invitation of the General's wife to be her guest for the duration of hostilities."

"But I don't know the good lady," Pat protested.

"That's a matter of small consequence to the old battle axe," Dan grinned. "Besides, that's easily remedied. Come over and I'll introduce you."

"Oh, but I couldn't accept, Dan," Pat said quickly. "I'm here to meet my brother, and he'll expect me to be here at the hotel."

"That's just the point," Dan answered. "The General's wife wirelessed your brother this afternoon asking him to be her guest while the fleet's in port. And, of course, without you, he won't accept. But with you already a captive to her bow and spear, she'll have no trouble in bagging him. And for some obscure reason the General is keen on having your brother as a house guest. Made quite a point of it, in fact."

Pat laughed. "It's a good thing you're in the Army and not the diplomatic service," she said. "In other words, the General's wife wants me, because without me she can't get my brother."

"Spoken like a man," he applauded. "Now may I tell her you'll be glad to accept?"

"You may not," she said. "But you may take me over to her table, so that I may thank her for the invitation."

Mrs. William G. Chenery proved to be the woman with the voice like a cultivated foghorn. She had the determined jauntiness of one bent upon retaining youth. Pat admired the skillful help of her dressmaker and speculated as to whether she had had her face lifted. From the way in which the ends of her red bobbed hair were pulled forward at the temples, it seemed likely.

"Why didn't you let me know that you were coming down?" Mrs. Chenery boomed, the idea apparently never occurring to her that a few minutes before Pat had never heard of her. "I'm so glad that you're going to stay with us. We'll have your things packed right away and taken up to Quarry Heights. You couldn't possibly stay here in this hotel. You'd be bitten to death by scorpions before morning."

"I'm sure it can't be as bad as that," Pat said, dimpling.

"My dear, you don't know these countries," Mrs. Chenery insisted, with solemn conviction. "Look at that man over there," she continued in a throaty whisper that carried to the far corner of the patio, and bobbed her head vigorously in the direction of an unsuspecting Spaniard who was seated on the opposite side of the place, dozing over a drink. "He's been watching me ever since I came in. He knows I'm the General's wife, so he doesn't dare, otherwise he'd have tried to lure me into one of those terrible seduction parlors long before this."

"Seduction parlors?" Pat queried, wide-eyed.

"Yes, the place is full of them. These Latins have absolutely no morals. Oh, you'll learn things if you stay down here long enough. So, my dear, you see the necessity of staying with us. You really need someone to put you wise."

Pat smiled. "It's awfully kind of you to want me, but . . ."

"No," Mrs. Chenery warned the world at large, shaking an admonishing finger. "I won't have it. Why, it's a part of the Army code of hospitality. The General would never forgive me if I left an Army woman down here in this perfectly frightful hotel to have her throat cut."

"But my brother isn't a regular Army officer," Pat protested. "He's a reserve officer doing a tour of duty in the office of the Chief of Coast Artillery, detailed to the Navy for the duration of the maneuvers, so . . ."

"Don't be absurd," the foghorn said placidly. "Of course he's an Army man. Everybody in the Army knows of Harry Fenton . . ."

"Leslie," murmured Pat, biting her lips helplessly.

"Harry Fenton," went on Mrs. Chenery determinedly. "You must come right up this afternoon, and I'll have the General wireless your brother that you're staying with us, and that we're expecting him, too. Dan," she turned to Martin, "tell those people at the desk that Miss Fenton is checking out. The General will send a car down for her baggage."

Dan raised his eyebrows inquiringly at Pat, a broad grin on his young face. Pat shook her head slightly. Oblivious to the fact that Dan had not moved from his seat, Mrs. Chenery's torrent of words flowed back toward Pat.

"My dear, I want you to look your best at dinner to-night. I've the most marvelous dinner partner for you . . . perfectly devastating."

Anger was rising in Pat like a tide at the unceremonious way in which her life was being ordered. She saw no way out of the situation save abruptly to countermand the order that had been given the young lieutenant.

She was about to speak, but Mrs. Chenery ran on as endlessly as the babbling brook.

"I know you'll find him the most marvelous thing you've ever laid eyes on," she ran on. "He only arrived this morning by plane . . . Nicholson, his name is, Captain Robert Nicholson."

"What did you say the name was?" Pat asked quickly.

"Captain Nicholson. Oh, don't tell me that you know him. That would be too frightfully thrilling."

"No," Pat said slowly, "I don't know him. But from your description I'm sure the experience will be an—er—interesting one."

She turned toward the waiting lieutenant.

"It's all right Dan. Please tell them at the desk that I am checking out," she said.

Chapter Five

THE MAN WHO CALLED HIMSELF Nicholson followed the Spaniard across the patio. At its far side he paused before a great door of *Moko* slabs, so hard that even the edge of a keen axe would be turned.

"We guard our treasures well," Mendoza said seriously.

"They are worth guarding," Nicholson responded.

The Spaniard tapped on the door . . . a rhythmic tapping that had in it something of the voodoo drum beats that the officer had heard in the hills of Hayti . . . an alternate tapping with the fingers and the base of the hand. It seemed incredible that the sound could carry through thick *Moko* slabs until Nicholson noted that Mendoza was tapping upon a little square of pierced copper inset in the wood. He smiled grimly. A microphone that picked up the sound and carried it to wherever the guardian of the door lurked. His mind subconsciously recorded the rhythm of the tapping; he felt his fingers moving in unison with those of the Spaniard.

The door swung open. Nicholson watched interestedly as the door opened, apparently without human agency. A flight of stairs, beginning just within the arched doorway, went downward into blackness.

Some trace of Nicholson's surprise must have shown on his face. The Spaniard smiled slightly.

"If a thing is worth guarding, it is worth guarding well," he said. "Keys may be lost or stolen. Passwords may be betrayed . . . or sold. But not even torture can wring a secret from a machine." He paused a moment and then went on with a certain amount of pride in his voice. "This door will open . . . from the outside . . . only in response to a series of electrical impulses set in motion by code rapping upon the microphone in the door. Without that"—he shrugged—"even explosives would fail."

He started down the stairs. Nicholson followed him. The door closed automatically and noiselessly behind them. And upon its closing a faint light tinged the darkness that shrouded the stair well . . . a light that came from insets of thick glass in the stone rises of the stairs. Just enough light to prevent a person from stumbling, yet not enough to illuminate the darkness. Ahead of him the Spaniard had become a pair of feet and legs that vanished into nothingness.

Nicholson had the peculiar sensation that the blackness was absorbing him, that in leaving the sunlit patio above he had left life itself. The luminous dial of his wristwatch wavered before him like a fleeting soul.

As Mendoza trod on the last stone slab of the stairs, the blackness was suddenly flooded with light . . . a brilliant, white, intolerable glare that came from dozens of reflectors inset in the ceiling, the wall—even at the jointure of floor and wall where the stair ended. In the glare the two stood out in ultra-clarity . . . in shadowless relief.

They were facing a wall of quarried stone in which there was a door.

"This," Mendoza told him, "is the entrance to what was once the treasure chamber of the Viceroy of Spain, when the laden mule trains moved over the Gold Road to dump their precious cargo onto the Plate Fleet at Porto Bello. Then this place was filled with ingots of silver from Peru, gold from Panama, emeralds from Colombia, pearls from the Gulf of Baja California. Its location was secret then. Now, all knowledge of its existence is lost, save to a chosen few."

He stopped. As if the cessation of his voice had been a signal, the lights in the little room dimmed and the door slid back noiselessly into the stone wall, revealing a passage somewhat wider than the one containing the staircase.

Nicholson took one step forward and then sprang back with an exclamation, icy cold chills playing an obbligato up and down his spine.

In the center of the passage, less than three feet away, reared the hood of a swaying cobra. Not the ordinary cobra of India, deadly though he is, but the King Cobra of Siam and Burma— vicious, swift and holding certain death in its fangs.

Nicholson's hand went swiftly to his pocket for the little automatic he carried.

It was gone.

From behind him came a little chuckle.

"I think you carelessly left your gun on the table upstairs," said the Spaniard's voice. "However, this is one instance when it will not be needed. Permit me to introduce one of the guardians of our—er—art treasures. No, don't be alarmed, Captain. He is merely a precaution to make sure that the person entering has a right to enter. Permit me."

Nicholson moved to one side, still keeping his eyes fixed on the deadly thing blocking the passage. Mendoza pressed forward steadily, and as steadily the cobra retreated before him until suddenly it had vanished in the shadows . . . under the pull of the horsehair cord noosed about its head.

"A most effective guardian to one not knowing that in boldness lies success," Mendoza said with his chuckling laugh. Nicholson assented grimly. A man would not be inclined to dispute the passage with *that* guardian.

They walked on. The passage, which was floored and lined with heavy masonry, was roofed in places by the natural rock, but there were spaces beamed with heavy timber, black with age. The floor and walls seemed very ancient, but the roof had been repaired more than once within the century. The level could not have been more than thirty or thirty-five feet underground, judging by the number of steps they had descended and, curiously enough, there was a distinct draught of fresh air. The passage took a sudden turn and Mendoza said:

"We are now under the sea wall."

At a heavy curtain of black that closed the further end of the passage the Spaniard stopped and turned, faced Nicholson.

"You go on from here alone," he said.

Nicholson nodded, stepped forward, passed between the folds of the curtain; stood on the further side in a dim greenness . . . a greenness that gave the illusion of standing in the midst of green water. He was at the far end of a great hall, a space many times longer than it was wide.

Inset in the stone walls, at regular intervals, were deep niches and in these were statues, illuminated by soft colored lights streaming up from below. Some of these Nicholson recognized. Opposite to him was an image of Janesseron, the three-eyed God of Thunder. Beyond that was a gilded statue of Han Chung-le, the greatest of the Taoist immortals, who was supposed to have found the elixir of life. Further down he thought he recognized a life-sized statue of Kwin-yin, Goddess of Mercy. He smiled a trifle grimly. Tibet . . . Old China . . . Mongolia. A curious mixture. But a fitting one.

Silence, it seemed, was part of the mystery that surrounded the hall. There was no light save the green, underwater tinge in which dim shuttles of the colored lights from the statues swam. The sensation was of being in a grotto under water and looking through it toward light shining through the sea outside. He almost expected to see fish swimming through the pale green air. There was nothing about it to understand. It stripped incomprehension naked and left it aware of itself.

But he was conscious of these things, rather than he saw them directly, for the thing that caught his eye, held him in breathless amazement, was the far end of the hall.

There, silhouetted blackly against some gleaming silvery material, was the gigantic shadow of a Chinese.

It took him a full minute to realize that the shadow was that of a man seated upon some dark object bathed in the shadows, his reflection cast upon the shimmering wall behind him by cunningly arranged lights.

It was Chu-Sheng, the Master, the Tongueless One, the central core of the mystery in which Nicholson was involved.

A sound . . . the soft whisper of bare feet on stone . . . caused him to turn. On either side of him stood a Chinese clad in black. They had materialized out of the darkness like somber ghosts.

A slim, keen knife gleamed in the hands of each man.

A voice spoke. A soft voice, with the oddest inflexion imaginable . . . a soft slurring that was like no accent Nicholson had ever heard . . . a tonelessness that was like that of a person speaking in a dream.

"Halt, Captain Nicholson."

Nicholson did not move. He strained his ears. Try as he might, he could not tell from where the voice came. It seemed to come from all points of the hall.

For a moment there was silence. Then the voice spoke again. And this time the language was the clipped Chinese of the North with the faintly guttural inflection of the Manchu, the conqueror. And there was a note of menace in the soft tones.

"Death waits hungrily in those knives, Captain Nicholson."

Nicholson switched to Chinese himself, speaking the Manchu with fluency, and his tone matched that of the unseen owner of the voice, inflection for inflection. He flung his words straight down the hall, at the gigantic unmoving shadow staining the wall at the further end.

"I seek not death," he countered, "but The Tongueless One."

"And if he whom you call The Tongueless One were to ask you, 'How can we do our duty by the dead, when we are unable to do it by the living?'—what would be your comment?"

"I would reply with the ancient wisdom of Confucius who answered the same question from Chi Lu by saying, 'Before we know what life is, how can we know what death is?' "

"Hao!" the unseen voice commented, and Nicholson did not know that the word of commendation was also a signal to the two guards that he had passed the test and that there was no longer need of their presence.

Then the voice said again, simply:

"Approach the Master."

As Nicholson neared the far end of the hall, he almost came to a halt in astonishment. He saw now what the dimness had prevented him from seeing before. Chu-Sheng was seated upon the head of a gigantic spider, a monstrous black thing that sprawled across the end of the hall almost as if crouched for a spring. Fat, horrible legs spread fanwise from its bloated body, its black eyes staring inscrutably into his. It took him a full minute to realize that its great shape had been cunningly carved and that the dreadful, inscrutable eyes were of jet-like jewels. But whoever the unknown genius who had cut it, he had created a marvelous likeness to a living thing. By some trick the eyes blazed out of it with the same living, jewel-like brilliancy of those of the man who sat upon its head.

He was aware of a curious mingling of feelings ... repulsion and a peculiar sense of familiarity, like the trick of the mind that causes what is called double memory, the sensation of having experienced the same thing before. There was something sharply familiar about it all ... a man seated upon the head of a gigantic spider. He had an irritated feeling that he ought to know it; that if he tried hard enough, he could remember it; that memory of it was just over the border of consciousness. Also he had the feeling that it meant something rather dreadful. Something better forgotten.

As he came nearer, involuntarily his eyes shifted up to the glistening shimmering fabric that hung flat against the wall behind the Tongueless One. By some trick of the lights it was made to seem convex ... a huge bubble of light suspended in green darkness. Little ripples of shimmering color ran over it as the fabric seemed to stir slightly. And yet, strangely enough, the shadow of the man did not waver. There was an odd touch of legerdemain about it, like the swift work of a master magician.

Little doors were opening in his brain . . . ah, he had it now! He remembered where he had seen a spider like that before . . . in the secret crypt of a ruined temple half buried in the drifting sands of the Gobi . . . What was it, Kendall, the archeologist had called it? . . . The Hunshuh . . . the Slayer of Souls . . . that was it . . . Hunshuh, the mythical spider that symbolized the principal that is inimical to life . . . not death precisely. More accurately annihilation. And he remembered, too, Kendall's statement that inner Asia was filled with ancient legends concerning it . . . that the symbol had been found carved on the blades of strange weapons unearthed in old Mongolian tombs . . . that he had seen it carved on the living rock high up in the Andes of South America . . . chiseled on stones of ruined temples in India whose history was lost in the mists of antiquity . . . What was the meaning of it here in this hidden room in Panama?

Desperately his mind grappled with the problem and found no solution, even as the nerve centers of his brain felt the tremendous force behind the eyes of Chu-Sheng sweeping across him like a paralyzing ray. He felt the cold, deadly shock of resistless malign power, intangible, inexplicable, yet terrifyingly real. His body, to his surprise, was tense, covered with cold sweat.

And then he stopped short in amazement.

Seated upon a cushion between the forelegs of the great spider, directly beneath its glistening black fangs, was a girl. And what a girl!

Outlined by a faint glimmer of light against the blackness of the crouching spider where she sat, her garments full and shimmery as cobwebs in the sun, and confined at the waist by a girdle of gold cloth that was only a shade or two darker than her marvelously smooth skin.

Then she spoke and by the soft tones of her voice he knew it was she whose voice he had heard before.

"Be seated, Captain Nicholson," she said.

He was aware of something that he had not noticed before, of a low stool directly in his path. He dropped upon it and studied her covertly. There was not one thing about her to give a clue to her race. No more than her lips, did her eyes or hair, coloring or body hint an answer. She seemed a slender figurine of age-old ivory . . . something created by a master sculptor of a vanished age into which life had been instilled by the rigid motionless figure of the man seated upon the head of the spider above her. He asked abruptly:

"Who are you?"

"I am the Voice of the Master," she said, and he noticed that she had an odd way of burring the words through her unmoving lips. Although she was staring straight at him, she did not seem to be seeing him.

Her level gaze brooded as though, for always, she had seen all and seen nothing. It was uncanny. The eyes seemed to be staring through him, as though fixed on some remote point in infinity behind him.

"Keep your eyes upon the Master," she ordered and Nicholson switched his gaze from the figure of the girl to the black robed form of the man upon the head of the spider, sitting there so motionless that he might have been carved from ebony and bronze. Only the eyes. They were wells of cold evil, agleam with sinister wisdom, older than mankind.

A lightening of the green dimness about him caused his eyes to wander upward. Colored lights were playing over the surface of the bubble of light . . . lights that gleamed and sparkled like shining silver in the sun . . . lights that, curiously enough, seemed to flow and ebb in waves. His eyes dropped again and encountered those of the gigantic spider. For an instant he had the absurd feeling that the dreadful, inscrutable eyes had become alive, were weighing him. He brushed the thought aside.

The girl spoke again, the vacant expression still filling her eyes, the level gaze still fixed upon some point behind him. Her voice still held that odd toneless inflection. He felt a queer shiver as he watched the scarcely moving lips through which the syllables edged their way.

"You come to me of your own free will, Captain Nicholson. Does the reward for one who succeeds balance the punishment for him who fails in the test?"

"It does," Nicholson answered firmly.

"Those who work with me are always under the control of Destiny as represented by me," the slow, passionless voice went on. "I use the talents of my servants to the uttermost, not waste them. I suitably and justly reward them, and where I punish . . . the punishment is just. And I do not choose a thousand haphazardly on the chance that a few will be of the right metal. I select the few and see that nothing prevents their development into what I desire."

Under the words Nicholson read truth. To this odd, monstrous intellect men and women were only puppets moving over a worldwide stage. Suffering, sorrow, anguish of mind or of body, were to it nothing but reactions to situations which it had contrived. Like the ancient evil whose symbol he rode, souls were his playthings.

"Your impersonation of Captain Nicholson, whose place you took, is clever," the toneless voice went on. "You have been accepted by the Commanding General as the man you pretend to be. But there is a test yet to be made. The Master does not entrust his secrets lightly."

"I am ready," the man who called himself Nicholson said quietly (and did not realize that even a master hypnotist prefers to gain the victim's own consent before beginning to exert his authority).

He *was* conscious of the fact that the eyes of the man on the spider's head were regarding him intently . . . twin black pools that were shutting him off from anything else . . . submerging him. He wrenched his own eyes away with an effort.

The girl began a low chant . . . a chant upon three minor themes, repeated and repeated and intermingled, and he was conscious of the odd fact that the chant was in rhythm with the flow of light across the surface of the great bubble of light suspended in the darkness. The sound of the chant seemed to call to him like some flying spirit in a storm; claim him. It seemed to summon him back to something he had forgotten centuries ago. It drew him as empty space draws a giddy man, to the very edge of the precipice. Steadily it gained in strength and massiveness until it had enveloped him completely in a silent, receptive atmosphere which he could not shake off, and at the very core of it, at the flaming center of his soul, was the sound of the chant.

And suddenly he knew. Knew beyond the shadow of a doubt. Knew the reason for that toneless inflection. Knew the reason for that fixed gaze that passed through and beyond him.

She *was* the voice of the Master. Through her lips Chu-Sheng, the Tongueless One, was speaking. She was hypnotized, and through some mysterious channel of telepathy he was communicating to her brain the thoughts he wished expressed in words.

That accounted also for the rigid pose of Chu-Sheng.

Something stronger than himself impelled Nicholson to look up at the bubble of light. He tried to keep his eyes away from it, as the girl's chant brushed his ears softly and subtly, but he could not. He could not understand the words of the chant. It was an ancient tongue that she was using . . . one whose roots struck far deeper down in the soil of time than any Nicholson knew.

And then he saw (or thought he saw) the first stirrings of the great spider. He knew that it could not be so, yet the monstrous legs were stirring, twitching as if life were flowing into them after centuries of absence. A breath that had in it the cold of outer space touched him as the great head seemed to lift and the black ageless pools of light that were its eyes focused upon him . . . he felt a sense of inhuman power surging about him . . . the great spider was moving . . . the great hairy legs were slowly drawing up beneath it just as if it were preparing to spring . . . something was probing, probing into his dulled mind . . . seeking to drag forth the secret that lay buried there . . .

Chapter Six

AN OFFICIAL CAR WAS WAITING when Pat and Mrs. Chenery left the Casa Central, the starred flag flying from its hood denoting that it belonged to the General.

They turned into Calle Central alongside the old cathedral where the Virgin of the Pillar, a plaster saint in scarlet and blue robes, stood in a tiny chapel open to the sidewalk, and then on through a rising sea of corrugated iron roofs, of stone and concrete houses, topped with red tiles, along narrow, twisting streets. A sharp turn and the new American town of Ancon flowed up the side of Ancon Hill. Their car sped along steep roads bordered by palms and flowering trees, passed the cool whiteness of the world-famous Ancon Hospital. Lining the roads were the houses of Canal employees, set back from the street, screened verandas almost hidden behind great clumps of hibiscus and oleander. The trunks of some of the trees were laden with clusters of orchids, brought from the jungle and wired to the trees, their sprays of tawny orange, brown, lavender and white blossoms making the gray trunks soaring pillars of color.

The car turned around the shoulder of Ancon Hill, and a panorama of tropical verdure lay before them, with the straight white ribbon of the Canal stretching through the marshy plain to the first set of locks at Miraflores. Then a plunge into tree-bordered streets again to the Army headquarters of the Canal Zone.

Sunset was furling its geranium petals when the car stopped in front of a two story building of white concrete, set on the edge of a cliff in the midst of trees and shrubbery. A few stars had already broken out like sparks of white heat on the torrid sky.

"Oh, how pretty!" Pat exclaimed.

"Pretty," snorted the foghorn voice of her hostess. "It's terrible. I'm always afraid that the house will slide down the side of the hill. Keeps me awake nights. Don't know why they ever perched the Commanding General's quarters on the side of a hill like this. Be all right for a second lieutenant."

Pat said nothing as she followed her hostess into the house. But she could have sworn there was a grin of half-concealed pity on the face of the enlisted man who acted as chauffeur. She was half inclined to grin with him, but sternly repressed the impulse.

"This is a perfectly dreadful room," her hostess said, throwing open a door near the head of the stairs on the second floor, "but it's really the best we've got. It makes me feel so terribly ashamed whenever we have a guest. But I'm sure you'll understand. Army people get kicked around from pillar to post so much, you know."

"Oh, but I think it's perfectly gorgeous," Pat said, surveying the wide, cool room, with its blue Chinese rug, the flaming San Bias Indian embroideries in crude blues and reds and raw oranges that hung against the cool whiteness of the walls. A wide verandah ran along one side of the room, screened against mosquitoes, and on the other a wide window looked out over the tree-clad slopes of Ancon Hill. The furniture was of split, woven bamboo, lacquered white, with a tiny edging of green.

She dropped down into one of the long bamboo chairs.

"You Army people may be knocked around from pillar to post . . . but if this is a sample of them, you're certainly to be envied," she said.

Pat was wishing frantically that Mrs. Chenery would get out of her room and allow her to unpack her bags in peace. She had a slight headache and the elder woman's aimless and endless chatter was setting her nerves dangerously on edge. But Mrs. Chenery had no thought or intention of leaving. Indeed, had any one suggested such a thing, she would have considered it unutterably rude. Her idea of sociability was to talk people into a dull stupor. So she sat on quite contentedly, rocking vigorously back and forth in the big chair by the window and fanning herself with a great palm leaf fan. Her cultured foghorn voice dove down to unsounded depths and again rose in a sort of lingering wail.

"I'm sure I'm going to have a stroke," she said, dabbing her lips with her handkerchief. "Did you ever see such heat?"

Pat had, but one soon learned not to argue with Mrs. Chenery, so she let it pass. True, the perspiration stood on Mrs. Chenery's brow in rows of little shining beads, but Mrs. Chenery was one of those people who carry their heat with them, who, even in the dead of winter, tear open windows in comfortably heated rooms, causing less warmly constituted individuals to scurry into protected corners because the Mrs. Chenerys on the scene never saw such heat.

"I wonder," Pat said, fluffing out a white organdie dress that she had just taken from a bag, "what time the fleet gets in?"

Mrs. Chenery looked grieved.

"My dear," she confided, "I'm sure the General knows. But it wouldn't do a bit of good to ask him. He doesn't tell me a thing about his business. Takes these maneuvers really seriously, and, like most men, is afraid a woman can't keep a secret. As if I'd tell! It's a positive shame, though, that you can't find out when your own brother gets in."

Pat hung her dress in the large dry closet, where an electric light burned all the time to dissipate the dampness of the rainy season, and stooped down for another.

"It's quite all right," she said. "I'll manage to struggle along until he gets here. I just thought if I knew the time it would be nice to meet him at the dock."

Mrs. Chenery's voice boomed out with such sudden explosive force that the blue georgette Pat had just picked up slid helplessly from her fingers.

"I've got it," the old lady cried. "We'll ask Sally."

"Who's Sally?" Pat asked, recovering her equilibrium and her dress at the same time.

"Sally? Oh, my dear! Didn't I tell you? Sally is my laundress. A St. Lucia girl, black as the ace of spades, but she's told me the most marvelous things. Last week she told me I was going to get a letter with a black border. It hasn't come yet, but poor old Cousin Charlie is very low. She's perfectly marvelous. And this week she told me I was going to meet a dark man to my sorrow. And would you believe it? That Hindoo I bought the ebony elephant in the living-room from yesterday charged me thirty dollars and I could have gotten the same elephant from the Chinaman down the street for twenty-two fifty. She's perfectly marvelous, that girl."

"Yes, I must meet Sally," Pat said desperately.

Ensued a pause. Pat wondered whether she could possibly ask the old girl, in heaven's name, to leave her alone, but Mrs. Chenery caught her breath and went on again.

"There's something I must tell you—about tonight," she said, a trifle uneasily. "Goodness knows, I hope you're broad-minded and will understand that in my position one has to meet and be nice to all kinds of peculiar people. Rank is everything, you know, and one has to be diplomatic. One just can't afford to ignore him."

"Of course not," Pat said with a smile. "Are you by any chance referring to this Captain Nicholson?"

"Oh, my dear, no! Captain Nicholson is quite delightful. You'll adore him. No . . . it's"—and Mrs. Chenery bit her lip and wrung her handkerchief in desperation. Then she burst out—"There's a Chinaman coming to dinner to-night." And the tragedy of it was written all over her round flushed face.

"A Chinese?" Pat queried. "Well, that's interesting."

"I'm glad you take it that way," Mrs. Chenery boomed, relief creeping into her voice. "Personally . . . I have no race prejudice at all . . . although my sister in Honolulu almost had her throat cut by a Chinese cook once . . . but after all, it's character that counts, isn't it? Character and personality and . . . rank. He's really a very nice person, even if he is a Chinaman. Goodness knows he can't help that. It isn't his fault he wasn't born white. He's a prince or something, so you needn't be afraid of having your throat cut or getting leprosy or something. The General has taken quite a fancy to him. He hasn't any race prejudice, either. People in our position can't afford to have any feelings in the matter. Would you believe it, we actually had to entertain an East Indian rajah once . . . and my dear, he was positively black."

"What time is dinner?" Pat asked, more for the sake of breaking the steady flow of words than for any other reason.

"Eight o'clock. Then after that we're going to the club for dancing . . ."

Pat glanced at her watch. "Goodness! It's after seven. I'll have to hurry, if I'm to bathe and be ready by eight."

Mrs. Chenery rose reluctantly.

"I must dress, too. But I hate to go. I've loved so talking to you. To-morrow morning after breakfast we must have a good long chat. I feel as if I'd known you all my life."

She disappeared through the door and Pat turned to struggle with the straps of a bag, vowing that the morning would find her deluged with duties that would take her far from the Chenery household.

In the shelter of one of the little islands that dot the Gulf of Panama, an oil tanker had dropped anchor. She was dirty, slovenly, that tanker, but beneath the grime struck out an occasional flash of snowy white, a passing glimpse of polished brass, as though the dirt were not accidental but deliberate. In the crow's nest a seaman kept a pair of glasses trained on the lights of the battle fleet as they passed across his view on the horizon. Below, in the wireless room, an operator listened intently, his ear phones clamped to his head.

Chapter Seven

AT ALMOST THE PRECISE INSTANT that Nicholson was entering the room wherein Chu-Sheng, the Accursed One, sat on the head of the spider, Prince Lai Chung was seated in a room on the second floor of the house he had rented for the duration of his stay in Panama.

It was a small room, as rooms go in the tropics; not more than fifteen by fifteen feet, the stone walls hung with heavy orange-colored silk and the windows closed by shutters that did not permit a single ray of light to enter.

On one side of the room, inset in a deep niche in the wall stood something curiously like the looped cross, the *Crux Ansata* which Osiris, God of Resurrection, carried in his hand and touched, in the Hall of the Dead, those souls which had passed all tests and had earned immortality. It was the height of a tall man, polished and glimmering as though it had been cut from some enormous crystal.

And at its feet, fettered to the *Crux Ansata* by tiny golden chains, was a replica of the hideous, monstrous spider on whose head sat Chu-Sheng . . . life fettering the enemy of life . . . rendering it impotent—holding it with the secret, ancient and holy symbol of that very thing it was bent upon destroying. And the great looped cross above . . . watching and guarding like the God of Life.

There were three lights in the room. Two thick candles burned unwaveringly in the hot still air on either side of the great looped cross. From them floated up the odor of incense, curiously and pungently sweet.

The third candle burned close to a great slab of some polished lucent substance, like a great curved sheet of clearest jade that stood upright on an ebony stand in the center of the room.

It was before this that the Prince sat. His face, in the light of the candle, was stern with a lurking hint of sadness in the eyes as he looked at the semicircle of men in orange robes who knelt beyond the sheet of jade (if jade it was). Men so much alike in motive and self-discipline, that a kind of unity had settled upon them, making of men of varying height and weight one pattern molded by unanimous desire.

He began to speak, using the Mongolian of the Inner Gobi, the tongue of the red-faced clansmen whose hereditary leader he was. In majesty, in intellect, and in impressiveness he was as far above those others who sat in a semi-circle as an eagle is above the ground over which he soars.

"Brothers," he began slowly, "an ancient evil has been loosed upon the earth. Knowledge that the Ancient Ones meant to be used for the good of the world is being used for its harm. It has been loosed by man. Therefore, man must balance the scales of justice by removing it."

He was silent for a moment. The silence grew like a tangible thing there in the silent room before he spoke again.

"All of you," he went on, "have witnessed the mysteries of Tu-lugum, have laid eyes on Yian the Holy, have set naked foot upon the Mother of Mountains and have meditated in the depths of the Azure Cavern of the Ancient Ones. To each of you has been imparted a fragment of the secret things that have been handed down to us from the days of the Ancient Ones. Each of you has sworn an oath in the smoke of the eternal fire that burns in the Azure Cavern to be faithful to your trust . . . that no word of the secrets pass your lips until the appointed time, because it is not good to meddle with knowledge before the time appointed for its understanding."

He paused and stared out into the shadowy room as if seeking there an answer to a problem. He was motionless, brooding, with the attitude of a man who has attained the stark simplicity of elemental knowledge and the kind of power that goes with it. In poise, calm, majesty of brow and magnetism he resembled more one of those temple images that sit in the gloom and stare through eyes of amethyst than any ordinary human being. He looked aloof from human standards. Then he lifted his head.

"Back there in New York when the affair of the resurrection of the Princess Nirgidma was finished, we believed that madness had descended upon the brain of Chu-Sheng, the Accursed One. But evil may not be bound with the twigs of the willow. Chu-Sheng is not mad. He is here, preparing a greater evil than that we halted by the purity of light. And now the time has come when you must put to use that knowledge that you have sworn never to use. The Wheel of the Law turns, and unless we, who are Keepers of the Secrets of the Ancient Ones, are alert, an opportunity is snatched or taken from us, for us or against us. In the name of the Ancient Ones, I absolve you from your oath."

A little hiss of expelled breath came from the semicircle of kneeling men. The Prince raised his hand. The sound died away instantly.

Reaching out one hand, the tall Mongol shifted the candle so that its light gathered like a pool in the translucent green of the slab before him. Then he shifted his position so that the reflection of the looped cross and its fettered monstrosity lay like a shadow across the slab.

"Bring Chu-Sheng, the Accursed One, to me," he commanded abruptly and, bending his head, plunged his gaze into the green depths before him.

For a long time he kept his gaze fixed, and for a long time not a sound came from the semicircle of kneeling men. Then, suddenly, a pinpoint of sea-green light grew and ebbed in the center of the green slab . . . swirled as if in moving water . . . increased and spread as a ring spreads when a stone is tossed into a quiet pool, until the whole slab was a trembling pool of liquid green light.

And then, slowly, as if the concentrated force of the kneeling men were opening the door to another world, in the transparent pool of light there grew a scene . . . a long room . . . a great spider that crouched beneath a shimmering globe of light . . . a man seated upon its head . . .

An almost imperceptible motion of the Prince's hand and from the lips of the kneeling men drifted a chant that rose in ripples of silver tone waves . . . spreading a network of infinitely delicate tone filaments like tiny, drifting ghosts of spring tinkling little lutes of fretted jade. There was triumph in it as it began to rise . . . the triumph of onrushing, conquering waves, the triumph of the free rushing wind. And there was peace and surety of peace in it that throbbed to some strange, lilting rhythm that sent the blood racing in tune and in time with its joyousness. The throbbing, singing notes were like tiny, warm vital blows that whipped the blood into ecstasy of life.

. . . And through it all the intent eyes of the Prince peered into the depths of the jade . . . a look of strain upon his face . . . concentrating . . . concentrating . . .

Back in the presence of Chu-Sheng Nicholson fought with deep stubborn resistance against the force that probed at his brain . . . seeking, searching . . . tugging at his will.

Try as he would, he could not keep his eyes from the globe of light that was like a softly shimmering, glistening rainbow, nor shut his ears to the evil evocation (and now he realized drowsily how utterly evil it was) that poured from the lips of the girl. They were not words that she uttered in that toneless voice; they were sounds whose roots struck back into a time before ever man drew breath . . . sounds the lips and throats of men were never meant to utter.

And always the monstrous spider moved and swayed in time to the chant . . . watching him . . . the eyes fixed upon him as if only waiting for the proper moment . . . He felt the surge of something huge and shapeless and evil hanging in the room . . . he felt the probing fingers at his mind redouble their effort . . . he felt himself slipping . . . Dimly he saw a shadow taking form on the shimmering bubble of light . . . taking shape and substance . . . himself . . . on the ship . . . Another shape was taking form . . . a woman . . .

He was listening to two voices. One urged him to pour forth his heart, his innermost secrets to the man who sat upon the head of the monstrous spider. The other whispered insistently that he must not . . . and that voice was the stronger.

There seemed to be a vast reserve of strength pouring into him . . . something was fighting with him . . . aiding him . . . a new strength . . . a clean strength . . . It drove through the mists that drugged his brain . . . a new sound was ringing in his ears, drowning out the sound of the girl's chant . . . a sound that was filled with the surge of the open sea and the rush of the wind through the trees . . . He struggled to his feet. How he did it, he did not know. But he found himself there and facing the Tongueless One . . . staring into his bottomless black orbs with grey eyes into which had been caught the clear coldness of a New England winter . . .

The girl's chant stopped abruptly.

"The Master has instructions for you," she said. "Listen carefully."

The odd toneless voice, which seemed to carry an undercurrent of weariness, went on.

He listened.

Some time later an exceedingly thoughtful young man passed out of the iron grille that led from the Casa Mendoza to the sea wall.

He would have been even more thoughtful had he known that Chu-Sheng, the Tongueless One, watching from the back of the

monstrous spider, and Prince Lai, peering intently into the translucent pool of light before him, had seen something of which he was
not aware. Both of them had clearly seen the face of a woman,
dragged from his mind and projected upon the bubble of light as
upon a screen, by the powerful will of the Tongueless One.

Just inside Cape Mala, which is the outermost sentinel of the Gulf
of Panama, a steamer was slicing through the calm sea, her nose
turned toward the Canal. She had the appearance and the super-
structure of an oil tanker, only no tanker could develop the speed
that she was displaying and her funnel lacked the insignia that a
tanker usually carries. Her course paralleled that of the United
States Battle Fleet which was steaming for the Canal, just over the
curve of the horizon.

Chapter Eight

NIGHT HAD DROPPED a sable mantle across the world and the channel lights at the entrance of the Canal were red wasps stinging the darkness, when Pat finished her bath and, wrapped in a kimono, stepped onto the balcony outside her room. Far below her, at the foot of Ancon Hill, lay the City of Panama, the new American city of Balboa, and a magnificent vista of bay and island that stretched out into infinitude.

A multitude of stars had swarmed out and dropped low over the Fortified Islands that seemed to lie almost at her feet. So low, in fact that Pat, standing there on the screened verandah, felt that she could reach out and touch them.

A light from the long French window behind her made a bright patch upon the gallery. But she stood outside the reflection, a shadow among other shadows. Her eyes were raised above the green of the rustling mangoes and aloes, swaying bananas and coco fronds below . . . and brooded upon the sea.

She was intent, absorbed, as though deciphering a code traced in the water.

Presently she sighed. Her mind held a picture that she had not been able to banish of the man she had known as John Sobieski, and who to-day was calling himself Captain Nicholson . . . more, was to be a guest in this very house to-night under that name. She wondered what his thoughts had been when she had spoken to him that afternoon in the hotel patio. And she wondered what he would do if he knew that she, also, was to be a guest to-night at that same dinner.

As a matter of fact, she was not sure herself what her actions were to be when she came face to face with him to-night. Denounce him? She thought not.

When she was again aware of the landscape outside, it seemed foreign, the fragrance from the garden suffocating. A vaporous breath, heavy with the scent of moist soil, brushed past her face. She was startled by the feeling that she was not alone. The presence she sensed was not tangible, but seemed, rather, the personality of some individual closely related to the heavy, suffocating night, a mental influence that had become incorporated in the atmosphere and now fused it with a troublous current. A vague but increasing uneasiness forced her to turn away from the verandah, back into the room.

A small clock on the dressing table chimed. A glance at it caused her to turn hurriedly. Seven-thirty. And she was to dine in half an hour.

She seated herself before the mirror, studying her replica. The dinner gown of flaming chiffon, she decided. It would look well with the uniforms . . . set off the darkness of her hair. She rose with easy languid grace; moved to a closet; opened the door.

As she dressed she hummed softly. And it was only when she was fully dressed that she realized that the melody was one to which she had danced night after night . . . in the arms of the man she had known as John Sobieski. She bit her lips . . . the tune died in a sigh.

There was no one in sight when she descended the steps to the floor below.

She knew quite well that the flame of her dress brought out the sheen of her hair, edged it with little dancing tones of flame, accentuated the lacquer-red of her lips into curved lines of beauty. She would not have been a woman had she not realized the arresting picture she made, and the shaded lights of the room brought out rather than dimmed the picture.

It was half living-room, half verandah, that room. A series of arches spanned two sides of it, the openings covered with split bamboo shades on rollers. A low parapet, about three feet in height ran between the arches with a top on which were placed urns. The vines with which they were filled spilled their blossoms down the sides and over the white plaster of the parapet.

She strolled to the far end and found that, below the parapet, the hillside broke away in a steep declivity, to end a hundred feet or more below in a pile of stone and rubbish. During the construction of the Canal thousands of tons of rock had been blasted from the side of Ancon Hill to form breakwaters at the Canal entrance, and army headquarters had been built on the bench thus blasted out of the side of the hill. Hence the name, Quarry Heights.

Far below her a necklace of lights was flung across the dark surface of the sea. She remembered seeing, as they drove up the hill in the afternoon dusk, a broad straight causeway that stretched out to Fort Amador and the islands in the bay. The Fortified Islands, Mrs. Chenery had told her they were called, where the heavy guns for the Canal defense were mounted. It seemed difficult to realize that, only a few years before, the expanse of well-lighted streets and houses lined below her had been impassable jungle and swamp, smitten with yellow fever . . . a pest hole avoided by the ships of the world.

She turned as a bell sounded somewhere within the house and her eyes followed the servant in white who glided to the door. He was fairly young; not more than 25, with ivory yellow skin underlaid with a dusky tinge that hinted at the admixture of darker blood, and his eyes were slightly oblique. A product of the mingling of Oriental and West Indian negro that bids fair to be a predominant note in the future population of Panama.

A little shiver ran through her, but so well disciplined were her emotions that she gave no outward sign of the tumult within as the man she had seen that afternoon stepped through the opened door.

He was in the white dress uniform of the Army in the tropics. She was conscious of his look, a look that swept her from lacquered hair to tips of slippers. But he gave no sign of recognition as he handed his hat to the servant. He held his emotions in powerful check, she told herself, to give no sign of surprise when he saw her. She remained standing at the far end of the room. He made no move toward her until the servant had glided out again.

Then he crossed the room swiftly. Now that he permitted his eyes to linger upon her fully she was even lovelier than he remembered—a clean, silvery loveliness that was breath-taking.

"I want to apologize for my attitude this afternoon," he began hurriedly. "I didn't dare admit knowing you there. To have admitted knowing you would have meant explanations . . . that I would not have been able to give."

"Does acquaintanceship with me call for an explanation?" she flashed. For an instant she looked at him, eyes flaming, then swung about. He put out a hand to stop her.

He lighted a cigarette; tossed the match away. In the amber flicker, his face was as rigid as bronze. When he spoke there was a bitterness in his voice, a bitterness that seemed insurgent against long suppression.

"I can't explain," he said. "It would be futile for me to attempt to explain. Absolutely. If I were so indiscreet as to tell you the truth, you wouldn't believe, and besides, just now the truth would be sealing my own death warrant. I'm compelled to throw myself on your mercy . . . and ask you to take me on faith."

Pat wanted to catch him by the shoulders and shake him . . . or strike him. She felt that she hated him. But, even in anger, she realized her animosity was not dislike, but a healthy resentment against the mystery of his identity.

She spoke in brittle tones.

"It's quite all right."

"I know, of course, that it isn't," he said. "An explanation is due you . . . and I cannot give it."

He paused as his mind flashed back two years. He saw Pat in a white dress dancing in his arms, her hair sleek and shining, her long earrings glittering down to her smooth, sun-tanned shoulders. It had been one of those white nights when men lose their heads under the magic of the moon; a night when he and Pat had danced through the door of the clubhouse and down the steps, and, still dancing, had come to the white sands of the beach.

He would have asked her to marry him that night, but even assailed by moonshine and madness, he had kept his head. What could he marry on? The little of his income that was left above his personal expenses went to the white haired father and mother in a little Connecticut town. He had left the next day without saying good-bye. And he had not written.

Standing there now, looking down at her half-averted face, he saw himself as a fool, perhaps. But even fools owed loyalty to their duty. Having her by his side again he knew that he had never stopped loving her. But he knew also that his moment had passed. He could not tell her now that he loved her. And yet he did not want her to go through life thinking that those days together that summer had meant nothing in his life.

"I would not have you think," he said awkwardly, "that those days we spent together at Montauk Point mean as little as . . . as my actions would indicate."

Stupid vague words, but he could find no others.

She turned toward the railing, rested one hand upon it and gazed down into the garden that ran along the edge of the cliff. Silence brooded within its hibiscus-bordered space, heavy with a thousand fragrances rising from the shrubs and flowers that blended into an unsubstantial pattern of gloom. A pool gleamed like a dark mirror.

"It was an interesting interlude," she said calmly, tossing the words over her shoulder. Her face was white, but her eyes were hard, as jewels are hard. He came up and stood beside her. She went on, still looking down into the garden. "I take it that you wish our acquaintanceship to date from to-night . . . as Captain Nicholson . . . and that the interlude of John Sobieski is to be forgotten."

"I wish I could explain . . ." he began. She cut him short curtly. "Please."

"I should be grateful," he said in a low voice, "if you would pretend that our meeting here—to-night—is our first."

The sound of the doorbell shattered the brittle silence between them. Carlos appeared like a ghost that had been waiting to be summoned into actuality and glided to the door.

It was Lieutenant Daniel Martin. He saw Pat and came forward with outstretched hands.

"Pat," he cried. "This is luck. I came early, hoping that you'd be down before the others."

Then he saw the other man, recognized him for a stranger and glanced at Pat inquiringly.

"Captain Nicholson, Lieutenant Martin," she said mechanically.

Dan glanced at the other man with a little crease between his brows. There was something vaguely familiar about him; something that stirred a memory that he could not place. He repeated the name thoughtfully.

"Nicholson," he mused. "You weren't at Governor's Island, were you?"

" 'Fraid not," the other smiled. "Hawaii, Arizona, the West Coast."

Seeing the boy there, his freckled face alight with eagerness, Nicholson felt suddenly very, very old and tired. Hunting for romance, the boy was, romance after the Richard Harding Davis manner; instead, when it was too late to clear his veins of wanderlust, he'd be disillusioned. He'd be achingly wistful of a home that he'd never have and go drifting on in a happy-go-lucky manner from one army post to another until he'd used up all his luck.

"Funny," Dan said, still puzzled. "Can't help feeling I've seen you before, somewhere."

"I'm afraid not," Nicholson said. "It's just one of those things. I've a fairly good memory for faces, and I'd have remembered you."

"Oh, this is perfectly terrible," cried the foghorn from the stair landing. "I'm a terrible hostess. It would be just my luck to have you arrive and me to be late. But I see you know each other."

"Oh, yes," Pat said, "Captain Nicholson broke the ice and introduced himself."

"That's a blessing," said Mrs. Chenery, as she swept down the last few steps and into the room.

Then, as the doorbell rang again, she called up the steps. "John, do hurry up. People are arriving."

Lieutenant Martin started as if stung.

John! The single word had freed the memory for which he had been groping. John! He knew now why the face of Captain Nicholson was familiar. He was the man with whom Pat had been in love at Montauk Point two years before . . . the man whose picture she carried in her bag . . . the same picture that he had seen that afternoon. John Sobieski he had called himself then . . . and to-night he was Captain Nicholson . . . What was it Pat had said . . . "Captain Nicholson broke the ice by introducing himself."

His eyes narrowed. A little steely glint came into their depths. Something was afoot here . . . something that called for an explanation.

Chapter Nine

FOR THE NEXT FEW MINUTES young Dan Martin's mind was like a squirrel in a revolving cage. It raced around and around endlessly. And always ended where it had started.

Pat had tacitly denied knowing Captain Nicholson.

Yet Dan knew, beyond the shadow of a doubt, that she did know him . . . that she carried his picture in her handbag.

He moved slowly across the room and, under cover of the chatter of arriving guests, attached himself to Pat and the Captain.

"Your first visit to the Zone, Captain?" he asked negligently, and at Nicholson's assent went on: "Quite different from Long Island, isn't it?"

From the corner of his eye he saw Pat's hand go to her throat in a fleeting gesture. But there was only grave inquiry on Nicholson's face.

"I imagine there is a great deal of difference," he said, "although I'm not familiar with Long Island."

The Lieutenant looked up in cleverly simulated surprise.

"Aren't you? My mistake. I thought you said you'd served on the Island."

Pat broke into the conversation with a swift "Oh, look. Who's that? Just coming in."

Martin glanced at the door to where a tall man in conventional black was following the ghost-like Carlos into the room. A ribbon across his chest blazed with orders. His features were unmistakably Chinese.

"That," he said, "is his Highness Prince Lai Chung. Chinese royalty of some sort."

A faint trace of a smile curved Nicholson's lips. "Chinese royalty of some sort." Didn't the young fool know that Prince Lai Chung was the hereditary ruler of the scattered tribes of Mongolia, the head of a royal house that antedated the rulers of Europe; a house whose written records antedated the birth of Christ. Then he caught his breath sharply. Did the presence of the Prince here mean that he was taking a hand in the game? If so, what was his game? Was he a foe?

The man was an Oriental of no common type. He registered an impression of bronze, almost beautiful bronze features. The face, almost, of a Buddha, and eyes . . . he groped in an effort to understand the eyes. He wore evening clothes with the air of one accustomed to Western clothing, and he had a poise, a finish to the minutest detail of dress. Nicholson remembered a fragment of information that the man was a graduate of half a dozen universities.

But there was no more time for conjecture. The Prince, with the General's wife beside him, stood before them.

"Your Highness," boomed Mrs. Chenery, "may I present Miss Fenton. And this is Captain Nicholson."

Prince Lai's acknowledgment of the introduction was gravely courteous, but for a fleeting instant his face held a queer arrested look; a chord of deep and abiding remembrance was touched. But not by word or gesture did he betray the fact that the face of Patricia Fenton was the face of the girl he had seen floating in the bubble of light that same afternoon . . . the image that had been wrenched from the mind of Nicholson by the will of Chu-Sheng.

Dan waited until a lull in the conversation left the General free for a moment. Then he said quietly in his ear:

"May I speak to you a moment, sir?" Then he added: "Alone, if you don't mind. It's rather important, sir."

General Chenery shot him an inquiring glance, then moved away from the chattering group near the door; leaned against the parapet. He was a short stocky man with iron grey hair, a grey mustache, and a ruddy complexion. His firm mouth and penetrating dark eyes belied the gentle quietness of his voice and manner. His campaign ribbons covered actions on four continents.

"What is it, Dan?" he asked quietly.

The boy flushed a trifle. He wondered for a moment if he were making a fool of himself. Then he plunged bravely ahead.

"This Captain Nicholson . . . do you know him, sir?"

"Personally, you mean? No. Never saw him before. Why, Dan?"

"Well"—the boy hesitated—"I may sound like a fool sir, but . . . well, something's happened, that I thought you ought to know. It may mean nothing at all. And again . . ."

Then he told the General of the episode of the afternoon, of Pat's implication that she and the Captain had never met before and of his own recognition of the man as John Sobieski.

"The man doesn't remember me. I'm sure of that," he ended.

"Hmmm." The General shot a glance from beneath grizzled white brows at the little group on the further side of the room . . . took in Nicholson's impassive face . . . Pat's troubled one. "It'll bear looking into. Just keep it to yourself, Dan, and let me handle it."

He crossed casually to where Pat, Nicholson and Prince Lai were engaged n conversation.

"Er—by the way, Captain," he said, "I believe you've been in China?"

"Yes, I lived there for some time," he responded. He had the feeling that the question had been asked for a purpose. Why, he could not have told.

"Do you know anything about ancient Chinese art?"

"Something," Nicholson responded. This was dangerous ground. Something was coming. Something that presaged danger. "Why?"

"I wondered . . . there's a question I've wanted to ask for a long time. That piece of bronze there in front of you . . . I picked it up in China while I was stationed at the International Settlement in Shanghai. Dealer charged me a stiff price for it. I've always felt that I'd been stung. Is it good . . . really good, I mean? Or just the ordinary run-of-the-mill stuff?"

Nicholson shot a glance at his host, but his bronzed features were falsely passive. This was a trap. All right. He'd play the game. He reached out and touched the oval bronze dish, filled with pink coral vine flowers.

"It's the usual heirloom type of sacrificial vessel," he said slowly, aware that the eyes of both Prince Lai and the General were upon him. "The shape is common enough, but the patina is remarkably good. You seldom see dark green streaked with prussian blue and the square dragon is interesting." He shot a look at the Prince. "It was probably made somewhere in Black China."

He caught a look of surprise on the usually impassive face of Prince Lai. He seemed to be seeking to surprise any unguarded look on Nicholson's face.

Then he murmured:

"Er, did I understand you to say Black China, Captain?"

He seemed to be more interested in the piece of bronze that had been under discussion than in Nicholson's answer. He moved it gently with his hands . . . long hands, they were; but they gave the impression that beneath their silken smoothness was sinuous, fibrous strength. Power.

Nicholson answered deliberately:

"Yes, Your Highness, Black China."

The General spoke.

"Where in the world is Black China. That's a phrase I've never heard before."

The Prince answered swiftly, almost as if he wished to prevent Nicholson answering.

"The phrase applies to a portion of Inner Mongolia and the border of Tibet, where Buddhism has not been generally adopted, and where a degraded form of Devil Worship is still practiced by a portion of the people." He turned toward Nicholson. "Was that your understanding of it, Captain."

"Exactly," Nicholson said, and his eyes met those of the Prince in a searching glance. But he knew that the Prince had not given the real explanation of the meaning of the word . . . and he knew that the Prince knew that he knew.

The glance of the Prince flickered after the retreating back of the General. Pat was engaged in answering some question of Dan's. Only Nicholson heard the low toned words of the Prince:

"Silence is an important thing in life, Captain. In the silence Wisdom speaks, and they whose hearts are open understand. The brave man is at the mercy of cowards, and the honest man at the mercy of thieves, unless he keeps silent. But if he keeps silent he is safe, because they will fail to understand him, and then he may do them good without their knowing it, which is a source of true honor and contentment."

He smiled gently and turned away again, leaving Nicholson staring after him in silence that was fraught with more than speculation.

Chapter Ten

WHATEVER MRS. CHENERY'S shortcomings might have been, they did not extend to her ability as a hostess. She had gathered together a group of unusually interesting and charming people, and at any other time Pat would have enjoyed herself thoroughly. But to-night she could not keep her thoughts away from the problem that confronted her.

Every now and then her eyes went to the smiling features of the man who called himself Captain Nicholson. But she knew that the smile was false. There was a curious strained intensity in his manner that did not match the casualness of his conversation.

The dinner table fairly reeked with rank. The governor of the Canal Zone and his wife occupied the place of honor, of course, because although only a colonel, by virtue of his position he outranked the Admiral in command of the Naval District. There was a lady with languorous eyes whose pompous husband called her Kitten (but for whom Pat at once thought of a more appropriate and more mature name), who had a disconcerting way of casting her odd orbs on Captain Nicholson and leaving them there. There was the secretary of Hacienda of the Republic of Panama whose name was Miguel MacGregor, and whose father had been a Scotch soldier of fortune in the revolution of 1904 that freed Panama from Colombia. His dark, vivacious little wife sat beside the British minister, Col. Brathwaite Wallis, whose tall, blonde and entirely charming wife sat on the right of the American minister. His daughter, a gawky young girl who seemed all teeth, was Prince Lai's dinner partner. After the rank came a scattering of colonels, majors, and lieutenant commanders and their dinner partners. Lieutenant Martin and Captain Nicholson were the only two men present below the rank of major.

Somehow the smooth impassive face of Prince Lai fascinated Pat. She wondered what was going on behind that carved mask. And once or twice, because she was frankly staring, she surprised a glance of his in the direction of Nicholson that puzzled her. Curiosity pricked her, like a needle flashing back and forth across the loom of thought. There was some connection here. But what? The thread was so slight, so tenuous, that to follow it was impossible.

Once, during the amused staccato talk with which the room reverberated, the Prince's quiet voice separated itself from the drone of conversation and she leaned forward suddenly. He was discussing with the General the leaping fires of war in the East, the steady swallowing of China by Japan. And the words of the Prince had seemed odd to her.

"The Western world," she heard him say, "can never realize, can never be made to realize, the tremendous potential power of an aroused East under the control of a will and an intellect greater than the sum total of all their wills and intellects. A mind greater than all of them to plan for all of them, a will more powerful than all their wills to force them to carry out those plans exactly as the greater mind has conceived them."

The Oriental's voice held Pat; gave her a picture of deft fingers inlaying a mosaic; thoughts chosen with care and spoken as though filtered through many translations before they left the tongue in English.

"I think," General Chenery said comfortably, "that the time to worry about that would be when such a personage actually appeared on the scene. Besides, why should a gigantic intellect, such as you have suggested, dawn upon the world in the East? Any more than in, say, the United States, or Germany or England?"

"Because," the Prince answered with a charming smile, "the world moves in cycles. It is the inexorable law of the universe. The East was the height of its glory about twelve hundred and twenty-five. Look at the leaders that were produced then. Then came Europe; now America . . . and after that?" The slender hands shaped themselves into an oddly expressive gesture. "The cycle repeats itself."

"Oh, dear," said Mrs. Chenery, "this is getting too involved. Don't let's get started on history. History invariably leads to war, and war leads to crime and crime leads to politics and politics leads to graft and graft leads to Prohibition and Prohibition leads to Repeal and Repeal leads to destruction. And there we are right back again where we started from."

It was with relief that, a moment later, Pat caught Mrs. Chenery's eye and they rose from the table. Coffee was served on the verandah. Conversation was general for a moment and then Nicholson said:

"I feel sure that I'm going to like Panama. It's my first visit to the tropics, you know."

"Anyone that can like Panama is an idiot," Mrs. Chenery announced. "It's nothing but a pest hole, full of roaches and sand flies and scorpions and sinister natives with knives lurking around dark corners and behind banana plants."

"Well," the General said cheerfully, "it's your own fault. You would marry me to see the world."

"See the world," she bellowed, and Pat started so violently that part of her apricot brandy leaped from her liqueur glass. "When it's a hundred degrees in the shade and you expect to drop dead from a stroke any moment?"

"Never mind, my dear," the General consoled with a twinkle in his eye. "When our tour of duty here is ended, I'll put in for duty in Alaska."

"I shouldn't be surprised," Mrs. Chenery said with conviction. "If you can't roast me to death, you'll try freezing me to death. What a depraved mind you've got."

A blonde girl with an expression as fluid as light slanted one lazy look at Mrs. Chenery and then winked at Pat, who had difficulty in keeping her face straight.

"I like your quarters," Nicholson said, rushing in where better informed acquaintances at Quarry Heights would have feared to tread. "They're delightfully situated."

"That's because you don't have to live here," Mrs. Chenery said. "I can just see myself falling down the cliff every time I look out of the window."

"You've the most marvelous flowers," Pat said desperately. "What are those lovely colorful things growing in the urns along the railing?"

"Those washed out things," said the General's wife with a shrug. "I've no idea. I was going to have them pulled up tomorrow."

"Oh, don't," Pat exclaimed involuntarily. "They have a perfectly marvelous odor."

"Have they really?" Mrs. Chenery asked in surprise. "Well, now, I really must smell them sometime."

"Speaking of colors," the General said to Pat, "Dan tells me that you have a handbag that shames the rainbow. Would you mind if I had a look at it? It sounds just like something that I'd like to send Marie for her birthday. She's in school in the States, you know," he explained.

"The one you had this afternoon," Dan put in, "with the hot diggety colors."

Pat laughed. "Of course you may see it. It's in my room. I'll get it."

"Don't bother," the General said. "It's evident you haven't learned the first lesson of the tropics yet . . . don't do anything you can get somebody else to do for you." He beckoned to Carlos. "Tell Carlos where it is. He'll get it for you."

"I suspect your tropical rule is pretty generally adhered to," Pat said with a smile. Turning to the waiting servant she told him where he would find her bag.

"In Mongolia," Prince Lai cut in, "we have a proverb quite similar. Never draw the cart and let the horse walk behind."

"Chi K'an Tzu said that, didn't he?" Nicholson queried.

The Prince nodded.

"You know our philosophers, Captain?"

"I was born in China," Nicholson explained. "I learned Chinese from the children and from the temple priests before I could speak English."

Carlos entered with the bag. Pat took it and handed it to Mrs. Chenery.

"Wish I had one like that," the lady said. "Wouldn't last in this wretched climate, though. Everything I've got is wretched."

"Except your husband, my dear," laughed the General.

"He might be improved upon," said the lady tartly, and there was a general laugh.

"Permit me," the General said and reached for the bag. His fingers snapped the catch and as he turned it over the contents fell upon the floor. Pat checked an involuntary cry of dismay. The snapshot. The snapshot of Nicholson. It was in the bag. And she had denied knowing him. She started forward to pick up the contents, but the General was before her.

"I'm so sorry," he said. Then his eye lit upon the photograph. "Ah, a photograph. The man you left behind you, Miss Fenton?"

"Oh, no," Pat said hurriedly. "Just a picture of no importance."

The atmosphere suddenly became taut, like gauze stretched tightly upon a loom. She felt that another word would rend the fabric.

Wordlessly she extended her hand for the picture. But the General seemed determined to tease.

"Now, now, Miss Fenton," he chuckled. "I may be grey-haired, but I can't have the wool pulled over my eyes that way. Girls don't carry around snapshots in their handbags unless the picture means something. I'll bet it's a handsome young man. Come on now, own up."

Pat was tense with fright. She realized that for Nicholson's picture to be found in her purse would reveal the fact that she had been lying, and not only that, might have serious consequences for him.

"It's really of no consequence," she said.

The General looked at her with a touch of sternness in his manner. Pat was conscious of the fact that Prince Lai, alone of the others in the room, seemed to sense the drama that lay hidden beneath the surface of the little scene.

"Sure, Miss Fenton?" the General asked.

"Quite sure," Pat said.

"It isn't anyone I know?"

"Oh, no, it isn't anyone you know."

"Then in that case," he said, "I'm sure you'll forgive the curiosity of an old man for looking at it."

With a quick gesture he turned it over.

Pat took a step forward in protest. But she was too late. The General was staring intently at the face of the picture. Her hands dropped helplessly to her side and she stared tragically at Nicholson.

The latter's eyes were invaded by an alert gleam. That was the only change in his expression. But there was something in his attitude, in the poise of his head, that likened him to a wild animal suddenly aware of danger. For he had read something in Pat's eyes that portended trouble.

The General did not speak. He raised his head and stared at Pat under knotted brows, his eyes as eloquent as the silence that had dropped about them. Then he said with abject apology in his voice:

"Whoever he is, he doesn't deserve a pretty girl like you," and passed the picture to her.

Pat had difficulty in controlling the gasp that rose in her throat.

It was not a picture of Nicholson. The face that gazed up at her was that of a man she had never seen before.

Chapter Eleven

FOR A MOMENT Pat could see nothing. Then from some inner reserve she found strength, controlled her rioting nerves. She raised her chin toward the light, her face filled with determination, her mouth a shining curve. Above it her eyes were sharp and alive.

Then she said: "I'm not sure he deserves anything at all, General."

She smiled at him gaily and with a swift gesture ripped the picture into fragments, crumpled them up into her hand.

"So you see," she said, "that was how much it meant to me." Her bright red lips quirked upward. "I hate to disillusion you, General Chenery, but I didn't even know the picture was there. I had thought it safe among a lot of other rubbish back in the States."

Her eyes met those of young Dan and she caught her breath sharply at the icy, black look that met hers. Suddenly realization dawned. *Dan knew.* He had seen the picture that afternoon, and, no doubt, he had told the General. Therefore, the interest in her bag. How stupid she had been. But that did not explain the mystery of the vanished photograph. She knew that the picture had been in her bag. And yet when the bag was opened, there was the picture of a strange man in it. Someone had changed pictures. Her eyes searched Nicholson's face. Not a muscle moved. Then she realized that it could not have been he. He had no means of knowing that she had treasured the snapshot. And if he had known, there had been no chance to remove it.

Convinced that it was not Nicholson, she considered for a fleeting moment the possibility of it having been Carlos. And dismissed it as absurd. Leaning against the parapet, she gazed out over the garden, as if seeking there a solution to her problem.

The foghorn voice of Mrs. Chenery admonishing her guests to gather their wraps informed Pat . . . and the neighbors . . . that the party was ready to leave for the club.

Young Dan and Nicholson reached Pat's side almost at the same moment. There was a puzzled look in Dan's eyes . . . the look of a child who has found by painful experience that fire will burn.

"We're leaving for the club," he said rapidly. "Will you go with me?"

There was an appraising look in his eyes as he waited for her answer.

Behind him Pat caught sight of Nicholson. The grey eyes were very steady and level, cornered by tiny wrinkles.

She hardly knew why she did it, but she said quickly:

"I'm sorry, Dan, but Captain Nicholson is taking me. He asked me at dinner."

Dan flushed hotly and his freckles were more pronounced than ever.

"Sorry," he said curtly, and turned away.

For a moment the chatter of the crowd at the other end of the room made sibilant overtones in the silence.

Then she said, half annoyed at herself for the thing she had done:

"I risked the possibility of your having asked someone else in telling Dan that, but I must talk to you."

"I came over to ask you to go with me," he answered, "but the youngster was ahead of me."

Pat's hair, catching the light from the moon outside and the shaded lights of the room, shone like black lacquer and her eyes were deep pools of gold-shot darkness. He turned his own eyes away from her for a moment. It was much easier, much less disturbing, not to look at her, to just stand back and try not to think. Letting the phrases that worried old memories slip through his brain unconsidered— that was the way to stop things from hurting.

"What I wanted to tell you," Pat said with little furtive glances about the room, "is that you're under suspicion."

Sudden gloom hardened the contours of his face as, in swift staccato sentences, she told him of the picture, of her belief that Dan, recognizing him as John Sobieski, had told the General, and then of the astounding climax when she found his picture missing and the snapshot of a strange man substituted.

There was a pause, then:

"Thank you for telling me," Nicholson said quietly.

"The muddle was of my making." Her voice was strained and off key. "If I had not been fool enough to keep that picture, it would not have happened. And in fairness I had to do what I could to remedy it. So I told you."

"Why did you keep the picture?" he asked gently, hopefully.

Confusion flooded her for a moment.

"Oh, I don't know . . . because a woman always looks back to what was, I suppose, just as a man looks forward to what will be. You'll find, when you've learned more about women, that we do a great many foolish things for no apparent reason." Then swiftly she changed the subject. "Shall we go? Everyone else seems to have gone. I must run up and get my wrap."

She vanished up the stairs. Nicholson waited until he heard the door of her room close behind her. The rattle of dishes and hum of voices from the rear told him that Carlos and the maid were engaged and were not likely to disturb him. Lifting the receiver of the telephone that stood on the table nearby he gave a number, and when the party at the other end answered, spoke a few swift cautious sentences.

There was the sound of a door opening in the rear of the house. Swiftly he hung up and moved over to the other side of the room, apparently deep in contemplation of the moon-drenched landscape outside. The telephone rang almost as soon as he reached the other side of the room. Carlos glided into the room and picked up the receiver.

"General Chenery's quarters," he said into the transmitter. "No, the General iss no here. He weel not return until late. Geeve me the radiogram and I weel see eet ees geev to him. *Un momento . . ."*

He picked up a pencil and wrote rapidly, then read back the message to the person at the other end.

"C.Q. Panama Dept.

"Quarry Heights, Canal Zone

"Re tel W.D. Jan. 28, 1933, assigning officers duty your department stop Captain Robert Nicholson found murdered here today stop Consequently unable join stop Orders cancelled stop Cancellation follows by mail."

There was a moment's silence as Carlos hung up the receiver, then Nicholson crossed the room toward him.

"Er—you have a message for the General?" he asked silkily.

"Si, Señor," Carlos answered, conscious for the first time of the presence of the officer in the room.

"I'll take it to him. We're joining him at the club."

"Oh, no, no, Señor, eet ees impossible. Theese message ees veree important. I mus' to the General geeve myself."

"But that's quite all right. The General wouldn't object to my having it."

"No, no Señor. *No es puerde.* To the General only mus' I geeve eet."

Almost as if by magic a flat little automatic appeared in Nicholson's hand. He jammed it into Carlos' ribs.

"Give me that message," he commanded in a low tone.

Carlos smiled faintly, a smile that seemed as unreal as himself. With a swift gesture he tore the sheet of paper into fragments and dropped them into a bronze bowl, used as an ashtray, which stood on the table.

"You should not be so hasty in attempting to shoot an ally, Captain—er—Nicholson," he said and his English was accentless.

Then he crossed to a side table, picked up the table lighter which stood there, and snapped it into flame. Nicholson watched him in amazement and neither of the men noticed that a vagrant breezed had picked up one of the scraps of paper and blown it to the floor. Carlos touched the flame of the lighter to the little white heap and in a moment only a few scarred scraps lay in its place.

Then he turned to the waiting man.

"You were quite right in being cautious, Captain—er—Nicholson. But it is quite unnecessary so far as I am concerned. I am K-50."

"K-50," Nicholson repeated mechanically.

"Quite so, Captain. I am K-50, and my instructions are to cooperate with K-92 to any extent that may be necessary. May I ask what your instructions are?"

"The first thing," Nicholson said, "is to make sure that the message you have just destroyed does not reach the General."

For answer Carlos lifted the receiver of the telephone.

"Quarry Heights 87," he called. When the connection had been completed, he went on, and Nicholson marveled at the perfect mimicry of the General's voice.

"This is General Chenery speaking. I want to talk to the operator on duty. Very good. You have just received for me a radiogram from Washington concerning a Robert Nicholson. I want all record of that message destroyed. It must not be discussed with your chief or your relief, when he comes on duty. Is that clear? Good-bye."

He hung up with a triumphant smile, then with a little exclamation pointed to the archway. Nicholson's eyes followed the pointing finger. Hundreds of tiny lights were creeping across the purple sea, while tiny pencils of light, searchlights, were playing across the sky.

"The fleet," Nicholson cried involuntarily.

"Aye, the fleet," Carlos said grimly. "They're proud enough to-night with their lights and searchlights. But the Slayer of Souls is awaiting his hour."

Chapter Twelve

IT WAS PURE CHANCE that gave Patricia Fenton her second clue to the mystery into which she had been unwillingly plunged; tossed her head first into its seething caldron.

Coming down the stairs she had heard the murmur of voices and there had come to her ears the single phrase in a strange voice, "The Slayer of Souls awaits his hour."

When she reached the verandah it was empty save for Nicholson who was staring out over the sea at the lights of the fleet below.

Wonderingly she looked about. Had her ears been playing her tricks? It had not been Nicholson's voice that she had heard, and yet he was alone on the verandah. It was on the tip of her tongue to ask him the meaning of the phrase when he spoke.

"Come over and take a look," he called. "The fleet's just coming in."

"Be there in a moment," she answered, dropping her bag on the table so that both hands might be free to tie the streamers of her wrap into a bow beneath her chin. The bag dropped to the floor and mechanically she stooped over to pick it up.

As she did so three words on a scrap of paper lying on the floor leaped up at her. "Nicholson found murdered" . . . she read. Her brain reeled. With trembling fingers she picked up the scrap of paper along with her bag. Read it again, furtively, her back turned, incredulity flooding her eyes. A nausea born of excitement rose in her. It seemed to touch her brain and bathe it in crystal clarity. Her thoughts settled, like bits of colored glass, into a brilliant pattern; a pattern that spread beyond her mind, that carried her with it, momentarily, the center of shifting lights and shadows. Then she slipped the bit of paper into her handbag and crossed to the railing. Leaned against a pillar. Her eyes were clear and untroubled . . . as though she had made up her mind about something and knew precisely what she was going to do.

Nevertheless, a hollow sensation, faintly cold, was spreading over her. It was a feeling of discovery, half of shock, half of horror. The hollow coldness increased, touching her thoughts and giv-

ing them an ultra clarity. She heard herself speaking in a tone colorless as ice.

"Did you kill this Captain Nicholson whose place you are taking?"

It was a quiet question, but Nicholson was assailed by something akin to panic. What did this girl know? He studied her face
before answering. Her profile, burningly white, seemed to cauter-
ize the darkness.

Finally he said in a hushed, flat voice: "No, I did not kill
Nicholson."

"Did you know that he was dead?"

He smiled, a queer little smile that quivered at one corner of his
mouth, whimsical and melancholy, and parried with an answer
that was a question.

"How did you know?"

For answer she opened her handbag, extended the scrap of paper to him. He glanced at it.

"Where did you find that?"

His voice was as dry and keen as a new-ground sword.

She told him.

"Oh." He shrugged. "So that," he said thoughtfully, "appears to
be that."

As he spoke she caught a hard glitter in his eyes. He could be
cruel, she decided. A dreamer, yes . . . but of a type that could di-
rect men to his purpose, making opportunities of their failures, or,
inspired by his illusions, sacrifice them pitilessly to his purpose.
Yet the picture did not match the mental snapshots her mind had
retained.

A long silence followed. The hollow sensation dwindled to a
fine point, pressed into her breast and hurt her with a sharpness
that was physical. She had a sudden, inexplicable desire to laugh.
He had opened the door to hidden secrets . . . and now the door
was sealed again. Irony. For a moment she felt frightened, felt that
life was transient and death immortal. Then she leaned nearer to
him.

"Hadn't you better go," she queried, "while there's time?"

"You mean," he questioned, "clear out?"

She nodded. "Before the General sees this . . ." She indicated
the slip of paper in her hand.

"The General hasn't seen it . . . and won't see it," he said
calmly. Silhouetted against the night his features had a vital qual-

ity that she had not felt before; he was . . . yes . . . in spite of what she suspected . . . rather likable.

She said shakily, her face uplifted to his, pale as a silver petal in the shaded gloom:

"Don't you realize you can't get away with what you're doing? I don't know why you're doing it. But whatever the reason, it can't be worth the risk."

He smiled a trifle grimly. The risk! How little she knew of the actual risk. Then she went on:

"Is it . . . are you doing it for money? If it is . . . I . . . perhaps I can help you." There was a feverish touch to her voice. "My brother is on one of the ships out there with the fleet. He has influence in Washington. If I ask him, he could find something for you there."

He turned, his face glimmering in the darkness, his thoughts dominated by a memory of two years before . . . of a white night on the sands with the moon distilling mad magic and pouring it over them. Curious, too, what the sound of a woman's voice could do to a man . . . futile, absurd, heartbreaking things.

"I must work this thing out myself," he said in a hard tone of voice. "There isn't anything that anybody can do."

"But there must be," she cried desperately. "You can't go on with this thing."

He looked at her sharply.

"Does it mean so much to you?"

"It's just because I don't want to see you in trouble," she said hastily.

"Is it because you care . . . Pat?" he asked gently.

"Care?" She kept her eyes lowered, so that they might not betray how much she did care. Deep in her heart she knew that she cared . . . for a murderer, perhaps. The shock of that realization cleared her head. She threw it back and laughed. But her voice was hard. The laugh lacked genuineness. "That's beside the point. I'm trying to help you. Can't you see that? Just as I would anyone who needed help."

"I see," he said quietly. His lighter spurted vividly into flame, laid a glow against a lean, disturbed countenance. For a second their eyes met through the gauzy smoke of his cigarette. He had cast off his indifferent, callous air, and his face had settled into a grim mould.

"Perhaps you don't care," he said carefully. "I've no right to assume that you do. But I care—for you. I thought I didn't. I told myself I didn't when I ran away and never wrote you. But I was merely lying to myself. I was being a coward, running away from the love that I knew was there. The reason that I did . . ."

She made a swift gesture that cut short his words.

"Need we go into that? It is water under the bridge."

"I can't let you go on thinking that . . . that I just left. . . that I looked on it just as a summer flirtation," he said earnestly. "It was because of money . . . there wasn't enough to support a wife . . . I couldn't ask you to share what I had to offer . . . so I played the coward and ran away."

She put out a hand blindly toward one of the pillars. She could not altogether keep the unsteadiness out of her voice.

"Money! Oh, I know the man's viewpoint. Women are to be sheltered. They can't have any blood in their veins. They must keep their skirts clear of the dust and make pretty pictures." She stopped, and then added. "Don't you suppose women want to take chances, too?"

"Not the kind of chance that I had to offer," he said gently.

"They do," she said. "The reason commonly given is that of love. But that is all in the past. Let it remain in the past. It is the present we are living in now. Are you willing to give up . . . whatever it is that you are doing?"

"I can't, Pat," he told her unhappily.

"Then I can't keep silent any longer," she told him. And wondered at her own strength. "You must either go . . . or I will tell General Chenery that the real Captain Nicholson is dead . . . that you are John Sobieski, a naval draftsman, masquerading in his uniform."

"Even though you knew it would mean prison . . . or worse . . . for me?" he asked, pain wrenching at his heart.

"I give you," she answered deliberately, ignoring his question, "until to-morrow morning. If by then you have not disappeared, I shall tell the General." She turned toward the door. "I think we had better go after the others. They will be wondering what is keeping us."

Together they went out into the purple darkness.

From a crack of the partly opened dining-room door Carlos watched them go. There was a curious smile on his face as he took from a pocket of his white coat the snapshot of Nicholson that he had abstracted from Pat's bag.

Below the house, in the Bay of Panama, the battle fleet of the United States rode peacefully at anchor.

Chapter Thirteen

THE UNION CLUB is built out over the water of Panama Bay, and when Pat and Nicholson reached the club the rows of tables set about the edge of the open air dancing floor were crowded. Women in filmy frocks, officers in white uniforms. An air of festivity, a buoyant spirit which is one of the charms of Panama, was everywhere. To-morrow most of the officers would be sweating in the jungle, as troops moved to repel landing parties of an imaginary invader. Fans waved, the sound of light chatter and laughter filled the air; white-clad waiters swarmed at the sound of clapping hands, which is the universal signal for a waiter in the tropics; from the bar came the sound of clicking dice and laughter as officers rolled the dice for drinks.

"Hello, there," called Mrs. Chenery as she pranced by in the embrace of a perspiring young officer performing his duty dance, and everybody within several blocks turned to see who was addressing them. "I thought you'd never get here."

Mrs. Chenery was light on her feet when she stayed on them . . . but not so light on other people's. She waved a fat hand at Pat and Nicholson as the two found an empty table, close to the railing, and then applauded vigorously, much to her partner's dismay, as the music stopped.

The orchestra began an encore, a slow waltz. The lights went out and the dance floor was illuminated only by the moonlight. In the dimness the little table floated in a sea of silver luster. Out on the floor couples swung in time to the lilting music. For a moment Pat's and Nicholson's talk was keyed to the soft mood of the night, a thing of pauses and low voices. To Nicholson, watching the play of moonlight in Pat's hair, the whole situation seemed to take on an air of unreality . . . a dream in which anything might happen.

He knew, though, what was going to happen. He knew Pat well enough to know that her threat had been no matter of idle words. He knew there was strength and determination beneath that sweetness and loveliness. And he knew that the morning would find him

a military prisoner. Unless . . . He shoved the thought aside resolutely and turned his thoughts back to the moment.

A sharp pain stabbed his heart as he realized with what little
compunction the woman he loved was ready to betray him. He
wondered what she knew—what she suspected. How she must
hate him. And then he clung to the forlorn hope that perhaps she
was placing what she considered her duty before love for him. But
immediately he dismissed the thought as the refuge of a weakling
who was afraid to face the truth. She could not love him or she
would not betray him.

Pat was sitting back in her chair watching the scene. For a moment Nicholson was content to study her. The slim oval of her
face, pointed and fresh, held a remote memory of trouble. It was as
if, seated there and staring out into the moonlight, she listened to
something in the dusk. A ragged, hungry restlessness streaked
along Nicholson's face as he watched her.

"Like it?" he asked after a moment.

Her acute inspection raked him. Then, just as if she had determined to forget what had already passed between them until the
morning dawned, she flashed him a smile.

"This"—she waved a hand at the crowd—"or this?" And the
hand indicated the frowning sea wall and an angle of a street,
dimly seen, where faces drifted by endlessly like leaves on a slow
black tide.

"All of it," he said.

She cupped her chin in her hands and stared out into the night,
drenched with tropic starlight, heavy with sweetness, a green
darkness pressing on hands and lips. Said musingly:

"I like Panama. It's just as if nothing here ever changes. As if
nothing ever would. It has permanency, the definite feeling that
the shadows have lain long and the hush given peace for a thousand years . . . dusty romance and old, shabby, colors . . . almost as
if time hangs soundlessly in the air and the heat and the smell of
frangipani wraps you around. And nothing could shatter the
peace," she finished.

Nicholson nodded and fingered the tall stemmed glass which a
waiter had just filled with champagne.

"It's a queer city," he said. "Spain in America . . . or America
in Spain, whichever way you want to look at it. Bad art to national
heroes erected in front of buildings with time-mellowed fa-
çades . . . imported French cars and ox-carts disputing the right of
way over cobblestone pavements."

He stared for a moment at the heavy jagged masses of the low mountains that rose against the moonlit sky on the further side of the bay. His nostrils were full of warm smells, a smothering blanket of sweetness, underlaid with a curious animal odor, like the breath of some great beast. He had the feeling that the jungle was creeping out across the moonlit water to meet them.

"Here"—and his head indicated the dancers—"we're dancing and drinking and talking, wearing the trappings of civilization. And out there"—and he flung out a hand toward the distant shore—"there are Indians who are living just as their forefathers were living when the Conquistadores landed and planted the cross on the sands of the Pacific. For four hundred years civilization has been marching across the Isthmus of Panama . . . and all the impression it has made has been the erection of a couple of cities . . . twin rails of steel from ocean to ocean . . . and the Canal."

"Well?"

She laid a long, deeply shadowed inspection upon him, every thought and emotion seeming to absorb his worth as he sat there.

He shrugged. The mood shattered. The orchestra struck up a Spanish air and he rose.

"Shall we dance?"

The music came as a bittersweet reminder of the last time they had danced together . . . that night of white magic. He was seeing her now as he had never seen her before. The lovely unawakened girl he had known was gone. The silver Artemis who had woven the magic of her presence under the pale chastity of the moon was gone. He saw her now . . . as he would always see her . . . a woman who had materialized from his world scroll into intimate palpability, bringing the rich gift of her presence . . . and leaving the bitterness of rue upon her departure. But life was like that. You took what came and you made yourself like it. But there was an ache, just the same.

And then . . .

Illusions faded and he was back in a remembered world, a world in which you could only try to forget the aching dreams you had, when young and gay, you went seeking for the pot of gold at the end of the rainbow . . .

Someone had tapped him on the shoulder. It was young Dan Martin, cutting in. Reluctantly he surrendered Pat to him; saw them swing out onto the floor together.

Chapter Fourteen

MRS. CHENERY WAS EXCITED. And when Mrs. Chenery was excited she was like a river in flood. Everything movable went down before her.

The cause of her excitement had been a fragment of overheard conversation between the British minister and the governor of the Zone.

Said the minister: "You know, Prince Lai is worth listening to. Aside from wielding enormous influence in Inner Mongolia, he's both a scholar and a mystic."

That had been enough for Mrs. Chenery. Followed a visit to the lobby, a short conversation with one of the attendants and a few moments later she slipped into the open air ballroom again. Prince Lai was alone at his table for the moment. She barged her way across the dance floor and dropped into the chair opposite to him; laid down on the table a deck of cards she carried in her hand. The Prince watched her in considerable amazement.

"Shall I make a wish?" she asked coyly.

"If you care to," he answered, mystified.

"Shall I cut?" she asked, fingering the cards longingly.

"If you don't mind, what is it to be?" asked the Prince. "Auction or contract?"

"Silly," she giggled. "You're going to tell my fortune."

"Tell your fortune?" echoed the Prince wonderingly. "With those?"

"Oh, don't you do it with cards?" She looked her surprise.

"I'm afraid I don't understand," began the Prince.

"The palm, then," and she handed him two fat and bejeweled hands. "The last time, it was a Spanish woman, and she told me the most remarkable things . . . of course, not that I believed them . . . but do begin. I'm just dying to hear it."

"My dear madam," began the Prince, "whatever gave you the idea that I read palms?"

"Oh," she cried in dismay, "you don't read palms either? Then what do you do? Crystal gazing? Or perhaps you read tea leaves?"

"I'm sorry to have to disappoint you, but I'm not a fortune teller," said the Prince.

"You're not?" she said suspiciously. "Well, that's very strange. The British minister said you were a. mystic."

"Oh," said the Prince agreeably. "That. I only go into trances. But I don't like to do that. I really quite forget myself. I'm quite liable to do things that I'd regret afterwards."

"Goodness"—she shoved her chair back from the table a trifle and looked at him with suspicion—"not dangerous things?"

"Quite dangerous," he said unsmilingly. "It's remarkable, but I feel extraordinarily in the mood for a trance right now. I'm glad you mentioned it . . ."

"Excuse me," the General's wife said, getting to her feet with such haste that her chair fell over backwards. "I see the General signaling to me. I really must hurry over to see what he wants."

And she skidded across the polished floor with all of the agility of a ten-ton truck on a slippery highway, nearly bringing ruin and destruction upon a young officer and his partner who were thinking more of each other than of their dancing. The glances she cast over her shoulder held the expression of a deer hearing the sound of the wolf pack on its trail.

If one of the followers of his Highness Prince Lai Chung, hereditary ruler of the princes of Inner Mongolia, Guardian of the Jade of Shingtze Po, Keeper of the Secrets of the Ancient Ones had seen his chief then, he would have been astonished. For the grave face with its hooded eyes was wreathed in the broadest smile it had held in many a day.

The smile faded into his habitual expression of gravity as he caught sight of Pat leaving the dance floor with young Martin. Rising, he crossed the floor in time to hear Nicholson ask the Lieutenant to join Pat and himself at their table. Martin's refusal was courteous, but somewhat strained, and the eyes of the Prince flickered reflectively from them to the retreating back of the Lieutenant.

"May I join you," he begged. "My partner has deserted me for the charms of a younger man."

"Glad to have you, your Highness," Nicholson said, rising. He watched the Mongol narrowly but covertly as he took his seat. Why had the man chosen them, out of all the party? But perhaps it was only his own over-stimulated imagination that made it seem odd. The Prince could not possibly know the reason for his being in Panama. And the sad eyes and impassive face made him instantly dismiss the thought that he was an ally of Chu-Sheng.

"It is a perfect night," the Prince said after a moment, his eyes watching a school of fish skim the glassy undulations of the bay in greenish, phosphorescent flashes as they sought to escape the relentless hunter that lurked beneath the surface. "Difficult to realize that beneath the peaceful surface of that water there are slayers just as there are on land."

Pat leaned forward.

"That reminds me," she said with a certain repressed excitement. "Do either of you know the meaning of the phrase 'The Slayer of Souls'?"

There was a little gasp at her side, followed by a sharp snap and a tinkle of glass. Nicholson's hand had been playing with the stem of his champagne glass and, suddenly tightening around it, had snapped it as though it had been made of brittle straw. A swift look showed her his face drained of blood and eyes wide in unbelief. "I'm sorry," he said, "clumsy of me."

The Prince's eyes dwelt upon him inscrutably. Even Pat, unaware of the significance of the phrase to both of the men, could not escape the feeling that the atmosphere about their table was suddenly tense with sudden drama.

But none of it was evident in the voice of the Prince when he spoke. It held all of its usual calm courtesy.

"Miss Fenton," he said, "that is a phrase rarely used in my country. Indeed, so rarely that I am puzzled where you could have heard it."

"Oh, then you can explain it," Pat cried. "Please do."

"There are three things to which man clings hardest," the Prince went on in his grave voice. "In the last analysis, they are all he has. One is contained in the other . . . yet each is separate. They are his soul, his personality, his life. By his soul I mean that unseen essence which your religion . . . and mine also . . . teaches us is immortal. By personality I mean the ego, the mind, that which says 'I am I' . . . the storehouse of old memories, the seeker of new ones. Life I need not define. Life, anyone may destroy, take. Science long ago learned that personality . . . ego, if you prefer . . . may be submerged, altered, destroyed. But whatever happens to these two, the soul remains unaltered. But if the soul be destroyed . . . obliterated . . . then the other two of man's possessions are as a ship without a rudder. Life becomes purposeless, living only in the present, knowing neither a future nor a past. Man goes on in the flesh like an amoeba of the sea, his consciousness submerged, a creature of the senses, but without Sense. The body becomes as an empty shell in which the kernel has been devoured by worms. When the soul is slain, the body is as a piece of animate clay in which the breath of realization has been snuffed out like a candle in the wind. It is the Living Death. Therefore, it follows that he who has the power to slay the soul is to be regarded with dread. For the victims of the Slayer of Souls join the ranks of the Living Dead. Have I made myself clear?"

"Perfectly," Pat answered in a low voice, conscious of Nicholson's intent gaze upon her, and of the fact that the eyes of the Prince were flickering almost imperceptibly from Nicholson to herself.

"Would you forgive my curiosity," the Prince begged, "and tell me where you heard that phrase?"

"I'm sorry," Pat lied, "but I really can't remember. I probably heard it years ago, and it stuck in my subconscious mind until just now. I've no idea what brought it to the forefront of my memory."

The Prince did not smile, but when he spoke there was an inflection in his voice that suggested he had thought of smiling.

"You will forgive me if I seem too serious," he said, "but the— the phrase that you mentioned is a symbol for something that is best left unspoken . . . and unthought. If I were you I would not mention it again."

But Pat was persistent. "Just one thing more, your Highness. *Who* is the Slayer of Souls?"

An odd shiver ran across the Prince's face at the question. It was like a tremor through ice. Then the inscrutable mask of the Oriental settled again.

"If I may answer a question with a question," he said, "who is Satan of your western theology?"

"You mean," she persisted, "that the Slayer of Souls corresponds to Satan?"

"I mean," the Prince said slowly, "that it is a term . . . and that in that term is comprehended all the evil, all the cunning, all the perverted spiritual intelligence of evil . . . its sinister might . . . its menace."

He turned his head slightly so that the inscrutable eyes were fixed upon Nicholson.

"You have been in China, Captain. Possibly you have heard of the Book of Iron?"

Nicholson's gaze was level. "Yes," he said evenly.

"It is called that," the Prince said, "because the leaves are made of exceedingly fine sheets of the metal, and it is engraved in the Book of Iron that no one shall face the Slayer of Souls and afterwards serve other than him.

"Possibly also," the Prince went on, "you know something of the usage of the Book of Iron."

Nicholson shook his head. "Only that it's supposed to be filled with incantations and magical formulas and similar rubbish."

"Rubbish, Captain?" queried the Oriental, drawing on the mask of patience that an Oriental early learns to use consummately or not at all. "Wiser minds than yours or mine decided about that years ago . . . several thousand years ago, if the chronological records of my House are true . . . and I know that they are. No, Captain. The Book of Iron is the record of secrets that used to form the basis of the Ancient Mysteries. Not religious secrets. Merely knowledge of natural laws. Compared to them our modern scientists are just as Alexander the Great would have been if someone confronted him with a bombing plan or an eighteen inch gun."

"I have heard . . . things . . . in China," Nicholson admitted with an odd hesitation. "But of course . . ."

". . . Of course," cut in the Prince swiftly, "in common with most Westerners you believe only in the things that can be proven. Which, if you will permit me to use your word, is rubbish. So long as a thing exists, why not accept its existence?"

"If a thing exists, it can be proven," argued Pat, resting her chin in her hands.

"Not necessarily," the Prince said. "This room is full of light, of laughter, of music and of color. Yet bring a man in here who is both deaf and blind and to him it is just another space of silent darkness. But does that prove that the light and the music don't exist? No, it only proves that the man's senses are not attuned to receive them. What, then, is to prevent there being other phenomena in this room, in this world, which you, in your blindness, in your deafness, cannot see nor hear?"

"You mean supernatural entities?" Pat queried.

"Nothing is supernatural, when you understand it," the Prince answered. "The only thing that exists is truth, but sometimes that is like a jewel at the bottom of a well—difficult to perceive."

"I guess I'm a die-hard reactionary," Nicholson said slowly, "but . . . well . . . if a thing is there, it's there. If it isn't, it isn't."

"Electricity was in the world from the beginning," said the Prince gravely. "How many men of how many ages observed its effects before one discovered it? Jewels were in the world from the beginning. How many men pass where they lie hidden, until one digs and finds them. Wisdom was in the world from the beginning, but only those whose minds are open to it can find it. As for example . . . that."

He waved a long slender hand before them.

Their eyes followed his outflung hand.

"Good God," Nicholson blurted. And sat dumb.

Far out on the moonlit surface of the Bay of Panama stood a city . . . a strange city . . . walls and golden roofs floating like a fabulous Atlantis in the silver moonrays . . . a wilderness of narrow streets and dazzling whitewashed houses (some roofed with blue tiles, others with dull red) rising to one great dominating structure standing sheer-walled upon sharply truncated rocks. Its massive bulk, longer than two city blocks, was pierced by row upon row of windows that seemed no larger than loopholes, and naked walls fell away from peaked roofs and terrace-like additions.

Pat's hand stole out and tightened upon Nicholson's arm.

"Do you see it?" she whispered.

"Yes," he replied through scarcely moving lips.

The thing was as impossible as water running uphill, and yet he was brought face to face with the actuality of the unbelievable.

From the main gate of the city before them a street cleaved between brick-walled enclosures. Beggars, ragged, repulsive looking creatures, crouched at the roadside and dogs and swine nosed in the black bubbling mud of the gutters.

Nicholson knew it was impossible, yet he could feel the keen wind that blew down from the snowcapped peaks encircling the city, feel it clearly through the thin white of his uniform.

Far and sonorous, quavering across the water from the city came the sound of bronze temple gongs.

Then suddenly there was nothing on the water, or beyond it, save the silver moonlight; no sound save the cry of a gull, sharp and querulous, flying above the sea wall, and the chatter of the crowd about the edge of the dance floor.

"That was Lhassa, the Sacred City," the Prince said politely.

"What . . . what did you do to us?" Pat asked in a little quavering voice.

"Only the Infinite knows what we living do to one another . . . or to ourselves," answered the Prince in a gentle voice.

"But . . . but it looked . . . real," Pat managed to say.

"All truth is real. Only *things* are relative, and pass when they have had their day. Truth *is* and all phenomena are delusion." The voice of the Prince was measured, slow, his words falling like the ticking of a great clock. "There are photographs of Lhassa, the Sacred City, in existence, taken by members of the Younghusband Expedition into Tibet. Some day it may amuse you to compare the photographs with the—original."

Nicholson moistened his lips and stole another glance at the still waters of the bay. Sky and water were blank and still, bathed in the moonlight.

"But the bells . . . I heard . . ." he began.

His reliance upon the laws of space and time, as he thought he knew them, was being wrenched from its foundations. His faith in the indestructibility of matter, in the continuity of force, in the fundamental laws of physics, was shaken and tottering. The universe no longer seemed a scene played in front of the great blank curtain of the unknowable across which filed an orderly progress of more or less predictable occurrences; it was becoming the playground of amazing things staged by this man who sat here at the table with him.

"Have you ever heard the bells of the Vatican across the radio?" the Prince asked.

"Yes . . . but this . . ." insisted Nicholson.

"This time you heard the gongs in the temple of the Sleeping Buddah in Lhassa . . . over my radio."

The two stared at him in bewilderment. The Prince smiled.

"No," he said calmly. "I do not carry tubes and a loud speaker concealed in my pockets. I am my own radio, just as you are yours. The only difference between us being that I have learned how to tune in."

"But I saw . . ." Pat began.

"Of course you saw," the Prince said. "Saw and heard. For a moment you were tuned in on my television. I merely made you realize what I myself have seen. A century or so ago your country would have burned me at the stake for it. To-day you would call it magic . . . shrink from it. But it is no more magical . . . no more extraordinary . . . than the television which permits you to see and hear objects a hundred miles or so away. Only, when you turn the dial of a television cabinet you know that behind its wooden exterior is a piece of machinery whose workings, in part at least, you comprehend . . . whose daily use has made its marvel a commonplace."

"It's uncanny," Pat said with a little shudder. "I don't know why . . . but I feel . . ."

"I know precisely how you feel," the Prince said gently. "To you it savors of the so-called supernatural. In actuality it was merely a simple exposition of the existence of one of those things that exist but that cannot be proven. Long before Christ was attempting to point the way from darkness into light, priests of China had discovered and were practicing fundamental laws . . . demonstrating that what is possible in one instance is possible in every instance. They are not secrets. At least not in the sense that you understand secrets. They are elemental facts whose roots strike as far below the surface of knowledge as the roots of the bamboo strike beneath the surface of the soil."

He paused a moment as if seeking the answer to a question within himself . . . and then seemed to come out of his meditation as if emerging from another universe.

"There exists an underworld of the mind of which the ordinary man knows nothing . . . the subconscious, where our lives and destinies are shaped without our knowledge. This is the force that controls us from the cradle to the grave. And it governs us while the body rests and the so-called intellectual faculties are inept and asleep. The conscious and educated mind of man is but a sharpened monkey cleverness, a few phrases learned by heart; a few ounces of viscid grayness subject to disease and decay.

"The subconscious is the real spirit of man; the immortal spirit within us which, save for a few, we have never striven to learn or understand. In our ignorance we follow the blind promptings of the material mind, which leads us into misery, illness, death. There is a Chinese allegory that the gods made man immortal, but hid the place of his soul, leaving him to discover where it was. Actually this is no fable. When a man comprehends the Higher Law through the teachings of the Ancient Ones, he can discover the secret of the subconscious and how to use it aright. Then he is master of his immortal soul and the dark universe in which he dwells."

He dropped into silence for a moment and then looked up, answering the unspoken question that trembled on Nicholson's lips.

"There are but few of us who can say that they understand the workings of the Higher Law. But those of us who do understand . . . and I am one, know that this knowledge is not always put to the use for which it was intended. Sometimes through the inscrutable working of the Higher Law, it is diverted to the purposes of evil. And, although justice is inevitable, evil may work havoc with the lives of those with whom it comes in contact."

He turned with queer sort of majesty, and faced Pat.

"That is why, Miss Fenton, I suggest you do not refer again to the Slayer of Souls. For evil brings evil, just as good brings good." He paused, then went on.

"I wonder," he begged, "if I might presume so far as to ask you to accept this."

He held something hidden in the palm of his hand. She bent over it. It was a small looped cross of ivory and fettered to it by tiny threads of gold was a spider carved in jet.

"It may be," he said gravely, "that this will be of service to you some day."

The voice of Mrs. Chenery, speaking from behind Pat's shoulder, came as a crashing dissonance in the quietness of the moment.

"Do you see that handsome young man over there, by the palm . . . the blond one with the soulful eyes," she said excitedly. "Well, my dear, he's been trying to flirt with me for the past half hour."

She slid into the empty chair next to Pat, entirely disregarding the presence of the two men, and heaved a contented sigh.

"I don't know what it is," she confided modestly, lowering her tones so that the orchestra could still be heard, "but you've no idea what a terrible time I have keeping the men at their distance. An attractive woman has to be so careful. Thank heavens the General doesn't realize. He'd be simply devoured with jealousy. Of course, being a man and blind, he thinks they're only paying homage to the General's wife . . . Oh, dear me, *he's coming over here!*" And there was genuine panic in the italics with which she underscored the words. She seized Pat's arm in a vise-like grip. "What shall I do?"

The blond young man came striding across the dance floor, dexterously avoiding couples, came right on toward Mrs. Chenery and . . . right past her.

She fanned herself vigorously.

"Oh, dear," she panted. "I thought I'd have a stroke. If he hadn't caught my frown in time my husband would be a murderer now and I would be an abandoned woman."

What Mrs. Chenery hadn't noticed was that the blond young man headed for a tall girl two tables further on whose attention he had been trying to catch for the past fifteen minutes.

Chapter Fifteen

SWIFT CLOUDS WERE SCUDDING across the sky as Nicholson strode down Calle Central with Carlos by his side. The moon was obscured and a little wind was blowing down from the hills. Somewhere a clock struck three, and had Nicholson been more familiar with the rainy season of Panama he would have known that the usual nightly downpour was due.

The two walked along in silence through the sleeping city. Now and then Nicholson stole sidewise glances at his companion. The man puzzled him. Obviously of mixed race, as obviously he was no average half-breed. Whatever his station in life, it was far above the position of butler he occupied in the Chenery household. And the man was cultured; not only educated but cultured. His English was flawless. It might have been the English of a graduate of one of the great colleges of the United States.

After a while, Carlos cast a glance at him and smiled.

"You are wondering why I serve the Master, are you not, Captain? I trust that you do not object to my addressing you as Captain? The only other term by which I could address you is K-92."

The latter part of the speech was obviously an opening for confidences. But one does not squander truth too lavishly on men who will repeat it. Nicholson contented himself with answering the first part of it.

"I have been wondering," he admitted.

"A great many people whom you would not suspect serve the Master," Carlos said. "You will meet many of them later."

"Not all of them Chinese," Nicholson hazarded.

Carlos glanced at him oddly.

"Chinese? Oh, I see. You take me for Chinese. I am Japanese." There was a note of pride in his voice. "Only half Japanese in blood—my father was of Nippon—but all Japanese in my heart."

They walked on in silence after that as Nicholson pondered the situation.

He had found Carlos waiting for him in his room at the Casa Central on his return from the club. He was the bearer of a message that inwardly filled Nicholson with misgiving, although it was the first major step on the path along which he had elected to walk . . . the first duty with which he had been entrusted by the Master.

The message had been brief, but it had been sufficient. Nicholson knew what was expected of him, although the reason for the thing he was to do was still shrouded in darkness.

It was his job to get Carlos into a secret room carved out of the living rock of Ancon Hill . . . a room that only he, as the officer in charge, and General Chenery himself, had access to . . . a room that was the nerve center of the Panama Canal . . . referred to in official correspondence as P.CD. Blue Plans . . . and it was his job to see that Carlos got out again unobserved when his mission in that room was accomplished.

But what the mission was, and the reason that he had been given orders by the Tongueless One to admit General Chenery's butler to the most closely guarded secret of the Panama Canal was still shrouded in secrecy, although some glimmering of the enormity of the plan which lay behind the instructions of Chu-Sheng was visible.

But now, with each step, as they entered the fragrant, tree-shrouded streets of Ancon and began the climb around the shoulder of the hill toward Army headquarters, apprehension rose in him like a chill and shuddersome tide.

And then he almost halted in his stride. Good God! Was *that* the thing contemplated by the Tongueless One?

Involuntarily his gaze shot off to the left where, shrouded now by intervening trees, the battle fleet of the United States lay at anchor.

Pat awakened with a start. Involuntarily she sat up in bed, staring drowsily about the room. It was buried in dusk. The moonlight, floating through the casement, crusted the floor with a band of pearl. As full consciousness wiped the threads of sleep from her brain, she wondered what had caused her sudden awakening. No noise, for silence shut down like a lid, made more intense by the sighing of trees beyond the stone terrace. The sounds of a clock on the table seemed to stitch the hush.

For a moment she sat there, vaguely uneasy; then swung her feet over the side and slipped them into bedroom sandals. Moving quietly to the dressing table she looked at the clock. After three . . . her sandals lisped on the polished floor as she crept to the window.

Below her Balboa and the entrance to the Canal lay asleep in the breathless night. Island, city, fleet and harbor. With a little shiver she returned to the bed.

Strange to awaken like this, she thought. The new surroundings probably. She sighed and settled deeper in the bed.

. . . She was almost asleep when a shadow flitted across her vision. At first it seemed a part of the slumber that had nearly overcome her, and she lay there contemplating the window casement where it had passed until it was borne to her suddenly, and not without shock, that she was fully awake and the shadow was not a shadow but a very substantial form that had stolen by the verandah. The realization drew her muscles rigid, and she lay motionless, listening to the hammering of her heart.

A faint scraping sound came from outside. What was it. A footfall? An oblong reservoir of darkness outlined the doorway. She could see nothing . . . she must move . . . call someone. But her body was locked in a temporary paralysis, her tongue dry.

Again the sound. Unmistakable. Someone was walking stealthily.

Her fright increased, swelled, became so acute that she could no longer endure it.

"John."

It was not a scream; a whisper. She found that she could move. She sat up, and her groping hand touched something cold on the table; closed about it. Slowly she got out of bed and crept toward the door to the verandah.

And then suddenly a voice rang in her ears; a voice that was not in the room; a voice that seemed to arise from within her brain; a voice that was clear and commanding.

"Back," it said. "Go back. Go back."

A faint amber light glowed on the walls of the room on the second floor of Prince Lai's residence, rendered more obscure the corners of the room, glimmered softly on the outlines of the *Crux Ansata* to which the replica of the monstrous spider was fettered, brought out in shadowy relief the semicircle of kneeling men and gathered in a pool of light in the center of the great slab of polished, lucent substance which stood before it.

From the semicircle of kneeling, yellow-clad men rose a thin, droning chant, faint but continuous upon one note, a note almost as high as that made by the rapid vibration of a bee's wings magnified a hundred times . . . a note that filled the room as the nave of a great cathedral is filled by the distant sound of an organ.

Prince Lai sat before the slab of green peering intently into the swirling pool of liquid light. And mirrored in its transparent depths was a room . . . a girl . . . Patricia Fenton . . . walking slowly . . . almost blindly toward an oblong of doorway. . . .

Prince Lai spoke and his voice held an echo of sternness:

"Back," he said softly. "Go back. Go back."

As if in answer to his command the slim, white clad figure in the pool of light hesitated . . . swayed . . . slowly moved away from the door and away from the figure which stood just beyond the doorpost, a figure invisible to the girl.

"Return to your bed," the Prince commanded in the same low, mellow voice. "And sleep . . . sleep . . . sleep deeply . . . you will remember nothing when you awake to-morrow."

Again, as if in blind obedience to a command she could not hear, the white-clad figure moved swayingly toward the bed . . . lay down . . . the droning note mounted. It held a concentration shattering quality, a blurring effect upon the mind . . . in a moment the girl upon the bed was sound asleep again.

And now the Prince spoke again, but this time his tone was sharp . . . commanding . . . full of menace.

"Ch'ing Fan," he cried in a terrible voice.

The shadowy figure lurking beyond the doorway obeyed the command . . . stumbled through it into the room as if impelled by a force greater than his own . . . The moonlight slanting through the window glinted on the blade of the thin, keen knife he carried.

"Halt, in the Name of the Ancient Ones," cried the Prince. "Thou knowest that to take life is forbidden to me . . . that I who know the secrets of the Azure Caverns may not slay . . . yet wilt thou, who came by night to take an innocent life, forfeit thine own . . . death waits for thou in this room, and not all the power of The Accursed One who sits upon the head of the Slayer of Souls can save thee . . . death that comes not by my hand . . . look now at thy feet . . ."

The face of the man in the lucent pool of light became livid with fear as he saw almost at his feet the swaying form of a cobra . . . a monstrous thing with inflated hood . . . wicked triangular head . . . the eyes glittering like mica discs with a filmy overglow; saw the tongue shoot out, reddish black, nervous, quivering; saw the steely whip of body slowly rise . . . rise . . . until the wicked head stood waist high with a wavy motion . . . a pitiless stretching of strength and cruelty, the black spots on the stripes of the sulphur-colored, scaly skin glittering like cressets of evil desire. He saw the jaws open wide, exposing the curved fangs. Then . . .

The bloated hood shot forward . . . struck . . . again . . . again . . .

The man in the pool of light stumbled backwards . . . backwards . . . through the door to the verandah . . . agony clearly to be seen on his face . . .

The miracle of lucent green light in the curved slab swirled as smoke is swirled by a breeze . . . the picture grew dim . . . faded . . . the green light narrowed to a pinpoint that danced and glimmered in the center of the slab.

The Prince turned wearily toward the semicircle of kneeling men.

"See that the body is found outside the house," he ordered and rose slowly to his feet.

Back in her room on the second floor of General Chenery's quarters Patricia Fenton slumbered peacefully in her bed. Clutched tightly in her hand was the hard cold object she had picked up from the bedside table . . . a tiny replica of the gigantic *Crux Ansata* with the fettered spider that stood in the room where Prince Lai had sat.

Chapter Sixteen

TAP—TAP—TAP. Pat stirred in her sleep. The bright morning sun poured into her room through the high open windows; there was a warm softness in the sea wind that lifted the long curtains. Lying there, in the always pathetic power of sleep, she looked like a little girl; an appealing little girl with her pale cheeks, even breath and little blue shadows under her eyes.

Tap—tap—tap.

The knocking was swifter, more determined. And at last it penetrated through layers of sleep consciousness, and Pat awoke with a start. She sat up. Nine said the clock on the dressing table. And a bright sun shining. Sunlight brought courage. She remembered her threat to the man who called himself Nicholson, made the night before. She would keep it. But a twinge of regret accompanied the resolution. It was pity, she told herself resolutely. Only pity. Nothing else.

The tapping began again, and she slipped out of bed, drew on her dressing gown and opened the door to Carlos standing there with her breakfast tray. He smiled cheerfully.

She returned the smile as he put the tray on the bedside table.

"The Señora, she say she like see you when you feenish breakfas', yes?"

"Certainly. Tell her I'll be down in half an hour," she said with a smile, and turned toward the tray. She was surprised to find that she held in her hand the little carving of ivory . . . the fettered spider . . . that Prince Lai had given her the night before and she dropped it onto the tray before picking up the silver pot to pour herself a cup of coffee.

The little tinkling sound drew the eyes of the lingering Carlos to the tray. Had she been watching she would have seen his smiling face grow livid, the color drain from his face and the smile fade exactly as an artist might wipe a freshly painted smile from the lips of a portrait.

"I tellum . . . haluf hour," he said in a choking voice and slipped from the room.

Slipping back into bed, Pat devoted herself to toast and coffee and her own thoughts.

And gradually, as the coffee began to warm her blood, the events of the previous evening came back with startling clearness. Nicholson . . . the affair of the substituted snapshot . . . the finding of the fragment of the message . . . Prince Lai . . . the whole tangled web started to unroll in a swift series of pictures.

There came a tap on the door, and at her call Carlos opened it. With him was a colored maid.

"The Señora, she no wait," he announced. "She go buy things. She say you come when you dress. She sen' Sally show you where come."

"Oh, but I've other things to do," Pat cried involuntarily. "I can't go shopping."

"Mus' go," Carlos said firmly.

The colored maid came further into the room.

"Mrs. Chenery will wait for you, Miss Fenton," she said in the broad accents of the West Indian Negro. "She said for me to tell you that she would wait until you came. Possibly it would be better if you met her, and explained that you were unable to go shopping with her."

Pat sighed. How like her hostess to make it impossible for her to do anything else but the thing she had planned. "All right, I'll go. I'll be ready in a few minutes."

It was twenty minutes later when she came down the stairs and found the little colored maid waiting patiently on the verandah. As they went down the stairs and into the garden the sun hit her like a physical blow. The glare from the sea bored into her eyeballs like a white hot needle. Long shadows were sliding across the purple hills on the further side of the Canal.

Sally pointed to a crushed place in the shrubbery.

"They found a dead man there this morning," she said with a little shudder.

"A dead man?" Pat looked at her with surprise. "In the garden? How extraordinary."

"Yes, ma'am," the girl said. "He died from heart failure, the doctor said. They think he intended to rob the house and had a heart attack in the garden."

Pat gave a little shudder and glanced back over her shoulder. Almost under her window.

Then she beckoned a dozing carameta driver, the maid gave him the address and climbed into the front seat beside him. After leaving the tree-shadowed streets of Ancon, the driver turned down a street of shifting shadows and color, an artery that seemed to come from the very heart of China itself. Yellow faces in the doorways and windows of gaudy houses, yellow faces beneath awnings, beneath crimson and gold signs, beneath balconies and quaint projections. Shops where silks from Yunnan and Pieng were sold; shops that smelled of perfumes and aromatic gum from Asia.

At last the carriage whirled around a corner and stopped before the blank façade of a house that stood flush with the narrow, winding street. The maid hopped nimbly out, while Pat paid the driver, and they walked through a tall, narrow door into the courtyard around which the house was built. Above the patio three tiers of balconies rose.

Water murmured somewhere and the faint breeze through the narrow slit of a door rustled the ragged skirt of a coconut palm that stood in the center of the patio. It was very quiet and the noise and bustle of Panama City seemed miles away. They walked around a tangle of hibiscus and cadenda, where a little plaster saint stood in her niche, holding a little fluted shell for holy water, and began to mount the ancient crumbling stone stairs.

The place seemed deserted save for a rotund negro squatting on the stairs who stared at them impersonally as they passed.

"Mrs. Chenery's dressmaker is on the third floor," the maid said.

They mounted another flight of stairs and at their head was a door bearing a faded dressmaker's sign.

The maid tapped and instantly the door was opened by a tall woman. Her eyes held Pat's for an instant and a chill passed over her. She did not seem the usual dressmaker.

"Is Mrs. Chenery here?" Pat asked.

"She's inside," the woman said. "Having a fitting. Are you Miss Fenton?"

At Pat's nod she added:

"Mrs. Chenery is expecting you. Won't you come in, please."

She held the door open and Pat stepped inside . . . and then whirled again. But she was too late. The door was closed and the woman was standing against it.

Facing her was a Chinese and in his face was something significant and terrifying. Suddenly she knew that she was afraid. Terror, the stronger for being suppressed, gripped her, producing the effect of ice on hot imagination. She longed to be out in the open street . . . anywhere . . . except in this little room on the third floor of an unknown house. Oh, why had she come? She turned hurriedly to look for the maid. She was not there.

Pat had one ghastly moment of horror.

And the Chinese . . . step by step . . . was coming toward her . . .

Chapter Seventeen

MORNING AND A BURNISHED SUN. Nicholson, rising early, looked out from his window into purgatorial glare and was not cheered. A glance into his mirror showed him a pallor beneath his tanned skin and dark half-moons beneath his eyes.

The night, or what had been left of it, had not been a pleasant one, arid now he was faced with the necessity of making a decision that he had no desire to make. And whichever prospect he faced, the outlook was not a happy one.

Damn the girl, anyhow. This was what happened when a man tried to drag the past out of dead ashes. Except for her, there would have been no hitch to his plans. He would have been able to carry through his scheme and then slipped into oblivion with no one the wiser for his part in it. And now . . .

She had given him until the morning to disappear. He smiled a trifle wryly. Disappear! Because of her he faced the exceedingly unpleasant fact that his disappearance was likely to be a much more permanent affair than she dreamed.

He glanced at his watch. He must gain time . . . someway . . . somehow . . . Two days at least, if the plan of the Tongueless One was what he suspected it to be. His face paled a little at the thought. Only the brain of a devil such as Chu-Sheng could have planned such a deed . . . could have imagined the horror of it. The Slayer of Souls. A fitting title. But there was something that bothered him. Something that did not click into place with the other pieces of the puzzle. There was just one thing that he could not fathom. And fathom it he must.

But first he must gain time. If Pat talked . . . if the General checked up on that wireless message . . .

He was shaken from his reverie by a sharp tap on the door. He opened it. Carlos stood there. Nicholson's face settled into a grim mask as he closed the door behind his visitor. Had it come? Was this a warning?

He waited for Carlos to speak not without a certain apprehension.

"Well," the latter said, "we must go."

"Where?" Nicholson queried.

"With me. The Tongueless One has commanded your presence."

Nicholson remembered vividly that episode in the long room. He had no desire to face Chu-Sheng again. But there was nothing he could do save follow.

"Any idea what he wants?" he asked.

"Not at all," Carlos answered. "There is something the Master wishes to tell you . . . and someone he wishes you to see. You needn't ask me. I don't know . . . and if I did I wouldn't tell you. Let's go."

Nicholson went with him wonderingly. The sun rode brassily over the palms now and the morning freshness was burned out of the air, leaving it hot and dead. They passed through the courtyard, through the door where the same ceremony of opening it was gone through and down the stairs. But this time they did not go through the passage that led to the room of the Slayer of Souls. Their coming was evidently expected, because another door at the foot of the stairs stood open, a door so cleverly camouflaged to resemble stone that Nicholson would have never detected its presence. It swung to behind them and Nicholson found himself in a small bare stone room. More a cell, in fact, than a room. In one of the walls was a small round hole, resembling a funnel, with the large end on the further side of the wall.

"Look through," Carlos directed. The place into which he peered was filled with that curiously clear and palely greenish light that gave the impression of water. It caused him to feel vague stirrings of repulsion, coupled with a sharp resentment. At first glance Nicholson thought that he was looking into a circular room of polished black stone. It took him a full minute to realize that the effect was obtained with curtains of black which swept around in an arc from wall to wall, reaching from floor to ceiling, and there was a shimmering tracery on them . . . like webs. They were webs; spider webs traced upon the black cloth and glimmering like those same silver traps beneath the moon. By the hundreds and thousands they were interlaced on the walls. They shimmered over the floor.

Placed at the rear of the semicircle, upon a low dais, was a black carved chair and a few feet in front of it a great curved dome of glass, more than three feet across and at least two feet in height.

Set almost in the center of the room was a post of some polished black substance resembling black stone some four feet high.

Even as Nicholson looked the lights faded . . . grew dimmer . . .
flickered out. Thick, impenetrable darkness replaced it.

There was a faint rustling. Then a gong sounded, producing
overtones that hummed away into infinity. Silence fell.

And then, slowly—almost like aurora borealis—soft light, beginning dimly in a dozen places, filled the room into which
Nicholson peered. It seemed to commence at the floor and slowly
to collect itself into a whole as water rises in a bowl, until the floor
was a glowing green jewel of light. As it lapped higher and higher
about the black walls, it framed the Tongueless One seated in the
ebony chair and, kneeling before the dome of glass the girl who
was the Voice of the Master. Her head was bent and she was staring into the depths of the glass dome. From it a soft light shone up
in her face.

Now Nicholson saw, chained to the post in the center of the
room, a man. A white man, clad in soiled crumpled whites. And if
ever agony rode a man's face, Nicholson could see it in his. His
feet were shackled to the foot of the post and his arms more
loosely.

The girl raised her head slowly, began to speak, and Nicholson
knew that through her lips Chu-Sheng, the Tongueless One, was
speaking. Again Nicholson had the feeling that her smooth body
was but a miraculous gesture of some Eastern craftsman immortal-
ized in ivory; that her hair gleamed so because of inlay and inlay
of polished rare woods; that her robe was an effect of cunning
light.

"Leslie Wells," the voice said, "you have tried to thwart me in
my plans. You sought to spy upon me. You dared set your will
against mine, in ignorance of the fact that no man may oppose me
successfully. There is no need for you to deny that this is so. I
know that it is. I know that you belong to the Intelligence Service
of the American Army. That is sufficient."

Her silver-bell voice had the same hypnotic quality that Nicholson had noted the first time he heard her speak, a quality utterly
outside the range of his experience. She employed no gestures.
Her breathing could not visually be detected. That slender body
retained its ivory illusion.

The man she had called Leslie Wells raised his head, squared
his shoulders and his voice held a firmness that was oddly at vari-
ance with the agony that had filled his face a few moments before.

"I have nothing to answer to that," he said, speaking slowly so that the tongueless deaf-mute seated upon the ebony throne might read his lips. "I am ready to die."

"Unfortunately, Leslie Wells," came from the lips of the kneeling girl, "death is not the punishment I have in store for you. At least not death of the body. That will live on—for a time. It is only your soul that I shall slay."

There was no answer from the shackled man and Chu-Sheng raised his hand. Almost imperceptibly the light in the room grew brighter until everything in view was outlined with sharpest accuracy by that clear and evil greenish light.

And then, at the top of the curtain, where it joined the ceiling, Nicholson saw something that caused him to catch his breath.

Clinging to the curtain was a monstrous black spider, fully a foot across, a perfect *living* replica of the great carved monstrosity upon whose head Chu-Sheng had sat. Even as Nicholson looked another appeared and another, apparently swarming over the top of the curtain, until the semicircular space was ringed with the hideous monsters. Some of them were as large as the first. Some of them smaller.

The shackled man saw them, too. Nicholson saw his agonized eyes sweep around; heard the throaty, whistling gasp that went up from him as the black spiders began slowly to creep down the curtains toward the floor. There were hundreds of them . . . possibly thousands . . . swarming over the curtains . . . creeping ever downward . . . nearer and nearer to the floor.

Nicholson shrank back, trembling. The thing was hellish. And he could see that the slow, inexorable march of the spiders was slowly stretching the mind of the fettered man to the breaking point . . . leading it into the path of madness.

And always the black-clad form on the ebony throne kept his eyes fixed on the shuddering figure shackled to the post . . . eyes that were like black holes in empty space . . . eyes that held nothing of reason or sanity within their depths . . . only force . . . a force that seemed to radiate also from the uplifted hand . . . a paralyzing force that swept the room . . . that seemed, through the opening through which Nicholson peered, to touch the very core of human fear.

A little choked scream went up from Wells as the first of the spiders reached the floor . . . another . . . and another . . . began slowly to creep across the floor toward the post in the center. There was nowhere he could turn and not see them, and one of the hellish things about it was, Nicholson knew, the fact that no man living could keep his eyes closed and shut out the sight of the marching spiders.

He jerked his head back from the opening, turned to Carlos, half incoherent, white lipped.

"For God's sake . . . enough . . . a bullet would be mercy . . ."

Carlos thrust him back to the opening.

"You must look," he said curtly. "You must see the end. It is the order of the Tongueless One."

Despairingly Nicholson looked again . . . looked with night-mare horror such as he had never known in worst of nightmares possessing him . . . the floor was black with the spiders now . . . a solid mass of them . . . crawling closer and closer . . . ever nearer to the screaming, shrieking man shackled to the post . . . the near-est one was only a few inches away . . . it raised itself as if to spring . . . Nicholson could see the great fangs . . . like the fangs of a snake . . . he could envision the shackled form in another mo-ment swarming with the loathsome creatures . . .

. . . Utter silence fell. Wells was hanging limply in his fet-ters . . . merciful oblivion had come to him.

Chu-Sheng raised his hand, the slim fingers writhing like bro-ken backed serpents.

And instantly every spider vanished. Just vanished. One mo-ment they were there. The next moment they were not.

Comprehension flooded in on Nicholson's brain. There had been no spiders. It had been nothing but hypnotic suggestion by Chu-Sheng. That gigantic brain had willed the man . . . and Nicholson also . . . to see the spiders. Mass hypnotism, like the Angel of Mons, the ghostly Bowmen of Crecy. It was the same thing, only infinitely more evil, as that ghostly city that rose from the waves of Panama Bay at the command of the waving hand of Prince Lai.

Shaken, horrified, he was about to withdraw his head from the opening when the girl spoke again.

"K-92, you who are known as Captain Nicholson," she said in that odd, toneless voice, "you have witnessed what happened to this man who opposed me. He will come out of this room without memory. He will not know his name, nor what he has been, nor anything that he has ever learned. He will know nothing of all these hereafter—ever. Like an animal he will know when he is hungry and thirsty, cold or warm. That is all. He will forget from minute to minute. He will live only in each moment. And when that moment goes it will be forgotten. Because I have slain his soul. I brought you here that you might see and be warned, lest some day occasion arise when you might be tempted to betray me. Now look."

Soundlessly a section of one of the black curtains was drawn aside.

Seated in a chair in the alcove thus displayed, arms bound to the arms of the chair, was Patricia Fenton.

Slowly the massive gates of Miraflores locks swung to behind the battleship *Pennsylvania,* flagship of the battle fleet. Muddy domes boiled and bubbled about her as water from Miraflores Lake poured down through the intake pipes, raising the giant ship to the level of the second elevation of locks.

Behind her in the Canal waited another battleship and behind her another and another. The surface of Panama Bay was dotted with the fleet; the airplane carriers *Lexington* and *Langley* and *Saratoga,* light cruisers, destroyers, submarines.

The greatest naval maneuver ever undertaken by the United States . . . an attempt to make the transit of the Panama Canal with the entire battle fleet within twenty-four hours . . . was under way. By morning the entire length of the Canal, from the locks at the head of Gatun Lake on the Atlantic side of the Canal, to Miraflores Lake on the Pacific, would be covered by the fleet.

Chapter Eighteen

THE SOFT, SLOW TONELESS VOICE went on, the words falling from the lips of the kneeling girl like slow drops of acid eating into his mind, the voice slowly, inexorably pounding the words into his brain.

"What you did last night was well done. By admitting my faithful Carlos to the room in the heart of Ancon Hill you fulfilled the major purpose for which you came here . . . enabled me to forge the last link in the chain. But no slightest suspicion must attach to you until my purpose is accomplished, else everything that I have done goes for naught. That is the reason for what you now see. She is not so much a hostage for your faithfulness, as a guarantee for your carefulness. Once the thing that I have planned is accomplished she will be released unharmed. But if you slip, Captain Nicholson . . . it would not be pleasant for you to witness the black servants of the Slayer of Souls creeping toward her."

The girl's voice stopped abruptly and with its stoppage the lights went out abruptly. Carlos reached out an arm and the opening in the wall snapped shut.

Nicholson whirled on him.

"You devil, you cold-blooded devil," he cried angrily, and threw himself upon the man.

Carlos caught his arms. Despite his slim form, he held Nicholson as easily as though he had been a child, while he kicked and writhed in futile attempt to break the inexorable grip. At last his fury spent itself. He went limp.

"I am not responsible for what you have seen," Carlos told him evenly. "The Tongueless One ordered it. It was necessary that Miss Fenton be removed from the scene temporarily. She knew that you were not Captain Nicholson, she knew that the real Nicholson was dead and that you had taken his place, and she had threatened to warn General Chenery last night. Therefore it was necessary to remove her, because for you to be removed from your post as officer in charge of the secret control room would have been disastrous. It might have started an investigation that would have undone all that I did last night."

He released Nicholson and stood back.

"You need not fear for her, so long as you carry on as you have been doing," he said quietly. "The Master keeps his word. In a day and a night the plans of the Master will be consummated, and she will be released. And she will be safer here than in the quarters of General Chenery."

Nicholson shivered a little at the cold evenness of the tone. He knew the import of that last sentence, and the words brought up a vision that whitened his lips. But he fought down the horror that all but choked him and said quietly:

"It was unnecessary for Miss Fenton to be kidnapped. She would not have betrayed me. And you can understand, also, how I felt seeing her there, after . . . after what had just taken place."

Carlos shrugged. "She was taken by the order of the Tongue-less One. Shall we go now?"

Nicholson followed him up the stairs again and into the sunlight that burned down over the ancient sea wall.

So preoccupied was he with the catastrophe that had befallen him, that he did not see the bundle of rags lying in a corner of the sea wall parapet stir and resolve itself into a man . . . a Chinese with the broad flat face of one from the borderland of China, where the blood of Tibet mingles with that of the Mongol.

Scouting planes from the airplane carrier *Saratoga,* flying over the Bay of Panama, could not help seeing the two steamers that lay at anchor there, one in the lee of a rocky little island only a few miles from Palo Seco, the leper colony; the other in an indentation of the coast where a river emptying into the sea had carved a deep channel through the mud flats and mangrove swamps.

Observers in the planes noticed nothing unusual about the two, except that both of them were anchored where ships rarely anchored. But then, naval aviators could hardly be expected to bother about that.

If the canvas awning that stretched over the entire length of the after deck of one of them had been removed, their curiosity might have been excited. There, all traces of catwalk, booms, piles that usually clutter the deck of an oil tanker, had been removed. There remained nothing but a broad expanse of deck on which little yellow men were working swiftly and efficiently . . .uncrating . . . assembling. And any one of the aviators flying overhead would have recognized the things that were being assembled.

They were planes. Fighting planes. Gawasaki Bvii's, to be exact, the deadliest fighting plane of the island empire.

Chapter Nineteen

IT WAS NEARLY NOON before Pat was permitted to leave the cabin of the launch into which she had been carried from Chu-Sheng's house of terror. When she emerged onto the open deck, she felt as though the launch was carrying her into a filmy unsubstantial world, a world of apple-green, of jade and olive. The boat was running along a channel between a reef and a mangrove swamp, the water a band of agate, its transparency clouded by foam as it rushed out of green twilight. Green were the mangroves whose roots writhed at the water's edge; green the growths that flung up a wild snare on the reef, hiding them from the open sea. Even the atmosphere was touched with the pigment that saturated earth, for an ice-green glow illuminated everything.

The beings that peopled this indefinite world seemed as foreign as the surroundings. Yellow torsos, sweat-bright, glistened before her. Standing in the bow was a little yellow man who turned as she emerged and came up to her.

He bowed with a little hissing indrawing of breath and spoke, his English blurred with only the faintest of accents.

"We reach our destination in a very few minutes, now, Miss Fenton."

"And where is that?" Pat asked uneasily. "What is to happen to me? How long am I to be kept prisoner?" she continued.

The little Oriental was courteous enough as he answered.

"You are to be placed aboard a steamer anchored a short distance ahead of us. My instructions go no further than seeing that you are kept safely aboard and given every possible comfort until instructions are received for your return to Panama. You will make the situation much pleasanter for yourself, Miss Fenton, if you accept it as it is."

"But don't you realize what you are doing?" Pat burst out, unable to dam up her anger any longer. "Don't you realize that you can't get away with this? By to-morrow every inch of these waters will be searched with planes; launches from the American fleet will be scouring every inch of the shore."

"By to-morrow, Miss Fenton," he answered gravely, "there will be no American fleet."

What passed in Nicholson's mind for the few minutes after he left the Casa Mendoza no man ever knew; it is doubtful if even Nicholson himself remembered afterwards. He was tasting the most bitter of all draughts which poor humanity knows . . . despair. His thoughts were laved in corrosive acid . . . he felt something of purgatorial fire . . . a burning of brains and nerves. But in the heat was a sphere of starry luster . . . a face . . . looking up appealing from the depths of a green mist.

He knew that he must make a decision . . . a decision upon which the life of the girl he loved was balanced on the scales by the thing he had set out to do. He walked slowly along the street toward the hotel. He entered the lobby. He watched his hand reach out to take the key from the West Indian negro clerk behind the desk. And all the while, his mind, like a captive bird, was beating against the cage bars of his intelligence, his typically Occidental refusal to believe the incredible . . . even after he had seen it happen. It was not until he opened the door of his room that his thoughts were brought back to a semblance of order.

Seated quietly in the big basket chair before the window was Prince Lai Chung.

Nicholson's nails dug fiercely into his palm. It was with an effort that he kept his face in an expressionless mold.

"Good morning, Captain Nicholson," said the Prince gravely. He rose to his feet.

Nicholson's response was courteous enough, but had one been able to see inside his head, a different story would have been disclosed. The spell of what he had beheld in Chu-Sheng's unholy room was heavy upon him. He had to fight a sense of futility. He was like a fly caught in a web in that room where the spiders had swarmed. And to find Prince Lai waiting in his room—with the door locked and the key at the desk—had not served to quell his discomfiture. What was he doing here? How had he gained entrance? Was he an emissary from Chu-Sheng? Or, if not, what was his purpose?

"You are doubtless surprised to see me," the Prince said amiably.

"Your visit *is* unexpected," Nicholson admitted bluntly.

His eyes searched the other's face; encountered a barrier of impassivity. The most important thing at the moment seemed to be to discover whether or not the Prince had penetrated his masquerade, and if not, to preserve its secret as long as possible.

"But . . . eventually . . . not unwelcome, I hope," the Mongol said.

They faced each other for a space of seconds, neither speaking. Then Nicholson said quietly:

"Do you come from Chu-Sheng?"

Something told him that there was no use fencing with this man.

The Prince answered in gliding, purring Chinese metaphor, in that cannily hyperbolic manner dear to Oriental minds and maddeningly annoying to Occidental.

"Do the wolf and the deer run together?" Then he added. "No, Captain, I come to you with an offer of help."

"Help!" The word snapped out in the stillness like an electric spark. Nicholson's gaze was like a knife. He no longer knew what to expect, now that the Shadow of Chu-Sheng, like an enormous omen of dreadful doom steadily darkening over his impotence, had fallen across the life of the woman he loved.

"There is no need for us to fence," the Prince said calmly. "I know why you are in Panama. I know what happened back there in Washington. You need not fear that I shall betray you. You have work to do . . . and I also have a duty to perform." He put out a restraining hand as Nicholson would have spoken. "I suggest that the two of us take advantage of the moment. I know that Chu-Sheng has taken Miss Fenton . . . I can guess the reason . . . and I know also that you will never be able to rescue her *before tomorrow* unaided."

Nicholson's head was whirling. How did this man know that Pat had been kidnapped? And what did the significant emphasis in his tone that underscored the two words mean? Did he *know?* Or was he reading his thoughts?

The Prince smiled a trifle wearily.

"I have been listening to your thoughts for some time, Captain," he said quietly, and Nicholson's head snapped up at the odd phrasing.

Listening to his thoughts? What did the man mean?

Then he threw discretion to the winds. The man's personality was beginning to win him.

"It almost seems as if you were," he admitted.

"The reading of thought is not a difficult matter," Prince Lai said. His tone was that of one teaching school. "After all, what do we know of the human mind? It has been proven that no thought can originate within that mass of matter called the brain. It has been proven that something outside the brain originates thought and uses the brain as a vehicle to incubate it. So why should it be strange that another mind should trap . . . receive, if you prefer the term . . . the thought force that is being conveyed to your brain?"

His long ivory fingers played a moment with a gayly colored bit of glass that stood on the polished surface of the table like a gay Chinese junk on the surface of a burnished sea. Then he added in a low voice:

"You have just left the house of Chu-Sheng."

It was not a question. It was a statement and for a moment the atmosphere was tense, suffused with a sort of honey-sweet violence. In the reflected glare from outside the window the purple black eyes of the Chinese held Nicholson's grey ones as a pool holds the picture of a stormy sky.

"And what if I have?" Nicholson challenged.

"The deeds a man does are the fruits that are weighed in the balance and from which the seeds of future lives are saved," the Mongol answered composedly, ignoring the challenge in the other's voice. "We live in the eternal Now, and it is Now that we create our destiny. There is a fit time for all things . . . an appointed time . . . and you are standing upon the threshold of an appointed time."

His face was an enigma . . . a mask with a marvelous smile; but the hooded eyes, to Nicholson, suggested excitement. At any rate, some emotion was shining through the self-controlled exterior.

The army officer got to his feet, his face set. He had reached the point now where his mind rejected speculation. Prince Lai might be a fiend or a friend who was sincere in his offer to help him. Into his mind leaped a memory of that shadowed, magical city which had risen from the sea before his eyes at the wave of this man's hand . . . of the mellow booming of the bronze gong that had drifted to him across the water from the city whose reality existed half way around the earth, tucked away in the giant folds of the mountain of Tibet.

A reckless impulse stormed the battlements of his control. He heard his voice in a queer, separated manner.

"Look here, I'm going to trust you. I've got to trust someone. This morning . . ."

"You need not explain," the Prince said gently. "I know what has happened. And I know that unless you succeed in freeing Miss Fenton to-night she will never be free."

"And I might have prevented the whole thing . . . if I hadn't been such a fool . . . if I had thought," Nicholson groaned.

"What a man cannot do is no weight against him. It may be the hand of destiny preventing a greater catastrophe. What weighs against him is failure to do the thing that he can do."

"I can talk to the General," the officer said rapidly. "The Army . . . we can surround the place . . . raid it . . ."

He stopped at a swift gesture from the Prince.

"The man who sets forth upon an unknown voyage should not stipulate that the pilot must agree with him as to the course," the Mongol made answer. "Miss Fenton is no longer in the house of Chu-Sheng. Within five minutes after your departure she was placed in a motor boat and was on her way to a steamer anchored in the Gulf of Panama. She will be kept there until it is . . . all over."

Nicholson could not suppress the feeling that there was something missing from the dialogue . . . something that should have been said that had not . . . something across which a veil had been drawn.

"How do you know all these things?" he demanded.

"I could talk to you about the stars," the Prince retorted, "but if you should meditate upon them and observe, you would learn more than I can tell you."

There was a sort of masked look on his face, as if he himself were still pondering the question.

And again there was that emotion shining through his self-control like the clear flame of a lamp through alabaster. Then he dismissed Nicholson's question with one firm, horizontal sweep of his hand.

"Are we," he asked gently, "to go into a discussion of what I know and why I know it? Or are we going to rescue Miss Fenton?"

"I am at your service," Nicholson said humbly.

"I am one who strives to tread the middle way from desire into peace," the Prince said musingly, "and he who would tread the Middle Way is patient, keeping both feet upon the ground and his head no higher than humility will let it reach."

A pause followed. The Prince sat like a carved Buddha; even his fingers ceased their restless playing on the arms of the basket chair. He seemed wrapped in brooding silence, like a man in intense thought.

Then he looked up suddenly.

"You must give me your cooperation, Captain," he said a trifle sharply. "I can do nothing to aid you without that. Words are useless things unless the mind and the heart are in them."

"Cooperation?"

Nicholson leaped to his feet, anger creeping over his tense, haggard face.

"Good God, man, what more can I do? I've told you that I'm ready . . . waiting. What else can I do or say?"

The Prince gave him a swift glance.

"You are right. But there is something . . . I cannot understand . . ."

He rose slowly; searched the room with a long, slow glance. Nicholson could not suppress the feeling that a new atmosphere was creeping into the quiet room as the Prince slowly paced up and down, touching objects, keeping always close to the wall . . . an atmosphere to which he did not like to give a name, but which, nevertheless was an atmosphere of taut suspense.

Slowly the Prince made the circuit of the room and Nicholson repressed an inclination to shudder—the inclination that forewarns a man of something that his eyes cannot see.

Abruptly the Prince halted before the door of a clothes closet. All expression was wiped from his face with such complete and startling abruptness that it left only a yellow Mongolian mask in which the eyes alone seemed alive.

He flung out his hand suddenly. Nicholson's eyes followed the pointing finger to the door of the closet.

"*T'hg ni kong ha,*" he said suddenly—not loudly, not commandingly, but softly, gently, urgently.

Slowly, ever so slowly, the command was obeyed. The door of the closet opened. A Chinese stood on the threshold, a dazed look upon his face.

The blood pulsed in Nicholson's temples. His stupefaction escaped the citadel of his impassivity. He stared . . . stared with the air of a man struggling to grasp something beyond his ken of thought . . . beyond possibility.

The man who stood there, a keen bladed knife in his hand, was one of the guards in the great hall where Chu-Sheng sat upon the head of the spider.

His face was absolutely devoid of expression, as though cast in stone; rather thin, with aquiline nostrils and a slit of a mouth, its predominant feature was the eyes. They were large, more oblique than is usual with Chinese of the coast cities. More on the order of the type to be seen where China begins to merge with Tibet. He seemed unable to take his eyes from the pointing finger of the Prince. It was as if that finger were a magnet which drew his staring gaze. Slowly he stepped forward, until the outstretched finger of the Prince almost rested upon his forehead between his fixed eyes.

The voice of the Prince broke the spell that held Nicholson . . . proof to him that what he saw was no sorcery of the eyes. In a silence in which the wing of moth in flight could have been heard, he began to speak.

"So," said the Prince in a wondering way, "it is Hoang-Ti, the Manchu . . . Hoang-Ti whose footsteps on the path of the Mother of Mountains faltered when the bronze gong thundered . . . Hoang-Ti the *Kuchar Khanpo* who stood upon the lowest stair of the Lotus Throne when the reincarnation of Guadama Siddartha was confirmed . . . Hoang-Ti who comes with naked steel in his hands . . . For whom is the death command I read in your mind, Hoang-Ti?"

The man, staring straight before him, made answer in a slow, hesitant manner, as if he found speaking difficult.

"For this man, O Great One, if he is found to be faithless to the Master."

"So Hoang-Ti would slay . . . and suffer in the lives to come?"

"For me, O Great One," came the toneless response, "there are no lives to come. The Slayer of Souls has slain mine . . . seized it in his black paws . . . devoured it with his great fangs . . . even as I sat in the great hall and watched my soul leave my body and go to its death. . . ."

His voice faded away and Nicholson, watching, saw his body shake and strain as though the memory of the ordeal still rose before him like a horrible accusation.

"You cannot undo the past," the Prince made answer in that strangely gentle tone. "Nor can all the gods, nor he who rules the gods, undo it. But now, this moment, and the next one, and the next, forever, ye create by thought and act and deed the very hairsbreadth of your destiny.

"And your destiny trembles in the balance. Your soul is not slain. It is only sleeping at the bidding of the Accursed One. I could show you your secret heart, and you would die in horror at the sight. But it is not good to slay, even with the rays of truth. So I present you herewith the gift of life that is forfeit to me."

His outstretched fingers brushed the man's eyes as delicately as the touch of a butterfly's wings . . . brushed them again and again as he spoke . . . first down and then across with the gentlest of gestures . . . weaving a pattern before the staring gaze.

"Return now to the Accursed One who sent you here," and his voice was low and soothing. "You have seen nothing in this room. You have heard nothing. When you pass across that doorstep, it shall be as if you never crossed it to enter. Nor shall the Accursed One be able to stir in you any memory to the contrary. And when you cross that threshold, your soul shall awake and reenter your body. The Accursed One shall not be able to capture it again. It is an order that no command shall break."

The voice of the Prince was low and gentle, yet, to Nicholson, it was as if the man were filled with some kind of elemental force that was inexhaustible . . . force that was pouring out upon the Chinese before him in a great overwhelming stream . . . tearing at the frail veil of human resistance . . . rending it into fragments . . . sending subtle roots down deep to tap that mysterious store of emotions which lies buried beneath the consciousness.

"It is an order that no command shall break," repeated the Chinese, and stumbled blindly toward the door.

Nicholson (or the man who called himself Nicholson) watched him go with a curious shrinking intensity. There came to him vividly the memory of that moment in the Great Hall when he had thought that the carved spider was wakening into life, that the great legs were twitching . . . crouching for a spring . . . would he, too, have had the illusion of his soul leaving his body to be devoured . . . A thousand other questions, equally insane, presented themselves in a gibbering horde.

"Was . . . was he . . . one of those . . ." The words died on his lips.

"He was of the ranks of the Living Dead," the Prince answered. The words were fraught with overwhelming sadness. "But there is nothing in this life that is not balanced by justice in the lives to come. The Wheel of the Law will turn and turn soon for Chu-Sheng, the Accursed One."

Then he turned to Nicholson.

"Now listen," he said. "There is only one way in which Miss Fenton can be rescued."

Nicholson listened as the Prince talked, a grim look upon his face. For the Oriental was raising veils behind which he had longed to peer.

Even as he listened, the last of the battleships cast off the moorings of the electric "mules" that had towed her through the Miraflores locks; steamed out into the calm, muddy waters of Miraflores Lake, headed for the second level of locks at Pedro Miguel, and the long stretch of the Canal ahead.

Before Miraflores locks the first of the airplane carriers made ready for the ascent.

Chapter Twenty

THE LONG LOW WICKER CHAISE LONGUE on the verandah of General Chenery's quarters was piled high with pillows. From their depths came a weak "Dan."

The foghorn had lost its power.

There was no answer.

"Dan."

This time there was a decided rumble in the distance. But no response.

"Daniel Martin, where are you?"

The foghorn was in full voice again.

"Here I am, Mrs. Chenery," said the harassed young lieutenant as he hastily entered the room.

"Where have you been?" the owner of the foghorn demanded.

"Why . . . I just went out to get a drink of water."

"A drink of water?" she snorted. "How many times must I tell you that I'm not to be left alone? Not even for a single second. How can I rest when the moment I close my eyes you sneak out to get drinks of water? I never saw such a thirsty person. Hereafter when you want a drink, ring for Carlos. But don't leave me again. Is that clear?"

"Yes, Mrs. Chenery," Dan answered between clenched teeth.

He did not permit his eyes to meet hers, lest she read what was written there, but let them rest deliberately on the landscape outside . . . a landscape of too much color, gold and heliotrope and lake and purple, picked out with glaring white lights, nicked with sulphur yellow and poisonous green and edged with chocolate brown and luminous blues. But for the moment he had no eyes for the landscape.

When Dan Martin graduated from West Point he was proud of his new status as an officer in the United States Army. He was delighted with his first assignment, of his appointment as aide to General Chenery. He adored the old man and had visions of himself sacrificing his life on a bloody battlefront to save his hero. The Army meant unbounded opportunity for heroism to his imaginative young mind, unbounded adventures, and now—in this time of need—instead of being charged with the sacred trust of going out and slaying the dragon, and bringing home the bacon as befits a gallant and brave young knight, he was detailed to play wet nurse to the General's hysterical and exacting spouse. Life was a bitter pill. At the moment he wished very much that he were not an officer and a gentleman, but an unscrupulous rogue who would not hesitate to take the old battle axe across his knee and give her the spanking of her life. The thought was exhilarating.

"Hand me my smelling salts." The voice went weak again.

Dan groped helplessly among the dozens of bottles and jars on the small table at Mrs. Chenery's side, lost in the pleasant contemplation of exercising physical violence upon her hapless person.

"That short fat bottle," she said, breaking in upon his reverie, and waving a chubby hand aimlessly toward the table. "No . . . no. On this side. The one with the crystal stopper . . . there . . . *no* . . . the lavender one . . . yes, that's it. At last." And she sank back among the pillows again quite exhausted, holding her smelling salts to her nose.

Dan wished, unholily, but none the less fervently, that they were knockout drops.

"To think, that if I had stayed in this house another five minutes those murderers would have kidnapped me instead of poor dear Miss Fenton," Mrs. Chenery said, sniffing at her salts. "They just took her by mistake, you know. When they find out she's not me, they'll come back, you'll see. Believe me, only my tremendous will power is keeping me from having a stroke, and if you dare leave me alone again, I'll tell the General and have you court martialed."

"But we don't know," Dan protested, "that Pat . . . Miss Fenton . . . has been kidnapped."

"Oh, don't we?" The foghorn roared. "Didn't she leave here this morning, and tell Carlos that she was meeting her brother and wouldn't be back until late to-night? And didn't her brother come up here looking for her, and hasn't found her yet? Don't tell me she hasn't been kidnapped. They're holding her for ransom. That's what they're doing, if they haven't already murdered her."

"What a ghastly idea," Dan said.

"The truth is always ghastly," Mrs. Chenery replied, bobbing her red head wildly. "Life is full of treachery. But"—and she became very confidential—"one must have the eyes to see it."

Dan glanced out through the arched openings of the verandah. Dusk was falling fast . . . that interminable translucent veil which, like a mist, screens and magnifies, transforms even the commonest of objects. In a few minutes he would hear the sunset gun from one of the forts. And Pat had not returned. It was absurd to think that anyone had kidnapped her. And yet, where was she? Why had they not had some word from her all day? He turned back toward Mrs. Chenery.

"Why should anyone want to kidnap Pat?" he asked.

Mrs. Chenery spoke slowly and precisely, much as one would to an imbecile child.

"They thought it was *me* . . . don't you see?"

How anyone could mistake the young, slim and altogether lovely Pat Fenton for the fiery-headed old battle axe, Dan couldn't see. But he held his peace.

"They saw her leaving the house," she went on mysteriously, "and thought it was me. They have probably taken her"—and Dan thought he detected a touch of wistfulness in the rumbling voice—"to one of those terrible seduction parlors."

Dan made a noise like a seal choking, but managed to keep a straight face.

"But why," he persisted, "should anyone want to kidnap you?"

Mrs. Chenery looked at him pityingly.

"Why should Paris want to kidnap Helen of Troy . . . or Caesar kidnap Cleopatra . . . or Dante go to hell for Beatrice?"

A slight difference in facts meant nothing to Mrs. Chenery so long as she made her point. Dan blinked at her. The point, to him, was slightly obscure.

She sighed and then went on meditatively. "The General doesn't realize the tribute I have paid him in being faithful to him all these years. Don't think he isn't jealous. He is. Desperately so. That's the main reason he made you his aide. He felt that you, being a relative, could be trusted not to flirt with me."

Dan agreed with her, mentally. The appearance of Carlos, bringing in a tray with two tall glasses on it ended the conversation abruptly.

Mrs. Chenery reached for the further one.

"No. No, Señora," Carlos said, indicating the nearer glass. "Thees one ees for you. I put seex sheeries en eet." He turned to Dan. "La Señora ees particularice fond of thees sheeries," he explained with an indulgent smile.

"So it would seem," Dan said dryly, taking the remaining glass.

Mrs. Chenery watched Carlos' retreating back suspiciously. When he was out of earshot she beckoned to Dan.

"Change glasses with me," she whispered mysteriously.

"But," the young man reminded her. "Carlos said yours had six cherries in it."

"Never mind," she snapped. "Change glasses with me."

Dan shrugged and changed the glasses wonderingly.

They drank in silence. Mrs. Chenery watching Dan's every move much as a cat watches a mouse. When they finished she said anxiously:

"Well, how do you feel?"

"Great," Dan said, "that certainly hit the spot."

Mrs. Chenery looked her disappointment. Then she sat up and, with a powder-puff from the table at her side, began to restore her face to something of its wonted expensive sheen.

"Then," she sighed, "he didn't try to poison me, after all."

In a tropical climate it is considered the height of folly, even bad form, for one to exert himself during the afternoon heat. The Americans have changed this, to some extent, in Panama, but even so, Panamanians of the old school still close their shops between eleven and two with true Latin regard for form when it is consistent with comfort.

In the silken hours following this siesta period, social Panama City emerges, driving out to the Savannas, where the country homes of the wealthy are located, or gathering over a cocktail in the patio of the Casa Central or (more American influence) an ice cream soda in one of the open air soda fountains.

The siesta period was just over when Nicholson emerged from the Casa Central, passed through the lobby to the entrance that opened onto the plaza and climbed into a car.

"Up Calle Central," he told the driver.

A few blocks up, where a façade of ancient masonry jutted out onto the sidewalk, he gave another order and the car swerved, dashed down a side street that grew steadily more narrow and crooked, to stop finally before a tall, lonely looking house, rising into the golden afternoon sun.

Not a soul was about. There was not even a sound. Which was odd, for tropical streets usually teem with life during the day. It was as if all life had been cut short at the entrance to the street. For a moment he stood undecided. Somehow he felt that it was the door of this house which stood between life as he had known it heretofore and the life of the future . . . whatever the future might bring.

Again he hesitated. Then, suddenly, a wisp of laughter drifted out of the nowhere, a woman's laughter, soft, tinkling, silvery, and he took a deep breath at the sound like a man about to dive, and lifted the door knocker.

A moment later the door opened and from the trooping shadows of the interior came a voice in swift, staccato dialect of the Northern provinces bidding him enter.

A smiling young Chinese in a woolen robe closed the door behind him, conducted him to a room on the top floor and signified that he was to wait there for Prince Lai.

It was a room severely plain, where the late afternoon sun splintered through the high, deep-set window to lose itself in the deep nap of the Tientsin carpet on the floor and find itself again on the mother-of-pearl insets in the great chair and flanking stool that stood before the window.

In one corner was a pedestal of teak and nacre which supported a Hanoto incense bowl of deep orange. Heavy smoke clouds floated and twisted about like a vaporous, gigantic furnace of opal colors, wreathing up into the ceiling, with a hot, honey-sweet smell of lilies and lotus buds and sandalwood.

Prince Lai's voice sounded behind him. He turned and dismissed the courteous apologies of the Prince for his lateness with a gesture.

"Everything is in readiness," the Prince told him. "A small boat will be waiting for you at Dock 15 in Balboa. It will take you out to the launch that will be waiting in the bay."

Nicholson studied his companion curiously. There was something he wanted to ask, yet dared not.

"You wonder why I do not attempt the rescue myself?" the Prince asked softly.

Nicholson stared. He had answered Nicholson's unspoken thoughts.

"I have wondered, yes," he admitted frankly.

"I send you," the Prince told him, "because I am powerless to act. I am forbidden to slay . . . because to slay would take from me the power that has been given me . . . even though the Law says that death is no more than the Gates of Life . . . and to-night there will be slaying."

Then, in that typical Oriental way which so distresses Europeans and which permits its possessor to pass rapidly, without jarring break and without the slightest feeling of ludicrousness or self-consciousness, from a level, drab plane of constructive, logically reasoning practicability to a gorgeously epic or religious height, he leaned forward.

"Captain Nicholson, in a place which only a few know there has been preserved for centuries a Truth . . . knowledge of a truth, that is; for truth is like skill. Unless used constantly, it disappears. The time will come, but it is not yet, when that truth will be given to the world with safety. Those in whose hands the ancient secrets are, being human, have made mistakes. Knowledge in the hands of criminals and fools is worse than ignorance. Let me illustrate.

"Once, when they who keep the secrets thought the time had come, they entrusted knowledge to some chosen individuals whom they believed to be pure embodiments of spirituality, who set the whole world first and themselves last, thus conquering the world. It was instruction concerning the scope of man's mind. But the time was not ripe. The hunger for human power burned in them. They were faithless, and from that one secret that escaped there sprang the whole evil of witchcraft, sorcery, necromancy, black magic, hypnotism, what is now called 'mob psychology,' the black art of propaganda, and inventions that are even worse."

For a moment he halted and looked out to where, above a sunset of somber, crushed pink, the gathering night was wrapping city and distant hills in her cloak of black.

"Many have sought those secrets to use them to their own selfish ends. Those who burned the great Library at Alexandria did so in order to secure them, and that was when men's memories were fresher than they are now. They failed. The Emperor Akbar tried to seize the secrets. He plundered India for them. But he died in ignorance of their whereabouts, although had he but known, one of the Keepers of the Secret was a member of his household."

Nicholson felt slightly self-conscious, slightly ludicrous. For he was an American, an average Occidental swinging, intellectually and emotionally, halfway between Christianity and biology, and what was all this painted, twisted, mazed Oriental tommyrot—all this mad talk about secrets and the Keeper of Secrets—but only for a moment. There flashed across his memory a vision of Chu-Sheng, the room of the Spiders, and the city that this man had summoned from the sea. And it no longer seemed ludicrous.

"Once a woman gained access to the Secrets," the Prince went on, "and was faithless to her trust. She turned them to her selfish use, and made of herself the greatest sorceress that China ever produced, the Princess Nirgidma, the Black Princess. And through her faithlessness Chu-Sheng has gained the knowledge that he uses against mankind to-day. Through many lives the family of Chu-Sheng searched for the lost knowledge . . . and finally their search was rewarded.

"So now the Wheel of the Law turns and you go against Chu-Sheng where I . . . even with the knowledge that I have . . . am powerless. But while I may not slay, I may aid. And I think that to-night you will see something that no man of your race has ever seen before . . . the unveiling of secrets that have been guarded for more thousands of years than you have fingers on your hands. But, *whatever you may see* do not be afraid, for justice is inevitable and its ultimate is peace."

He lifted a slender hand.

"May the Source of Light illuminate thy thoughts," he murmured. "Now go upon your appointed errand."

Chapter Twenty-one

THE WORLD DREW on sable armor; steely chinks were the stars.

It had been a trying day for Pat. Locked in her cabin, she had been a victim of her own thoughts and they had not been pleasant ones. She would have preferred the society of her captors, distasteful though it was, to being locked in her room, because through them she might have dredged up from their reticence some inkling of her future.

Luncheon had been served in her cabin, but when evening fell, her door had been unlocked and a courteous young Oriental had asked if she cared to have dinner in the saloon with them. It was a meal of awkward silences. The men were courteous enough, but seemed merely to tolerate her presence. Her questions were met with either blank stares or noncommittal answers. When the meal was over she felt profoundly relieved.

She remained on deck until nearly ten, her sole companion the moon that was racing through the clouds like delicate ivory flotsam. Then she retired to her cabin. It was when she heard the key turning in the lock from the outside that her composure snapped.

She shivered and swallowed the lump that had pushed up into her throat.

"I won't cry . . . I won't," she told herself bravely.

And she didn't, for a miracle, as she waited tensely, and the long minutes marched by, each second a throbbing beat of anguish.

All day there had danced and beat in her brain that sentence of the young officer's on the launch.

"By to-morrow there will be no American fleet."

And now that she was alone again in her cabin with the night pressing around, she tried vainly to unravel the tangled skein which his words presented. "To-morrow there will be no American fleet." The words hammered at her brain insistently, but never for an instant did their true significance penetrate. The reality was too stupendous for an inkling of it to penetrate.

She rose; went to the window and opened the porthole, looked outside. The somber trees on the distant shore were merged with the sable sky; water met land blackly. All about her was blackness made more intense by the stars. In the direction of the shore a single light rocked through the gloom like a strayed and drunken star. The night was as oppressive as a prison, and with a little shudder she turned aside.

Time wore on, but her faculties were too thoroughly aroused for sleep. She lay in darkness and stared at the ceiling, wishing some noise would break the quiet. The stillness . . . the hush of a tropical night . . . was profound except when a languorous breeze whispered through the open porthole. Once she heard footsteps outside her room; another time voices in a strange tongue somewhere close by. The silence evoked recollections and staged a pageant, a pageant imposed upon the shifting backgrounds of the past few weeks. She saw herself with Nicholson . . . at General Chenery's . . . at the club; visualized the city which Prince Lai Chung had summoned from nothingness before their eyes; heard again the slow words from the lips of a kneeling girl warning Nicholson that she was hostage for his carefulness . . . carefulness in what? Faces and scenes became confused and clogged her mind. She shut her eyes; tried to sleep; failed. The moments lengthened into eons.

She was growing drowsy when she started involuntarily and raised herself on one arm. The cause was a sound, ever so faint . . , something foreign to the tropical night. But just what it was she did not know. But as she listened, she heard only the increased palpitations of her own heart. After a moment she decided, without being convinced, that she must have been dreaming, and dropped back on the pillow.

And then it came again, ever so clear in the stillness. The call of a Bob White.

She sat up, her heart thumping loudly. A bob white? Out in Panama Bay? It could not be. And then her mind flashed back to Montauk Point and she had a sudden memory of the man she now knew as Nicholson standing beneath the window of her room, sending out the musical call of a bob white until she made her appearance.

She reached out an unsteady hand and pressed the light switch, and as she did so the call came again, clear and distinct, from outside. There was no mistaking it now.

She crossed to the porthole and, ever so faintly, sent an answering call into the night.

And then a faint whisper:

"Pat."

A face was framed in the porthole. It was Nicholson.

She ran toward him, and instantly came his whisper.

"Quiet. Keep quiet."

His warning came just in the nick of time. She was vibrant, almost hysterical.

When she reached the opening he said swiftly:

"No time to talk . . . I took a chance . . . thought you might remember the old call . . . listen . . . how is your cabin situated?"

"It opens on the dining saloon . . . the only one. All the others are further back," she whispered back rapidly.

"Good," he answered. "Now listen. Lock your door . . . if there's no bolt shove something against it . . . and whatever you do don't open it unless you're sure that I'm on the other side."

The face disappeared . . . grey darkness, stars and the loom of distant trees took its place. She tried to look out. But the side of the ship fell away so that she could see nothing.

The time that Pat stood there in the center of her cabin might have been an hour for the multitude of thoughts that flashed through her brain. Standing there, with the sound of his voice still fresh in her ears, it seemed that life, for the first time in months, possessed some coherent purpose. Her slim figure seemed possessed of a sudden throbbing suspense as she waited for some sound from above. The winter light, that had possessed her eyes since that fateful afternoon when she had first glimpsed this man in the patio of the Casa Central, suddenly faded; they were lit with a new illumination; the lens of suspicion crashed into a thousand fragments. She realized now, what she had known all along; that no matter what he had done, no matter what, she loved him, and would always love him. The knowledge brought such a deep inner wonder and content that the question of who he was or what he was doing in Panama didn't seem to matter at all. For the moment nothing mattered except the one glorious fact that she cared for him, and that he had come for her.

Quiet lay heavy now, save for the low murmur of wavelets slapping against the hull. Then a voice raised in challenge . . . a cry that died suddenly in the sound of a gun . . . padding feet outside her door . . . yells . . . a confused babble of voices . . . a sound of hammering. . . .

Footsteps outside her door.

She held her breath.

A voice spoke. Nicholson's.

"Pat," he said. There was the sound of the outside key turning in the lock.

She flung open the door, held out her hands to him a little blindly, and the tremble in her throat and the look in her eyes betrayed the agony she had gone through. It was a look that sent a flood of joy to his heart, even when he saw the torture behind it. He held her hands close, and into her eyes he smiled in such a way that he saw them widen, as if she almost disbelieved; then she drew in one sudden breath and her fingers clung to his.

She gave a little cry, so low that it was scarcely more than a broken breath, a little sob that came of wonder . . . understanding . . . and unspeakable faith in this man in the face of tragedy. He gathered her into his arms as the blessed gift of tears filled her eyes. He held her tightly a moment, then released her.

"Everything's all right now," he told her.

"What happened?" she asked weakly.

"Brought out a boat load of men," he said grimly. "Came alongside and boarded before they knew we were anywhere in the neighborhood. Cut 'em off from the deck before they knew what had happened. It's stalemate. They can't navigate the ship, because we've got the deck and the bridge, but we can't get under way, because they've got the engine room. And I want to bring her into port . . . I must. I'm sending the launch back to Balboa with a couple of men to tip the authorities off to what we've got, and I'll send you back with them."

"And you ?" she asked.

"I'm staying here," he told her.

"So am I," she answered simply.

"If you love me," he said gently, "please go."

"No," she said fiercely. "I stay here until you go."

"That's impossible," he told her firmly. "I've got to stay here. There may be trouble. This is a big thing . . . bigger than you can conceive . . . and I've got to keep this ship under control."

"I'd rather stay here," she told him, "with you. Please."

It was a sheer breathless moment, a moment detached and charged with exquisite suspense. Pat's look had revealed a naked soul. And it was a soul transparently clear with the motive that lay behind it.

Nicholson did not argue further. Together they went on deck. A late moon was rising, spreading a silver luster over the water. There were half a dozen men on the deck . . . pitifully few to have surprised and taken a ship like this. They were Chinese, all of them.

As Nicholson and Pat came out onto the open deck, the former stopped short with a little exclamation.

"Good lord," he cried in dismay. "The radio aerial. I'd forgotten it." He gave a few swift orders and a man swarmed up to the top of the radio cabin and snipped the wire which led to the aerial. The radio operator had been trapped below with the crew. But this ship was not like other ships. There was a possibility that he might have access to another instrument.

Pat watched the motor launch in which the raiders had arrived shove off from the side of the ship leaving her behind—without a qualm of regret. Nicholson was remaining there, and she was content to remain. They could spare only two men from the pitiful handful who held the deck, a man for the engine and a steersman.

Nicholson turned to her as the stern light of the launch vanished in the darkness that surrounded them.

"You'd better get some sleep," he said kindly. "It will be hours . . . possibly daylight . . . before anyone from the Canal arrives."

She shook her head. "I couldn't sleep," she said, and her hand stole out and touched his arm. "Besides, I couldn't stay in my cabin. I'd be imagining every moment that something was happening . . . up here."

With a pile of rope and a cushion from her cabin he made her comfortable on the deck; sat cross-legged beside her. For a long time there was a silence that was like a seed planted, to germinate, sprout, grow and blossom as inevitably as any other plant. Finally it blossomed.

"They—the Chinese who took me—told me that I was being taken away so that I couldn't betray you."

There was a curious breathless note in her voice, as if she dreaded the answer.

"I know," Nicholson answered.

The silence lasted a few minutes longer. Then Pat spoke again.

"What would have happened to you . . . if I had betrayed you?"

"I should have been imprisoned . . . not for long . . . but long enough for catastrophe to break."

"What catastrophe, John?"

"I can't tell you," he returned somberly. Then he turned to her, facing her squarely. "Pat. . . my name is not John Sobieski. That summer when you knew me, I was doing special work for the Army Intelligence Service that necessitated my using a false name.

There had been reports of a strange vessel seen off Montauk Point and the Department sent me there to determine if it were merely a rum runner, or, as reports indicated, something more sinister. I *am* Captain Robert Nicholson, Pat. You never knew, because I never wrote you after leaving."

She sat upright, eyes sparkling with excitement.

"You . . . Captain Nicholson . . . But I thought . . . the radio-gram . . ."

". . . Was a plant." He laughed shortly. "No such radiogram was ever sent from Washington. The night before I left an attempt was made on my life, so that an agent of Chu-Sheng could take my place . . . use my orders . . . assume my identity as Captain Nichol-son and report to the Commanding General in my name. But I had been warned. The Chinese shopkeeper to whom this man went for information and aid is actually a very valuable member of the Se-cret Service. The other man was killed . . . and I assumed *his* iden-tity . . . posed as an agent of Chu-Sheng. That was why I dared not risk any question of my identity being brought up. I should have had to prove myself to be Captain Robert Nicholson, which would have at once destroyed my usefulness. I knew that the people against whom I was working *must* have a spy in the house of the Commanding General. It was only logical that they would. And it was necessary for my own safety that I know the identity of this spy."

"Then the radiogram was a trap?" she exclaimed.

"A trap," he agreed. "I had authority from the Secretary of War superseding even that of the Commanding General. Using that, I had the radio operator on duty at the Balboa radio station tele-phone a fake message to the General's butler, making sure that it did not come into the hands of the General himself. It worked. The fake message, which was at once reported to Chu-Sheng by Car-los, gave him complete assurance that I was his own agent who had assumed the identity of Captain Nicholson, and also put me wise to the identity of Chu-Sheng's spy in the General's house-hold."

The cloak of silence fell upon them again. From the shore came the eerie roar of a howling monkey. Once a scream of something stricken rose in the ambient darkness. With the passing minutes fatigue gnawed at Nicholson's brain, and he found himself on the offensive against the insidious attacks of drowsiness. Repeated inspections of his watch appraised him of the advancing seconds.

In spite of herself Pat dozed off, secure in the knowledge that

she was safe with Nicholson. Watching her quiet rhythmic breathing made it even harder for him to keep awake. He had had only
an hour or two of sleep the night before for his mission with Carlos, after leaving the club, had consumed several hours.

The coppery moon rose above the charred tracery of the trees
on the shore. With it came a breeze, languorous and burdened with
the earthy odor of the jungle. These fragrances were potent wine to
his already tired senses. Several times on the very verge of sleep,
he nodded and jerked himself back into position.

A cry.

He sprang to his feet instantly. From the lookout on the bow
floated back a voice.

A ship was coming . . . a ship without lights . . . dimly seen in
the moonlight. . . driving toward them at full speed.

He had not realized that Pat was awake until she stood beside
him. Felt the touch of her hand upon his arm.

"There's a ship coming," he said. No need to frighten her any
more than necessary.

"Rescue?" There was joy in her voice.

He shook his head. " 'Fraid not Pat," he said quietly. "There
hasn't been time. It may be nothing . . . or it may be trouble."

He felt her tremble, and then she said bravely.

"Whatever it is, we'll stand together."

The oncoming ship loomed up in the moonlight. She was very
close and coming up rapidly. Unless she changed her course, she
would strike them amidships.

"What's the matter with them? They're coming straight at us,"
cried Pat, panic ringing in her voice. "Can't they see us?"

"I don't know," Nicholson said, then turned to fling a rapid order to one of the men. A handful of waste, soaked in oil, flared up
on the bridge.

The ship kept on. Indeed, she seemed to change her course the
merest trifle as if her helmsman were using the flaming waste on
the bridge for a target. A chorus of yells went up from the men on
the deck.

"She's going to ram us," Nicholson yelled, and, seizing Pat by
the hand, ran for the other side of the deck. Almost before they
reached it came a tremendous crash that flung them against the
rail.

Chapter Twenty-two

ALMOST AS SOON as the other ship struck there was a clatter of rifle shots from the Chinese on the deck of the raided tanker . . . a pitiful sound. In the moonlight Nicholson could see that the deck of the other ship swarmed with men, some of whom were already dropping to the deck on which they stood.

"Is there anything we can do?" It was Pat's voice, and there was no tremor in it.

"Stay out of range," he said quickly, as another volley of rifle shots came from the trapped Chinese and was answered from the deck of the attacking vessel. "You're likely to be hit."

Her hand tightened on his arm. Something like an electric thrill passed rapidly from her body to his, bringing with it a voiceless message, a terrible steely encouragement.

"You're in as much danger as I am," she said quietly.

"The only chance we've got is to stand them off," he said. And then a memory flashed into his mind. "There are guns in a rack at the foot of the saloon stairs."

They ran down the companionway together and he hastily scooped up a couple of automatics and several magazines from the rack in the dining saloon.

Regaining the deck, he found his Chinese putting up a futile and feeble resistance. The attack had been unexpected and had found them unprepared. And they had not been armed to ward off an attack in force. It was only a question of minutes before the vessel would be in the hands of the attackers.

Then, as the remaining members of the defenders were driven aft, toward the poop deck, he saw his opportunity. In a second he seized it.

"Run . . . the bridge . . . the only chance," he said to Pat. Then, automatic in hand, he lunged across the deck.

With a sweep, in passing, he snatched up the automatic that had fallen to the deck and ran up the bridge ladder, three rungs at a time. The girl followed him. In the confusion no one witnessed what they had done.

He ran the length of the bridge. There was only one ladder and the sides were of sheet steel, waist high, and strong enough to turn a bullet. One man could do much to stem a rush up the single ladder. But he realized with a sinking heart that there could be but one end. Balked in an attack on the bridge, the assailants had only to abandon them to achieve the same end . . . death. Once the prow of the other vessel was withdrawn, their vessel would sink.

He turned to the girl.

"There's no hope," he told her swiftly. "Fighting is only delaying the end. If they promise not to harm you, to put you ashore, I'm afraid they wouldn't keep their word."

"There is always hope," she told him quietly, lifting her face so that in the bleakness of the night the almost flower-like whiteness of her face was apparent to him. "There is a chance . . . just a chance."

"We'll fight it out," he said grimly, "as long as we can. But I wanted you to know the truth. I'll have to make every shot tell."

"I can shoot," the girl said calmly.

"Get down in that corner," he growled.

A bullet struck a corner of the chart house, close by, spattering them with splinters, as if to punctuate his remark.

But there was a timbre in his voice which made her smile at him . . . a steady magical smile, quite different from anything he had ever seen on her face before. The sheer warmth of it, here in the face of death, thrilled him; before it the blood seemed to dance in his veins; the world about him was misty, and he could see nothing but the glorious light in her eyes.

The sound of the uproar died away but a man's voice rose, an angry note in its suavity, speaking what Nicholson took to be Japanese. The ship was being searched. Presently they would be found and the struggle continue. But steadily Pat's warm, soft body pressed against his, her courage, her trust, armed him against the devastating sapping of his confidence. There was a way. There must be a way. A few schemes glimmered brightly for an instant, and then went glimmering like will-o'-the-wisps.

The merciless searchlight from the bridge of the other ship illuminated the scene with relentless clarity. Nicholson moved cautiously into the bridge wing . . . a steel and canvas affair where the officers took their noon shots at the sun. From there he could peer cautiously down upon the deck without being seen.

A voice came from below, speaking English with a Japanese accent.

"Yes," replied Nicholson calmly, but no volley of shots answered his voice, as he had expected.

"Only a fool puts his hand between the wolf and his prey," came the silky tones, "and you are a wise man. It is only necessary for me to order my engineer to reverse his engines, and you will drown like a rat. But I have no desire to do that. Be sensible. Let us keep the girl in safety until this affair is over."

"I am not bargaining," Nicholson said curtly.

"If I have to take her," the silky voice said, "she will never live to see land again."

"Bargain with him," the girl whispered urgently. "Every minute gained is that much to our advantage."

Nicholson called down to the man on the deck.

"How do I know you'll keep your word?"

"It is the order of the Master."

Came silence: silence that bloated like a balloon of evil anticipations. Still Nicholson said nothing. Ten minutes . . . ten precious minutes. Pat stared out into the menacing darkness from which death might come at any moment. Something she saw on the after deck of the attacking vessel caught her eye—held her. She touched his arm, whispered. He nodded.

"I know. Planes. She's a midget airplane carrier. Built to look like a tanker, but capable of being converted into a plane carrier at a moment's notice. This is the supply ship we're on now."

A man's impatient voice from the deck below cut short his sibilant whisper.

"Well, how about it? This boat is leaking badly. Do you accept?"

Nicholson braced himself for the inevitable. Time for talking was over. He must act now.

"No," he said curtly.

"Then you'll have to take the consequences," the man said.

Silence fell again. Seconds passed with the glittering clarity of crystal drops falling into a bottomless pit.

Nicholson expected the storm to break immediately. But he was wrong. Instead, the searchlight that had been illuminating the deck with its cold glare flashed off. Darkness closed in like the fall of a velvet curtain.

Suddenly there was the patter of bare feet on the deck plates. Nicholson crouched at the head of the bridge ladder, automatic in hand. The head of a man came above the level of the deck plates. The ladder swarmed with attackers.

Nicholson waited until the figure was head and shoulders above the deck and then fired. The man fell backwards with a choking cough, a gaping hole blown in his forehead, but so crowded was the ladder with men that, for a moment he stood upright, upheld by the press behind him, his face a bloody mask. Then he disappeared from sight and the rush was on.

Again and again the staccato sound of Nicholson's gun rang out. At such close range he could not miss. It was more than human flesh and blood could stand. The rush broke up, leaving the sprawled forms of the dead to dot the deck plates at the foot of the ladder, and an automatic lying on the lip of the ladder. An addition to the armament. Nicholson snatched it up promptly. Silence swooped down on the ship again like a living thing.

For ten minutes the silence grew, an aboriginal, empty silence, as of life withheld. The two waited tensely. That hush was pregnant with foreboding, with disaster. Their enemies were planning something . . . a new attack . . . a surprise. But where would it fall?

Once Pat leaned forward. "They're Chinese. What are Chinese doing here, like this?" she asked.

"Not Chinese . . . Japanese," he told her tersely. "Watch the deck forward. They're hatching something."

Protecting his body by the steel windbreak, he peered down into the deck. It was deserted save for the sprawled forms of the dead. And the silence continued. Evidently the leader knew the psychology of keeping an enemy waiting for the attack . . . of keeping the nerves taut until they reached the snapping point.

A volley of bullets rattled off the bulkhead . . . slugs so close to the bridge ladder opening, that Nicholson risked his life in exposing his head for a moment. Echoes of the explosions rang sharply through the still air. Bullets ripped splinters from the chart house, ricocheted with angry whines from the steel bulwark. It was evidently a covering fire for a rush, for the steady firing kept up.

Crouching there, Nicholson found his mind skipping nimbly from fact to fact. One thing stood out in ultra-clarity. If ammunition did not fail—and it was not likely to—sooner or later a bullet must find a crevice and end it. It seemed incredible that he had not already been killed. He dwelt with a strange calmness upon the immutability of circumstances that had brought him to this end.

There passed before his mind's eye a parade of the vessels of the battle fleet . . . proud, majestic, as they steamed through the

Canal, passed beneath the frowning, scarred face of Culebra Cut . . . and he shuddered at the picture that followed.

Then the coup was sprung . . . sprung with such suddenness that, despite their watchfulness, it all but swept the two off their feet.

A steel grapnel, to which was attached a rope, suddenly appeared on the forward windbreak, tossed from below.

Nicholson's heart sank. Attacked in front and in rear under a barrage of revolver and rifle fire that was proving itself deadly accurate, how could he hope to stem the rush?

Heedless of danger he pumped bullet after bullet down into the close packed mass of men below, but from the angle from which he was compelled to shoot, only a part of them were within his sight.

And then . . . a scream from Pat and from behind a bullet slapped by him with a vicious whine, telling him that their enemies had gained the bridge in the rear.

The last of the light cruisers had completed the transit of the first level of locks. Steaming slowly through the Canal, the tropical verdure on their banks brightly illuminated by the searchlights playing upon them, were the battleships, followed by the airplane carriers and a long line of cruisers.

There remained only the destroyers, the submarines and miscellaneous vessels to make the transit before the entire Naval fighting force of the United States was in the Panama Canal.

Chapter Twenty-three

BUT IT WAS ONLY FOR AN INSTANT that danger threatened from the rear. On the heels of the shot from behind him came another and a sharper report from close at hand and a yell from the man perched on the rail.

Pat had entered the fight and her first shot had gone home.

The next few minutes were hectic ones. The men rushed again and again and each time Nicholson stopped them, until his automatic was empty and the ammunition in his pocket exhausted.

"Pat . . . gun . . . empty . . . yours . . ."

Coolly Pat took the gun and handed him hers. And none too soon, for a man was thrusting up the last steps of the ladder. The shot that killed him blackened his shirt, for the gun was almost against his chest. His tumbling body, for a moment, blocked the advance of the others. Rapidly Nicholson pulled the trigger until the hammer fell with a thickening click.

And now Nicholson was forced to swing a length of pipe, picked up from the scuppers, smashing heads as fast as they came into range. He was in plain view from the deck and there were immediate consequences.

Someone, possibly the leader, began to snipe. A bullet ripped through Nicholson's coat, bit into the fleshy part of his thigh. Another plucked at the cloth between the upraised arm and breast. Involuntarily he recoiled. The movement gave the man at the top of the ladder a chance to gain a foothold on the bridge. He swung a knife.

The blade descended, clanging upon the length of iron pipe, bearing it down toward the deck.

Before Nicholson could lift the pipe to a defensive position the man with the knife was upon him. There was no chance to dodge.

Over his left shoulder a rapier of corrosive flame stabbed the night, a rapier of flame that reflected hideously upon a distorted face and sank its hot shaft into a man. His face was almost blown away at that close range. He dropped, toppled backwards, and rolled over the lip of the bridge ladder.

The unexpectedness of the shot, its fatal effect, the falling of the stricken man was a quick negative snapped and imprinted upon Nicholson's brain. He had no time to look around, but he knew that it was Pat who had saved him. The next instant the automatic dropped by one of the men in the first attack was in his hands. It was their last reserve.

Then, without warning, disaster came leaping. Over the edge of the bridge canopy a squirming figure dropped and landed upon the bridge.

Nicholson shoved the gun into Pat's hands.

"Watch the ladder," he called and leaped forward to meet the man.

Dodging a knife thrust, he made a futile grab for the piece of pipe. But it was beyond his reach. Then in a second he found himself tangled in battle. His opponent was evidently an expert with a knife.

A quick slash and his coat was laid open from shoulder to shoulder. A shot and then another sounded. Pat was evidently keeping guard over the ladder. Nicholson's hand went up to seize the wrist that held the knife. Instinctively he lunged forward to get inside a thrust. His left hand went out to grapple for the man's throat, and the man seized his wrist. Thus they stood, two bodies straining against each other, the attacker concentrating on loosening the hand holding the knife, Nicholson struggling to throw the man.

The steel-like body pressed close to his, bending as he bent, tightening as he tightened. In the flashing second of opportunity, Nicholson realized that his only advantages were that the assailant's hand held a knife, which may not have seemed an advantage but was. Relaxing suddenly, Nicholson recoiled, and then before the other had divined what was coming, plunged his head against the other's chin. The trick broke the man's hold. With his left hand, Nicholson drove the man's body against the steel windbreak. The knife flew to the plates. The man's head thudded against the corner of the steel plates.

He dropped limply to the deck.

Nicholson did not wait to see how badly he was hurt. He turned to the bridge ladder. As he did so, the tanker lurched to port. The two, swept off their balance, slid to the windbreak and brought up with a crash. It was not until he had reached his feet that Nicholson heard a new sound above the turmoil . . . the deep throb of an airplane engine.

At the same instant the tanker's searchlight flooded the deck with a blinding glare. There were cries and shouts from the main deck below. The doomed vessel continued to roll. She seemed about to turn turtle.

With a sinking heart Nicholson realized the new danger. The other boat, frightened off by the arrival of the airplane, was leaving them to their fate. Falling astern, she had wrenched her bow out of the hole and the yacht was sinking fast.

Nicholson leaped onto the windbreak and looked up into the sky.

Between two smaller lights a searchlight played down from the sky. Even as he looked a red flare dropped swiftly to the sea where it rode the waves, painting scarlet the two boats.

Pat cried out joyously: "We're saved!"

Nicholson knew there was no time to lose. He sped down the bridge ladder. The deck below was strewn with dead men. His feet slipped in the sticky mess. The survivors had fled back to the other boat.

The port rail of the yacht was awash. It would be only a matter of minutes before she sank. There was no boat handy, but there was a life-raft, two steel cylinders covered with a wooden grating, partly buried in the gentle swells. He cut it loose and, with Pat by his side, stepped into the water from the rail and struck out vigorously for the raft.

They were just in time. It was not a moment later that, with a sucking and gurgling, the tanker disappeared beneath the water. Only an overturned boat, a few pieces of wood, and a dead body or two marked the place where it had been.

Nicholson peered into the night for the other vessel. It had vanished into the darkness. In the watertight compartment of the raft he found a rocket, placed it in the tube and touched a match to the priming cord.

It hissed skywards for fifty yards and blossomed into a shower of stars that slowly descended to flicker out into the water. The roar of the plane immediately began to grow. Nicholson fired another rocket. A magnesium landing flare hit the water and splashed into white glare not fifty yards away. By its light a man's arm was seen to wave from the window of the plane. Then it landed a short distance away and slowly taxied up toward them, a small searchlight picking them up full in its glare.

Nicholson vigorously paddled the unwieldy raft closer until he could step from it to the pontoon of the Douglas amphibian.

A doorway in the side of the cabin opened. Nicholson assisted Pat in and then scrambled up himself.

Facing them was Lieutenant Dan Martin, a revolver in his hand. "You are under arrest, Captain Nicholson," he said.

Into Nicholson's mind flashed a picture of the battle fleet steaming in close-packed array through the Panama Canal.

Chapter Twenty-four

IT WAS A STRANGE TABLEAUX there in the cabin of the plane, rising lightly to the swells of the gulf of Panama. Martin, his face set and stern, revolver in hand, Nicholson facing him, face equally grim, and Pat, white-faced and weary.

The tension was broken by Nicholson. His movement was as swift as the lunge of a striking snake, his timing perfect. Martin, taken entirely by surprise, had no defense against it. The edge of Nicholson's palm, striking his wrist, sent the gun hurtling into a corner of the plane. A second blow, fair on the chin, dropped the astounded lieutenant to the floor.

Before the open-mouthed pilot could spring through the door that opened into the cabin of the plane, Nicholson had retrieved the gun and had him covered.

"Take it easy, buddy," Nicholson snapped. "Don't get hasty."

The pilot dropped back into his seat.

"Okay," he admitted. "You win."

"Give 'er the gun," Nicholson said. A glance told him that Martin was stirring. "Get her in the air and make it snappy."

"Okay," the pilot said again. "Where to?"

"Panama City," Nicholson told him. "Land in the bay and taxi up onto the beach just below the Union Club."

Then he turned his attention to Martin, who had raised himself on one elbow, dazed, as the engine of the plane roared into life.

"Sorry I had to do it, Lieutenant," he said, "but there wasn't time to talk."

"It was a sweet one, all right," Martin admitted, rubbing his chin, watching the other with a certain reckless defiance in his eyes. "I suppose you know what you'll get for this. You can't get away with it."

"I'll risk it," Nicholson told him. "How about you? Willing to be a good boy, or will I have to tie you up?"

"Tie me up," the boy said grimly.

Nicholson shook his head. "No sense in it. All I ask is that you don't try to start something while we're in the air. After you're ashore, I don't care what you do . . . corral all the military police on the Zone and come after me."

"It might make things a little easier for you," Pat put in, "to know that Captain Nicholson is here on a secret mission for the Secretary of War. I only learned it myself to-night."

The boy looked his unbelief. Nicholson nodded.

For a moment or two, silence filled the cabin of the plane. Nicholson sat there with an air of attention, of expectancy, of suspense. Before him lay life or death, and he knew it. Then he glanced out of the window of the plane. The Bay of Panama below him was a polished slab of mahogany. The lights of the fleet were gone. The knowledge bit into his mind like a grim engraving. He turned back swiftly to Martin.

"When is the last ship of the fleet scheduled to make the locks?" he said.

"I don't know . . . sometime around daybreak," the boy answered. "Why?"

"Because," Nicholson answered, "when the last vessel of the fleet enters Miraflores Lake, hell is scheduled to pop. Every mine in the bed of the Canal will be exploded simultaneously . . . every fortification on the Zone . . . Fort Sherman, Fort Randolph, Fort Delesseps at the Atlantic Entrance, the Fortified Islands, everything on the Pacific side, will be a mass of smoking ruins."

"Good God!" The boy gazed at him wide-eyed. "How . . . why it's impossible!"

"The control room," Nicholson told him grimly.

"But they're disconnected . . . the switch panels removed . . . even the wire leads capped so that there's no possibility of an accidental contact."

"Not now," Nicholson assured him briefly.

The boy looked at him, his face a white mask of incredulity.

"You mean . . . but why didn't you report it . . . Good God, man, don't you realize what may happen?"

"I do," Nicholson said grimly. "To have reported it would have meant only a brief postponement. The mines will be exploded by remote control . . . from where I don't know, although I've a strong suspicion. And rest assured that the man behind this hellish plot has more than one string to his bow. Destroy one and he uses another. No, the only thing is to destroy it at its source."

The pilot was cutting across an arm of the city that jutted into the bay, swinging around for a landing in the bay against the wind. Below them the lights of the city gleamed . . . and stretching out through the darkness, seemingly into infinitude, were the lights of the fleet steaming through the Canal.

Nicholson turned to the boy.

"Listen," he said. "When we land I'm going to run for it. Don't try to stop me. I'd hate to shoot you, but if you interfere I'd have to. There's just one chance in a million that I'll be able to stop this thing before it's too late. If it does happen . . . nothing on God's earth can save the fleet. But you may be able to do something. Warn the General. Get every man out of barracks and out of the range of the mined areas as fast as they can. And tell the General this. Within ten minutes after the explosion comes . . . if it does come . . . there'll be a fleet of Japanese planes swooping over the city dropping gas bombs. There's a tanker out in the gulf . . . really an airplane carrier . . ."

The plane landed with a little bump, headed for the beach. Nicholson opened the door, almost blinded by the salt water thrown up by the pontoons. There was a grating noise as the plane grounded on sand and instantly Nicholson was out . . . splashing through shallow water to shore and then up the stairs that led to the sea wall, headed for his gamble with destiny.

A faint pallor was growing in the east as he reached the top of the sea wall. For a moment the terror of the human imagination . . . in which rest all possibilities of terror . . . increased the coldness in his heart. At any moment now might come the roar that signified the destruction of the battle fleet and of the forts, the failure of his mission. But until it did come there was hope.

The Casa Mendoza was in darkness when he reached the iron grille that stood across the opening. The grille was locked. He picked up a stone and hammered on the iron. Empty, echoing silence and the chatter of a parrot, awakened from his sleep among the fronds of a nearby coconut palm. He hammered again. There came a shuffling step and a man came to the door; peered out— and found a revolver jammed into his stomach through the iron grillework.

Nicholson knew no Spanish. But knowledge of a revolver jammed into one's stomach sharpens the perceptions. The man grasped quite readily, from Nicholson's gestures, that he wanted the grille opened.

Once opened Nicholson found himself in a quandary. What to do with his prisoner. He had nothing with which to tie or gag him. The problem was solved by shoving him outside the grille, locking it again, and intimating, with graphic gestures, what would happen if the man made noise.

Then he made his way across the patio toward the door that led down to the room where Chu-Sheng waited. As he crossed there came from somewhere in a room close by the rattle of a clock preparing to strike the hour. It seemed to Nicholson as a thing of abominable violence—like countless swift hammer strokes on the innumerable frayed ends of his nerves.

Almost on its ending came disaster. The purple pool of shadow where a great earthenware *olla* stood in a corner of the patio was agitated and from it sprang a man . . . Diego Mendoza.

Nicholson did not hear him. He certainly did not see him, but he could feel the breath of peril at his back. He glanced back swiftly, just as Mendoza closed in on him with a glitter of steel plunging for his back.

There are some reflexes of the human body that are too quick for perceptions to follow. Nicholson did nothing wittingly, accomplished nothing for which he was consciously responsible, yet he crouched low and hurled himself against the oncoming man, knocking him to the paving, himself with him.

The knife clattered to the paving also, but not before Mendoza had gotten in two quick slashes . . . one on the shoulder, another and a deeper one that bit into the flesh of his side.

Ignoring the wounds Nicholson was up like a lithe cat, even as Mendoza got to his feet himself. Back and forth across the patio they battled, wrestling, striking, insane with blood lust, reeling and stamping there in the darkness, fighting silently and with maniac fury. But Nicholson had a wiry strength, and he was in the pink of condition. Moreover, he was spurred by a homicidal craving to overpower this assailant of his. Before his eyes danced a vision of the battle fleet . . .

His fists beat swiftly into the Spaniard's face. Dazed by blows that fell with the force of a club, Mendoza's head sagged backwards and Nicholson's fingers dug into his throat. Ten seconds . . . twenty . . . half a minute . . . and flesh and sinew gave way. He sank to the patio floor.

With a quick movement Nicholson snatched up the knife and sprang to the door of *Moko* slabs. Fingers and the palm beat the rhythmic tattoo that he had heard twice before. The door swung open silently and he plunged down the stairs. Again the blinding light at their foot that silhouetted him in ultra-clarity, then that door swung open and the passage lay before him, the cobra rearing its ugly head to bar the way. But he pressed resolutely forward and the deadly thing retreated as it had done before. He went rapidly down the passage until he reached the black curtain at its end, slipped through it—and stopped abruptly.

Awaiting him, long keen knives ready, were two Chinese guards, barring the way.

Chapter Twenty-five

"TAKE ME TO THE MASTER," he said in fluent Cantonese, with all the arrogance he could muster. He had no definite plan, although there was the faint glimmering of an idea. His feelings were tossed together into too violent confusion for immediate disentanglement.

He stood there in the long room where he had first seen Chu-Sheng. But now there was no glowing ball of light, no monstrous spider. Instead a somber black curtain shot off the far end of the hall.

Hands slipped over his body, searching for a weapon. He smiled grimly. They could not search his brain. And his white man's brain, at that moment, was a more potent weapon than any the Tongueless One could muster. Silence filled the long room like wine rising in a cup.

He was weak, but he knew that he must pretend that he was even weaker. Then the caution of the cunning, which permits an injured and weaker thing to approach unchallenged, would not be stirred by alarm. So he stood swaying, facing the somber curtain at the further end of the room where shadows danced a purple saraband.

Then suddenly the curtains slid aside and the setting at the far end of the room jumped at him with a brutal massing of colors and sounds.

For a moment there were no words spoken and for a moment the room seemed pregnant with death. And then he almost laughed in the face of the Tongueless One, the Master. The answer? The answer to the riddle. He had it. He knew now what he must do. And the knowledge pushed back the licking tongues of pain; killed everything in his mind but the fact that the safety of his country, the safety of the battle fleet and its thousands of men lay in the hollow of his palm. If he failed, they went to death in a flaming hell of horror. With an anger, deadly because it was backed by the brain of a man who had just learned the meaning of hate, he faced the Tongueless One.

Chu-Sheng was at the far end of the room, seated behind a polished table of ebony or some dark polished wood on which stood the complicated radio apparatus with which he planned to send the United States battle fleet and the fortifications of the Canal to destruction in a roaring, blasting inferno of death . . . the radio apparatus whose receiving end was in the secret control room in Ancon Hill, placed there by Carlos the night when Nicholson had admitted him to the room.

Seeing him there, black eyes fixed unwinkingly upon him, Nicholson could almost feel the black thrill of the death lust rising from him, and hanging in the air like a tangible thing. A cruel smile animated the yellow face. Nicholson wondered if by look or gesture of his, or intuition on the other's part, the Chinese had guessed the plan that had been born in his brain. And then he realized that it was only the inherent savage in the man which made him savor, in anticipation, the cruelties he would wreak upon this white man who had defied him, who had threatened to wreck his plans, who now stood before him, wounded and helpless.

A sudden uprush of hatred poisoned Nicholson, swept through him as a sudden gust of wind goes through a house, scattering the common things of life, breaking the mirrors of vision and leaving in place only the basic emotions.

The toneless voice of the girl seated rigidly on a carved ebony chair in the corner broke in on his thoughts, shattering the mood.

"The Slayer of Souls welcomes you, traitor."

A slow coldness swept through Nicholson's veins. Momentarily he was seeing again that scene in the black semicircular room . . . the crawling spiders in the greenish light. But his face was a carved mask as he replied.

"There is something that I must say."

"Punishment waits, Captain Nicholson. Nothing can be said to alter that."

The cold black eyes of Chu-Sheng stared at him as his thoughts were given utterance through the lips of the girl. Hate flickered in his eyes like the shimmer of a naked blade. Nicholson felt it reach out and prick him like a sword point. And it seemed to bring up from his brain and heart unexpected, rather forgotten, qualities, as a storm-whipped wave brings up mud and gravel from the ground bed of the shore . . . the surging rhythm of the refrain in his brain rang louder in his ears.

Kill . . . Kill . . . Kill!

"I must tell you something . . . before I die . . . I'm not pleading to live . . . but you must listen to me. Disaster threatens . . ."

Whether the brain of the girl transmitted his words through that strange, secret channel of communication, or whether the Tongueless One, watching his face intently, read his lips, Nicholson never knew, but a new look came into the face of Chu-Sheng. The fish had seen the bait.

"You have not long to wait," the Tongueless One said through the lips of the kneeling girl. "Soon you will go forth again into the daylight. But you must leave behind you all your ego, all your memories. It will not be dangerous, Captain Nicholson. Just a few hours . . . perhaps a few days . . . alone with lights and mirrors and sounds . . . and you will emerge as one new born. For, from you will have been taken forever all recollection of what you have been. Like a child you will set forth upon your new pilgrim-age.

"My voice is weak," Nicholson made answer. "Your threats mean nothing to me. I am going. Death calls me. If you are to hear me I must come nearer."

An inscrutable expression flitted across the face of the Tongueless One; the dropping of the Oriental veil. His right hand flashed up and the fingers writhed and twisted as they spelled out a message to the two men who stood guard beside Nicholson. They stepped back a pace.

The smile of the Tongueless One bit into Nicholson's consciousness like a grim engraving. Fear ran through every nerve channel, and his eyes were dark sick pools. But these factors had no connection with the analyzing power of his brain. He knew why the Tongueless One had leaned across the table toward him; read it in the movements of the long, slender fingers that he knew itched for his throat; in the smile that held something of the snarl of the animal crouching for the kill; in the depths of the eyes that held an unholy lust of hate.

For fear passed swiftly. In its place was only a fierce exultation. The first trick had been scored. And at its winning fear had been shed as a dreamer sheds the last rags of his dream; stands stark and bare to the world once more. Now the game was on . . . and thronging the Panama Canal . . . unaware that a game was being played with their lives as the stake . . . were the ships and men of the battle fleet. A clawing pain clutched at his brain.

"Speak and be swift," came from the lips of the girl.

The face of Chu-Sheng was like a mask of yellow enamel that threatened each moment to shatter from tremendous pressure applied from within. It told Nicholson clearly that he had no time to lose.

He took a step nearer the table. The world seemed closing in on him. A haze was creeping over the world. Only the knowledge of that line of ships steaming through the Panama Canal and that he alone stood between her and destruction, kept him on his feet.

"The authorities . . . the soldiers . . . they know that you are here . . . they plan to raid this place . . . you may destroy the Canal . . . but unless you make preparations now . . . you will be destroyed also."

Chu-Sheng lifted a hand threateningly . . . as only an Oriental can threaten with a gesture. It was more than a mere waving of hand and arm. It seemed like an incident which cut the air like a tragic shadow.

But Nicholson did not recoil from it, as the man had expected. Instead, he took a step forward. He must get nearer to the Tongueless One before he could pour the black brewage of fear down his throat until it choked the life from him. By a tremendous effort of will he kept his thought from showing on his face. And he must convince the man that there was no strength left in him.

The girl spoke sharply.

"Fool. To come with a message like that. There will be no soldiers, no authorities left."

Nicholson played a trump held in reserve. Cobwebs seemed to be dropping around him, cobwebs whose multitudinous strands were held by one master hand, and pulling him, pulling him, irresistibly . . . toward what?

"But the Prince . . . Prince Lai Chung . . . he is planning . . ." His voice died away.

Chu-Sheng leaned forward. His body was stiff, taut. His face was not set and cold now, it was fiery, livid, evil. Energy flamed and seethed in every sensitized atom, even the end of his black cloak, the tips of his pointing fingers threw some vibratory shock into the air.

The girl's voice came back at him swiftly and it seemed to Nicholson that there was an undercurrent of fear in the words.

"What is this dog of a prince planning?"

"I can't think," Nicholson said wearily. "My head . . . I'm bleeding . . . my brain won't work . . . ."

Blood from his wounded shoulder trickled down over his shirt. He left it there.

He took another step nearer the Chinese, swayed, and then with a low moan crumpled to the floor. But he kept his gaze fixed intently on the Tongueless One through eyes that had narrowed to tiny slits. A false move, one single bit of suspicion awakened in that cunning brain and his one slim chance was gone. He crouched on the floor, gripping his leg.

"He plans . . . plans . . ." his voice died away in a moan.

"Speak," came harshly from the lips of the girl.

Exultation swept through Nicholson like a tidal bore up a sluggish river. A smile crept to his lips in spite of the pain that gripped him, but he crushed it back. The white man's brain was winning. The trap was ready to be sprung.

"He plans . . . plans something . . . I do not know the details . . . something that he says you cannot combat . . . cannot resist . . . I overheard . . . talk . . . the General . . ."

Slowly as he talked, he had crept toward the immobile figure behind the table. The stretch of stone flooring between himself and Chu-Sheng seemed as vast as interstellar space; the time it took to cross it, dragging along on his hands and knees an incalculable eternity.

"Repeat the conversation," came from the girl. "All of it . . . what were the words?"

The hand of the immobile figure came to life in an expressive gesture, the fingers crawling like evil, slimy things.

In answer to the message they conveyed, a guard sprang to Nicholson's side . . . dragged him to his feet roughly. Then stepped back to the table again.

Nicholson stiffened in resentment against the rough handling before he remembered. He must grovel. But hate poured new life into him, new strength, while only agony was stamped upon his face. No single gleam of that hate was permitted to show. The end was near. The end of Chu-Sheng . . . or of himself and the United States battle fleet.

He strained upward, clinging to the legs of the table, struggling to keep his feet, his voice so low that it was hardly audible. And all the time his eyes were fixed on the intricate mechanism on the table, searching for a vital place . . . for the heart of the machine. Chu-Sheng was within arm's reach. It might be possible for him to reach his knife and drive it home in the man's breast before guards could intervene. His brain toyed with the thought . . . his eyes even searched out the little hollow at the base of the throat where the knife should go home. But he thrust it resolutely aside. Better to smash the machine. Dying, Chu-Sheng might still have strength enough to throw the switch . . . or one of his men might do it, establishing connection with the control room deep in the heart of

Ancon Hill. No. Better to smash the machine. If time still remained after the smashing of the machine he might try for the man's throat.

He knew that the moment had come to strike. It was the most propitious moment that he could hope to find. He swayed, almost went down, and his hand crept stealthily beneath his trouser leg for the knife secreted there.

The moment had come. With a swift movement he straightened up.

Again the room of shadows where Prince Lai sat before the gleaming pool of liquid light in the slab of jade . . . the candlelit gloom was rich with color . . . the deep yellow of the row of yellow-clad men almost lost in the baffling shadows . . . the richer sheen of the jeweled robes of the Prince.

The eyes of the Prince were plunged into the depths of the lucent pool of green light. From the lips of the kneeling men came a low chant. . . words that were ancient when much of the store of human knowledge disappeared with the burning of the great Library at Alexandria . . . words that were ancient when Wise Men from the East chanted them, as the cap stone was laid upon the top of the Great Pyramid . . . words whose echoes seemed to agitate the gloom of the room as though some tenuous living force agitated its depths . . . was drawing sustenance . . . strength . . . from their repetition. . . .

Chapter Twenty-six

WITH ONE CLEAN SWEEP Nicholson demolished the heart of the machine on the table. Tubes smashed with a tinkle of glass . . . tiny filaments of wire were torn loose from their fastenings by the blade. From the center of it came a flash . . . another as wires fused and short circuited . . . Smoke rose . . . the odor of burning rubber entered his nostrils.

Long in the telling. Brief in the doing. So short, in fact, that the deed was a thing accomplished before the two guards at his back could interfere . . . before Chu-Sheng himself realized what had happened.

Then . . . nightmare.

It was neither a shriek nor a scream that came from the lips of Chu-Sheng, but from some hellish region in between. It was high and shrill, yet it had a vowel sound in it, a blat that stabbed the ear. It was a cry of anger that spouted up, a terrible geyser of sound as the Tongueless One saw his plan to blow up the American fleet shattered in a single instant by this man who had betrayed him. For a moment death peered at Nicholson from the other man's eyes . . . death, swift and merciless . . . giving no quarter, no opportunity for battle, for strategy.

Then Chu-Sheng's right hand darted forward, and the twisting, writhing fingers communicated a message to the two guards.

They sprang toward Nicholson . . . and halted in dismay.

A gridiron of terrible living light (or what appeared to be light) sprang up between Nicholson and the guards . . . drove them backward until the two guards, the girl and Chu-Sheng himself were penned in the rear of the great hall by the bars of living light which reached from wall to wall and from floor to ceiling.

From the secret depths of Nicholson's consciousness rose the frantic empty assurance that what he saw was incredible. That it was not possible.

Chu-Sheng flung out one hand before him . . . with his forefinger drew a barrier through space . . . bar above bar. And where his fingers had been sprang into being a barrier of *dark light* . . . light that was black as ebony . . . yet light that seemed incandescent with terrible *black* heat . . . heat that seemed to carry with it the absolute zero of evil . . . a clinging shrouding aura of horror . . . of terror . . . heat that seemed to detach itself in floating black particles from the barrier which the forefinger of Chu-Sheng had reared and drift through the air toward the gridiron of living white fire which stood before it . . . to cling to it as ice forms and clings to a telegraph wire during a sleet storm . . . seeking . . . ever seeking to shroud the bars of fire in a blanket of black . . . and ever being consumed in the fierce energy which glowed along the bars of the white gridiron.

Nicholson stood rooted to the spot. He dared not move . . . he was almost stunned by the tremendous thing being enacted before him . . . There was no sanity in it at all . . . no stable point upon which he could grasp. He was conscious of tremendous forces swirling about him . . . forces that battered at his brain . . . shook his body as a tree is shaken in a hurricane . . . Great whirlwinds in which something huge and black and irremediably evil tugged and tore at him . . . touching the very core of human fear . . . and were dissipated for the moment by a wedge of silver light which bathed him in its luster . . . a light which clung to him like a protective aura . . . And then grew dim, wavered and was almost dissolved into floating shreds of silver mist as the whirlwind of evil tore at him again.

The utter impotence of any resistance which he could oppose to such titanic force struck him suddenly with a dismay that was paralyzing. A hundred, insignificant memories, all infinitely irrelevant, disconnected and futile, rose from the back of his mind and occupied his attention insistently, though all the while he knew his every faculty was engrossed by the danger which threatened him.

There was creeping over him a compelling urge to keep his eyes fastened upon Chu-Sheng . . . He watched that figure of terror behind the bars of black light as one watches a creature uncreated, who figures horribly in some disordered dream . . . The clinging touch of horror . . . of terror . . . grew thicker . . . seemed to hang in the air about him like a mist . . . seemed to be enfolding him . . . making him one with itself . . . He had the sudden impression as if something in his brain was being wrenched violently loose from its fastenings. It was as if his entire soul life and soul understanding were shifting within him with utter completeness. At that moment something old and ancient and evil seemed to be born within him. A new perception of life came to him, certain new sensations which he felt instinctively, without being able to classify or describe . . . a huge irresistible whirlwind which swept out of the womb of the past and back into the present . . . He put one foot forward tentatively . . . desperately he tried to halt the movement. He could not. Something stronger than himself was tugging at him . . . tugging at something inside of him . . . tugging at his soul . . . he could feel some gigantic, nameless power clutching at it with a myriad fingers . . . tearing at it as if with great claws . . . He took another step forward . . .

Instantly he was bathed in the wedge of silvery light . . . light that seemed to thicken and congeal as water does when gelatine is added . . . light that clung to him . . . impeded his movements . . . The tearing sensation within him vanished utterly . . . there welled up in him a horror of the thing that lay behind the bars of black light . . . a desire to escape from it. . . .

. . . The great gridiron of living fire seemed to be moving . . . it *was* moving . . . slowly, inexorably, it was gliding down the hall toward Chu-Sheng, the crouching fire of the girl and the two guards as if moved by a relentless intelligence.

He was conscious of a sound that was ringing in his ears like a gigantic rush of splendor . . . some flooding, massive energy, like a tide of unknown power and beauty and glory that surged through him . . . that seemed to be carried on the wedge of silvery light . . . A sound of chanting . . . a chanting as melodious and sweet as the stone *klings* of Yuran when struck by a sturdy finger . . . and under it rolled and thundered the word that signifies the absolute . . . the perfect . . . the holy . . . the magic syllables . . .

O-O-O-O-O-OM-M-M-M-M-M-M

There flashed into his mind Prince Lai's words—"To-night you will see something that no man of your race has ever seen before . . . the unveiling of secrets that have been guarded for more thousands of years than you have fingers on your hands. But *whatever you may see,* do not be afraid . . ."

The strength that was carried to him on the wings of the chant grew and grew, as if the sound were a guidon pointing the way to a Life of To-morrow beside which his Life of Yesterday and To-day faded to a wretched, meaningless dream.

Chu-Sheng flung out his hand again . . . flung it out again and again . . . and each time black light seemed to dart from the writhing finger-tips and re-inforce the barrier of black light he had erected . . . and each time a terrible geyser of sound rose and fell and rose again from that tongueless throat . . . The wedge of silvery light that enveloped Nicholson was spreading now . . . creeping beyond him . . . following in the path of the gridiron of living light as it relentlessly pushed back Chu-Sheng's barrier . . . it reached the white gridiron . . . passed beyond it . . . and with sudden stabbing force plunged through the barrier of black light . . . The blackness gave before it as steel before a mighty projectile . . . the edges crumpled back . . . began slowly . . . slowly to fade . . . The light reached the kneeling girl . . . crept around her knees as water rises in a pool . . . higher . . . higher . . . the chant coming from her lips faltered . . . died . . . when the light closed over her head as a rising tide closes over the head of a statue . . .

A shriek rose from the lips of Chu-Sheng . . . a mighty, stabbing blat . . . a shriek that was cut short abruptly as the girl sprang to her feet . . . whirled . . . standing very straight and still in a strange, supple, agonized attitude, her left forearm across her eyes, her right hand clenched, her slender body twisted slightly to the left.

She began to speak, slowly distinctly . . . *And the voice that came from her lips was the rich, full voice of Prince Lai.*

"Hai, Faithless One," the voice of the Prince rolled out from the lips of the girl in sonorous tones, "the Wheel of the Law turns. Justice is inevitable . . ."

And then Nicholson's overstrained nerves gave way; inside his brain something like a colored rocket burst into a thousand iridescent fragments . . . Unconsciousness carried him into its shadowy corridors.

Chapter Twenty-seven

EVERYTHING WAS VERY STILL. The afternoon sun shining through the drawn Venetian blinds was lying in narrow golden bars across the white wall above the immaculate white bed. An electric fan buzzed lazily on a little table at one side.

Nicholson opened his eyes. For a moment he lay there, staring into the fretwork of delicate purple and heliotrope shadows that cloaked the room like a silken veil. Then he was conscious of Patricia Fenton's face bending over him. He started to speak, but she laid her hand softly over his lips.

"Don't try to think," she said slowly. "Just relax. You've been awfully sick, John, and you mustn't talk."

He grinned a trifle in spite of the pain in his side.

"Robert, not John," he corrected her.

"Robert," she said gently.

His eyes flickered about the strange room and she interpreted the meaning of the flicker.

"This is Prince Lai's house," she told him. "Something happened . . . nobody seems to know just what . . . and the Prince had you brought here. He had a talk with the General and they decided to leave you here instead of taking you to the hospital."

Nicholson closed his eyes for a moment. There rushed over him in a flood a memory of those last few minutes before he lost consciousness . . . it all seemed like a dream. His hand groped about the coverlid until it found hers; gripped it tightly.

"Chu-Sheng," he whispered. "What happened to him?"

"I don't know . . . nobody knows," the girl said, with a touch of strain in her manner. Mention of that name brought back to her memories that she had wanted to forget. "But you mustn't think any more about that. And you mustn't talk any more."

"If you think," Nicholson said, "that I'm going to lie here and not ask questions, you've got me all wrong."

"You can ask," she said serenely, "but if nobody answers, what good will it do?"

In her eyes, as she bent over him, was a new and thrilling expression, an expression that registered on Nicholson like sunlight on film . . . that gave him a strange sense of exhilaration, yet, at the same time, a dreamlike content.

Whatever his answer was, it was drowned in a sound from outside, a sound strangely reminiscent of a foghorn on the East River at night . . . but a cultivated foghorn.

The next moment the door was thrown open. Prince Lai stood there, and with him was Mrs. Chenery and Lieutenant Martin.

She swept across the room and Nicholson braced himself to withstand the flood of words that gushed forth. Dan, after a quick glance at Nicholson, leaned against the window sill, trying bravely to look glad that Pat was happy.

For a moment the Prince eyed the little group. It was well, he mused, that two people in love needed no language, for Mrs. Chenery was using up all the words in that steady stream that was so characteristic of her. Fortunately it didn't matter particularly to the good lady whether anyone listened or not, so long as one didn't interrupt.

She had seated herself by the bedside, fanning herself intently, a look of triumph on her flushed round face.

"What did I tell you," she demanded of the world. "This place is full of scoundrels, ready to seduce the innocent, ready to plunge knives into their hapless victims. They thought I was crazy when I insisted you had been kidnapped. But I knew. I knew they were after me, too. That they are still after me. My honor, my very life are in constant peril. But I am brave. I realize that is the penalty that all famous women of history who have the unconscious power of maddening men, must pay for their allure. When I found out that I had been harboring a vicious spy in my house, I thought I would have a stroke . . . I really did. Dan can tell you. I fainted dead away. To think that I let that murderer feed me for nearly a year, and all the time he was just biding his time to poison me." She shuddered delicately, her double chins trembling like a bowl of jelly. "I hope now you'll listen to me, my dear, and get yourself a bodyguard, as I have done. Dan here, is an angel. He doesn't leave me out of his sight."

The angel made a not so angelic a face as she leaned over and patted him playfully on the arm with her fan, and for a fleeting instant there was possibly as much trace of amusement on the lips of Prince Lai as may be seen on the granite monument of one of the old Pharaohs.

"I'll never step out of my room without a bodyguard again. Not as long as we have to stay in this terrible hole. You just can't trust these foreigners. They all have axes to grind, and they're just as liable to grind them on your neck as not. Present company excluded, of course," she added hastily bobbing her red head toward Prince Lai.

"You're really not like a foreigner at all, Prince . . . well . . . I mean you're not treacherous . . . I mean, you're just like any human being . . . I mean, you're . . . I could trust you. I really could. It's because you're a Prince, I suppose. Which just goes to prove that blood will tell, even in a Chinaman . . . Yes, indeed, I've found that out. And you're a mystic, too. You see things. Perhaps"—and she tilted her fan coyly on the end of her last chin—"some day you'll see something for me."

The Prince strode toward her. His long slender fingers were outstretched toward her and those dark hooded eyes were bent upon her in a piercing look. Mrs. Chenery's heart began to beat audibly. For once she was speechless.

"I see something now," he said in a deep and solemn voice. "I see your home. I see your husband. He has someone with him. She is young, and very lovely. He is saying, 'I hope she doesn't come in for an hour or so yet. I want to surprise her, my darling. We are going to Alaska.' "

Mrs. Chenery squawked in the manner of a stuck pig. She rose, red and belligerent.

"Come, Dan, we're going home," she shouted, grabbing that surprised young man by the arm. The light of battle was in her eyes as she swept unceremoniously from the room.

Pat and Nicholson looked their utter bewilderment.

"What in the world kind of nonsense did you tell the poor dear?" Pat demanded.

"It wasn't nonsense," the Prince said, smiling at the closed door. "The General had just called up to say their daughter arrived unexpectedly from the States, and that he had received his orders transferring him to Alaska. He wanted Mrs. Chenery to come home. Besides, it was high time she went. Our young friend here needs rest."

Pat rose instantly.

"May I come back to-morrow morning?" she asked the Prince with a touch of wistfulness.

"Of course you may," he said.

She bent over and kissed the man on the bed quite unashamedly.

"Until to-morrow," she whispered, and passed out through the door the Prince held open for her.

In a moment or two the Prince was back again.

"I'm going to leave you alone now," he said. "Try and get some sleep. But if you need anything, just ring this." And he indicated a bronze gong that stood on a table beside the bed.

"Just a minute, please." Nicholson put out a restraining hand.

"Yes?" the Prince asked.

"Sit down a moment, your Highness," Nicholson said. "There's something"—he seemed awkwardly, obviously groping for words—"that is . . . there's something I've got to tell you about . . . something that's been rather . . . well . . . rather troubling me. You know I want to marry that girl . . . and . . . well, the point is, I'm perfectly normal, am I not?"

"Normal," the Prince said in surprise. "But of course."

"I mean mentally," Nicholson asked uneasily.

"My dear boy," the Prince said in distress, "what on earth have you on your mind?"

"Well, it's . . . it's about those visits to Chu-Sheng," the man in the bed said slowly. "Especially that last one. I must have been out of my head. I saw the damndest things. I saw a fight between white light and *black* light . . . *black* light, mind you . . . I saw Chu-Sheng produce it out of the air . . . just cause it to appear from nothing . . . and I heard *you* talking through the lips of that girl slave of his. God, it was a hellish nightmare!"

There was a slight pause. Then he asked, and there was a touch of uneasiness in his voice:

"It was a nightmare, wasn't it?"

The Prince looked at him long and slowly, and all of the wisdom of the ages rested in those dark unfathomable eyes.

"Yes, my son," he said at last, quite calmly, "it was a nightmare."

YELLOW MAGIC

Chapter One

TARA TRAVERS cocked an inquiring ear as a fragile web of music
drifted through the thin partition of her dressing room. Then, as
the strongly accented rhythm of the tom-toms resolved themselves
into a woven ribbon of sound, she turned back to her mirror. The
Voodoo number. Half an hour before her own number. She dipped
her finger into a pot of grease paint and deepened the shadows
above her eyes, then surveyed herself critically.

It was not a flattering mirror, but even its flawed surface could
not conceal the beauty of the tall, slim girl who sat before it. An
oval face, almost startlingly white, with curved vivid lips and dark
eyes that, in certain moods and in certain lights, seemed black. The
face was tinged now with the slightest film of cold cream and her
black hair was of that fine, evenly brushed darkness that is faintly
blue when you look through it. The Chinese makeup she was carefully applying gave the flawless features an even more mysterious
and arresting beauty.

She dabbled her face deftly with grease paint, her thoughts hurtling thousands of miles of distance, remembering each individual
scene as it rose out of the unknown to take its appointed place in
the puzzle picture in the mosaic of her past—a past that had been
different from most girls', in fact, different and stranger, possibly,
than that of any other girl of her race. Which may have accounted
for the touch of sadness and the premature wisdom in those dark
eyes and for the touch of wistfulness about the crimson lips. It was
a past she was striving eagerly to forget, as she was living eagerly
every moment of the present in her new-found and still so strange
freedom. A little smile touched her features as she remembered
how ill equipped she had been to face the future upon her release
from bondage . . . a veritable babe lost in the woods. And then that
strange and awful knowledge of things unknown to the Western

world came to her rescue. Overnight, miraculously, through this knowledge, she had become the sensation of Broadway. Yet, strangely enough, she kept a calm and level head.

She was still surveying her make-up when there came the faintest of sounds from the door. The door that she had locked (for she had learned from experience that an unlocked door was an invitation to trouble). Her eyes flashed to it. Suddenly, tragedy came to her like the rush of black waters sweeping her away forever from everything that was hers—all youth and life and the right to be free.

The man who came through the door that she had most certainly locked was a Chinese ... tall ... slim ... young.

She turned from the mirror. Her poise did not desert her; she only drew a swift breath as though she had known from the first who stood beyond the door and this meeting was no more than was expected, even anticipated.

There was no fear in her eyes (even though there was cause for fear) because she knew too well the danger of permitting fear to sap her will. Instead there was a slight smile upon her face, beneath which there was combat and the power to sustain it.

The Chinese—he, too, was smiling—bowed. His slender, almost feminine hands gleamed sharp cut in the light as he greeted her with a gesture that was ancient when Timur the Lame overran a continent.

The smile did not disarm the girl, as, perhaps, was intended. She knew too well that ancient evil, refined to an exquisite degree, looked at her from beneath the bronze lids. She waited for him to speak.

"Greetings, Little Azalea Blossom," he said, and the tongue he used was old when Atlantis sank beneath the waves; words whose roots were buried in the beginning of time.

"Greetings, O T'Sang Kee Meng," she replied in the same tongue.

"I have come for you," he told her quietly.

The girl flung her words back at him. Flame, as of black opals, danced and flashed in her eyes as she gazed at him.

"Then your mission is in vain. I do not return."

"The Master commands."

"You forget that I am not one of the Company of the Living Dead. I am free from the commands of the Tongueless One. Since that night in Panama when my mind slipped from his grasp, he has had no power to command me ... no power to seize my mind . . . to force me to peer into the crystal . . . to compel me to utter the words that his own tongueless throat cannot bring forth . . . No longer must I play the Trilby to his Svengali . . . I am free—and free I shall remain."

The man she called T'Sang listened very quietly, his head a little to one side, seemingly unaffected by the words.

"You will return," he said quietly.

"If fate wills, an ape will sing a love song, a stone will swim in the water, a courtesan will find affection in her heart, a pig-faced woman will be crowned Queen of Beauty. But the Tongueless One is not fate."

"The power of the Master has not waned," he suggested quietly.

"Neither has mine," she flung at him. "All the power that he so foolishly gave me and taught me is mine and will remain mine. That and many other things that he does not dream of. Think ye that I am afraid of the Tongueless One's accursed magic? I, who am younger and stronger than he? I, who have seen mysteries that you can never hope to see . . . mysteries the sight of which would blind you . . . I, who am a *Trapas* better than any of those who make magic for the ignorant in Chorten Nyma and Lhassa . . . I, who spent a night in the company of the Tongueless One at the feet of the Ten Kings of Hell in the cave temple of Lung Men . . . think ye that I am afraid of him . . . of you . . . or of any living thing?"

"You *are* afraid of the Master," he returned serenely.

"That is a lie. You know it."

"A lie is a fleeting word which flies away on the wings of the wind, to be forgotten the next moment, Little *Azalea* Blossom," he said quietly. "Thus it is with a true word. That, also, flies away and is forgotten. Truth and lies are but words. And who can tell where one ends and the other begins? But servants of the Tongueless One do not lie to one another. That also you know."

"I am no servant of the Tongueless One," she said calmly. "And now, you must go, O T'Sang Kee. It is nearly time for my performance."

He smiled gently. His features were pleasing, smooth and regular; his cheek-bones high, his skin fine and of a pale bronze tint . . . eyes of Lucifer and face of Buddha. Once, those black, beautifully shaped eyes wandered to the automatic which she had clutched in her hand, and a slightly ironical expression veiled his face for a moment. It was like a swift glimpse behind the serene, Buddha-like exterior.

"Bullets," he murmured gently. "Do you think then, that I fear death?"

"Ai!" She spat the agreement at him. "You fear death. So do I. And because I fear it, I have no desire to have the Tongueless One bathe me in the rays of the Lamp . . . make me a member of the Company of the Living Dead who walk through life with Death as a boon companion . . . Nay . . . life is mine, and I mean to keep firm grasp upon it. I will fight to keep it. I am coward enough to hold my tongue for the sake of living. So . . . I bargain with the Tongueless One. If he will but let me be, I keep my peace. If not— I fight. Oh, I have no wish to defy the Tongueless One. I know the power of that which he has stolen from the Keepers of the Secrets of the Ancient Ones. But if I must . . . I will."

The sensitive lips quivered in a quick smile, and his right forefinger sketched a swift gesture in the air. The girl shrank back momentarily, shuddering, face blanched, knowing full well the significance of that gesture.

Then she leaned forward. The bronze face was as expressionless as that of the Buddha it resembled. Nor was Tara's face any less impassive. It was as if the two had drawn armor about them.

"Think you, because I have confessed to a fear of death, to frighten me with the Gesture of Death?"

She laughed, and there was in the laugh a hardness that did not match the sweetness of her face, the youth of her form.

"You make the Gesture of Death. But can you slay with it? Nay. I know that you cannot. *But I can.* And I know other things. Things that I shall use if I am compelled to."

She came a step toward him. "Do you remember that night at the portals of the Temple of Lung Men, buried a hundred feet beneath the yellow sand of the Gobi . . . that night when the flaring torches in the hands of the Living Dead painted the long stone steps with crimson? Ai . . . I see that you do remember . . . Remember your own terror when the acacia blossoms scattered on the steps suddenly came alive and began crawling toward you in a wave of deadly things—scorpions—the tiny red spider whose bite is death . . . the little yellow rock snake from whose fangs no man recovers . . . It was I who did that! I, Hing Mee-Yin, the flute girl, who mocked you and laughed and flung still more acacia blossoms—or were they acacia blossoms or something more harmful—after you as you fled down the stairs. I knew more than you did, then. And I have learned much since then . . . things that the Tongueless One himself does not know that I have learned . . . Now go, and take to the Tongueless One my message . . . I shall fight if it is a fight he wishes—but it is peace I seek. And tell him this: It will be useless for him to seek to seize my mind again, because I have freed my mind from his power, and I know how to keep it free. And, much as I desire to live, I will seek death myself before I return to him."

She leaned forward menacingly, forefinger raised threateningly in the air.

"Now go . . . before *I* make on the air the Gesture of Death."

She held her position until the door closed behind the Chinese. Then tears rose perilously in her eyes. For a moment she fought them down; they stung in the corners of her eyes; then the film of them blinded her, and she slumped into the chair before the dressing table, her frame trembling as with a chill. The orchestra outside was playing the overture for her act, the act that was the sensation of Broadway.

Chapter Two

DALE REYNOLDS arrived in town on a late train, all unmindful of the finger of fate that had twisted the threads of his life the moment he had stepped aboard that train. It was raining, so he drove to his apartment. There he exchanged his tweeds for evening clothes and a raincoat and went out into the downpour again, not, however, disdaining the proffered services of a taxi to his destination, which was the Flyers Club.

In the cloakroom there were men he knew, being divested of wet hats and coats; in reading room, card room, lounge, billiard room, squash court and gymnasium, men greeted him with that friendly punctiliousness which indicates popularity; from the splashed edge of the great swimming pool men hailed him; clerks and club servants saluted him smilingly as he sauntered about through the place, driven into motion by an inexplicable and unaccustomed restlessness. Bobby Gregory discovered him coming out of the billiard room.

"Have a snifter," he suggested affably. "I'll round up a couple of the boys for a couple of rubbers of contract, if you like."

Dale shook his head smilingly. He was tall and solid enough, but the evening clothes made him seem even more so. His hair stood short and crisp off a wide forehead; and beneath that were features long and straight of line.

"I've an engagement early in the morning, and I believe I'd better go to bed early."

"But good lord, you've only just come to town. Bed's a place you can always go to when there's nothing else to do. Besides, you must see Tara Travers."

"Who is Tara Travers?" Dale demanded.

Bobby's mouth dropped open and his eyes grew wide.

"You don't mean to tell me," he asked in amazement, "that you've never heard of Tara Travers?"

Dale laughed at the other's incredulous expression. "You sound like it was a criminal offense," he said. "After all, I have been away, you know."

"Yes, but man, Tara Travers is the talk of New York."

"Say, what is this? A new breakfast food?"

Bobby's sensibilities were even more outraged.

"She's the flute girl, the Bride of the Flame, and she's at the Silver Slipper, you ignoramus," he blurted out, all in one breath.

"Oh, a night club girl," Dale said distastefully.

"She's not. That is, not really," Bobby insisted loyally. "She's just opened there, and boy, she's a wow! You wait. She'll be in the movies soon."

"And if you're not her press agent, you ought to be," Dale laughed. "You've got it bad. Sorry I can't see the girl wonder to-night, but I've an important business conference on in the morn-ing, and you know the old slogan, business before pleasure."

"You and business. Lord! The amazing alliance. What are you going to do? Instruct your lawyer to sell a few bonds, you bloated plutocrat?"

"No, this really is a serious matter."

"Oh, yeah?" Bobby retorted. "In what show and what row does she cavort, dear friend . . . speaking in an exquisitely colloquial metaphor."

Dale shrugged. "I'll play you a couple of rubbers of contract before I turn in. Come on, you suspicious sport."

"What show?" demanded Bobby obstinately. He did not mean it literally, but Dale's easy popularity with women originated con-tinuous gossip, friendly and otherwise; and his name was often connected with this or that attractive woman in his own circle. But the surmise was idle, and the gossip vague, and neither the one nor the other disturbed Dale, who continued to saunter through life keeping his personal affairs pleasantly to himself.

So now he merely contented himself with saying, "Better change your brand, Bobby. Might be better to switch to good old bootleg stuff, if this is what repeal liquor does to you."

Then he linked his arm in Bobby's and guided him toward the card room. The two had been friends for years, and Bobby could say a great many things to Dale that the latter would have resented from others. However, they found no card tables vacant, the hour before dinner being a popular one with contract players, so Bobby again suggested his snifter. And Dale accepted.

The snifter, as Bobby ordered it, turned out to be long and tall and cool, of a pale greenish color with little slices of orange float-ing in it and a lingering, tantalizing tang. They were a specialty of the barman, who had received his training behind the bar of the

Myrtle Bank Hotel in Jamaica, where the mixing of a drink is a serious matter.

"Dinner?" Bobby suggested, after a somewhat surprised look into his glass to find it empty.

"Not with you," Dale told him firmly.

"Why not?" demanded Bobby reasonably. "I'm house broken."

"Experience," Dale reminded him, "is a great teacher. I remember the last time I allowed myself to be persuaded to have dinner with you."

"It was a good dinner," Bobby argued.

"It isn't the dinner I remember so vividly. It's the bill for breakage in the night club, your unwillingness to believe that you aren't man enough to uproot a lamp-post, and your firm belief that one-way street signs didn't apply to you."

"It was a grand night," Bobby sighed.

Dale snorted, and finished his drink.

"Anyhow," Bobby pleaded, "let bygones be bygones and have dinner with me to-night."

"Sorry," Dale said decidedly. "I need a clear head in the morning."

"I'll promise not to break a single glass, and to read and believe every street sign we see.

"And no night clubs," warned Dale.

"Nary a night club," agreed Bobby with upraised hand, "except the Silver Slipper."

So, an hour or two later they found themselves at a table in the Silver Slipper, the city's newest, noisiest and most expensive night club. And little did Dale dream of what awaited him because of his failure to stick to his original resolve.

"Here," Bobby declared, "is where you will find the cream of the town's night life."

"Uh huh," Dale agreed. "Sour cream."

Already he was regretting having come there with Bobby. The noise annoyed him. The hot, smoke-laden air of the place clogged his lungs and he looked with a jaded and jaundiced eye upon the fully revealed charms of the young things who made up the chorus. He fully determined that one drink, or at the most two, would mark his limit, and then he would yank Bobby out of the place.

The sound of a brazen gong, struck three times, broke in upon his reverie. The lights slowly went out and the curtains on the little stage at the far end of the room split open.

A shimmering radiance grew upon the stage, disclosing a huge gold and green dragon of porcelain on its faience pedestal. And there, high cradled between the forepaws of the huge Mongolian monster, sat a slim figure in silken robes of turquoise, rose and scarlet, a Chinese lute across her knees, slim feet pendant beneath the rainbow skirt.

Her headdress was wrought fantastically of openwork gold, inlaid with a thousand metallic blue feathers, accented by fiery gems; across the silky golds of her slitted tunic were embroidered in iris tints the single-winged birds whirling about each other in floating clouds; little clog-like shoes of silk and gold, embroidered with moss-green arabesques inset with orange and scarlet, shod the feet.

Ancient Cathay, exquisitely, immortally young, sat in jeweled silks and flowers under the huge and snarling dragon. She gave the illusion of being a slender figurine of age-old ivory . . . something created by a master sculptor of a vanished age into which life had been instilled. Presently, string by string, her idle lute awoke, picked with the plectrum, giving forth note after note in strange and unfamiliar intervals. Looking straight in front of her she began to sing.

Almost, as if in accompaniment to the sad slow notes of her song, the lights on the stage faded into a blue. But the blue was not permanent; almost imperceptible pulsations were stirring and modifying it toward a warmer and less decisive hue, and through it throbbed and ebbed elusive sensations of palest turquoise, primrose and shell pink. This waned and deepened into a yellow which threatened to become orange.

Suddenly, at a shattering note from her lute, all was washed out in unaccented gray; the gray gradually became instinct with rose and gold; the blue was split by a violet stream; then virile scarlet tumbled through clashing scales of green, amethyst, crimson, into a chaos of chromatic dissonance and vanished, engulfed in shimmering darkness.

A tiny spot of color, like a flickering candle flame, grew in the center of the stage, grew and grew until a fire burned there; leaping flames roared up almost to the ceiling, smoke poured up and spread in a thick layer about the ceiling of the stage.

The girl dropped her lute beside the dragon and stood up; walked slowly toward the roaring fire, stepped within it; stood in its center. The flames writhed about her; the silken robes of turquoise, rose and scarlet blackened, burst into flames; the white flesh of her body was visible for a moment as the flaming silk dropped away, then her body was hidden as the flames swirled higher; embraced it with their hungry tongues . . .

A gasp of horror went up from the audience . . . and suddenly the flames were not . . . like a candle flame snuffed out in a puff of wind the stage was empty save for the smiling figure of the girl standing where the flames had been, the silken robes untouched by the hungry tongues of fire that a moment before had been swirling about her.

The curtains swung to, cutting her off from the audience. A moment's silence—that greatest of tributes to the artist—and then a storm of applause swept the crowded floor. People were startled, dumfounded, jaded senses were thrilled unexpectedly. A babble of voices filled the room. Tara Travers was the sensation of Broadway.

Back in her dressing room Tara found Dan Hurst, manager of the Silver Slipper, lounging in a chair. Fresh from her success, with the applause of the audience ringing in her ears, she faced him with a smile that gradually faded. She looked at him steadily and the man avoided meeting her eyes. A bitter look came into her face.

"You have come to tell me," she said quietly, "that you do not wish my performance any longer." It was not a question. Merely a fact stated by one who knew it to be a fact.

Hurst looked startled. "I'm sorry," he began.

"There is no need to be," she said evenly. "I am not surprised."

"Well, I am," he burst out. "And I want you should know it ain't me. If it was up to me I'd double your salary. Honest, I don't know what's come over the boss. I think he's going plain nuts. He was out there to-night. He heard the hand you got. He knows you've more'n doubled business in the time you've been here. And just as soon as your act's over he comes and tells me to let you go. You coulda knocked me over with a feather. He looked kinda scared, like he was afraid you'd put poison in his soup. I tried to argue with him, but it wasn't no use. And you, with the biggest illusion act in the business. . . ."

"It's not an illusion act, Dan," Tara interrupted.

"Well, whatever you call it. Anyhow, it's a knockout. A honey," Dan continued, chewing on his cold cigar, "and the boss cans you. I don't get it."

"I get it, Dan," she said evenly. "I get it perfectly."

Dan Hurst studied her, his head cocked to one side.

"Say, has that mug been trying to make you, baby?" he demanded.

Tara smiled. "No, Dan. Mr. Bradford has been quite proper in his behavior toward me. And now, if you don't mind, I really must dress."

For a long time after Dan Hurst had taken his awkward leave Tara sat there and stared straight into her mirror.

She was a brave girl. She was conscious of the fact in her own honest way. But she knew that her dismissal was an act of war . . . that through the owner of the Silver Slipper Chu-Sheng, the Tongueless One, had struck the first blow in a series designed to bring her mind back to the slavery in which he had held it. Standing at the edge of her consciousness was the thought of the Tongueless One, like an evil abyss licked by a flame of fire.

Chapter Three

MEANWHILE: The second floor of No. 62 Mott Street, in China-town, was a cistern of gloom where tiny yellow lights, flickering squat candles, blossomed in the darkness. Forming a semi-circle about the far end of the room, they revealed a man seated crosslegged on a throne (just as Sayki-Muni, the Buddha, sat in a similar posture in a buried century), revealed his bronze-yellow features, his orange-yellow robes and the semicircle of men who knelt before him, a man to each candle, and murmured *mantras;* men so much alike in motive and self-discipline, that a kind of unity had settled upon them, making men of varying height and weight one pattern, molded by unanimous desire. The man on the throne was motionless. In majesty, in intellect and in impressive-ness he was as far above those others who sat in a semicircle as an eagle is above the ground over which he soars. Only his lips moved, and his eyes. A hint of sadness was in his face. He re-peated a *mantra* automatically, and his fingers told the carved car-nelian prayer beads mechanically, for his thoughts were elsewhere.

Behind him, on a tall pedestal, stood something curiously like the looped cross, the *Crux Ansata* which Osiris, God of Resurrec-tion, carried in his hand and touched, in the Hall of the Dead, those souls which had passed all tests and had earned immortality. It was the height of a tall man, polished and glimmering as though it had been cut from some enormous crystal.

The draperies of the room were orange. Orange-colored scrolls and black-and-gold paper prayers, inscribed with ideographs, were fastened to the beams of the room with filigreed dragons. Anyone seeing that orange and yellow would have known at once that here was one of high rank in the Yellow Hat hierarchy, whose influence is flung from one end of sprawling Asia to the other.

Except for that *Crux Ansata* . . . That secret, ancient and holy symbol of Life whose origin was already old when Wise Men brought it with them out of the East . . . those same Wise Men who built into the Great Pyramid of Egypt the sum total of knowledge that the world has ever known. It contrasted oddly with the orange robes, the prayer wheel, the paper prayers.

The patter of bare feet on the flooring caused the man on the throne to shift his gaze to the gloom at the far end of the room. A figure with shaven head emerged from the coiling shadows. The dim glow from the candles disclosed the keen arrogant face, the ruddy complexion, the aquiline beak of a nose of a Man-cho-jen. He wore a hastily donned yellow robe beneath which could be seen the trousers of Western dress. The lamaist emblems woven into the fabric of his robe proclaimed him to be a Ringding Gelong Lama, and while a Ringding Gelong Lama does not rank as high in the Lamaistic scale as a cardinal does in the Roman Catholic Church, there are but few to whom he bends the knee. And the obeisance he gave the man on the throne was that of a man who knows secrets to a man who knows yet greater ones . . . and keeps them. There is no more marrow-deep obeisance in the world than that.

Uttering the habitual Manchu phrase of felicitation: "Kungski-kungshi," the Lama straightened up and waited for the man on the throne to speak.

A single brief word gave the required permission. When he spoke, the tongue he used was the guttural Mongol of the Gobi, of Inner Mongolia . . . the tongue of the red-faced clansmen who once buried China under a bloody avalanche —the native tongue of the man who sat upon the throne—His Highness Prince Lai Chung, hereditary overlord of the princes of Inner Mongolia.

"I followed T'Sang Kee Meng, as you instructed, O Great One," the man said. "He went to a dancing place which is called the Silver Slipper, and there he talked to one of the dancing girls named Tara Travers. I do not know of what they talked, but whatever it was, it was not to his satisfaction, for there was black anger upon his face when he emerged."

"You have your instructions," the man upon the throne said. "Keep this girl always within your sight, but always remain beyond the sight of any one who may be engaged upon the same errand. And remember the words of the Precious One, 'A flaw in a jewel may be ground away by skillful hands, but not even the Buddha can remedy the deed done wrong.' "

He raised his hand in blessing, and the man bowed and took his leave. Again the patter of naked feet until the falling curtains blotted out the sound.

The man on the throne resumed his prayer.

In the corner an aged man, orange-clad, slowly turned a prayer wheel, as his lips monotonously formed the words:

"Om Mani Padme Hum . . ."

The semicircle of kneeling men took up the words in a chant that rose in ripples of white tone waves, silver-flecked, spreading a network of infinitely delicate tone filaments, drifting on the air with an abandon of throbbing cadences like tiny, drifting ghosts of spring tinkling their girdle gems of fretted jade . . .

The man on the throne raised his hand in a commanding gesture. The chant died away.

"Brothers," he said. "All of you have witnessed the mysteries of Tugugum, have laid eyes on Yian the Holy, have set naked foot upon the Mother of Mountains where death lies in wait for him who knows not the secret way; and have meditated in the Azure Cavern of the Ancient Ones. To each of you has been imparted a fragment of the secret things that have been handed down to us from the Ancient Ones; knowledge that the Ancient Ones meant to be used for the good of the world when the world should be ready to receive it. But Chu-Sheng, the Faithless, has taken of this knowledge in defiance of the Law and, as you know, is using it for evil. It has been loosed upon the world by Man, therefore Man must balance the scales of justice." He paused and stared out into the shadowy room as if seeking there an answer to a problem. He was motionless, brooding, with the attitude of a man who has attained the stark simplicity of elemental knowledge and the kind of power that goes with it. In poise, calm, majesty of brow and magnetism he resembled more one of those temple images that sit in the gloom and stare through jeweled eyes than any ordinary human being. He looked aloof from human standards. Then he took up the thread of his thought again.

"The Wheel of the Law turns, and unless we, who are Keepers of the Secrets of the Ancient Ones, are alert, an opportunity is snatched or taken from us, for us, or against us. But Evil may not be bound with the tender stem of the young lotus. Darkness must be opposed with light. And Chu-Sheng, the Accursed One, must be fought by the Keepers of the Secrets of the Ancient Ones with the knowledge, a part of which he has stolen." For a moment he sat there silent, a figure curiously detached and aloof from human affairs. He spoke again after a long pause, as dispassionately as a big clock ticking in the dark, asserting measured, elemental facts.

"There is a balance in the universe and an intelligence that governs it. No man can escape the consequences of his own acts, though it takes him a million years to redress the balance. There is a fitness in all things, and a time for all things. If you light a torch at midday, what does it accomplish? To discern the right time and to act precisely then, is as important as the knowledge how to act."

He was silent again for many minutes. Not until the silence had grown like a tangible thing there in the dimly lighted room did he go on speaking. Then he said unhurriedly:

"This is an appointed time—a time when the Wheel of the Law turns, using Man to balance the Good against the Evil. I call upon you Brothers to use the secrets that are yours to crush Chu-Sheng, the Accursed One."

The answer rolled from the lips of the semicircle of kneeling men in magic, long-drawn syllables that were sacred before the civilization that was Atlantis rose to its height and sank beneath the ocean, and new gods rose and were forgotten in undiscovered continents . . . the syllables that signify the ultimate, the immeasurable, the absolute, the beginning and the end: . . . O-o-o-o-o-m-m-m-m-m-m.

Chapter Four

DALE LEFT BOBBY at the door of the Silver Slipper, electing to walk to his apartment, rather than share Bobby's taxi to further ports of pleasure, so dear to the latter's heart. He walked leisurely across town toward the East River. Ahead of him a woman walked briskly. She was only a silhouette against the street lights and lost in the shadows between. Dale would never have noticed her, had she not been carrying a small dressing case which she shifted frequently from hand to hand.

The one thing in life that rarely happens is the unexpected. If the actual thing does occur, then the manner of it sets up so many unforeseen contingencies that only the subtlest mind, and the sanest, and the least hidebound by opinion, can hope to read the signs fast enough to understand them as they happen.

Dale had crossed Lexington Avenue when suddenly forms detached themselves from the coiling shadows of an alley and hurled themselves upon the form of the woman. There was a cry, choked off suddenly . . . the high-pitched cry of a woman in terror.

There is an element of sheer pugnaciousness, unchristian stubbornness in most men that is said to damn while it saves the best of them at times. Dale's common sense told him to look for a policeman. That stubbornness inherent within him urged him to act. He acted.

He had no clear purpose in mind as he dashed down the street toward the spot where the girl struggled with her assailants. The thought that they might be armed . . . probably were . . . never occurred to him. And if it had, the thought would have made no difference.

So preoccupied were the men that they did not hear the sound of his running feet or glimpse his oncoming form in the semidarkness of the street. It all happened in a flash. The next thing Dale knew he felt the bite of his knuckles in the neck of one of the men as, his hand firmly clutching his collar, he tore him backwards. Flung to one side, the man's head struck the edge of a flight of stone steps and he went down. Lay still.

By now the other man was aware of his presence. There was murder in his quick black eyes as he turned. His hands clawed for his hip pocket, but Dale was at him at once, driving for his face. The man dodged the blow, but a second one landed on the point of the chin. He stopped dead, his eyes goggling, his head sagging on his shoulders. Then he crumpled up in a heap at Dale's feet.

He turned to the girl. She was huddled on the sidewalk, where she had fallen when the man released his grip, her breath coming and going in quick gasps. He bent over her.

"You shouldn't have done that," she said, struggling to her feet with the aid of his arm.

"You're hurt?" he asked concernedly.

"My ankle," she admitted, white about the lips. "It's nothing. It will pass."

But she kept a tight grip upon Dale's arm as he raised her, and a little spasm of pain swept her face as she tried her foot tentatively upon the pavement. Her color came back. She flexed her ankle this way and that. "No bones broken," she announced. "Not even a sprain, just wrenched I think. Thank you. You've been very kind."

He steadied her and said: "There never is a policeman around when he's needed. But there ought to be one somewhere in the neighborhood."

"Don't call one," she said quietly. "I'd prefer just to let the matter drop."

He regarded her in surprise.

"But those men attacked you," he protested. "You might have been badly hurt . . . robbed . . . kidnapped . . . heaven knows what, if I hadn't . . ."

"Yes, I know," the girl said nervously. "And I appreciate what you've done. You were very kind. But if you'll just let me go on home now . . ."

Dale looked puzzled, but refrained from urging her further.

"As you wish," he said courteously. "Do you live far?"

"Several blocks," she said.

"You can't walk with that ankle," he said decisively. "I'll get you a taxi."

She cast an uneasy look at the men upon the pavement.

"I'll manage to get to the corner," she said. "I can get a taxi there."

"Very well," he said, picking up her dressing case and keeping a firm grip on her arm as she hobbled down the sidewalk to the corner, where he signaled a cruising taxi.

"I'll see you home," he said, and, despite her protests, climbed in also.

In the dimly lighted interior of the taxi she regarded him quietly for a moment. Superficialities of strength did not impress her. She passed over the fact that the youth beside her was tall and keenly muscled, that his hair crinkled above his forehead and that the nose seemed sensitive and finely cut. Only the quiet brown eyes held her gaze. She had long ago learned to gauge the honesty of men by their eyes.

Then he broke into her thoughts. "Wouldn't you prefer to see a doctor before going home? That ankle should be bandaged."

She shook her head. "I'll bandage it when I get home. I know something of first aid."

Pulling off her hat she leaned back against the cushions, one slim silken foot with its injured ankle stretched out before her. The passing lights picked up her face in almost breathless perfection and let it sink reluctantly back into shadow.

"You know," he observed after a moment. "You really should have allowed me to call a policeman. Those men should be punished."

"They will be," she returned enigmatically. Her words seemed to hold a definite significance, and the thought of them kept hurrying through his mind like a wan ghost scurrying through the dark for the rest of the drive.

The taxi stopped in front of an old house. Dale made a gesture toward his pocketbook, but at the girl's: "Please, I'd rather you wouldn't," he withdrew it.

He shot a glance at the house as he helped her out. Obviously there was no elevator, and stairs are not easy to negotiate with an injured ankle.

Then Dale did the reckless thing; did it impulsively, with a careless gesture in the direction of fate.

"Which floor?" he asked, and at the girl's look of inquiry, added: "I hope that you're not going to be foolish enough to attempt to climb those stairs with that ankle of yours. It won't help it any. And since I'm here, I might as well be made use of."

Had he but known it, by those few words he altered the whole course of his own and her existence, for few people have the abil-

ity to recognize the linked consequences that hang on every decision which life puts up to them to make.

"Oh, you mustn't," she protested earnestly, and he wondered if
the look that came into her eyes could have been fear. "I'll . . . I'll
get up somehow. Don't think I'm not grateful, but you really must
go now."

"You act as though you were afraid of me," he said, a little
puzzled. "I'm quite harmless, I assure you. Truly I am."

"I'm not afraid of you," she said gravely, "but *for* you."

"Ah," he said lightly. "An irate father or a jealous husband,
eh?"

She dimpled suddenly. "Neither. I live quite alone, thank you.
But you really are in danger if you remain here any longer."

"You mean because of those men?" he queried.

"Yes," she said guardedly, not meeting his eyes. "That is the
reason."

But in some intangible way he knew that she lied, and that the
danger lay not in these men, but in something else.

"But what about you?" he probed.

"Oh, I can manage," she said with a little nervous laugh.

He smiled at her, admiration for her pluck shining in his eyes.

"You're very brave," he said, taking her arm and a step upward
at the same time. "But also very foolish."

She shot a sidewise glance at him. He was a most distressingly
determined young man, she decided. So she said nothing further
and together they negotiated the stairs to the third floor. Fumbling
in her purse the girl produced a key and unlocked the door.

"I want you to know how truly grateful I am," she said, extend-
ing her hand in farewell.

"Are you sure you don't want a doctor?" Dale asked, releasing
her hand.

The girl opened the door, then turned to face him.

"I can manage quite well without one," she responded. "Really,
it isn't as bad as I thought it was at first."

"I'd sleep a lot sounder if I could believe you," he said.

For the first time he heard the girl laugh. Soft. A husky, throaty
laugh . . . delicious.

"I see you're one of those dreadful people who need proof of
everything," she said. "It's quite all right. You need not worry."

She touched the switch by the door and the room flowered with
light. For the first time he had a clear look at her.

"Why," he exclaimed involuntarily. "You're Tara Travers. I saw your act at the Silver Slipper to-night."

"Oh, you were there?" For a moment a look of suspicion crept into her eyes. Then she saw the clean-cut lines of his face recklessly etched in the burst of light from the room. He was so obviously what his bearing and manner proclaimed him to be . . .a gentleman.

"I . . . this is rather informal," he said awkwardly. "But I'm Dale Reynolds, free, white and over twenty-one, and awfully glad to know you."

Tara smiled. "Well, I should say that, coupled with what you did to-night, is sufficient introduction for anyone. If you don't mind waiting while I bandage this ankle I might attempt to repay you with a cup of tea."

He surveyed the room in which he found himself as he waited for her to return. The floor was covered with an ordinary carpet, never good, and now worn at the thresholds and under the table; the wallpaper was old and faded, peeling in corners; the woodwork was dull white mottled with broken blisters. Yet, flung across the back of one of the chairs was a silken veil, heavy with a pattern of hammered gold and silver. The faintest odor of oil of geranium came from a slim-necked crystal bottle, inlaid with gold, upon the mantel and, veiling the door into which the girl had vanished was a screen over which a shawl was flung, a thing of silver and black . . . heavy black silk which (had he but known) was ancient tribute silk on which japónica fluttered their silver petals. The room was like a human wreck filled with memories.

He could not have said why, but a weight had begun to fall upon his spirits, which for lack of a better word he called a premonition. There was not the slightest trace of superstition in his eminently practical make-up, but he felt there was something in this situation that he could not understand, something disquieting, something strange. Perhaps it was just as well that the feeling went no further than a premonition, that he could not see with greater clarity what awaited him—what awaited the two of them—at the turn of the next few hours.

Chapter Five

DALE TURNED AT THE SOUND of the opening door. The girl's ankle was bandaged and she was wearing slippers of orange leather as she limped across the room.

"Don't bother," she said as he started toward her. "I can manage all right. Besides, I'm not going to sit down. I'm going to make you a cup of tea."

"Please don't," he said. "I really don't want it. I'm only going to stay long enough to satisfy myself that you're all right."

She walked across the room with her straight admirable shoulders touched by the merest swagger, which was like a grace not in smooth rhythm; the smoky darkness of her eyes laid a lovely line across her brow.

"I'm quite all right," she said as she sank into a chair. "By tomorrow my ankle will be as good as new."

She was an individual, this girl, he told himself. The cut of her clothes, the very tilt of her head, combined to make a foil for an individual who created her own setting. Add a straightness that made him frown . . . a straightness in her bearing, in her glance and in the manner she moved and you had a sum total that was not inconsiderable.

She was no young child of the woods, he knew. The glance that whipped across his was very sharp. It changed the quality of her face for a moment.

"I hope you're right," he said. "It would be a pity if you were forced to cancel your performance to-morrow night."

"That? Oh, that is finished. To-night was my last night."

He misinterpreted the remark.

"You don't belong in a night club," he said. "You belong in one of the big revues."

"The management of the night club evidently agrees with you on a part of that," she said. "You see, they fired me."

"Fired you?" His astonishment was evident. "But . . . but that was the most marvelous thing I've ever seen. It was like something magical."

She lifted somber eyes, hesitated, and then said as though she did not care whether he believed it or not: "It *was* magic . . . what you would call magic."

An odd shiver passed over him. For a second he took her literally, suddenly convinced that the things he had seen were magic, and not tricks of the professional. He tried to push from him a sense of impending disaster which was steadily creeping over him; tried to laugh himself out of the feeling. Powerless to do anything about it, he sat for a moment and watched her, his thoughts racing in circles. Vague, formless misgivings were being evoked in him. There was nothing tangible, but the whole atmosphere which surrounded him here in this room awoke a creeping terror which he could not shake off.

"I'm sorry," he told her. "It was thoughtless of me to attempt to pry into professional secrets."

"I meant exactly what I said," she returned I evenly. "The things you saw there to-night were not tricks. They were things that I learned in China—childish things, to be sure—but nevertheless things from the lore of a man whom you would call a magician."

There was a moment of silence during which he regarded her with the baffled interest of one who is aware that something dramatic is happening, but does not as yet comprehend what it is. Then he inquired smilingly:

"You don't expect me to believe that even in unexplored China there exists such a thing as a real magician, do you?"

She shook her head.

"No. Of course not. You are much too logical, too literal. But it's true, just the same. There are those in this world whom you would call magicians who perform miracles of good or evil, according to their lights. Those who can project their astral bodies to far places, or send their thoughts around the world to other minds attuned to them, who can live without food, and be dead without dying, or do any number of mystic things as easily as you can change your clothes."

He cocked an inquiring eye at her and kept back the smile that crinkled the corners of his attractive mouth. She was much too pretty and vital, this girl, to have her head filled with such wild and impossible things. She had evidently been too much alone, read too much and dreamed too much until she probably believed that things such as that could actually happen.

"I used to believe in fairy tales, too," he grinned.

Color flooded her face. She bit her lips, wishing desperately that she had not said so much. There was insolence in his smile, mockery at her beliefs. He was rude, this young man. Rude and stupid. She was surprised that she had not noticed it before. And for some strange reason the discovery made her heart ache. She wished he would go. Wished that he had never come with her. She regarded him calmly, her eyes frigid as northern lights.

"You don't believe me, do you?"

She looked at him squarely—indeed, held him with a slight widening of the irises that seemed to him at first astonishing and then altogether childish and delicious. There had been an intense directness in her words which startled him. Her slim figure seemed possessed of a certain throbbing suspense as she waited for his answer. She had turned a little, so that the almost flower-like whiteness of her face was clear to him. With her smooth, shining hair, the pallor of her face under its lustrous darkness and the clearness of her eyes, she held him for a moment, while his brain struggled to seize upon and understand the something about her which he had noticed before and which made him interested in spite of himself.

"Oh," he stammered, covered with confusion. "I didn't mean it quite that way. I . . . well . . . it is a bit hard to expect a practical-minded man to accept anything like that on faith . . . out of a blue sky, as it were. After all, seeing is believing, you know."

Her head was cocked to one side, and she studied him for a moment, thoughtfully. Then mischief twinkled in her eyes. She said quite soberly:

"So! Seeing is believing. Then do be careful, or you'll burn yourself."

He turned, and leaped backward instinctively.

The wall of the room, at which she was pointing, was ablaze. Flames were creeping up from the baseboard . . . little tongues of red reaching out hungrily for something to devour. He could feel the heat. Even as he looked a licking tongue reached out and the scrim curtain at the window blazed up.

Chapter Six

"SO SEEING IS BELIEVING," Tara repeated mockingly.

And suddenly the fire was not. Just was not. A moment before it had been there. He had felt the heat from it as the flames danced. And now there was nothing . . . just emptiness where the flames had been. And the wall was undamaged . . . the curtain that he *had seen burn* again hung white and fresh at the window.

For a moment Dale had the dizzy delirious feeling of a man confronted suddenly by a thing that could not happen. For an instant the normal perspective of the world around him had shifted and he had a swift glimpse into a world where the happening of the supernatural could cause no disturbance of the natural—or rather supernatural—laws; where rabbits' feet have an acknowledged potency and the evil eye may be averted by the making of the sign of the horns.

He passed a shaking hand across his forehead, and dropped back into his chair. The girl was smiling slightly.

"Of course," she said in delicate mockery. "You do not believe in magic."

He stared at her in utter bewilderment.

"But . . . but I . . . the place *was* on fire. I saw it."

She shook her head. "There was no fire. I merely caused you to believe that you saw the flames."

The muscles of Dale's jaws moved perceptibly at the announcement; otherwise he stood motionless, eyes upon the girl.

He was a rational enough young man; and if his own, inner consciousness had whispered to him just then that a mysterious, invisible force was tugging at his heart strings and that the silent soul of the East was whirling about his own soul and trying to edge into it . . . to merge with it . . . if his inner, secret consciousness had whispered to him any of these things, he would have laughed. But he did feel slightly self-conscious, slightly ludicrous. For he was an Occidental, an average Occidental, swinging halfway between Christianity and biology, and what was all this mazed, Oriental damn foolishness?

"You mean . . . your performance to-night . . . all of those things you did . . . you didn't actually do them . . . I mean . . .?"

"All those things you saw were illusions," she said quietly. "But not illusions in the usual sense of the word. Not tricks of the professional. The things that I caused you and those others in the audience to see were done by mental, not material, means . . . just as I caused you to-night to see a fire that did not exist, by suggesting it to your mind."

He leaned forward, his face terribly earnest.

"Do you realize," he said, "that with a power like that you can do almost anything . . . *anything?*"

"I am fully aware of its power . . . and its danger," she said crisply.

"Tell me," he urged. "How do you know these things . . . how did you learn?"

Ensued a bracket of silence. Then Tara brought her attention back to him. For an instant her eyes had been fixed on his face, her head cocked slightly to one side as though she were listening to something . . . some voice . . . inaudible to the man.

"You wouldn't believe," she said quietly.

"After that," and he glanced at the wall where the fire had been, "I could believe anything."

"Then why shouldn't I tell you?" she said recklessly.

Her tale was amazing. It painted the quiet room with crowded processions of lost ages. It dwelt with the stupendous ghosts of Asia's dead set square against a background of the infinitely deathless. It gave to him the solution of many things about which he had wondered—gave him the key to many an unsolved enigma of ancient history, clear back to the days when Christ was a living figure and America not even a dream in the minds of men, back through the days when Genghis Khan emerged from the Mongolian deserts and challenged the might of the world; to the misty past when Alexandria was the hub of the known world. Then swinging ruthlessly into modern days, as far as China, as far as New York, he saw the seal to it all put on by the hands of a girl who had received her education under the strangest circumstances that ever human being dreamed.

And the tale was complete, swinging through the centuries with neither crack nor fissure; clear to him who wished to read; the tale of an infant left alone in a Chinese city through the sudden death of both parents by cholera—her passage from hand to hand until she reached those of the most mysterious and sinister figure in the whole of the mysterious East—Chu-Sheng, the Tongueless One, Chu-Sheng, the descendant of Chinese magicians; a tale of her education at the hands of a man whose brain was the repository of most of the secrets of the world since human history began to be remembered; a man whose family had been magicians of China in unbroken line back to 1090 B.C. Mute this man was, therefore his name of the Tongueless One, but through this girl he had been able to speak. Under the influence of hypnosis imposed by him, the Tongueless One had transferred his thoughts to her brain; given utterance to them through her lips. She had accompanied Chu-Sheng to America, and when one of his schemes had been blasted, and his power over her temporarily removed, she had fled.

When she had finished she lifted somber eyes to him.

"So that," she said, "was where I learned these things that I know. The things that I did to-night and—the things that are not—respectable."

"Respectable," he protested, "but . . ."

He stopped and peered suddenly at her. She seemed to have gone away—spiritually—somewhere, leaving an unashamed vacuum. She was leaning back in her chair, her face blank, her fingers limply holding the arm of the chair. It was eerie, this utter departure; almost as though a corpse or a changeling had taken the place of the girl. And he was startled, almost frightened, at the expression that had come into her face. Panic, it was . . . nothing short of it. Every drop of blood seemed drained from her face. Even her lips were white.

And then, almost as though the stoppage of his voice had brought her back from wherever she was, she rose to her feet, facing him.

"O God," she murmured in a strange trancelike voice. "Chu-Sheng. He is after my mind again, I can feel his brain groping to seize my brain and get possession of it. I must fight . . . I must fight or I am lost."

Dale rose, too, a worried expression on his face. It was quite obvious that the girl was on the verge of a nervous collapse. The things that she had been through, her fear and dream of this old Chinese, her struggle to fight his influence, imaginary or otherwise, was telling on her nerves, endangering her very sanity.

His heart went out to her in pity, and a firm desire to help. He took her hands in his. They were deathly cold.

"My dear child," he said in as light a tone as he could muster, "you really must pull yourself together. You'll go to pieces. There's nothing to be afraid of. Do you hear? Nothing."

She drew her hands away and held her throbbing temples.

"Oh, isn't there?" she whispered in a choked voice. There was a crooked, twisted smile on her mouth. Her eyes stared wide and unseeing before her. "You say that because you don't know, because it's not you, because it's me he's after . . . me . . ." She turned toward the door with a desperate gesture. "I'm going away."

"Where?" Dale asked.

"I don't know . . . anywhere . . . away from Chu-Sheng."

Then suddenly she went limp; sank into a chair. He thought that she was about to faint. But she spoke, and her voice sounded small and thin and utterly lifeless.

"It's no use," she said. "I can't run away from Chu-Sheng. No one can run away from him, any more than they can run away from the day, or the night. Wherever I go he will follow. I must carry on—here—as best I can . . . somehow . . ."

"I'd like to help you . . . if there's anything I can do," Dale said.

She looked at him searchingly.

"I think you're the kindest man I've ever known," she said gratefully. "If I weren't such a coward I'd tell you to go . . . before you, too, get involved in this. But I need someone . . . so desperately . . . something firm and solid that I can cling to."

She paused and seemed to be listening, that same look of tranced terror on her face.

"Yes . . . I hear you," he heard her say clearly, and he knew that she was not speaking to him, but to someone—to something—to which his own senses were not attuned. It made his flesh crawl. Suddenly she put her hands before her eyes, and a low moan escaped her lips. He came over to her in alarm and shook her slightly.

"What is it now?"

Tara looked up at him.

"It is you," she whispered. "You . . . and it is my fault. I heard his thought so clearly . . . the thought that you must die."

Chapter Seven

THE HOUSE THAT STOOD opposite the Bowery Mission in Chinatown had not even a trace of the patina of antiquity, that bitter and
morose grace which clings about old houses like ghosts of dead
flowers. There was nothing there except the marks of the present—hard, gray, scabbed, already rotting before having lived
overmuch—a house that presented a blank and incurious front to
the world, and yet seemed a house that had secrets and guarded
them well.

And there were secrets hidden behind that rotting façade. There
was not an Oriental in the whole of Chinatown who did not know
that the house was the residence of Chu-Sheng, the Tongueless
One. But not a white man, from the members of the narcotic squad
(who know most of the inner secrets of Mott and Pell Streets) to
Harry Burgess, who lived with a Chinese wife over the Palace of
Seven Gustatory Delights, suspected the secrets that lay behind
that blank, impassive front.

Its appearance was thoroughly in accord with the two hard-
faced men who came down the crooked, winding street and
stopped before the door set flush with the wooden wall.

"The Chink's gonna be sore that we didn't get the dame," ven-
tured one of the men, as the other beat a tattoo on the door.

"Nuts to the Chink," said the other vigorously. "Let him be
sore. I've handled tougher babies than him."

"I dunno," returned the first speaker doubtfully. "He's a funny
one, that bird. Didja ever notice the way he just sits there and
looks right through you and seems to know what you're gonna say
before you say it? It gives me a creepy feeling."

"Nuts again," said the other as the door swung open silently.

A little Chinese servant in a black robe stood in the large square
room into which the door opened. The most remarkable thing
about him was his eyes, cold, opaque sort of eyes that were dead
and lifeless looking, and yet at times seemed to burn with a faint,
greenish glow, like the eyes of a cat in the dark . . . those strange
eyes that were the only outward manifestation of the Living Death

that overtook every one who became a follower of the Tongueless One. The room was bare, with a single naked electric light burning in the ceiling. The man asked no questions. Simply flung open a door on the further side of the room and motioned the men to precede him down the hallway.

At its further end a door opened as if the sound of the footsteps had been a signal. The two men passed through it, without their guide, and found themselves at one end of a long room whose further end was lost in obscurity. The only light was a dim glow which enveloped a form seated in a high carved chair against the back wall, his shadow staining the wall behind him with the soft impalpability of a creeping bat. Another young man sat on a low stool beside him.

There was only the hazy impression of a man's face to be seen in the dim glow that illuminated the figure in the high carved chair; of a projecting predatory chin, a deep chasm of broad-set eyes. But there flowed from him the impression of something gigantic.

For a long moment the deaf mute's silence, his impassivity, made a screen between them . . . an ever-thickening, although invisible, barrier.

Then his right hand flashed up and stabbed out like a dagger . . . a hand like old ivory . . . ivory that had been left out in the sun and rain for a long time . . . high-veined . . . slim . . . the hand of a man who has grown ancient in the practice of a craft delicate and minute . . . its fingers twinkling in the light, moving with an uncanny dexterity, spelling out a message which the man on the stool translated for the two others.

"You have failed," he said quietly, and before the joint impact of that quiet message and the light in the eyes of the man in the chair that were like bottomless pits of chalcedony, the two men quailed.

They could feel the dark, secret thrill that emanated from him like the electric tingle in the air that foretells a thunderstorm. There was power behind this man, immense power, power that gave the impression of tremendous forces dammed up and waiting for release; not the power of muscle, which these two men could understand and fight, but something far more subtle, something uncanny, inexplicable and oddly disturbing. It was all the more disturbing to them because they could feel its presence, but could not understand it.

"There is no need," the man on the stool went on, as the hand rose again and the twinkling fingers spelled out another message, "to report upon your failure. The Tongueless One knows."

"But look here," began the bolder of the two and then stopped abruptly as the hand of the Tongueless One lifted in a threatening gesture . . . as only an Oriental can threaten with a gesture. It was more than a mere waving of hand and arm. It seemed to cut the air like a tragic shadow. And in that instant the two men felt the chill of the tomb strike them.

"You have tried and failed," the interpreter said again, reading the message of the flying fingers. "You were promised, if you delivered the woman here, a reward such as you never dreamed of. You failed. But the Tongueless One is generous. There will still be a reward. A rich one. Look there!"

The eyes of the two men followed the pointing finger. At first they could see nothing. After a moment or two the darkness, heavy, black and imponderable, began to shred away into a vague gray. The wisps of gray took form slowly, growing more solid minute by minute, gathering weight and substance until they wavered into the shape of a room . . . a room whose floor was completely hidden beneath a shimmering stretch of ancient Ming rug that was like moonbeams on running water. Lustrous embroideries hung on the walls in a mysterious blending of blue and green and purple, like the plumage of a gigantic peacock, or the darting of countless dragonflies.

And on the couches against the walls were women . . . women whose necks were hung with jewels. . . women who played with handfuls of jewels, pouring them from one hand to the other like sparkling water.

With the gradual opening up of the scene there had come the sound of a chant, low at first, and slowly growing in strength as the figures began to coalesce from the mist—a chant that cried and whimpered huskily through broken, suspended phrases, over and over, dying away behind a sustaining undercurrent like recurrent drumbeats.

"There," went on the voice of the man on the stool, "lies the reward the Master has provided for you. The jewels are yours."

Slowly, as if impelled by some strange force that was not their own, almost as if the rhythm of the chant was calling to them, the two men moved toward the room that held the women and the jewels. Neared it. Stepped across the threshold . . . and vanished utterly as two men would vanish who walked straight through an opaque curtain.

For a long moment there was silence, broken only by the subtle call of the chant.

Then from the spot where the two men had vanished a scream filled the room with a soulless quaver, rose twice, loud, inhuman, ripping the sensitive membranes of the night and then was still. It was an unbearable sound, the sort that unhinges thought, that makes one cringe from its repetition. It resembled a call of despairing madness that summons death to strike and have done . . . The scream of a man, but so demoniac and anguished that the hearer would shrink from superstitious imaginings. It was a fearful thing, with fear in it, and the agony of death and the limit of pain. It was like some horrible echo, a dreadful cry of despair that beat against the ramparts of the world. It split the darkness as a knife might split a sheet of taut cloth . . . and was snuffed out in a hideous parody of echoes as one snuffs out the flame of a candle.

A faint smile flitted across the yellow mask of the man in the chair.

The glow about his figure slowly faded until it was replaced with blackness, as if a curtain of velvet had dropped.

The chant died away. . . left an aching void of silence.

Chapter Eight

TARA'S WORDS RANG in Dale's ears. "The thought that you must die." He rose slowly to his feet. This thing was getting uncomfortable, to say the least. Perhaps there was more to this stuff about magic than appeared on the surface. Evidently the girl was horribly shaken by what she had just experienced. It was all terribly real to her. And then there had been that physical manifestation of fire which she had conjured out of nowhere and as mysteriously erased. That was, at least, partial proof that there was something behind all this talk of evil influences and death. And now that fiendish old Chinese, who was, as yet, only a legend to Dale, was after him too, the girl would have him believe. It was preposterous . . . laughable . . . he wondered why he didn't laugh.

Being superior to the fears of others is one thing. But when those fears attack our own lives, that is another thing again. All his carefully built and practical theories regarding the absurdity of superstitions, and beliefs in the existence of things or forces beyond the ken of human senses came tumbling about his ears like a house of straw.

"But why me?" he asked quietly, only his unsteady fingers as he crushed out his cigarette betraying the fact that he was not calm inwardly.

"Because you have befriended me," the girl replied soberly.

She turned her head away from him for a moment and a subtle essence of weariness seemed to creep over her entire body, causing it to droop like a wilted flower. Then she unclenched her small, slim hands slowly, staring down as though in the cupped palms an invisible light shone, terrible and beautiful. For a moment the terror and the beauty shone across her still face . . . and was gone. When she spoke it was in the silverest of voices, but with some bright dark fire leaping behind her eyes. She kept her head turned as if there were something in her face that she did not want him to see, and went on, as though a stranger were talking through her scarlet lips.

"I feel his fingers . . . the fingers of the Tongueless One . . . touching me . . . feel his brain moving stealthily to surprise me and

grasp my thoughts . . . I know what he is doing . . . I am fighting . .
. fighting . . . fighting . . ."

Her face was a composed mask but within every curve of her
body he sensed a curious rigidity. Her eyes were frozen pools, in-
expressive, but behind them Dale knew (although how he knew he
could not have told) there was stirring a deep hypnotic fear.
Fear . . . for him. She was quiet, quiet as if life were over, as if she
were listening to something across the gulf.

"Is this what you believe to be magic?" he asked uneasily.
"Something that is threatening you and now me?"

"Yes. It is Chu-Sheng. He is seeking to bring me back under his
influence again . . . to make me again the Voice of the Master . . .
to force me to give utterance to his thoughts through my lips. And
he thinks . . . because he threatens death to you . . . that my defense will be weakened . . . because he knows that I will protect
you . . ."

She moved closer to him.

"Give me your hand," she said tensely. "Hold it tightly. Whatever happens, don't let it go. My mind is battling his . . . battling
the mind of the Tongueless One . . . and I might fight him for both
of us."

His hand clasped hers and her free hand closed over it tightly.

"He is after your brain also," she whispered after a moment,
and although she was staring straight at him, she did not seem to
be seeing him. Her level gaze brooded as though, for always, she
had seen all and seen nothing. It was uncanny. The eyes seemed to
be staring straight through him, as though fixed on some remote
point in infinity behind him. "Don't be afraid. Fix your thoughts
on me. Keep your mind clear of his . . . don't let the groping fingers of his mind seize yours. If you do, you will never be free."

She clasped his hand more tightly, pushing her voice out over
the stillness of the room like a little sled over thin ice.

"Look at me. Believe in me. I can defend you."

He felt ridiculous, but he followed her instructions.

"Does your head feel confused?" she asked after a moment.

"Yes, rather," he confessed. "I seem to feel sleepy."

"Don't give in to it. Don't close your eyes. Keep them open and
fixed on me. If you sleep you will never wake up," she said with
terrible energy.

It dawned suddenly on Dale that something was clutching at his
brain as if with myriads of tiny hands; stealing beneath the surface
of his mind and stirring that mysterious store of emotions which

lies buried so deeply beneath the consciousness. He was becoming aware of tremendous forces stirring within him, elemental, incredibly ancient and primitive. The girl, close as she was, seemed veiled in a mist. He saw her as one sees a figure on a fog-shrouded night.

"I can scarcely see you . . ." he said drowsily.

The noises of the outside world seemed very far away. There was just a memory of street cries; just a memory of the clamor of automobile horns, the rumble of the elevated. And yet something from the outside world, the unreal world of facts, seemed to brush in on unclean, sardonic wings, to disturb the perfect peace that was enveloping him.

"You must see me," the girl told him sharply.

"My eyes are heavy," he said sleepily.

The figure of the girl was becoming dimmer and dimmer. "I can't see you . . ."

Something in him told him that he must fight this feeling that was clutching at him, seeping through the enveloping fabric of his consciousness; breaking down his will. A part of him wanted desperately to flee from the room into the clean night outside. But he could not. He was more and more at the mercy of old, dark influences that lay like a sediment at the bottom of his soul. Old impulses, too powerful to resist, were being set free.

The voice of the girl was coming to him from a great distance.

"You must keep your mind clear," she was telling him over and over again. "Keep your mind clear. Don't you understand? The Tongueless One is after your mind. Believe in me. Believe that I can defend you . . . save you . . . if you do not you are lost."

His heavy lids lifted and he tried to look at her. Even in his half stupor he could see that the girl was fighting something . . . something unseen. Her face was tense, drawn, set.

"Can you see me? Can you?" she demanded desperately.

He opened the eyes that had dropped shut and tried to straighten up.

"I can't . . . see . . . anything . . ." he gasped.

"Look at me," she ordered.

"I can't," he gasped. The world was gray before his eyes. A gray that was shrouding him, pressing in on him, seeking to smother him. And yet, strangely enough, he seemed to have no desire to resist it. Rather, to welcome it.

"I tell you that death lies behind sleep for you," the girl said urgently. "Can't you believe me? Can't you hear? If you sleep he will seize your mind . . . and then you will become a slave to the Lamp . . . join the Living Dead . . . oh, you must fight . . ."

"Why can't you let me sleep?" he asked drowsily.

"Because to let you sleep is to let you die," she cried.

Seizing his arm she dragged him with her as she went from light to light, jerking off the shades, touching the switches of others until the room blazed with a strong white light. Then she snapped on the radio, dialed it until the sound of a musical program came in strong and discordant . . . twisted out of recognition . . . distorted so there was no rhythm to the music . . . nothing to lull the senses . . . nothing but a hideous, discordant blare.

"That will help," she whispered to herself, and then began to walk Dale up and down the room, never stopping, dragging his stumbling body along with her as one does a person who has been drugged.

"He can't seize your mind," she said in his ear, again and again, her cool voice cutting through the din of discords. "Can you hear what I am saying?"

He did not hear her. Instead there was a new voice in his consciousness, a voice that he *felt* rather than heard . . . a voice that was whispering . . . insistently . . . urgingly . . . a voice that he knew was not speaking English or any other language that he knew, yet whose meaning he comprehended perfectly.

He took a side step . . . cunningly . . . slowly . . . obeying the urging of that voice so quietly that the movement passed for a part of the dizziness that enveloped him. But he was no longer dizzy. His brain was clear . . . crystal clear . . . focused upon one thought . . . to get his hands upon the keen-edged paper knife that lay upon the table . . . the most desirable thing in the world . . . the only thing in the world . . . was that paper knife . . . and the urge to use it as that insistent, compelling voice directed.

Another slow side step. He could see the knife. He could see nothing else. The keen, shining bit of steel lay in the center of a pool of light. Everything else was blackness save that one spot of light with the slim blade in the center of it.

Another lurching step. His hand went out slowly behind him. The trailing fingers touched the steel . . . closed about the hilt . . . the arm tensed . . . a single swift gesture and the point was at his breast . . . cutting through cloth . . .

"No!" cried the girl in a voice like a clear-toned bell.

Freeing one hand she brought it against his cheek with a resounding blow.

The shock opened his eyes. The paper knife clattered to the floor.

The gray fog that surrounded him was clearing . . . fading away as a fog does under the rays of the sun.

Then suddenly she released him; sprang to the center of the room with upraised hand.

Not five feet away from her Dale saw (or thought he saw) the most incredible of all the incredible things that had happened in that house that night.

The shadow of a man was taking form in the room . . . a blurred, indistinct figure through which the further wall of the room was clearly discernible . . . a figure that was rapidly taking on thickness and substance . . . almost as though wisps of fog were solidifying to form the figure of a living man.

Chapter Nine

TARA'S HAND WAS FLUNG UP, palm outward, in an arresting gesture.

"I know you, Wang-fi," her voice rang out, the words sounding like a hammer on a silver bell, producing overtones that hummed away into infinity. "Your mind has shed your body as the oak sheds its leaves for the winter, and the body that stands before me is only the shape created by your mind . . . it is only the evil will of the Tongueless One that keeps it here. You come in this guise to do murder, so that I may not make the Gesture of Death on the air and slay your body as your soul has already been slain."

The atmosphere was perfect for any kind of illusion . . . stifling, electric, full of panic. Dale wondered dully if he were mad and this a part of the hallucination.

The girl took a step toward the figure that was no longer a shadow but a solid; it was living, breathing flesh and blood.

"It is only your will and that of the Tongueless One that keeps your shape here before me," the girl went on. "But somewhere your body lies asleep . . . and my mind is seeking it to slay it as it sleeps."

The infinitesimal fraction of a minute that Dale stood there in the room, swaying, might have been an hour for the multitude of things that flashed through his mind. He started to move . . . and something . . . some force . . . flung him back. The girl had not moved . . . indeed he doubted if she had seen the involuntary movement on his part, but now her voice came to him, low, urgent.

"Don't move. You can do nothing. This man's body has no real substance. It is only a shape created by his will and projected in here."

Then, there in that little room began a strange and horrible struggle . . . the more dreadful because the struggle was not physical and the combatants never touched each other . . . scarcely moved at all. It is doubtful if any man had ever before witnessed so fantastic a scene.

The shape of the man confronted the girl whose eyes were ablaze, her lips parted with the violence of her breathing. And, visibly, the shape writhed and squirmed under the terrific concentration of her gaze, her mind locked with that other mind in deadly battle.

"I have found your body," she said slowly, distinctly. "It is out there in the hall, standing behind the opened door of the linen closet. . . there is a pain in your chest, Wang-fi . . . a pain that stabs . . . and stabs . . . it is going deeper . . . soon it will reach your heart . . . there is a knife in your breast, Wang-fi . . . Ah . . . You flee . . ."

Almost on her last words Dale saw the solid shape of the man before him dissolve . . . float and eddy like whitened ashes stirred by a wind on the hearth; then drift through the room, fading, dissolving, lost gradually in thin air.

The girl flung up a slim hand.

"I bar your pathway to life," she cried in a terrible voice. "Before your mind can regain your body I claim it. I call you, Wang-fi . . . I claim your presence here . . . I bar your mind from your body, Wang-fi . . . Come . . . come to this room."

Slowly, before Dale's horrified eyes, the door to the hallway opened and a man moved into the room . . . *the man whose body he had seen dissolve into thin air not thirty seconds before . . .* A man moving with short, jerky steps as a mechanical doll moves . . . a Chinese who held in his right hand a long, slender knife.

The girl made a swift gesture with a slim hand, a gesture that cut through the clustered shadows of the little room like a dramatic incident, that brushed through the sudden, clogging stillness like a conjurer's wand, sweeping away the suspense. And at the movement the man halted, just as if her hand had been pressed firmly against his chest. Actually, he seemed to be leaning against it.

"A knife, Wang-fi?" she questioned mockingly in English. "Is not that a poor weapon to use against *me?*"

The man lifted his eyes to her . . . cold eyes that were dead and lifeless looking, and yet that seemed to burn with a faint, greenish glow, like the eyes of a cat in the dark.

"The knife was for him, not for you, Hing Mee-Yin," he returned dully.

The girl's eyes flickered to Dale. He was no longer swaying, and the dazed look had gone from his face. She turned back to the Chinese.

Her silver-bell voice had the same hypnotic quality that Dale had noticed before, a quality utterly outside the range of his experience. She employed no gestures. Her breathing could not be visually detected now. That slender body retained its ivory illusion as her out-thrust hand seemed to keep the man at bay.

"Once to-night," she said in ringing tones, "I sent a message to the Tongueless One . . . a message that I would fight if he wished me to fight . . . I see now that he wishes to fight. So be it. And not all the stolen secrets of the Ancient Ones twisted to his own dark usages . . . not all of the things taught the Keepers of the Secrets themselves in the depths of the Azure Cavern shall succeed in compelling me to return. And, as I strike the first blow in the battle, so shall I strike the last one."

Her words died away. And hardly had she finished speaking when there came from the man a low and awful cry. His face was a horrible mask.

Dale, too, stared in horror. His eyes were fixed on the man's hand where, a moment before, a knife had gleamed. Now, there was no knife there. In its place the man grasped a slender snake that was coiled about his bare arm and wrist; a slender dust-colored thing with wicked, triangular head.

Even as he looked the snake struck, and struck again.

In a low choked voice the man said:

"It is death."

To which the girl replied quietly: *"Solei . . .* you die."

Slowly the stooped figure straightened itself to its full height.

"Solei, " he answered. "I die."

Stoic and fatalist, he stood motionless, waiting for death to overtake him. A look of horrible fear—of torture—crept over his face. It suggested a formless phantom of despair. Doubled up, tortured, his hands clawing at his throat, the perspiration of a man in terrible agony pouring down his face; his eyes were strained, staring, seeming about to jump from their sockets, the veins in his forehead strained to the breaking point.

Then death struck. One moment the man was swaying on his feet. Then he crumpled to the floor, writhed in agony for a moment, then lay stiff and quiet, his face twisted into a horrible mask.

And from the clenched right hand that a moment before had grasped a deadly snake, *the gleaming knife blade clattered to the floor boards.*

Chapter Ten

FOR A MOMENT Dale stared horror-stricken at the form on the floor. Then he brushed his hand across his eyes as if to rub this vision from his sight; caught the fingers of one hand in the other, examined them carefully, looked down at them as though he had never seen them before, examining them carefully, turning them over and over in the light. He heard his own voice, excitedly pitched, unreal. He knew there was madness in the utterance.

"Is he dead?"

"Yes," came the girl's still, small voice. "He is dead. I . . . I killed him."

For a moment it was as if all the sounds, and all the movements of the world had passed out of existence; their very memory seemed to have died. Then the girl's racking sobs stabbed the quiet.

"What nonsense," Dale said unsteadily. "It . . . it was suicide."

It was not the first time that he had come face to face with death, but he had never been able to lose the sense of human bafflement, of doors too swiftly shut on human understanding; the feeling of sharp and sudden reversal of all that has gone before.

"God forgive me," the girl whispered, a tortured look upon her face, "if what I have done this night is in vain. But this is one member of the Company of the Living Dead that will no longer be a slave to the Lamp."

A shiver passed over her, and then she was blessed with the gift of tears.

"Don't cry," Dale murmured. The quiet cataclysm of her tears began to touch his nerves in a different way. The realization, brought home so poignantly, of what she must be undergoing, brushed him like trailing fingers of distress. He took her fluttering hands in his and held them gently. "Don't cry. Please. Don't cry," he repeated. "Everything will come out all right."

She smiled for a moment through her tears. "You're an optimist," she whispered. They sat for a moment in silence. The touch of his hands seemed to steady her. Something of the tenseness of her attitude died down; some of the dazed look vanished from her eyes. She turned to him. Her face was like a beautiful mask; immutable, expressionless.

"I would have spared you what has happened Mr. Reynolds, could I have helped it."

"How—how did you do it?" he questioned almost in a whisper.

"He died," she said quietly, "through the power of suggestion, which touches so closely on the shadowy boundaries of the unknown, that no man living can say where it leaves off and the realm of a far greater mystery begins. There was no snake, but he—and you—believed that there was—a snake of a deadly species. He was made to believe that it struck him again and again. He knew that the bite of that particular snake meant death. And so the deep-rooted subconscious thought brought death as swiftly and surely as though a snake had actually bitten him. That, I suppose, is one of the things you would call magic . . but actually it is only knowledge."

Dale drew one hand across his moist forehead, as though to wipe away the dregs of a nightmare. The recollection of that moment when his hand had snatched up the knife came as a hot accusation. His lips had touched the cup of death, and of shuddering memory there remained the chill knowledge that had she not acted, that keen blade would have been buried in his breast by his own hand.

"I don't know what to call it," he said somberly. "You might tell me that this man was killed here in this room by magic . . . and I would not believe you. But that would not change the concrete fact that he is dead, and that I cannot explain his death."

The girl made a weary gesture.

"What I did was no more than you could have done, had you the knowledge," she said. "Knowledge forced by the strength of intelligence into the domain of high powers. The greatest of all man's gifts is his will. If a man possesses enough knowledge . . . and the will to use it . . . he can do anything; shape the destinies of those about him, influence the comings and goings upon the surface of the earth, cause wars and the break-up of nations, and even, when the seed has sprouted and the tree has flowered, defeat the purpose of death. All by the force of his will. And what you saw here to-night was not quite what it seemed. I did not slay a living man, but only a man who seemed to be living."

Dale brushed his hand across his eyes mechanically.

"I'm afraid I don't understand," he said. "You mean . . . he isn't . . . wasn't . . . dead . . . I mean . . . he was dead when? . . ."

The girl stopped him with a gesture. The brilliant lights of the room made a fluid outline of her slim body.

"It may not be possible to make you understand," she said slowly. "He was living . . . and yet dead. Years ago, the Tongueless One slew his soul, but left the spark of life in his body . . . a piece of animate clay responsive only to the mind of the Tongueless One . . . obedient to his commands . . . his brain living only in the brain of the Tongueless One."

"Slew his soul?" Dale's mind was dazed. He had the curious thought that this was some strange glimpse of an alien life that had come to him out of the dark, a mere fragment of an alien existence, and that it would pass back into the dark, leaving no trace. And he was irritatingly conscious of a puzzling and inexplicable desire to share whatever lay ahead of this girl in the adventure. "What in heaven's name are you talking about? Do you actually believe that a soul can be slain?"

"I do not believe. I know," she said with deadly calm. "For years I lived in the Company of the Living Dead, yet not of them. And long ago I made up my mind to one thing: that I should never become one of them. The Tongueless One shall not steal my soul from me . . . make me a member of the Company of the Living Dead . . ." she stopped abruptly, and gazed at him, her face holding a quality of helpless, appealing fear, as if she had been brought face to face with some horror too great for the human soul to understand.

Misunderstanding, he said gravely:

"I do not understand what you mean, but I know that nothing can slay a soul. No matter what you do, what you have done, the soul is intact. I'm . . . I'm not much of a religious fellow, but . . . well . . . I know that it just can't be done."

Tara made a swift gesture.

"You wouldn't understand. What I know, I know. What I was thinking about was you . . . you have been so courteous. . . so kind . . . and you don't know . . . Oh, you don't realize that by being kind and considerate you have signed your own death warrant."

Dale brushed his hand wearily across his forehead, straining at the threads of amazement which still entangled him.

"I guess I must be an utter fool," he said, running his hand through his hair in bewilderment, "but I must confess I don't get the whole damn thing. I can understand this Chu-Sheng wanting to get you back in his power again. And of course I can understand your struggle and desire to avoid this. But why should he pick on me?" He threw out his hands in a gesture of bafflement.

"Don't you see? Your action in saving me from those men to-night has earned you the enmity of Chu-Sheng," the girl said crisply. "Men who earn the enmity of Chu-Sheng do not live long."

Dale struck his hands together in light persistent blows, unconsciously, in his disquietude, racking his brains for some concrete thought, some solution to fasten upon.

"It seems to me," he said, "that if you are afraid of this Chu-Sheng, the best thing to do is to go to the police and tell them the whole story."

"And be locked up as a lunatic," the girl said quietly. "What should I tell them? That I am afraid of a Chinese magician? Can you imagine how your unimaginative policeman would look upon a story such as mine?"

Dale could, and said so.

"You must not leave here to-night," the girl said thoughtfully. "You would never reach your own home. Because the Tongueless One failed a little while ago, do not think that he is finished. He will try again . . . other things . . . and unless I am there, he will succeed with you. And I must have time to think—to plan."

"Stay here," Dale repeated, "but . . ."

The girl cut him short. "I know what you are going to say, but this is no time for conventions. Your life is at stake. And," she added ironically, "if anyone suffers through the shattering of conventions, it is the woman, not the man. No. I got you into this, and I have no intention of permitting you to walk out of that door to your death."

"Don't you think," Dale asked gently, "that your own terrible experiences with this man have shaken you to such an extent that you magnify the ability of this Chu-Sheng to . . . to do the things you attribute to him? After all . . . it is rather incredible, you know."

"It should not be . . . to you . . . after what you have seen and heard here to-night," the girl said with definite significance.

"Have you forgotten that I stopped your hand just in time to prevent you plunging a knife into your own breast? Were you doing that of your own accord—or at the bidding of another mind? No, Mr. Reynolds, I tell you I *know*. I know that if you go out of this house to-night, you will never reach your own home alive. I can protect you if you are with me. But away from me . . . no."

Dale was finding it difficult to shepherd his facts into logical alignment, because his mind was heavy with a sense of the impossibility of it all. And the more he thought of it, the more confused he became. Back of it all he could sense some plan, an intricate, diabolical purpose which his processes of ratiocination could not follow, much less combat. And this slender girl with the wistful eyes and the soft, sweet voice, what was her part in it? He did not want to admit the possibility of anything occult in the night's happenings, but . . . his mind shrank from the possibilities that the thought opened up.

In the tensity of their conversation the two had forgotten utterly the still, prone form on the floor. Sight of it brought back to Dale certain concrete facts.

"Look here," he said earnestly. "We've got to do something about—about the body," and he nodded toward the still form of the Chinese. "The police . . . there's nothing they can really do . . . but it will be unpleasant . . . there will be questions . . . Publicity . . ."

The girl nodded somberly.

"They will never know," she said.

She turned, so that she faced the door and spoke in a low, penetrating voice. Chinese, Dale thought, or some Asiatic tongue. Hardly had she finished, when the door swung open silently and two Chinese entered. Without a word they picked up the body and bore it silently out of the room.

The girl looked at Dale with level eyes.

"That," she said quietly, "is what would have happened to you. You would have been taken away secretly, and no one would ever have known what had become of you. Just another mysterious disappearance. You would have vanished without a trace. And that danger still hangs over you. Now do you see the necessity of staying here?" She held up an imperative hand as he started to speak. "Please, Mr. Reynolds, I am responsible for the position in which you find yourself, and I must protect you from your own unbelief. You must stay here to-night."

"Very well," Dale agreed unwillingly. "I'll stay."

"You will find the couch fairly comfortable," she said quietly. "Try to sleep a little. Good night," and she went into the next room, closing the door quietly.

Chapter Eleven

DALE AWOKE WITH A START. Morning sunlight streamed through the window. Then he leaped to his feet in dismay as he realized that Tara Travers was seated upright in a chair on the further side of the room, wide awake, her face the face on a silver coin.

Realization of the position he had placed the girl in by agreeing to spend the night in her apartment flooded him. The previous night's happenings seemed much more gruesome when viewed in the bright morning sunlight, and he felt rather silly and ashamed that he should have allowed the girl's fears to persuade him to jeopardize her reputation.

She smiled a little tired smile and answered his unspoken question.

"No," she said, "I have slept." But the shadowed lids gave the lie to her words. If she had slept it had been but briefly. "I have prepared coffee," she went on. "And it will take me only a moment to make toast for you."

As he took his seat at the table in the center of the room, after washing up, he smiled rather ruefully at his evening clothes. She caught the glance and interpreted it correctly.

"You must have other clothes," she said. "But you cannot go for them alone. I dare not let you."

"I've never met anyone quite like you before," he said with a smile. "And, in a sense, I'm grateful to you. You have violently interjected romance into my perfectly commonplace existence. Murder and magic and sudden death in silken, exotic form. You have taken the book of my life and not only illustrated it with vivid and colorful pictures, but you have unbound it, sewed into its prosaic pages several chapters ripped bodily from the best selling thrillers. And then you have rebound the whole thing, pasted your own picture on the cover and written underneath it: 'Continued in our next.' "

"You're taking it as a lark," she said gravely. "And it isn't. There is nothing at which these people would stop to achieve their purpose. You must not leave alone."

"But how long will this keep up?" he burst out.

"Until it is ended, one way or the other," she stated simply. "And until that time, you must stay here."

"But my dear girl, that is impossible," he expostulated. "There's . . . well . . . there's business, for one thing."

"Your business will be of little consequence to you when you are dead," she stated shortly.

He stared at her soberly.

"Then you still think that I am in danger?" he queried.

She drew her slim brows together in the queer absent way of one whose thoughts revolve about things which have happened long ago. Her hands lay against the table-cloth. They looked slim and lovely. She looked slim and lovely all over in her simple little frock. Her hair was a shadow against the light walls. Then she looked up and said gravely:

"I know that you are."

"But . . . no matter . . . don't you understand?" he wanted to know. "I can't go on staying here. It was inexcusable to stay last night. There is bound to be . . . unpleasantness."

She gazed at him without flinching, eyes frank and resolute.

"You mean gossip."

For all her poise and assurance there was something virginal in the shyness with which she approached the word.

"Yes," he admitted.

"That is something we cannot consider now," she said with grave certainty. "I dare not trust you away from me. I got you into this; I am responsible if you are murdered. It's a ghastly responsibility for a girl to have upon her shoulders."

He looked at her, wholly serious now, and spoke in a taut, ragged voice.

"But . . . your reputation."

'What does it matter," she said thoughtfully, "if the world thinks I am good . . . or bad, so long as I know that what I do is right?"

"It matters very much," he insisted.

"But in this instance the world would be wrong," she went on. "For, in doing the conventional thing, the thing the world would consider good, I would really be bad . . . unspeakably bad. I would be sending an innocent man to his death."

He lifted his eyes toward her, and she saw in him the strong pride and the flash of courage that lifted him above the common rut.

"I can't let you do it," he said decisively. "Even at the risk of . . . what you think."

Her eyes pleaded and her lips were about to protest.

"Please," he went on. "You don't seem to realize what my staying here would mean to you. You're very young. Your whole life is before you, and if I kill your reputation now, you'll have no happiness later, when this thing has blown over."

She gazed at him steadily.

"And do you think that I would have any happiness if I knew I had killed a friend, to save my honor? What honor would I have in that? I would hate myself for the longest day I lived."

"Then isn't there something else that you can do . . . some way in which you can use your . . . your knowledge . . . to fight this thing off—end it quickly?"

The assurance had gone out of his voice. His earnestness was making him realize something of the never sleeping vigilance of this thing that she feared, and the depths of the cunning of the man she called Chu-Sheng. It was all completely over his head. His brain whirled from the effort of trying to make a complete picture of the contrary jig-saw fragment of events that had followed from one dramatic moment to the other.

"I could try," Tara said thoughtfully, "but it would be dangerous. Perhaps open the doors to dangers as yet unguessed. No . . . I should not dare risk it, except as a last resort. You see, Mr. Reynolds, you haven't the slightest conception of the tremendous thing you're up against. I have. Why, I have seen a whole tribe of people sicken and die in their black felt yurts when Chu-Sheng and the Living Dead gathered in the Temple of Lung Men and prayed . . . can you understand the terrible, the terrific power of hundreds of minds all *willing* in terrible unison, the destruction of a people . . . or a mind? You can't—because you've never experienced it—because you don't realize that thought is electric energy . . . force . . . generated by the brain . . . That life is electric energy. Matter is the same. Thought. Life. Matter. All three are basically the same, made of the same stuff. And you fighting Chu-Sheng is like matching a tiny electrical force against a greater one. The smaller will inevitably be snuffed out like a candle flame. No! I can't let you die. As you will, if you try to fight this thing alone. I must stay with you, day and night."

He bit his underlip. In his eyes was an absent look, as though he followed a derelict idea. Followed a moment's scowling silence under the merciless scrutiny of her eyes. Then, a robust energy swaying his words as trees are swept by wind, he said:

"Then you must marry me."

The solution was all so simple. As simple as a law of mechanics which, whether we like it or not, goes on serenely holding the universe in place. But beyond the immediate present, even his shrewdness could not foresee the consequences.

It was some time before she answered. For a second or two he sustained the searching quality of her gaze. And in her face was something he had never expected to see there . . . a turn of the mouth . . . a shape behind the eyes . . . something bitter and very lonely . . . a barren bough in the gale.

"It's kind of you to ask me," she said, raising somber eyes to his. She let the silence drag, then said in quietness: "But I'm afraid that's impossible."

He looked at her curiously. For an instant he seemed to see behind her eyes, into her heart. There was a message there, clear and pure as if air had written it on a tablet of mountain snow, but a message that he could not read, for it was written in a strange language, and to him the characters of that language were as mysterious as marks carved on a Druid stone.

"Impossible?" he questioned. "Is there someone for whom you care?"

She shook her head.

"Then I'm afraid I don't understand."

She hesitated. "I mean . . . it could never . . . that is . . . it would only be a mockery of marriage."

"I quite understand," he said stiffly. "You need have no fear."

She cut him short.

"What I am trying to say is this"—a tide of crimson flowed over her face and then receded, leaving it again a lovely Benda mask—"that if I . . . if I ever really become married . . . you know what I mean . . . both of us are lost . . . You see . . . these things that I know—these powers that I have—are only possible for me as long as I am . . . single."

He turned pink. "It will be quite all right . . . your liberty— privacy—I shan't bother you—annoy.. . ."

For a moment she gave him a slow smile, lustrous and heavy lidded with the contentment of faith. For an instant, seeing that smile, an edge of a shadow of misgiving crept over him. An irrational sense of helplessness. It was deeper; it was wonder. There was a little touch of unbelief in his heart as he looked at her. It was incredible that she should be the girl that she was. . . incredible that she should be concerned in this fantastic mystery which swirled about the two of them.

"After this affair is settled," he went on, "in a month or a year . . . at any time . . . you can very easily get your freedom, and you'll have all your life before you." He rose, youth settling affairs that belong to the Gods, and said, "We'll always be friends."

She had also risen, standing slim and calm. ~

Her eyes seemed to draw and absorb the light and burn of themselves with a diffused sort of luminosity, a light of dreams rekindled; a brooding, avid light of hope recaptured and bound.

Then with a swift gesture she turned and faced Dale squarely; raised her eyes to his with a rather particular concentration of trustfulness, her lashes making a softly wistful shadow upon her face.

"You're a grand person," she said seriously, "but I—I really shouldn't let you."

But now, having stepped into the shadowy depths of his decision, there was no hesitancy upon his part. Once he had arrived at a conclusion, he clung to it with almost pagan resolution.

"You must," he said decisively. "After all, it's just a simple sort of business arrangement for . . . for the protection of both of us."

Her eyes searched his intently. "Well . . . the way you put it, it does seem the easiest way out of an awkward situation."

"There's a sensible girl."

She studied him narrowly. "You're sure there's no one you would hurt in taking this step?"

"No one."

"It's very generous of you," she said. "But remember, I don't ask it. Really I don't."

"But I do."

"Then, in that event," she flushed prettily: "Thank you . . . and . . . I'll marry you whenever you wish."

"Good! Let's shake hands on that."

They clasped hands laughingly. It was their first light moment since the beginning of that ghastly night.

"Get on your things. There's no time like the present. We'll go out and get the license at once."

Chapter Twelve

TARA TRAVERS AND DALE REYNOLDS had been married at noon. All the way back to his apartment he had been striving to realize that she was his wife. But he could not then, any more than now, bring himself to realize that the new ring upon her finger really signified anything to him . . . that it had altered his own life in any way. But that had not prevented his incredulous eyes returning to her slim finger, banded with the narrow circlet of gold.

And in the face of it he did not seem to know exactly what to do or say . . . what attitude to assume . . . what effort to make.

Tara came into the big living room from her own bedroom, removed her hat and came slowly over to the window where he stood, gazing out over the roofs of the city.

"It's lovely here," she said with a little sigh.

"I'm glad you like it," Dale answered awkwardly. "I . . . I hope you'll be comfortable."

"Thank you," she said.

"It . . . it seems rather odd, you being here like this. I mean, you living here . . . and all," Dale went on.

"Does it?"

"Yes." Then, on a sudden impulse he blurted out: "I really can't bring myself to believe that we are married."

He was embarrassed, although smiling.

Her upward startled glance arrested him. Her voice was odd, stilled. Her smile was a faint glow in her eyes; the rest of her face, in the afternoon sunshine, was untouched, reflective.

"Regretting it already?" she asked, without a touch of coquetry.

"No," he admitted, "there hasn't been anything to regret."

"I know how you feel."

"The first thing to do is to face this rather funny situation and take it amiably and with good humor," he went on. "You'll have your freedom whenever you want it."

"Yes . . . I know. We belong to different worlds, you and I. Perhaps the two worlds touch here, at this moment. But they won't stay that way. They'll carry us apart, so far apart we couldn't even talk."

Looking at him, standing there on the other side of the window, Tara was stirred by the sharp vigor of this man, the sureness behind his charm. Her nerves quickened; and all of the savors of the day were more acutely pleasant. He lifted her up and carried her along . . . his personality did.

"I wonder," he said reflectively. "You see, when two people are as oddly situated as we are, they're likely to be afraid of being in one another's way. But they should be happy so long as they are quite confident of each other's friendly consideration, don't you think?"

For a moment she seemed to be thinking of something else. Then she turned toward him in a pose very like his own, her head resting against the edge of the window framing. The deep, friendly eyes held a queer wistfulness.

"I like you," she said slowly. Her smile flickered all over her face like a pale light. "You're simple and clean and honest and . . . I haven't had many friends. I think we should get on splendidly."

There was an almost imperceptible hesitation before the last two words. But he caught it and wondered. She glanced at him swiftly and then averted her eyes. Nervousness, Dale thought, noting the movement. No doubt she was wondering, as he was, how or from where the next blow would fall.

"You are tired," he said gently . . . "tired and lonely and unhappy."

"Tired," she answered in a small, odd voice. She tried to be casual about it but she wasn't casual. "But not . . . the others."

"Not unhappy?"

"No."

"Aren't you lonely?"

"Not with you."

The answer came so naturally, so calmly, that the slight sensation of pleasure it gave him arrived only as an agreeable afterglow. Her faint smile was fixed on the distance and her slender fingers ran the hem of the window curtain back and forth between them. Whatever restlessness she possessed was expressed by those fingers.

"It was thoughtless of me to bring you here," he said after a moment. "It never occurred to me that you might have preferred to get away from New York . . . go on an ocean trip, perhaps."

She shook her head and a strange look came into her eyes . . . a look of admiration mixed with some form of fear that he had never before seen. Her supple body, encased in the simple linen frock in which she had been married, abruptly came alive. Her eyes shone, her cheeks glowed, and her lips were parted in a faint smile. He admired her beauty without reservation.

"It is peaceful here . . . so peaceful and quiet after Lung Men that it does not seem possible that the two places could ever exist on the same planet."

"Just where is Lung Men?" he asked. "You have spoken of it before, and I do not remember ever having heard the name."

Tara did not answer for a moment, but turned back toward the room; crossed to the long library table and picked up a cigarette carefully.

"Lung Men," she said, "is a city that does not exist upon any map."

She sank into a deep chair, snapped the table lighter into flame and drew a deep puff of smoke.

"In the days when the ancient silk roads from the East and West were new," she went on, "it stood among the hills of Chi-jen . . . that is on the edge of the Gobi Desert. But the shifting, blowing sands of the desert buried it, until now the only evidence of it that shows is a black pagoda standing above the yellow sands."

She shivered a trifle as if the thought brought up unpleasant memories.

"That is the home of Chu-Sheng. And buried beneath the sand is the great Temple of Lung Men. There, in the Month of the Snake, things are done that have not been done elsewhere since the time of the Ancient Ones . . . the lifting of the veil from secrets that have been guarded for a thousand years or more. I have seen . . ." she stopped abruptly, then went on. "It is in the Month of the Snake that men come from all parts of Asia to swear allegiance to the Tongueless One. And some of them remain. . . to join the ranks of the Living Dead."

Dale stirred uneasily in the chair into which he had dropped. He did not meet her eyes. He had a queer feeling that a sense of shame, of horror, held the girl as she told him these things, and that it would be kinder not to look at her.

"The Living Dead . . . You have used that phrase more than once. Just what does it mean?" he asked.

"There are three things to which man clings most tenaciously," the girl said gravely. "His soul, his personality, his life. One is contained in the other . . . yet each is separate. Each is based upon hope. And Chu-Sheng destroys hope. By one of the stolen secrets of the Ancient Ones he slays a man's soul—yet with these same secrets he keeps him alive, so that the man, walking, living, breathing, knows that the slightest whim of the Tongueless One can—and does—send him out of existence completely. Hope . . . of life . . . of the soul . . . of personality . . . is snuffed out like a candle in the wind. It is the Living Death."

"Horrible," Dale said. Then resolutely changing the subject he glanced at his watch. "I did not realize that it was so late," he said. "Shall we dine out, or here?"

"Here, please," the girl said instantly. "I'd rather just be . . . be quiet and peaceful for a few days, if you don't mind."

Meanwhile, sunset lay like a fan of flamingo plumes across the streets of Chinatown, casting a film of color across the gray, scabbed houses, deepening the shadows in the maze of dim, narrow streets. Here and there a hand, a face was struck by the light and stood out pallidly in the growing shadows . . . a black-clad figure lurking in a doorway . . . a self-satisfied face peering from the door of the Bowery Mission . . . store windows with strange fruits and vegetables.

But in the great room where Chu-Sheng sat in a high carved chair, the sunset did not penetrate. There was only a green light that seemed to emanate from nowhere—a light like the glowing heart of a flawless emerald, giving to the room the curious impression of an undersea cavern with the sunlight streaming through placid water.

In that light the eyes of the Tongueless One seemed gentle, mildly curious. But they only served to accentuate the horror and the evil and the ancient timeless power of the face. There was nothing weak about the face. There was nothing in it of stupidity, or indecision or compromising kindness. It was all power . . . Strong, *non-human* power.

At his feet sat T'Sang Kee Meng. He was speaking.

"It is true," he admitted slowly, in the tongue that was spoken in the city of Lung Men long before the civilization of Atlantis sank beneath the waves, "I am afraid of her. What happened two years ago on the stairs of the Temple of Lung Men happened there in her room. Then she made a host of poisonous things out of the soft petals of the acacia flower. There, in her room, she made a yellow death adder out of nothing and from its bite Wang-fi died."

The hand of the immobile black-robed man in the chair flashed up. The twinkling, writhing fingers wove a question upon the air.

"You chatter like a temple ape," was the message the fingers flashed to the younger man. "Does she return or does she die? That alone interests me."

"She must not die," the young Mongol said in sudden fierce defiance. "I love her."

All the wrath of the world seemed to gather and congeal in Chu-Sheng's eyes. That slender, yellow hand was raised high and menacingly; the fingers flashing with vehemence.

"Love!" the angry fingers flashed. "How dare you speak of love? Where has my training gone? Who are you to bow to such softness? You, the disciple of the Master—one day to be a Master yourself. Love is for common men, for weaklings, not for such as we whose destiny it is to some day rule the world. Love is the enemy of ambition. Desire? Yes. But love? No." The twinkling fingers halted a moment, then went on. "She returns here . . . to live. She remains there . . . to die. That is final." T'Sang hesitated, moistening his pallid lips. "Her powers are greater than mine."

"The wise man," the twinkling fingers spelled out, "laces on his sandals backward, when he flees from the spot where an enemy has felt the steel of his knife. Her power is great. But not great enough to overcome this. Go thou to . . ." and for the next quarter of an hour the slender young Mongol read the instructions that poured in a flashing stream from the twinkling fingers of the man in the chair.

Chapter Thirteen

THREE DAYS IS A LONG TIME for two healthy young people to be cooped up in an apartment. By the afternoon of the third day following their marriage the sense of strain—of waiting—had reached a tremendous pitch and a chafing at the chains of their quiet, almost cloistered existence was making itself felt. Nerves were taut.

Tara found both laughter and tears not far behind even the most trivial remarks.

Dale became moody, uncommunicative and smoked almost incessantly.

The desire for movement, for gayety, as a relief from the strain, was becoming a necessity for the two of them.

That the Tongueless One had altered his purpose, Tara never considered. She knew the quality of his patience. He would wait until the proper time and then strike. Whether it would come that night, or the next, or the night after, no one could tell. Perhaps he was planning some new method of attack; striking from ambush, from unexpected sources. All she could do was keep constantly upon her guard for some sign, however slight, that he was about to strike. With this thought she had comforted herself during the past few days, and with a fatalism which even an Oriental could not have surpassed, had waited for events to show her what, finally, would be the manner of her defense.

But she was young and healthy and, so when on the afternoon of that third day, Dale had suggested that in heaven's name they get out, do something, anything . . . perhaps a drive into the country and a dinner somewhere out on Long Island . . . she eagerly agreed.

She was in yellow, daffodil yellow, which looked exquisitely simple. Her slipper heels were high and slim and her hair was sleek. Perhaps only a woman can appreciate the astounding change of mood that a change of dress can give her. And Tara, putting a final dab of powder on her face, and patting her already flawlessly groomed hair, gazed with satisfaction and a touch of frivolity at her reflection in the glass. To-night she seemed a woman without responsibilities . . . only pretty feminine whims . . . like something fragile and exquisite that must be handled with care.

It was a new Tara that emerged from her room, humming a little tune, a Tara in a gay yellow gown and a mood to match. Seeing her thus, one would never have suspected that beneath her gayety lay a real fear of a fate too horrible to put into words.

"Have I known you long enough to tell you that you're pretty darn beautiful?" Dale asked, as she came into the living room.

"Not quite," she answered gayly.

He smiled then, and the touch of isolation that had been gripping him was momentarily gone; light flashed across her face, gave it a quick restlessness.

It was just that velvet hour before dusk when they started out, when the raw tints of sunset have begun to fade into an amethyst veil shot with colors, as perfume rises from an ancient garden. Light ran thin blades of saffron across the silvered river surface as they crossed Queensboro Bridge and headed out on Long Island. In silence Tara lay back in the roadster and watched the distant skyline slowly grow shadowy as it was shrouded in the haze which gave it an air of remote mystery, as a woman of the East is shrouded in the mystery of her veil.

Holding the wheel with one hand, Dale lighted a cigarette and offered her one as an afterthought. There was a keen relish in the smoke, a thin and effervescent flavor to the night. He glanced at her. The glow of her cigarette ran back and betrayed the upward tilt of her features; they were faintly shining. Then, for a long time silence flowed between them . . . a contented silence . . . like the current of a deep stream.

Dale had chosen an inn on the north shore, a famous place where a famous orchestra played and the newest blues singer moaned her woes.

He had no sooner parked the car and they had started together for the entrance than they ran into Bobby Gregory with a party of friends. It seemed to Dale that a whole eternity had passed since that night when he had gone to the Silver Slipper at Bobby's urging and embarked on the queerest adventure that ever befell a man.

Bobby's eyes widened in astonishment at sight of them.

"Well, I'll eat my hat," he cried, "if it isn't the little Reynolds boy sporting a new flame. How did you manage to get a date with the hard-hearted Tara, you Don Juan? I tried, notoriously unsuccessfully, for two weeks. You're a fast worker."

Dale waited until he was through. Then said, a trifle stiffly:

"May I present my wife?"

For a moment Bobby looked at him like a shipwrecked man might gaze at the hungry king of a cannibal tribe. His mouth opened and the match with which he had been lighting a cigarette burned his fingers before he came to.

"Huh?" he asked foolishly.

Dale grinned then, and the slight stiffness was instantly gone.

"I said, may I present my wife?" he repeated.

"Your wife?" Bobby sputtered. "Well, say," and his self-control and good nature came rushing to the rescue. "You are a fast worker."

He pumped both their hands enthusiastically. Tara's laugh was instant and gay . . . and pleased.

"Boy, we'll sure have to celebrate." He turned toward the others, two pretty girls and a nondescript young man who might have been a bank clerk or a millionaire's son. Introductions and congratulations followed and nothing would do short of Tara and Dale joining the party.

Tara smiled, and Dale, catching her dancing eyes, agreed.

Bobby had reserved a table on the edge of the dancing space and swift, deft work on the part of the waiters enlarged it to accommodate six in almost the twinkling of an eye.

"Champagne," Bobby called to the waiter. "Champagne, and a toast to the bride and groom."

Bobby may not have been the perfect companion for all occasions, but his very carefree tomfoolery was the perfect antidote for these two serious-minded young people who had crammed so much of the drama of life into one short week-end. And through Bobby's infectious good humor the six were soon laughing and talking together like old friends in the joyous unrestraint of young people the world over.

Across the little table Dale watched Tara in the soft rain of light that filled the room. The pretty particles of dancing light did not foolishly invest her with frivolity; rather, she seemed steadily to shine through them as a star can shine through the fuzzy fragments of a cloud. They touched her hair with dancing highlights, warmed the pale tranquil curve o her throat.

The orchestra began to play. The party rose in laughing pairs and joined the gay kaleidoscope of whirling color on the floor.

Tara answered the unspoken question in Dale's eyes with a slight shake of her head.

"Do you mind?" she asked softly. "It's so terribly pleasant just to sit here, surrounded by pleasant, gay people and imagine—for a little while, at least—that the past is only a dream."

"Let's make it a dream—just a bad dream—from which we've awakened," he said.

She shook her head. "It wouldn't work. That's the trouble with life. You get a glimpse of what you want . . . and then it's gone. Like a bird against the night sky. Peace and happiness and beauty fill you like a brimming cup . . . but only for a moment, then you've got to drop back to all the jangle of jarred nerves and shaken faith; all the confusion of shattered hopes and ideals . . . and may never be achieved again."

The music stopped. Their party trooped back to the table and he observed how swiftly she could change; how easily her complex, rare personality slipped elusively away. Her tone went light, faintly provocative.

There was a little bracket of silence between them, during which chatter from the others flickered back and forth across the table, and Tara watched the captain lay the foundation of crepes Suzette in the chafing dish on the little serving table. She was playing idly with her fork, twisting it so that it shone in her fingers like a pale, metallic splinter of light. Then she glanced around the room.

Dale's eyes followed hers, for with the sixth sense that is a part of the make-up of many men he had sensed the presence of something inimical . . . there had come to him the sense of exposing his back to a shot or a knife whichever way he turned. Once before . . . in a narrow twisting street of Havana during the recent revolution. . . he had that odd impression, and had heeded it just in time to save his life from a prowler.

He thought that the girl's eyes lingered just a shade too long as they swept over a man who had just entered alone. Dale did not watch her openly, but his mouth had grown stern, had grown thin all at once. But when her gaze returned to him, she betrayed nothing. And nothing of it was reflected on Dale's lean, impassive face.

Nothing queer about this man, Dale reflected, as he studied him furtively. Except perhaps, his eyes . . . cold, opaque sort of eyes that were dead and lifeless looking, and yet at times seemed to burn with a faint greenish glow, like the eyes of a cat in the dark. The clear olive of his face was set off by a small, waxed mustache under a slender, aquiline nose. The hands were long and slender; almost the hands of a woman . . . or a professional killer.

As the dinner went on the feeling grew to a certainty that the girl and this man knew each other. A certain nervousness came into her manner. More than once she let her eyes trail around the room. Once, one of her slim shoulders lifted with impatience as she caught the man's eyes flickering away from them.

She rose abruptly to her feet, as the music started again and slipped into Dale's arms.

As they moved away from the table she said: "Do you mind if we go outside for a moment? I'd . . . I'd like a breath of fresh air."

Dale nodded and guided her expertly toward the entrance door. They stopped just abreast of it, and slipped through into the hall-way together.

From the corner of his eye he saw the man rise also and make his way toward the door.

A hint of fear flickered in the girl's eyes as she, too, observed the move, and Dale felt her hand tighten upon his coat sleeve. To-gether they stepped out into the tremulous violet shadows of the clustered trees. The night was blue and moonless; no ordinary blue, but the clear, rich shade found in the depths of a sapphire, and it poured out as if from an invisible fountain, blending the sky and sea; it caught a thousand stars in its flood and they, like dia-monds caught in an unstirred pool, pulsed with lazy insolence.

Off in the distance a single island rose toward the skyline, soft yet clear, like a purple bubble dreaming between violet sky and a sea like a floor of passionate blue. In the stillness all the colors of the night were intensified, all shadows dark as purple night, all far things looked astonishingly near.

Dale shot a glance behind them as they strolled down the gar-den path between walls of shrubbery. The man of the dining room was no longer visible.

About them, as they walked, the tree tops were limned against the lazy, purple sky in dark tranquility. The scent of wood flowers came to them on the cool air, more a released projection of some magic essence distilled of the night than an odor, and Dale felt that, although invisible in the darkness, the slopes must be covered with the blossoms. The inescapable feel of it crept through him. They seemed suddenly to be shut into a lane of thought unexpect-edly intimate and isolated. They walked in the very heart of silent beauty.

It was a sensation, as moonlight and high snow are sensations, that disturb the secret fibers of the soul. The garden and the night seemed to have cast a spell on him. He shot another look behind him as they made a turn in the garden path.

"Our friend has vanished," he observed.

"Friend?" She turned and her inspection was alert, suddenly searching.

"Yes. The man who was watching us in the dining room."

The words that she had been about to utter died on the girl's lips; her face blanched. For once she was not concealing enough with the swift lashes; for a second there flashed from the eyes upturned to him something that was cold, frozen fear . . . fear that he knew, in some curious way, was for him.

"Then . . . he was watching us?"

She touched Dale's hand, a soft fugitive pressure that somehow seemed to link them together in a subtle league against a common enemy. It left him startled and curiously thrilled. Then he lit a cigarette, the match cutting his steady profile out of the purple shadows; he turned his head and showed a stir of excitement in his eyes.

"I'm afraid so. Did . . . do you know him?"

"I recognized him," she said slowly. "He has come to the Temple of Lung Men several times. But I did not think that he would recognize me . . . the temple girl . . . here in this place. I hoped that his presence was an accident."

She turned a trifle and her face was further away; moonlight swelled along the earth and the dark began to heave as the radiance struck the shadows. An earring flashed; below the thin stuff of her dress her shoulders stirred faintly and went still, like a gesture of resignation.

"But I know now, even without what you told me, that it is no accident."

Dale was on the verge of speaking when the words died in his throat. There was a dark patch on the whiteness of the sanded path before them. Dale stared.

"What is it?" Tara gripped his arm, shook it. "What is it?" Her face was upturned to his. She had not seen what he had seen.

He relaxed, let out a slow breath. "Seeing things!" He laughed a bit unsteadily. "Just a patch of shadow. Sorry! Wait here and I'll take a look."

He stepped forward. Shadow, of course. Couldn't be anything else. Or some discoloration of the ground, maybe.

Her small slippers pattered behind him. He turned with nervous exasperation. "Wait, I tell you. Damn it, it isn't anything."

"Oh, don't be so stupid." She was staring down at it, her breath coming quickly. "Wha—what is it?"

Cold fingers fumbled for matches in the pocket of his coat. "Oil," he heard himself saying. Why oil? Oh, never mind. He said it again: "Must be oil, or something."

The match spurted blue. He shielded the flame. They stooped.

There was a flash of time, infinitesimal and yet endless, while the stuff winked up at them . . . red, shining, horrible in the yellow flare. The match fell from his fingers, hissed out.

He blinked, the flame still dancing before his eyes. There was a sick, sweetish reek in his nostrils.

He felt for his matches again. "Wait," he snapped. "Don't look." The match crackled. He bent again, touched it with a forefinger. Wet. Red. Sticky. And it was oozing slowly from a tiny image lying in the path . . . the figure of a woman with a gaping wound in her side carved (although he did not recognize it) from a gnarled Buddha's Finger, the citrous fruit that the Chinese place before godlings, signifying immortality. Death coming to immortality.

He stared at his forefinger in sick revulsion.

"It's blood," he heard himself saying almost as if another person were talking. "Blood . . . and it's coming from a little image of a woman."

There was a sound that was almost a whimper beside him. The girl's hands went up to her face. "It isn't—it can't be."

"It's blood," he repeated, as if in protest against something that could not happen, "and it's flowing from that . . . that *thing* just as if it were really bleeding."

"I should have known," she said in a hushed voice.

"But . . . how . . . who could have put it there?" Dale demanded, his eyes fastened on that dark pool in the starshine.

"The man you saw in the restaurant," the still, quiet voice went on. "He came out here before us."

Fear for her leaped to his eyes . . . fear stalking the dark with iron steps that filled the stillness and beat in his brain.

"What does it mean?" he asked.

"It is the Sign of Luanghai . . . and it is meant for me," the girl said in the same dull tones. "It is a warning that . . . that I have only twenty-four hours to live."

Chapter Fourteen

DALE REYNOLDS OPENED HIS EYES into a darkness that was only less heavy than that of a dream. He found himself sitting up in bed, with all his senses alert. Consciousness had come back at a bound, just as if he had been aroused by the shake of some invisible hand. And with consciousness had come fear . . . a creeping and soul-shaking fear such as he had never experienced before. It was sheer terror which turned him cold and sick and he knew that it sprang from the presence of—something—in the room with him.

How that knowledge came to him he did not know, but he was as certain of it as he was of his own existence. And more than that: some uncanny instinct, some inward sentinel of the spirit which watches over man while he sleeps, warned him to watch the doorway.

And presently he discerned it dimly, a dark rectangle on the further side of the room. Dark . . . like a hole. The thought made the blood race tumultuously through his veins. The door had been shut and locked when he turned in. Was it open now? Were unseen eyes staring into the gloom of the room from the threshold? And then he heard the faintest shuffling sound and the dark rectangle seemed to disappear.

Terror touched his soul like a flame. Who . . . or what . . . had closed that door? His eyes were dragged toward it in the expectation of seeing some sinister and appalling sight. Nothing! No, there was nothing there. But he knew, nevertheless, that something lurked and watched in the darkness of the room.

And then, as he watched, he became aware that the room was becoming slowly lighted, as if from some phosphorescent element. There was a pale spot forming on the far side of the room . . . an indefinite sort of moon, vaguely round . . . a spot that seemed to pulse and glow feebly as if from within itself . . . a spot that seemed to be filled with little dancing, sparkling flecks of light, as a sunbeam is filled with dust motes . . . something blurred seemed to be moving in it . . . becoming more definite . . .

The reality of the thing was ice about his heart. In that moment he lay with his hands tightly locked, his lips parted, hardly breathing, hearing—incredulous of his own ears—a soft and cautious slipping of feet across the floor. Coming nearer—and as it approached the dancing sparks of light assumed form . . . solidity . . . showed him the outline of a face, a Chinese face.

For a moment it seemed to him to be the nebula of a thought from his brain, showing what was going on in his own mind. It seemed, so to speak, a projection of the thoughts that were taking place in his brain. But only for moment.

The next instant he had touched the light switch beside his bed; swung to his feet.

Standing only a few feet from his bed was a tall slender Chinese.

The man stood for a moment in silence as the light went on, as if realizing that his appearance there produced the effect of ice upon hot imagination.

"What do you want?"

Dale's question lanced through the air with a sudden, quiet vehemence, the edge of a blade so sweetly keen that it seemed to caress even while it cut.

Then: "Sit down," the stranger said in English. His voice was as magnificent as his appearance . . . as surprising.

Dale was not the sort of man to probe and dissect his own emotions, to wait for psychical developments before acting physically; for he was the type that felt that dissection of emotions and registering of impressions spoil the surety of one's aim and muddy one's clearness of action.

So, now as always, he felt, perceived, and acted at exactly the same time. His senses worked together with the instantaneous precision of a camera shutter timed to the hundredth part of a second.

He turned and swung for the jaw of the yellow man.

The blow failed. It glanced off as if guarded by a pugilist. Yet the man had not moved.

He merely said in the same quiet, unemotional tone:

"Sit down."

And then Dale knew that the other was attempting to hypnotize him. Knew that to obey would be the beginning of the descent into subjection. The first step. The others would follow swiftly. There flashed into his mind the thing that Tara had said . . . the surest way to stand up against hypnotism . . . to instantly switch your thoughts to another object—anything whatsoever, so long as it served to concentrate the will and was outside the thought of the practitioner.

The smooth yellow mask smiled at him as Dale tried to stare beyond it—concentrating—working with ice-cold frenzy at a mathematical formula—eliminating all else, visualizing the fig-ures—winning back to self-control and sanity.

The tall Mongol just stood and smiled at him; inflexible, im-movable, like a graven image. Dale could see him, although he kept his eyes resolutely away, could feel the force of him although he was using every ounce of will power to concentrate on the mathematical formula. And he knew that he was slipping; knew his efforts were no match for the perfectly trained mind and eter-nal patience of this yellow man.

Unconsciously he sized up the other's physical resources and he did not fancy matching strength with him, despite the yellow man's slimness. Suddenly a thought struck him. One of those eleventh-hour inspirations that strike some people like a bolt from the blue in emergencies. He remembered that he was backed against the night table at his bedside, and on that table stood a ca-rafe of water.

Slowly, stealthily, his arm crept behind him, closed about the heavy object and swung it high.

And as suddenly the yellow man moved and his fingers brushed Dale's arm. A shock like electricity shot up the member from wrist to shoulder, and he dropped the carafe because he could not help it. The yellow man, still smiling through his smooth mask, sent it spinning away into the shadows with a touch of his foot.

"Childish . . . and useless," he commented.

Step Number Two, Dale told himself, for he knew from Tara that the hypnotist works by rule and uses one trick after another until his resisting victim yields. Dale hung onto his resisting self-control like a man overboard clings to an oar. Nevertheless it was disconcerting to note that the mask of carved ivory before him had not changed by the flicker of an eyelash.

"Get out," he commanded, although he knew it was useless. But he needed to gain time; to divert the man's attention for now, instead of a mathematical formula, his mind was fixed upon Tara . . . the thousand invisible fingers of his brain groping and stealing through the darkened apartment seeking to establish con-tact with her brain. Tara . . .! Tara . . . the call went out from him like a despairing prayer . . . Tara . . . where are you? . . . Tara . . . and all the while his brain was sending out that frantic SOS his lips kept up an incessant babble of demands . . . of questions . . . trying to build up a barrier between himself and the Mongol.

The smile of the man facing him never varied, but the dark eyes changed; they were considering Dale's resistance, speculating as to the source of its strength, calculating which trick to play. Slowly, the way a serpent moves advancing on a spellbound bird, the Mongol's right arm lifted until it was on a level with Dale's eyes . . . slowly he advanced toward Dale, every faculty he owned concentrated in one immense magnetic effort to induce a corresponding state of mind in Dale.

And the latter knew that if the finger touched him he would go down under it . . . beaten.

Chapter Fifteen

WHAT IT WAS THAT WOKE Tara she never knew. Perhaps it was that sixth sense that never deserts some people when they are in danger that caused her to lift her head and listen carefully.

Involuntarily she restrained an impulse to sit up in bed and stared drowsily about the room. The moonlight, floating through the window, crusted the floor with a band of pearl. She wondered what could have caused her sudden awakening. No noise, for silence shut down like a lid, made more intense by the faint sound of the surf on the beach.

Her thoughts flew to Chu-Sheng. He was starting something again. At once she was fully awake. Tense. Alert. She listened, scarcely breathing, her heart beating audibly.

And then she knew. Her own name. "Tara" she heard. It was ringing in her ears, hammering insistently at her brain, echoing and reechoing through her mind. Dale's voice calling for aid.

She swung herself out of bed, groped for her slippers and, standing up, threw a negligee hurriedly about her shoulders; stole quietly across her room and opened the door of the living room. It was in darkness. But a thin streak of light glimmered from beneath Dale's door on the further side.

Unhesitatingly she crossed the room and flung the door open. A voice halted her on the threshold, the smooth voice of T'Sang Kee Meng, the Chinese.

"Greetings, Hing Mee-Yin," he said.

"You!" she said harshly. "What brings T'Sang Kee here?"

"You," he retorted with a bow. "One does not send a boy to do a man's work, and it were but folly to underestimate a foe."

Her eyes went beyond him to the figure of Dale Reynolds standing motionless on the far side of the room . . . a Dale whose hands hung limply at his side and whose eyes, wide open, stared straight before him.

Her eyes went back to the tall, slender Mongol who stood in the center of the room.

She flung one word at the bronze man . . . a word in a language that is dead . . . extinct. . . that never did exist according to authorities . . . and then went on bitterly.

"What have you done?"

The Mongol shrugged.

"You see," he said.

"I warned you," she said evenly, and her right hand went slowly up into the air.

"Careful," he said swiftly. "If you make the Gesture of Death *he* dies also."

One hand indicated the still, motionless figure of Reynolds.

"I have implanted deep in his subconscious the thought that I, and I alone, can awaken him. So if you slay me, his life will speed after mine."

The girl stared at him incredulously for a moment. The uplifted right hand dropped to her side. Hurtling thousands of miles of distance, her mind leaped back to a temple plunged into bitter, blotched darkness, yet with sudden brutal flickerings and stabbings of light that showed sights that she would have preferred not to see. And she knew that he was right; knew that his death would mean also the death of Dale Reynolds . . . knew that he would never awaken from the hypnotic state into which he had been plunged.

"You will die for this," she assured the Mongol with terrible earnestness.

The man shrugged. "Death rides the black camel to the door of every man at the appointed time," he said. "Even the knowledge of the secrets of the Ancient Ones cannot ward off death forever."

"Yours," she told him pleasantly, her might seeking a loophole in the wall which presented itself, "will not be an agreeable one."

"Nor will his," he said calmly, nodding at Dale. "I will give him the command to awaken, when the first blast of the trumpets sounds, and then as the sound of the drums begins, and the Living Dead take up the chant of the Ancient Ones, he will be able to see—"

"No!" Tara's voice rang through the room clearly. She, even better than he, knew the horror that lay behind that low, humming chant of the Living Dead . . . Many times, from behind the stone lacework that screened the gallery in the Temple of Lung Men, she had watched the Living Dead take their places for the ceremony . . . flaring torches painting the scene with scarlet . . . had turned her eyes away in aching horror as the ceremony reached a climax . . . had closed her ears as a despairing scream rose and rose above the humming chant . . .

She faced the Mongol resolutely.

"Not that. Better that I slay you."

And again her right hand went up. And again the Mongol interposed swiftly.

"There is a gateway through every wall," he said.

She watched him cautiously.

"And a gatekeeper to exact his fee," she made answer.

"But the key is in your hand to open the gate and set him free," and a motion of the Mongol's head indicated the motionless Dale.

"And the price?"

"Your return."

She shook her head decisively.

"No. I am free from the Tongueless One. And I shall remain free."

"Then he dies."

The girl watched him quietly for a moment. Then helplessly she said, "Very well. I return to the Tongueless One. On condition that he is never to know . . . and a pledge that he is never to be harmed."

"It is pledged," said the Mongol gravely.

Chapter Sixteen

NOW HAD T'SANG KEE MENG given thought to the matter (for by all odds he was no fool) he would have realized that the hypnotic suggestion of paralysis with which he had bound Dale's limbs, holding them prisoner as rigidly as might bands of steel, had not affected his mind. The effect of the hypnotic spell had been like that of the drug curare, paralyzing the action of the nerve centers, yet leaving them free to feel and think as acutely as ever. Dale could not speak, but he could see and hear and understand everything that passed before him.

In not remembering this fact lay the single great error which the Chinese made during the evening.

At Tara's word of surrender he bowed slightly.

"You are wise," he commented.

"Do not count your gold before it is minted," she told him coldly. "I go with you, T'Sang Kee . . . but remember that hate walks by my side. And there is no love so strong as the hate of a woman. There is no honey so sweet as the gall of revenge to the woman who dreams of revenge as the damned dream of salvation. The wits of man are as yoked oxen plowing heavily through the fields of thought, turning furrow after furrow. But the wits of women who hate are like wild birds which loom and fade out of the summer sky. So, I warn you, T'Sang Kee Meng, I go with you . . . but hatred of you and of the Tongueless One is my shadow."

"A woman whose mind is red with the mists of love is useless . . . as useless as horns upon a cat or feet upon a fish," T'Sang commented amiably. "Let us go. There is nothing here that you need take."

"There is nothing here that I need," the girl said tonelessly. "Let us go."

She flung a glance at the rigid form of Dale . . . a glance in which was mingled many things . . . and then turned toward the door. And stopped short.

"Your pledge," she said quietly.

"He will awaken when you are in the house of the Master," T'Sang responded.

The girl flared angrily.

"I keep my pledges. Either you awaken him now. . . or I do not go."

The Mongol made a faint gesture (it might have been resignation) and moved closer to Dale, placing his hand upon his shoulder, his eyes fixed intently upon the other's.

"T'Sang bids you awake," he commanded.

And then his error bore fruit.

Dale awoke. His left hand snapped up and seized the Mongol's wrist . . . at almost the same instant that his right hand landed squarely upon the man's chin . . . a short chopping blow swinging up in an arc that not even the hardest chin could resist. And it floored T'Sang.

"That," Dale said thoughtfully, "gave me more pleasure than anything else I've ever done in my life. I guess that stops him."

"Would you scoop up the sea in a cup . . . or halt the stars in their course, Mr. Reynolds?" a quiet voice from the doorway said.

They whirled.

Standing just inside the doorway was a tall Chinese with a square, expressionless yellow face. In the downflung rays of the electric light, Dale could see that he looked out upon the world from hooded eyes in which rested a hint of sadness. A man who might have checked a royal progress. There was evidence of majesty about him, but nothing whatever forbidding in his whole surroundings. His quiet, mellow voice gave Dale a picture of deft fingers inlaying a mosaic; thoughts chosen with care and spoken as though filtered through many translations before they left his tongue in English.

Dale's temper thrust up like the frosted edge of a blade.

"Who are you?" he demanded bluntly.

"What matter if the knife fall on the melon, or the melon on the knife, the result is the same," quoted the man. "However, if my name will be of assistance to you, it is Lai Chung, and my race is Mongolian."

A little gasp came from the girl.

"Prince Lai Chung," she said, taking a step or two closer.

A little numbed wonder was rising in her heart. The Keeper of the Secrets of the Ancient Ones . . . the leader of those from whom the Tongueless One had stolen his knowledge . . . the man whose powers had freed her from the chains of Chu-Sheng's mind once before . . . here . . .

The man inclined his head with a slow smile and then said gently:

"Will you inform your husband that he need have no fear of me?"

The girl turned toward Dale, but there was a curiously speculative look in her eyes.

"Prince Lai Chung," she said quietly, "is the one man in the world upon whose word you can rely implicitly . . . and the one man in the world whom the Tongueless One fears."

"The Tongueless One has no fear of me as a man," the Prince corrected her. "Only a fear of the things for which I stand."

His glance flickered toward T'Sang Kee who had groped his way to a chair and now sat there, immovable. Not a feature moved. His wrists were unbound but he had crossed them and held them as if they were bound. He hardly seemed to breathe. He did not blink. He did not so much as glance at the others. He was like a dead man at a feast.

Then the Prince turned back to the girl, spoke to her in swift, staccato accents. She listened quietly, answered him once, and then, bowing assent to whatever it was that he said, turned, and with a swift movement had crossed the room and reached the door of the sitting room.

She turned toward Dale.

"I must go," she announced calmly.

"Go? Where?" he demanded.

"I have pledged myself to the Tongueless One," she explained, "and I must keep my pledge."

It seemed to him that the Tara he beheld was an absence rather than a presence. She seemed to have returned to another world. Aloof, her hands hanging loosely at her sides, her spirit seemed untroubled, secured by distance.

Her words set playing some emotion that he had not known before. He tried to analyze, as he talked, the tumult of his emotions toward her . . . this new and bewildering force in his life which threatened to sweep him from his known moorings. Despite the mystery which enveloped her (or possibly because of it) and the indisputable fact that she was deeply concerned in it, she seemed to him a kind of symbol of all the youthful loveliness in the world.

"But a promise made under such circumstances doesn't have to be kept. It isn't valid."

"A pledge is a pledge," she said steadily. "I must go."

Anger streaked through him, and his lower lip folded slowly across his upper.

"Don't let this man influence you," he implored. "I don't know what his object is, but, believe me, he is wrong."

Tara looked at him. There was resignation in that look, and the courage of conviction in her voice.

"A promise must be kept, regardless of the risk . . . or of the consequences," she said slowly.

"I won't let you go," he stormed.

She smiled, a mirthless, sad little smile.

"You can't prevent me." Her voice was as passionless as fate, as if the single phrase were a calm statement of premeditated fact.

She turned and walked from the room, head high, a brave tragic little figure in her frail negligee.

It is a strange thing how a single word or a single gesture can change a person's previous opinion of another. All his previous ideas of Tara's strength, her independence, her unconquerable powers came crashing about his ears. He saw her now, pitifully young, and pitifully inadequate in the face of a desperate situation. Not an Amazon ready to battle and match wits and strength with gods or men . . . just a woman licked by her own pledged word . . . desperately in need of help . . . a brave but defenseless young Daniel walking calmly into the lion's den. Suddenly he wanted to protect her, to hold her close. In one blinding flash he knew that he was in love with her. He knew that he had loved her from the moment he saw her there upon the stage in the night club, but until then he had not realized it. The discovery shocked him into action.

He rose and reached for his clothes.

"Where are you going?" the Prince asked gently.

"After my wife."

He started forward . . . and halted instantly. It was as if a gigantic hand had been placed against his chest . . . had pushed him so that he sank back into a chair, although the Prince had not stirred from his position in the center of the room.

"Wait," the Prince said quietly. "First, there are things to find out."

"There is no time to be lost," Dale insisted.

"Life is long . . . and there are many things to be done before the priest burns prayers above your coffin," the Prince advised him. Then he said more gently: "Nothing can be accomplished without faith."

For a long breathless moment the East and West stared across a racial gulf. The Prince did not speak for what seemed an interminably long time and there was an air of almost unsupportable weariness as he gazed across at Dale. There were ridged lines in his forehead and a sense of strain about his body, as though kept tautly in leash.

Then he continued quietly:

"I am about to try an experiment, Mr. Reynolds. An experiment that may be fraught with incalculable danger for us, because I may bring into play forces that even I cannot control. But there are certain things that I must know . . . and I can find them out in only this way."

"More mystery," Dale said wearily.

"Everything that we do not understand is a mystery," the Prince answered gravely. "It is an inexplicable mystery to a dog why a man throws him a bone . . . but the man understands."

He turned toward the motionless figure of T'Sang Kee Meng in the chair; stopped directly in front of him.

"I think," he said softly to the motionless figure of T'Sang, "that it is you who will provide the solution of our mystery for us."

Chapter Seventeen

T'SANG'S EYES OPENED SLOWLY, almost as if they were opening against their owner's will. And then . . .

Hurling himself clear of the chair, he seized a massive vase upon the table and lifted it to brain the Prince.

The thing was so heavy, and the arm of the Prince, raised to intercept it, would have been mashed to pulp had it struck.

Yet it was the hand of the Prince . . . smooth, soft palm upward . . . that met the full force of the blow, arrested it midway . . . a hand that looked as if it could not lift the vase, let alone resist it. And he said one word in a language that Dale did not recognize, a word that seemed to stiffen the prisoner again from head to foot, so that he stood transfixed with the heavy thing in his hand arrested in mid-motion.

"Now sit down," the Prince said quietly, switching into English, and T'Sang Kee put down the heavy vase and seated himself like a man in a dream.

"He imprisons himself," the smooth, even tones of the Mongol Prince flowed on, as the man's face settled into an immovable mask. "You see before you the embodiment of fear and not the slightest need of it. He is self-hypnotized. He is afraid with a fear that is within him . . . that he has cultivated in himself . . . that he has used to govern others. Dynamite could hardly loosen it. Yet that is the very thing that will guide his mind into the channel I wish."

His outstretched hands brushed the man's eyes as delicately as the touch of a butterfly's wings . . . brushed them again and again as he spoke . . . first down and then across with the gentlest of patterns before the man's staring gaze . . .

"T'Sang Kee . . . all forms are only temporary . . . illusions of the flesh . . . you are asleep . . . T'Sang Kee . . . you are asleep . . . you are throwing off the shackles of the mind of the Accursed One . . . you are forgetting the illusions . . . you are asleep, T'Sang Kee . . . you are asleep."

The man did not seem to hear at first, but finally his body began to relax and Dale, watching, saw some of the tense look fade from his face. His eyelids began to droop.

"You are asleep," Prince Lai went on, his voice low and gentle, yet, to Dale, it was as if the man were filled with some kind of elemental force that was inexhaustible . . . force that was pouring out upon the Chinese before him in a great overwhelming stream . . . tearing at the frail veil of human resistance . . . rending it into fragments . . . sending subtle roots down deep, to tap that mysterious store of emotions which lies buried beneath the consciousness. "You are asleep . . . asleep . . . asleep . . . T'Sang Kee . . . asleep . . . asleep . . ."

The man's eyes closed. He seemed asleep.

"Sleep has you in its embrace, T'Sang Kee," the Prince went on. "You will sleep until I bid you wake."

The man's lips moved. He murmured, "I am asleep. I will sleep until you bid me wake."

"You must answer my questions," the Prince went on.

"I must answer your questions," the monotonous voice answered.

"Why does the Accursed One wish Hing Mee-Yin, the flute girl?"

"For me," came the whispered response.

"Why for you?" went on the Prince's voice insistently.

Dale strained forward.

"That through us may be founded a dynasty that shall rule the earth," T'Sang said hesitantly.

"Why has he selected the two of you?" came the Prince's question.

"Because in us is the mingling of the East and the West. . . and because I am his son."

For a moment the last phrase seemed suspended in the air. It was as though each one in the room repeated it, echoing it again and again against some distant mountain of understanding.

The Prince straightened up slowly. He did not start, but he gave the impression of one tremendously and profoundly impressed. Not so much as a muscle quivered in his impassive, pale-bronze face, but into his eyes came almost a look of fear. Something that was lurking terror coiled in the depths of those eyes and rendered them stony, glassy, shallow. It was as if a curtain had been drawn across them from within, hiding anything that might be disclosed to an observer, leaving only that suggestion of terror, of fright, imprinted upon the retina.

Then the low rich voice of the Prince began again, going on endlessly like smoothly flowing water.

"But you . . . you are of the Living Dead."

"No," came the slow, hesitant answer. "I have not been bathed in the rays of the Lamp . . . nor will I be . . . but *she* will be . . . on the eve of our wedding, so that never again can she leave me or the Master."

His voice broke off, trailed away to a whisper difficult to catch. Dale was conscious of a chill breath of air surging past him. For a moment he had the sense of feeling something huge and shapeless and irremediably evil as it brushed by him . . . a presence that was beyond description and vision filling the room. Trembling chills, icy-cold, ran up his spine.

Then the Prince leaned closer and spoke again.

"Sleep. . . sleep. . ." he urged the man in the chair. "You cannot awaken. When will the ceremony of the Lamp take place?"

"I cannot answer . . ." the words came out jerkily, as if by a tremendous effort.

"I order you to talk . . . You *must* answer."

"I . . . cannot," came the slow, laborious voice . . . and then came the thing that capped the climax of the whole series of events . . . the impossible coming to pass . . .

T'Sang's body suddenly shook and strained as though tremendous impulses were moving within him . . . little beads of sweat stood on his brow.

And coincident with it, Dale had that queer impression of a cold wind blowing across him . . . a chill that struck through clothes and flesh to the very bones.

The Mongol strained forward suddenly in his chair . . . strained horribly, terribly . . . dropped back again.

And from his half-opened lips came the voice of a different person.

"Chu-Sheng will," the voice said, and Dale knew that he had never heard, and would never hear again a voice charged with such tremendous sinister evil. "O arrogant Prince of the Mongols . . . Keeper of the Secrets of the Ancient Ones that are secrets no longer—Chu-Sheng will answer your question . . . The Tongueless One will answer through the lips of his son . . . To-morrow night Hing Mee-Yin, the flute girl, will be bathed in the rays of the Lamp of Life . . . and not all your knowledge Keeper of the Secrets, can prevent her becoming the bride of the son of Chu-Sheng."

And then. . . anti-climax.

It was neither a shriek nor a scream that came from between the lips of the son of Chu-Sheng, but from some vague region in between. It was high and wild, yet it had a vowel sound in it, a blat, that smote the ear rather than stabbed it. It was not a cry of anger, so much as triumph . . . of strange and maniacal triumph. It spouted up, a terrible geyser of sound . . . and Dale knew instinctively that it came from the throat of a man who could utter no other sound.

Chapter Eighteen

MORE THAN HALF AN HOUR had passed since that terrifying moment when a man who had no tongue had spoken through the lips of his son. In that half hour T'Sang Kee had been waked from his hypnotic trance, released, and had fled like some evil thing into the night.

The anxiety that was seething within Dale cast his features in a mold of grim resolution. Like the agony of scalding water on an open wound was the knowledge of the fact that she had sacrificed herself to save him. Impatience at the Prince's delay in searching for her finally burst out in an angry flare.

"Only a little while ago you hoodwinked me into permitting my—my wife—to walk out of that door . . . God knows why I did it. I must have been out of my mind. But there's still time to stop her before she reaches this madman."

The protective instinct, in varying degrees a part of every love, possessed him. If only there was a way . . . any way at all . . . to shield her from the danger into which she was stepping. To think she . . . an hour ago . . . had held safety in her hands and had thrown it away . . . for him. Like a chord of poignant sweetness the thought brought a lump into his throat and a momentary frostiness before his eyes.

"My friend," the Prince said quietly, "you must realize that you are pitting yourself against something, the evil depths of which you have no conception; you are fighting a man who combines a mastery of mental science with a knowledge of laws of nature to a degree of perfection . . . A man whose evil, diseased mind has twisted these laws . . . meant originally for the good of the world . . . to uses never before dreamed of by the men from whom they sprang."

"The whole damn thing hasn't any meaning for me," Dale returned. "I'm not afraid of the occult. There's no such thing to me. Whatever happens . . . happens. There is a natural and logical explanation for it, whether you know that explanation or not. We've got concrete facts to deal with. To save me from something that she thought threatened me, my wife has returned to the man she hates . . . a man who holds some sort of hypnotic control over her . . . and I'm going to find that man and set her free if I have to kill him."

"How will you find him?" inquired the Prince.

For a moment Dale was nonplused. He faced the facts squarely. Refusing to see them made them no less real . . . or less hopeless.

"I don't know," he admitted. "Go to the police would be the best thing, I suppose."

"They could find nothing," he said quietly. "As well search for a bird at the bottom of the sea. The police are not fools . . . but even the wisest of them cannot follow a trail on water. And what will you tell them? . . . That a man has died before your eyes, willed to death by the mind of the girl you wish them to seek? No . . . before you even came near the place where your wife is held she would have been bathed in the rays of the Lamp . . . be numbered among the Living Dead who serve the Accursed One. And better that the life be sped from her body than she be numbered among them."

"The Living Dead," Dale echoed.

The same phrase that Tara had used. What cheap trifles, what thin bubbles, words are; a thousand drifting across an idle day, spoken lightly, dropped carelessly here and there, fading away like snowflakes on water . . . and yet reappearing out of the void of the memory to strike with a blow like a cudgel.

The Prince paused and looked across the room. His eyes were filmed, trancelike, and he seemed to be looking inward at the secret growths of his mind.

"My friend," he said finally. "All the knowledge that the world will ever know and has ever known is contained in these books which are hidden in a certain place. They are books whose very alphabet only a handful of men know, written in a language compared to which the oldest known tongue is modern. There are individual books among them that contain more true scientific knowledge than all the works of the modern scientists put together. There are books among them that contain rules for the application of mental knowledge, the general knowledge of which would devastate the world. And among them is the knowledge of how a man may be made to die, yet live."

"I don't believe it," Dale said flatly.

"You saw a snake that did not exist kill a man by its bite," the Prince reminded him gently, and Dale wondered, with a start, how the man could have known this. "You saw a man appear from nowhere and disappear into that nothing from which he came . . . you had a man bind you with the power of his mind more securely than you could have been bound by chains of steel . . . Whether you believe in what I have said or not, these things have happened . . . They are all a part of the knowledge which Chu-Sheng, the Accursed One, has stolen from the Books of Knowledge and turned to his own evil uses . . . Your wife shares a certain part of that knowledge . . . Enough to make of no avail the efforts of Chu-Sheng to make her will subject to his own—but not sufficient to prevent the rays of the Lamp of Life from claiming her as a new recruit to the ranks of the Living Dead."

"What is . . . are . . . the Living Dead?" Dale asked.

"Among the secrets that were stolen from the Keepers of the Secrets by Chu-Sheng," the Prince said quietly, "was the knowledge of a mineral unknown to your scientists—as radium was unknown to them until a comparatively short time ago—whose rays possess the power of destroying life. A person subjected to these rays dies within a certain period of time . . . Dies certainly and surely unless subjected to a counteractive before the period of time expires. That is how Chu-Sheng makes certain that his servants are faithful to him," he went on. "Each of his followers has been bathed in the rays of the Lamp of Life. And he knows that death dogs his heels more closely than his shadow each hour of the day. If he fails to return to the Accursed One within the specified time, death follows surely."

For a moment Dale sat there as if he had been struck; then he came to his feet with a movement astonishingly agile. His eyes took on a queer, luminous glaze.

"Then . . . then Tara . . . he means to—to subject her to these rays?"

The Prince did not answer at once. For several minutes he sat in brooding silence, like a man in tense thought. At last he raised his head and said with slow significance:

"The Accursed One means to make sure that she shall never leave his abode again."

"God!" Dale choked. "Then let's get going. We're wasting precious minutes. We'll never find her by sitting here and talking."

The face of the Prince was immobile. He did not stir.

"Perhaps we will," he said calmly. "Strength can be guided into the grooves of destiny only with the lever of knowledge."

"Damn your platitudes," Dale said furiously. "Will you help me? Or won't you?"

"I *am* helping you," the Prince responded softly. "I have thought while your mind has been tossed on the sea of anxiety. And I think I have found the way. Provided you have the courage and the singleness of heart to follow. I will tell you how your wife may be saved from becoming one of the Living Dead . . . but you must be willing to look unmoved upon things that no man of your race has ever seen before . . . the unveiling of secrets that have been guarded for more thousands of years than you have fingers upon your hands . . . and be willing to run the risk of yourself becoming one of that company that marches through life dead but alive . . . the Living Dead."

"Tell me," Dale said grimly. "I must find my wife."

Chapter Nineteen

IT WAS NEARLY EVENING when Dale and the guide furnished him by Prince Lai Chung reached Chinatown.

The tide of cool spring twilight was rising in slow pools of intangible shadow, breaking in soft waves against the islands of deeper shadow cast by the ancient houses; the night pulse of the city, which is like the pulse of no other city in the world, was picking up its beat of tinsel and tragedy and laughter. The rumble of the "L" was like the beat of distant surf.

The shop before which they finally stopped was swollen and bulbous with merchandise that tumbled across the counter and through the open door, spilling into the street itself in a motley, crazy avalanche. There were bolts of silk and linen and wool; wooden boxes filled with Turkish and Greek sweets: figs in strings and pressed dates, raisins from the Isles of Greece, and brittle, yellow Turkish tobacco, tied up in bundles; pyramids of strange, high-colored vegetables; slippers of flimsy red and orange leather, dried fish and incense in crystal bottles; attar of roses from Bulgaria and oil of jessamine and geranium in slim bottles picked out with gold leaf; carved walking sticks from Saigon; inlaid tortoise shell from Ceylon; black and white veils, heavy with hammered silver and gold, and rugs from many lands.

The place seemed prosperous and prosperous too seemed the youngish Chinese merchant who stood in the doorway, hands in pockets, contentedly puffing at a fat cigar. Peaceful he looked and rosy and well fed; pleased with himself, his neighbors and the world in general. Only a man well versed in the Orient would have suspected that an immediate ancestor of this placid merchant had once worn the coral button.

The two men, the guide and the merchant, looked at one another swiftly; a quick, veiled lightning flash of understanding that Dale caught as he studied them under half-closed lids. A quick low word in the sonorous Chinese of the Manchus with the rounded syllables of Pekín, and they entered the store.

A screen in one corner masked a doorway; a screen of jade-green and pigeon-gray on which the brush of an artist long dead had traced in glowing colors the marvels of some city now forgotten beneath the blowing sands of the Gobi. A strange and rare treasure for a shopkeeper of Chinatown to have in his shop.

Passing behind it, Dale's guide opened the door and motioned him through. They passed through several rooms until finally they reached a brick wall that barred further progress. A pressure of the hand upon one of the bricks, and a section of the wall swung outward, disclosing a passage that led downward into darkness so deep that the voice of his guide bidding him enter seemed to come from another world. Then the light of an electric torch wavered upon damp walls; upon mud underfoot. Cold, earthy odors fouled the air.

Before they had proceeded far, loose rocks rattled underfoot and Dale, glancing down, saw that he was treading upon chips and small particles of stone.

His guide answered the unspoken thought in his mind.

"The Tongueless One knows naught of this passage," he said. "Only the Keepers of the Secrets and those whom they wish to know, such as yourself, are aware of its existence."

The tunnel continued its gradual downward course for what Dale calculated must be at least three hundred feet. If he judged right they must be somewhere near the street on the further side of the block. Suddenly the subterranean corridor made a series of turns, then sloped upward, running straight after that and bringing them at length into a cellar. The smell of oil hung in the air and Dale identified it with the iron-bound door at one side. The guide fumbled at the formidable portal, and; following a grating noise, it swung soundlessly on well-oiled hinges. The torchlight impinged upon the darkness of a stairway.

Near the top of the stairway the guide halted and directed the light upward. It swept another door at the very head of the stairs; the lines where it fitted into place on either side were scarcely visible.

"From here on you go alone," the guide whispered. "It is a double door. The inner one . . . this one . . . opens inward. The other is apparently not a door but a tapestry backed with a panel of wood and mounted upon a frame. You must be careful that no one is in sight when you open it. And remember! There are many corridors, but only one is safe. *To wander from the correct path is death.*"

He swung the inner door open noiselessly. A smooth panel of wood confronted them. A touch upon its frame and it swung outward, half an inch or so. Dale peered through, then swiftly pushed it open further, stepped through and then swung the panel back so that it remained open about an inch.

An atmosphere outlives the man who made it. It is easy to feel lawless in a pirate's den . . . brave and determined between decks in a ship that has just won a battle. It was easy to feel, there in that room, that it was the door to the impossible, and that therein all things waited for accomplishment by him who dared and knew. There was a sense of being in the very womb of faultless destiny.

Nervously he felt for the little tube in his inner pocket. It was still there.

The place was in darkness, such utter darkness that the senses were almost swallowed by it . . . and the atmosphere of the place seemed to strike him like a blow in the face. It was surcharged with the presence of that which is forever unsaid. There was silence, an aboriginal empty silence, as of life withheld . . . that silence of the tomb that precedes the advent of evil. It inspired a creeping chill of fear in Dale.

He switched on the electric torch; flashed it upward . . . and looked into the eyes of death . . . of (had he but known it) of Kali . . . of the Goddess of Destruction . . . into the eyes of Siva's bloody bride. One of her four arms reached out toward him from the darkness.

Living snakes (or so they appeared in that light) encircled her hair like the tresses of Medusa, writhing as if in torment. Skulls, that might have been of children or manufactured—there was no telling in that light—rattled faintly like dry gourds on a rope about her shoulder. There was a faint smell, not exactly of a charnel house, but something that suggested blood about the statue.

With a shudder he moved the light further on. Another statue. The three-eyed Tibetan God of Thunder. And still further on another. The entire wall seemed to be lined with them, each life size, and each inset into a niche in the wall.

Satisfied that he would recognize the statue that guarded the hidden door, he turned away. And as he did so he gained an impression of vastness and gloom and many indistinguishable objects. From somewhere out in the gloom that confronted him came a faint sighing noise, like a faint wind under dried leaves . . . or the whisper of silk trailing upon a polished floor.

Swiftly he snapped off his torch. Listened intently. Was it man or beast? He dared not look to see. If he were discovered now, at the beginning of his search, all would be lost.

There was something sinisterly significant . . . a devil's portent . . . in the sound. He could not free himself from the thought as he groped his way, step by step, across the vast space, listening every now and then for a sound that might betray the presence of another person or give him a hint of their whereabouts.

Had he known the source of that noise it is doubtful if he would have gone forward. Could his eyes have pierced that gloom he would probably have fled in helpless, headlong terror. But the darkness was kind. It cloaked the source of the sound and he went on.

It is a curious thing that a man in a mask is generally a coward. Similarly, stealing through the dark saps the nerves of even the bravest of men, and now, as Dale groped his way in the silence that lay over this place, teeming with the gray ghosts of dead centuries, the suspense became almost unendurable. The very silence seemed to ache with it. He felt an insane desire to shout or send a volley of shots cannonading about the walls. He could feel the sweat trickle down over his face and hands. But he still moved forward under the looming crests of that awful silence which seemed to gather and build on itself like a great wave that rises and rises until the crash of its finally overtoppling walls spells the sheerest music of relief.

His destination was three tiny points of light on the further side. Three lights, he had been told, each one of which marked a corridor, one of which would lead him to Tara, the other two to death. Slowly he made his way across the room, afraid to use his flashlight (and never knew that his fear saved him from a horrible death) until he reached a dark opening above which a tiny pinpoint of steady light burned. He stepped across the threshold, felt his way along the wall until his trailing fingers touched a doorway.

Cautiously he opened it, and, feeling again for the tiny vial in his pocket, figuratively gave himself into the hands of his kismet.

He stood upon the threshold of a little alcove on the further side of which a passage opened up again. In a niche of the wall of the alcove a light gleamed, and in the passage he could see another light burning. They were steady, unwinking globes of light that burned without any sign of fuel atop a tiny tripod of metal. The three legs of the tripod were elaborately carved and decorated. It was a thing that looked at once very ancient and very modern. The pattern and decoration of the tripod were archaic beyond belief. But the lights . . .

He stopped short, as if halted by a gigantic hand. On his finger was a diamond set in soft gold . . . the ring which Prince Lai had placed upon his hand. And it was glowing vividly, even when he held up his hand so that the diamond was in shadow. The stone seemed to glitter as if on fire.

Hastily he stepped back and closed the door.

In bold relief in his mind were the words of the Prince:

"There are three corridors that lead from the temple. They are lighted with lamps of identical design. Two of them carry death in their rays . . . they are the rays that make of you a member of the Company of the Living Dead. The third is harmless."

Only a diamond could distinguish the presence of the deadly rays, the Prince had said. The rays made it fluoresce. Nothing else would. And he knew that he stood in the presence of death.

Softly he tried the second of the passageways. It was identical, even to the intricate designs on the legs of the tripod. But the diamond did not glow. He knew that the passage was safe.

The corridor was short, hardly more than fifty feet. At its further end a flight of stairs led upward. He mounted them; pushed tentatively upon the door at their top, and stepped through into the hallway into which it opened . . . and stopped short.

From somewhere came a faint pulsation of sound . . . the sound of Tara's voice chanting the song that he had heard that night in the Silver Slipper. Following it he advanced guardedly down the narrow, uncarpeted hallway.

His search was rewarded by a narrow pencil of light beneath a door. There could be no mistake about it; the room behind that door was lighted, and from behind it the voice of Tara was coming.

And then . . . the sound of a footfall approaching around the turn of the corridor.

Chapter Twenty

DALE'S MIND MOVED in certain channels with the speed and precision of infinite experience. There was only one thing to do. He did it. Without a moment's hesitation he opened the door, slipped through it and closed it behind him. At the sound of the closing door the girl looked up slowly, unwilling, as though she dreaded the sound. Dale's uplifted hand checked her voice and then he indicated the slow footsteps in the corridor outside.

Tara looked whiter than ever, delicate as a carved rock-crystal tree. She stood where she had risen from her chair, her back against a tall, three-paneled screen, with her hands pressed flat on either side against the taut silk. She looked like a flower straightening up after rain, like a dead woman come to life.

Both waited tensely until the sound in the corridor died away. Then Dale crossed the room swiftly to her; took her hands in his.

"Oh, why did you do it?" she asked despairingly, her voice dropping to a low whisper, a frail sound that struck into Dale's heart like a thin knife because of the poignant quality it held.

"Because I love you," he said softly, taking her hands in his.

And, although he did not realize it, never before had he been so naked of heart and soul and spirit. His face, for the moment unguarded, held the answer to the eternal question of defeated understanding. Before that look her own eyes dropped. When she raised them again and spoke, her voice was as soft as a gentle April shower . . . a voice that slurred over its notes.

"Oh, my dear," she said quietly, raising his hand to her cheek, "it was wonderful of you to come. But you shouldn't have risked it. I don't know how you got in, but you'll never get out again."

"We'll both get out," he assured her. "I know the way. Just trust me, won't you?"

"I do trust you," she said somberly. Her eyes looked straight ahead, strangely steady eyes in a strangely unsmiling face . . . the face of a woman who looked as if she were paying dearly for the privilege of being alive. "But it is all so useless. And even if we did get out, what would be the use? It would only be the same weary battle over again and again until we were compelled to give in."

"Trust me," he repeated again confidently. Precious time was passing. At any moment someone might enter the room, give the alarm. "Don't think about anything else but getting out of here. Let the future take care of itself."

"You must go," she repeated wearily. "Every moment is precious. It would be fatal if he found you here. Perhaps—perhaps I can come later."

"I won't leave without you," Dale said stubbornly. "If you stay . . . I stay. And whatever happens to you is going to happen to me. You forget," and his voice was edged with tenderness, "that I said I love you."

And then tears came into her eyes. Her hands freed themselves from his clasp and went blindly, flutteringly up toward his face, as if to reassure herself by the magic of touch that what he said was indeed true. And the look she gave him resembled the sudden trembling of a bed of white phlox under the moonlight, heavy with rain and sweetness. Then she relaxed against him, and it seemed to Dale that he had never seen such exhaustion. It was as if she had been holding herself upright by sheer force of will, all strength being gone from her body.

"I'll do whatever you say," she whispered. "We will go together, make our fight together, and whatever happens to us will happen to us together."

He took her arm gently. "Let's get going," he urged.

He took her back, cautiously, the way that he had come, carefully avoiding the wrong corridors. . . mechanically the turns had registered on his mind . . . one to the left . . . two to the right . . . and so on. Everything was deathly still. They dared not speak or show a light. But Dale was confident. He had found his wife. In another moment they would be free of this place and all the sinister horror that hung over it.

They had reached the long hall with its life-sized statues and were groping their way stealthily toward the secret panel at the far end when suddenly the place was flooded with light . . . an emerald light . . . ghastly . . . weird . . .

Chu-Sheng stood in their path.

Behind him stood the man who acted as his interpreter, flanked by two armed Chinese.

Came silence; silence that floated like a balloon of evil anticipation, that lunged forward like a beast of prey about to pounce and tear. And in that silence Dale could feel the dark, secret thrill that poured forth from the man like the electric tingle that fills the air before a thunderstorm breaks. For an instant he was paralyzed and trembling chills played up and down his spine.

Chu-Sheng was clad in a long robe of dull black, Imperial tribute silk, had Dale but known it . . . the gift of a governor of a province to a sovereign. It was shot with curious designs in gold thread. The slanting eyes of the man were riveted on Dale's face with the lidless, unwinking stare of a serpent. It was as if his face had been carved out of some yellow, fire-hardened wood. But for all the age that was evidently his, his movements were as light and as smooth as a cat's.

From the lips of the girl came a low, despairing cry, and she flung herself in front of him as if to protect Dale from the gaze of the Chinese.

"You shan't harm him," she choked.

That slim ivory hand flashed up, the slender fingers writhing a message and Chu-Seng's features, ivory-yellow as old parchment, curled in a slow, flat smile. Dale knew then that he could read lips.

The girl took a single step forward as Chu-Sheng's hand finished its message and dropped to his side.

"No," she answered clearly. "The answer is no, and no it will be so long as there is a single spark of life in my body. Bathe me in the rays of the Lamp of Life, if you will . . . make me one of the Company of the Living Dead . . . even place me before the altar and let the Living Dead begin the Chant of Death . . . and my answer will still be no. I will never become the wife of T'Sang Kee."

She might as well have uttered the words to something sardonic, without nerves, without heart, without soul; alive, but having none of the attributes of life.

Chu-Sheng's hand flashed up, the fingers twisting and writhing like serpents whose backs have been broken, and the girl's face turned white as she interpreted the message. Dale knew, instinctively, that it referred to him.

"What is he saying?" he demanded. His voice was flat, dry, bitter . . . but unfearful.

A thought was evolving in his mind. He did not capture it wholly; say, rather, the thought cast a shadow across his mind, was gone, returned with doubled intensity.

"He says," choked the girl, "that to-night at eight o'clock I shall hear the Chant of Death . . . and that I shall have the right to change my mind at any time before . . . before I die . . . and that after I die . . . you, too, shall hear the Chant of Death . . . and meet the Death that it summons forth."

"Can't you stall him off . . . gain time?" he whispered tensely. They would search him. But if only that search was not too thorough.

She shook her head. "One cannot lie to the Tongueless One," she said.

Suddenly his temper thrust up like the edge of a frosted blade.

He straightened up. "Then tell him to go to hell for both of us," he flung out.

And now the thought that had been working in his mind lay crystal clear before him. A plan, desperate, almost impossible . . . and yet . . . Powerful though Chu-Sheng might be, there was one power stronger even than all of the secrets of the Ancient Ones that he had stolen.

If only he might be given the chance to utilize it!

Chapter Twenty-one

DALE WAS MARCHED out of the room by two Chinese guards, down a corridor and then along another cross-corridor. A heavy door shut with strident clamor behind him. He saw neither lock nor bolt as he entered, and, after waiting for several minutes, he tried the door—a purely perfunctory act. To his surprise it swung back . . . and showed him, in the gloom of the corridor, two armed Chinese.

He turned back to the room. His was the despair of a gambler who has plunged, who perceives defeat for himself in the first hand and after that plays without hope, with only the will to hope.

For a long time he sat motionless as a graven image except for an occasional glance at his watch. The germ of his idea was beginning to crystallize in his brain. At first it had startled him by its sheer daring, then had fired his imagination, quickened his blood and taken possession of him. But he knew that his decision must not depend upon impulse. He was brooding upon it now with the patient care of a hen hatching a long egg. His mind was charting every inch of the course, every possibility of success, every danger of failure.

There were two uncertain factors which must be explored. Either of them would spell failure to his plans. And his only weapon was the tiny hope which was glowing in his heart . . . a slim weapon with which to fight a more cunningly armed opponent.

He returned to his seat to wait . . . wait for the hour that preceded eight o'clock. A supreme restlessness ruffled his blood; it irked him to sit there passively awaiting a chance which might never come. Yet to move now, sacrificing all his patient endeavor to the urge tormenting him, was to steep his act in folly. Yet, with all this reviewed in his mind, it was hard to hold himself in check, for he knew that unless he could act swiftly, in that one hour that preceded the advent of doom, his only chance, slim as it was, would be finished. As the minutes dragged by his nerves underwent a gradual disintegration. Anxiety, mental and physical weariness . . . they were the destroying forces. He walked the floor . . . it was exquisite torture, this waiting; something inquisitorial about it. He fled from it, in thought, to Tara, as a persecuted worshiper to the healing coolness and quiet of a cathedral nave.

The thought of her was like something remote and beyond reach, something dim as a dream . . . and beyond her the memory of that phrase which had shimmered from Chu-Sheng's brain to hers, like a baby spot upon a stage . . . the Chant of Death . . . what could it mean . . .? It had an ominous sound that fitted in perfectly with the things that had gone before . . . Was it some new form of torture . . .? His mind shrank from the thought.

As the luminous hands of his watch approached seven o'clock he walked to the door and swung it open. The two men on guard in the corridor straightened up.

"I wish to send a message to Chu-Sheng," he said.

"I will take it," one of the men answered, with only the slightest trace of accent.

"Tell him," he said, "that I yield. That if he will release me, I will tell him how he may make Miss Travers do as he wishes."

The man bowed and slipped away down the corridor.

Dale retreated to his room. A few moments later the door opened. A hand beckoned to him. Between the two armed men he left the room and descended to the lower floor. Almost exultantly, as they traversed corridor after corridor, Dale thought that he was getting into a position to get somewhere at last. Then one of the men threw aside a black curtain that veiled a door and motioned Dale to enter.

He stood there for half a moment staring into the fretwork of delicate purple and heliotrope shadows that cloaked the room like a silken veil. His chance had come. But if the gods denied him luck the game was up.

Crossing the threshold of that room was like passing from the twentieth century into a vanished era.

Chu-Sheng sat in a great carved chair at the foot of a tall pedestal of ebony and nacre which supported a great Tibetan incense bowl. Heavy smoke clouds floated and twisted about it like a vaporous, gigantic furnace of opal colors wreathing up to the ceiling, with a hot, honey-sweet scent of lilies and lotus buds and sandalwood, and it seemed to Dale, standing there on the threshold of the room, as if he were standing on the borderline of dim, half-forgotten things, on the frontier of a new life . . . new, yet, somehow, subconsciously remembered . . . which was remote, not in years nor in distance, but in principles of civilization, from the life, the personal experiences, the very physical and psychical reactions he had known heretofore . . . as if the gaunt black figure in the chair were a finger pointing the way to a life of To-morrow beside which his life of Yesterday and To-day faded to a wretched and meaningless dream.

It was like a rush of giant splendor that threatened to over-whelm his mind, his sober, prosy, saving occidental common sense and prejudices . . . and then, out of the trooping shadows came the gentle, purring voice of the man who acted as the inter-preter of the Tongueless One.

"The Master bids you enter."

Dale entered. The heavy black curtain swung to behind him, and Dale had the odd sensation that their swinging folds were cut-ting him off from everything in the life that he had known.

"The Master bids you speak," the gentle purring voice went on.

Fishing a cigarette from his pocket he stuck it into the corner of his mouth, and struck a match. The flame did not tremble as he lighted the cigarette. Across it, as he drew the first few puffs, he looked at the black-robed figure.

"I speak to Chu-Sheng alone," Dale said softly. "What I have to say is something that no other human being shall know. I do not need an interpreter. But first ask him if what I tell him is satisfac-tory . . . if through it he succeeds in persuading Miss Travers to yield to his wishes . . . then shall I be released?"

Those twisting fingers flashed up with a question.

"The Master wishes to know why you are willing to tell him this."

"Because I am not a fool . . . because I know when I am de-feated," Dale answered. "There is no sense in dying, just for the sake of dying. Shall I be released?"

The black-clad figure read the words on Dale's lips and bowed assent.

"Unharmed?" Dale insisted.

Chu-Sheng stared at him a long time, so long that it seemed as if he had been turned to an idol of black and yellow stone with malevolent eyes of jet. Then, with an almost imperceptible nod of his head, he gave assent.

"Then get out," Dale said to the interpreter.

He knew that the last supreme moment of balance had come. In another minute he would know whether he would ever see the sunlight striking down through Manhattan's canyons . . . would know whether Tara and himself faced life together . . . or death.

The interpreter shot a look of inquiry at the silent figure of his master, received an almost imperceptible gesture of assent. Getting to his feet he crossed the room and lifted an oblong panel of embroidery which hung against the wall. Dale noted with quickened interest that the tapestry veiled a door.

Once it closed behind the interpreter, he shot a quick look about the room. Save for the pedestal and its bowl, and a small table on which lay a hooded ceremonial bowl of black, there were no other furnishings.

Then he turned back to the man in the carved chair and found himself looking into black pools that were shutting him off from anything else; that threatened his mind and composure. The eyes grew larger, became enormous and bizarre. Dale knew that he must face those eyes . . . that to drop his own might give the man an inkling of the truth—that he was lying—and yet he knew that it was necessary not to let those eyes submerge him for a single instant . . . knew that once his guard was beaten down he was lost. He stared back with gray eyes into which, for the moment, had been caught the clear coldness of a New England winter. But the effort not to flinch made his eyeballs ache. A tenseness seemed to hold the frail body of the deaf-mute and he seemed to grow with this tenseness, to enlarge until Dale could not have said whether he were six feet tall or twelve. It was an illusion, he told himself . . . well, he would throttle the fears that threatened to master him and surmount the barrier of illusion that this man was creating.

He took a step forward . . . another . . . until his hands rested on the edge of the table . . . His mind was reeling from the impact of that other mind. He knew that he could not keep this up . . . that in another moment his mind would falter . . . go down . . . and he . . . and Tara . . . would be lost . . . Already he felt a strange drowsiness creeping over him . . .

Chapter Twenty-two

MEANWHILE: In the hall below, the Company of the Living Dead had begun the Chant of Death.

Rank after rank of kneeling men and women filled the far end of the great room . . . Chinese most of them, but here and there an Occidental . . . sucking in their breath through thin lips, their faces like carved masks, their eyes—those lifeless eyes that held the greenish glow of a cat's in the dark that were the mark of the Living Dead—fixed on a high altar that stood at the far end of the hall . . . and from their lips came the words of a song lost in ancient mystery—a strange off-key chant . . . a chant that was old when Christ was born . . . a song as old as the mysteries of Delphi, and as little understood . . . a chant that rose, imperceptibly, bit by bit, from a sweet whisper, up the scale so gradually that its progress was almost indistinguishable. Under its influence the centuries seemed to be racing backwards on purposeless wings.

There was no light save a green, underwater tinge in which dim shuttles of shadow swam; The sensation was of being in a grotto under water and looking through it toward light shining through the sea outside. There was nothing about it to understand. It stripped incomprehension naked and left it aware of itself.

On either side of the altar stood a tall Chinese clad in black. A slim, keen knife gleamed in the hands of each man.

A note of drumbeats had come into the chant, although there were no drums visible. Subtly the chant strengthened and rose, following the increased violence of the drums, until one could almost see the toppling of a hundred centuries in the space of an instant, could visualize the years falling like a house of cards before the attack of that rising chant.

And, in some strange way, the light seemed to rise and fall with the violence of the chant, as the tide follows the drag of the moon. When the chant sank to a low, husky whisper the lights . . . that evil, greenish light . . . flickered and sank like the glow from a million dying fires, and when the chant rose, the light rose with it until it filled the great room like a brimming wine glass.

But always the light seemed strongest about the high altar at the far end of the room. It seemed almost as if the altar glowed from within itself with the evil greenish light, pulsating in rhythm to the beat of the chant; at times it was almost translucent as if the light within were so strong and so fierce as to pierce even the stone of which the altar was made.

The chant wailed and sobbed and ached, carrying with it a subtle rhythm that held nerve-tearing excitations, so that the room was filled with a strain almost unendurable; the strain of a keyed-up violin string that is ready to break.

And at its height a door at the right of the altar was flung open and Tara entered, guarded on either side by a Chinese garbed in black.

She wore a long robe that was like a current of silvery blue, embroidered with trailing silver clouds and sprays of plum blossoms and along the bottom of the skirt was embroidered an endless line of lotus plants of the color of the coral lotus that grows only in the lily pool behind the temple at the First King of Hell on the road to the Ming Tombs. On her head was the traditional jeweled headdress of the Chinese Bride.

At her advent the beat of the chant changed, became slower, heavier, seemed to sink into a deeper, duller key; but the illusion of far-off booming drums strengthened, so that the insistent beat seemed to press outward against the walls. It was as if a deep, hopeless hunger had come into the chant, an unassuageable torment.

Slowly the girl paced her way across the room toward the high altar. Her visage was like sculptured wax, the greenish light giving an illusion of transparency to the flawless skin. Lips, incarnadine.

Her eyes flickered about the room seeking Dale. But he was not in sight.

As she approached the altar there came into the chant a subtle, syncopated undercurrent, gradually growing stronger. Without rising in strength, it seemed to fill the room, holding them all in a dull hypnotism of sound . . . and it was big and thin and crying; so that although the voices had lost none of their timbre, they seemed to be sighing, heartbroken, the age-old victims of unsatisfied desire that was the essence of all pain . . . voices calling . . . urging . . . calling for something to come forth . . . to show itself.

The light—that greenish light—grew and grew until the hall resembled the interior of a great glowing emerald. The altar pulsed and glowed as if green electric fires burned in it. Every eye in the room was fixed upon the altar; united wills concentrated upon one single definite purpose.

Coming through the high, keen sound of the chant, there came now a heavy scraping sound, as of a great bulk being dragged over a floor. The chant rose up and up and up.

And, as the chant rose, from behind the altar a great head reared itself, a huge, diamond-shaped head with immense cruel jaws and a pair of lidless, cold eyes that stared out dispassionately at the throng watching from the darkness of the hall.

Chapter Twenty-three

TARA STARED AT THE HUGE GREEN HEAD in horrified fascination. It was not the first time that she had seen it slowly emerge at the call of the chant that now filled the hall with its broken, whimpering phrases, distilling the essence of fear from the brains of the chanters and spreading it in the room like a palpable mist. But never had she witnessed the consummation of the ceremony. Invariably she had hidden her face in her shuddering hands until the last agonized shriek told her that it was finished. This time, she knew, she would be unable to hide her face. For this time it would be she who would feel those coils tighten about her. This she knew, but never, once had she faltered from her refusal to wed T'Sang Kee Meng.

The head was followed by a huge body that flowed resistlessly to the altar . . . a body thicker than an ordinary barrel and longer than any other reptile she had ever seen.

She was conscious of the fact that the lidless eyes were fixed upon her, and she wrenched her own away. Too many times had she seen someone who occupied the position she now occupied drawn toward those eyes, as empty space draws a giddy man, to the very edge of the precipice.

Slowly the great reptile dragged its length to the altar, coiling itself slowly, with head poised some ten feet above it, weaving back and forth, a forked tongue flickering like lightning as the enormous green mass rippled and heaved.

And still the chant flowed on; seemed to be attempting to call to her like some flying spirit in a storm. It was like a giant canticle of all the hidden and savage forces of nature; terribly symbolic with a brooding evil; without key, without distinct melody . . . the terrifying rhythmic outpouring of something dark and mysterious and evil.

A small platform was being dragged to within a short distance of the altar on either side. She wanted to close her eyes, but could not. She knew the purpose of those platforms.

Now, a guard mounted each of the platforms and from some-where above a rope was lowered above the altar where the snake swung its head back and forth in time to the chant. The man on the right-hand platform, almost beside her, was attaching a bundle of silver-colored cloth to the rope. Finishing his work, he swung the rope across the space, directly in front of the great snake.

As it passed swiftly by the reptile drove at it with its mighty head, its massive jaws open so that one could almost look down into the cavernous throat. But the bundle swung too swiftly by, and the snake missed. It was deftly caught on the far side by the man on the platform and swung back again. Again the huge crea-ture lunged at it and missed, his jaws gaping wide. Back and forth the silver bundle swung until the eyes of the snake were flashing with cold green fire, his heavy coils twisting and writhing angrily.

And then, as if in response to a spoken cue, Chu-Sheng, the deaf-mute, stood in the center of the high platform back of the al-tar. How he had reached there, she could not have told . . . one moment he was not there . . . the next instant he was. The envelop-ing black robe with its cowled hood covered him from head to foot, and the clear emerald light which seemed to stream up from the base of the platform on which he stood, made of him a gigantic black shadow, a thing incredibly sinister.

At his appearance the chant swelled up until it seemed to be licking at the brain with tongues of flame that had the chilling qualities of ice, numbing, freezing with the cold touch of ter-ror . . . rose until it beat against the walls of the room in recurring waves of sound . . . sound that suggested a hidden world of mys-tery and barbarism that was too horrible for words.

For a moment Chu-Sheng stood there . . . remote . . . calm . . . surveying the room and its chanting rows of the Living Dead. Then he flung up his hands in a swift gesture that gave him the appearance of a gigantic bat about to take wing.

The clinging touch of horror, of fear, of terror, grew thicker and thicker about the figures which swayed and flowed to the ebb and flow of the unceasing pulse of sound like a palm tree in the trade winds.

At the movement of Chu-Sheng's hands, Tara's guards sprang forward. She was seized, her wrists bound before she could utter a sound, and carried to the top of the platform beside the altar; the loop of the rope fastened about her waist.

Then she was dragged to the edge of the platform, held on either side by a Chinese who prepared to shove her swinging off into space in front of the gigantic snake.

She gave one last despairing look about her. Dale was nowhere in sight. Then, as the chant rose into its last phase, she closed her eyes and waited for the end.

Chapter Twenty-four

THE CHANT that had been smashing its way against the walls subsided. Its long dying was like the rushing away of vast waters that have broken and destroyed their barriers; all unsatisfied subsidence, full-bodied and insatiable, dying only because the peak of its strength was past.

The girl nerved herself for the swing out into space—and death—that would follow the dying of the chant. And then opened her eyes again at the sound of a soft purring voice calling her name . . . the voice of T'Sang Kee Meng, son of Chu-Sheng.

The tall slim Mongol stood at the foot of the platform. He was clad in the conventional wedding garments of a Chinese of the upper classes.

"Greetings, Little Azalea Blossom," he said conversationally, his voice as calm and as soft as though the girl stood on the threshold of her own home, instead of before the gates of death, and this were a visit of ceremony.

"What now, T'Sang Kee?" she asked, her eyes flickering desperately about the hall. Nowhere in the green gloom could she distinguish Dale. Above the altar where the huge snake was coiled, Chu-Sheng in his long black-hooded robe, stood motionless, silent, immovable as a figure of death.

"One last chance," T'Sang Kee retorted.

"I do not wish it," she flung back at him.

"Death is not easy for one so young," he said. "Think well of the two roads that stand before your feet."

"I prefer the road that leads to the snake to the one that leads to life . . . and you," she said calmly.

The half smile faded from T'Sang Kee's face; there was in his eyes a glow that hid all of the beauty of Buddha that had shone upon the bronze features.

"There is nothing in life that will not be yours," he urged. "You will be Empress of the World. With the power of my father at my back we can conquer the world."

"The world conquered by such means as you possess is the world lost," she flung back at him clearly.

"Take life," he urged. "Life is sweet. Take it as a gift."

"Whose gift?"

"The gift of my father."

"And at what price?" the girl demanded.

"You know the price," T'Sang Kee said gravely.

"It is written," she said slowly, "that we belong to God and we return to him."

Chu-Sheng walked slowly toward the edge of the little platform upon which he stood, looming incredibly tall, incredibly menacing up there in that weird green light.

Sweat stood like beads on T'Sang Kee's brow. His eyes implored her.

"My father grows impatient and the fangs of the serpent are hungry and sharp. Think well, O Little Azalea Blossom. One last chance. Is it life with me? Or death?"

For a full moment silence covered the vast hall like a sheet of ice. Tara's eyes searched the unfathomable eyes of Chu-Sheng's son. She thought of him, and of what life with him would represent. Untold splendor. Untold evil and degradation. And then she thought of Dale. Of Dale, who had failed her . . . Ah, well . . . she threw back her head and her voice rang out, high and clear:

"I choose death."

A shudder, and something akin to a gasp, ran through the huddled forms on the floor.

T'Sang Kee Meng straightened up as one who has received a stinging blow across the face. Hurt pride, chagrin, defeat, lay smoldering in his eyes. He made a futile gesture of resignation.

"So be it then," he whispered, in a voice that scarcely reached her ears, and motioned to the two black-clad figures on either side of the platform on which she stood.

The two guards stepped forward, seized her; watched that black-robed figure there on the platform for a signal.

Slowly that arm beneath its somber covering began to rise. Every eye in the room watched it . . . and then . . . the thing that happened was so swift, so breath-taking that Tara could not believe her eyes.

Miraculously a revolver had appeared in the hand of Chu-Sheng there upon his high platform . . . from it the Tongueless One poured shot after shot into the body of the huge snake coiled upon the altar.

Then the enveloping robe, the hood which had cloaked his face in shadow was cast aside.

It was Dale Reynolds.

He leaped lightly from the high platform to the floor, and his fist crashed against the jaw of one of the guards who stood beside the altar. The man crumpled, and with his right hand Dale seized the long knife as it fell from the guard's nerveless fingers, and in another second he was upon the little platform where the girl stood; had slashed at the bonds which held her wrists; cut loose the rope.

And then, as though it were all part of one single, smooth, flowing movement he had whirled and driven the blade forward in a lightninglike dart at the other guard, piercing his throat.

Pandemonium broke out. Panic ran through the crowd like flames under dead leaves. Where was Chu-Sheng? That was the question in every mind, on every lip.

After the first shock of surprise a frantic call for aid rose from T'Sang Kee's mind. He summoned all his forces, all his resourcefulness, calling his father over and over again. The call was carried to that other brain. But there was no reply, either in deed or thought. No manifestation of Chu-Sheng's mastery, either in physical violence or spiritual forces. In his hour of need his father was failing him.

Meanwhile, Dale, driving at the next guard, felt the point of his weapon strike bone, and heard a scream from the man as he withdrew the steel. At that second he felt a paralyzing grip upon his arm, and turning, he saw a huge Chinese closing in upon him. The pain was excruciating, but somehow, in spite of it, he managed to swing his adversary around toward the front, between himself and the others, and hacked at him with the long knife. The man fought silently, his talonlike fingers gripping for Dale's throat. At that distance the long knife was useless, and he let it clatter to the ground, carrying on the fight with his fists, his feet and his whole body . . . fighting desperately, savagely, smashing again and again with his free arm at his adversary's face, turning and twisting meanwhile to avoid the knife point which one of the guards from the further side of the altar was thrusting at him.

Then, high above the tumult of the crowded room he became aware of a voice, and caught sight of T'Sang Kee. The tall, slender Chinese was evidently urging a mass attack upon Dale and, heartened by his words, a group of men surged forward.

Summoning a reserve of strength Dale swung his adversary in close to him and his fist, swinging up in a long arc, crashed against his chin with all of the weight of his body behind it. The man swayed, shuddered and then crumpled to the floor.

The crowd was closing in, under the lash of T'Sang Kee's tongue, in a great half circle, a thickly packed half circle that stretched from wall to wall. There was no escape. Snatching up the knife he had dropped Dale sprang to the little platform beside Tara.

As he did so the girl flung out her hands in a commanding gesture. She flung one word at them . . . a word in a language that Dale did not recognize . . . and then he caught his breath in astonishment.

Little licking tongues of flame had sprung up all around them, forming a perfect circle. Little flames that crawled along the floor toward the throng of men . . . flames that licked their boots and reached up for their clothing . . . Flames that rose higher with each passing moment and sent up great columns of smoke . . . flames forming a hot, translucent wall between them and the maddened men beyond.

The men in the forefront saw the fire first. Dale watched their agonized eyes sweep around looking for an opening. Heard the throaty whistling gasp that went up from dozens of throats as the flames began slowly to move toward them . . . and then a scream of fear went up and the men in front turned and strove to fight their way back through the rear ranks. The panic spread and in the space of seconds the mass of men was fighting its way through the exits . . . all save one.

T'Sang Kee stood alone in the center of the room, a scornful smile upon his lips. Then he strode forward . . . and the flames gave way . . . vanished at his approach.

From somewhere beneath his robe he had drawn a revolver. He stopped just below the platform, the gun poised in his hand.

"My father was wrong," he said. Each word was separate, as if etched. "He should have killed the two of you at once. But his son will rectify that error."

He raised his gun.

Chapter Twenty-five

DALE EXPLODED LIKE A VOLCANO. One-tenth of a second then would have been plenty for the whole of his plan to go up in smoke. But he was squandering no tenths. His movement was so abrupt, so unexpected that T'Sang had no warning.

Like coiled springs, his legs had launched him into the air, hurling him down at the man standing on the floor beneath him. T'Sang's revolver exploded while he was still in midair, but the bullet went wild, missing him only by the width of the gooseflesh on his shoulder. A second later Dale had landed squarely on his head and shoulders, knocking him to the floor, sending the revolver spinning across the room. Almost instantly both men were on their feet.

Dale wasted no time. Seizing the slim, wiry body of the Chinese he drew it close. T'Sang tried to use his knee viciously, fighting the while for mastery of Dale's hands. No python ever wrapped and unwrapped coiling energy so fast, nor struck so savagely. T'Sang was strength and hate and savagery all compressed into the heart of charged springs. Dale gave way. Then he swung himself against the man, swung one quick hand behind T'Sang's back, and caught the other's exposed chin in an iron grip. T'Sang found his head snapped back abruptly so that his spine threatened to crack. He fought, but helplessly. His back bowed further and further. His breath choked in his throat.

Then, for one unexpected half-second, he was free, completely free. Dale had released his hold. T'Sang sought to regain his balance. But even as he straightened up a terrific blow crashed on his chin, and he crumpled to blank unconsciousness in a heap on the floor.

Dale straightened up . . . and a voice behind him said quietly:

"Well done, Mr. Reynolds."

Dale whirled, on the defensive, then dropped his hands.

Prince Lai stood there, clad in a long orange robe. Behind him was grouped a semicircle of orange-clad men.

Tara gave a little cry and ran down the steps of the platform.

"Prince Lai," she gasped. "I'm so glad you've come."

"I have been here for some time," he said gravely. "And I have not been idle. Other things in other parts of the building needed attention and they could only be done while the occupants were all concentrated here."

He took a deep breath and went on.

"I have destroyed the Lamp of Life."

The tremendous importance of this statement left Tara stunned for a moment.

"You have destroyed the Lamp of Life!" she exulted. "Then I need never again fear becoming a slave to the Lamp—need never again fear joining the Living Dead."

Her face clouded for a moment again.

"Oh, the poor Living Dead."

The Prince inclined his head.

"Better that the Living Dead pass forever from the earth, than remain slaves to the Lamp," he said with a touch of sadness in his voice. "But do not think that while I was off on other missions I had forgotten you. I had two men stationed in this room with guns. If anything had gone wrong they would have used them . . . but, as things turned out—it was not necessary."

"Two men with guns?" Dale asked, a puzzled frown between his eyes. "But surely, two strangers would have been detected and thrown out or killed."

"Hardly likely," the Prince said with a smile. "You see, they are still here, and you have not detected them yourself."

Tara's eyes swept down the long empty room.

"Still here?" she asked incredulously.

The Mongol Prince clapped his hands and gave a command in swift staccato Chinese. From the niches in the wall two of the life-sized statues of gods came to life . . . stepped from their pedestals and climbed to the floor.

The Prince watched the two young people's faces with amusement.

"Just a little trick in camouflage," he explained.

"Wonderful," Tara said.

Dale looked around him, his fingers twitching restlessly.

"This place has gotten under my skin. For God's sake, let's get out of here."

The three walked toward the hidden door, now swung wide open.

Tara turned toward Dale.

"But what has happened to Chu-Sheng?" she demanded. "How

did you take his place?"

Dale could not help looking like a very wise and most superior canary who had reversed matters and eaten the cat.

"He's in his room," he said innocently.

"Locked in there?" the girl asked.

Dale shook his head. "Oh, no. The door is open. But don't worry," he added hastily. "He won't come out."

Tara stopped. "Oh . . . he's dead."

"No," Dale said, "he's not dead."

"But how . . . what did you do?" the girl insisted. "You came out wearing his robe. You took his place on the platform. How did you do it?"

"Chloroform," Dale answered succinctly.

"Chloroform?" Tara repeated in astonishment.

He nodded agreement.

"I had a fragile glass tube of it with me," he amplified. "Thought it might come in handy in overcoming a guard, or some such thing. When the guard searched me he overlooked it. So I managed to get into Chu-Sheng's presence by a ruse . . . crushed the tube in my handkerchief and clamped it over his mouth and nose before he could try any of his tricks. His magic, or whatever it is he uses, can't overcome chloroform."

Tara shuddered. "Come quickly," she urged. "He's liable to come to at any moment."

"You need never fear Chu-Sheng again," the Prince said gravely. "His power to harm you has gone forever."

For a moment it was as if an alien life, an alien existence enfolded him away from the world in an incomprehensible and inhuman quietude.

"What do you mean?" Tara asked breathlessly.

"No man can halt his destiny, and every man's destiny is written upon his forehead from the hour of his birth. If the trend of that destiny is downward, it keeps on going downward to the inevitable end. And I think that Chu-Sheng's destiny has reached the end of its downward path. When I found him there . . . unconscious and bound . . . I had my men carry him away. He will accompany me to China, there to stand before those whom he has wronged—the Keepers of the Secrets of the Ancient Ones from whom he stole the knowledge that he had misused. I may not take a life . . . but the Keepers of the Secrets will mete out to him the punishment that he deserves."

He paused and smiled. "A journey of a thousand miles begins

with but a single step," he said. "I have yet the first step of many to take . . . and so have you. Go now, the two of you, and take the first step in the journey of life together. And may the Source of All Light illuminate that journey."

He lifted his hand in blessing, then turned and strode toward the passageway down which his followers had vanished.

Gloom lay like a heavy fog in the living room of the Reynolds' lovely apartment the next night. The golden drapes were drawn and the amber-shaded lamps cast soft pools of friendly light on the deeply piled blue carpet and the linen-covered chairs. A tray stood invitingly on a little table with a silver cocktail shaker and two brimming untouched glasses.

Dale, slumped among the pillows of the sofa, tried to read, but his mind was fastened on Tara; on her sudden frigidity, since the affair with Chu-Sheng was ended, and he turned the pages of his magazine mechanically, the words a blurred mass before him. She had seemed warm and impulsive and altogether adorable when he told her that he loved her, he thought bitterly. And he, fool that he was, had flattered himself that she cared for him, although she had never said so in so many words. He thought then, it was only the danger of their situation that stopped her from yielding to him completely as her eyes had done. But it seemed her concern in his welfare—in his safety—was only a maternal one, a sort of protective instinct . . . She was evidently easing her own conscience by being kind to him, for a complete change had taken place in Tara's attitude. The warm, unrestrained friendliness had given place to a frigid formality which puzzled and hurt him. He decided he could hate her very much indeed if he did not love her so much. Altogether it was a most uncomfortable situation. Here he was, married to an animate icicle, who treated him as though he was some particularly nasty insect that had to be handled with tweezers for fear of getting warts.

Tara was seated at the grand piano picking out a lonely tune. Her black velvet gown made her neck and shoulders look like sculptured wax. Dale was keenly aware of her beauty, but it was strangely unconsoling.

Her thoughts, too, were far away, and her eyes were filled with tears. Hurt and bewildered by Dale's changed attitude, his stiff-lipped, almost insulting politeness, she stayed on, swallowing her pride, hoping against hope that he would reopen the subject so dear to her heart. He had said back there in Chu-Sheng's place that he loved her and she had believed him. But, neither by word or gesture, had he reaffirmed that statement. The fear was growing within her that he had said it only to comfort her . . . to make her feel that she had his complete support. Yes, that was it, undoubtedly. He didn't love her, really. He said what he did under stress of the moment. He had thrown out a lifeline for her to cling to and now that the need of that lifeline was over, he had withdrawn it. She was a fool to imagine that he could care for her. Why, he hardly knew her . . . or perhaps he knew her too well. He had witnessed too much of her powers . . . had seen a man die at her hands. She must seem terribly foreign to him. Perhaps even— uncanny. If she had only not allowed herself to love him. But then, she realized that love had taken possession of her without her knowledge. She was alone and quite heart-free, and then, suddenly, there was this stranger, and she loved him. That love made the stranger into someone quite dear and intimate, someone she might have known all her life, and many lives before.

The little tune ran sadly on under her faltering fingers. Painful self-consciousness made the room unbearable. In sudden determination Dale flung his book to the floor.

"Tara," he said abruptly.

The sad little tune broke into fragments. The girl turned, her eyes large and somber.

"Yes?"

His own eyes dropped before her searching gaze. He kept them fastened upon the floor. Ensued an awkward pause.

"Yes?" she said again, a little fear gripping her heart at his evident discomfiture.

"I . . . you . . . you're free now," he began slowly.

"Yes, I'm free now," she agreed dully.

He did not raise his eyes. His lips were drawn in a tight line. "So you can get that divorce any time now."

It had come. Panic seized her heart. Color flooded her face.

"I . . . I'll get it whenever you wish," she said in a small choked voice.

"Whenever *I* wish?" He looked up then—came over to her. Gently he raised her head until her brimming eyes, like violets in a rain, met his.

"Oh, my dear . . . are you doing what you think *I* wish?"

She nodded, unable to speak.

A great gladness shone in his eyes.

"Well," he said, his voice vibrant with emotion, "if you're going to do what *I* wish . . . then kiss me . . . my wife."

RAMBLE HOUSE'S

HARRY STEPHEN KEELER WEBWORK MYSTERIES

(RH) indicates the title is available ONLY in the RAMBLE HOUSE edition

The Ace of Spades Murder
The Affair of the Bottled Deuce (RH)
The Amazing Web
The Barking Clock
Behind That Mask
The Book with the Orange Leaves
The Bottle with the Green Wax Seal
The Box from Japan
The Case of the Canny Killer
The Case of the Crazy Corpse (RH)
The Case of the Flying Hands (RH)
The Case of the Ivory Arrow
The Case of the Jeweled Ragpicker
The Case of the Lavender Gripsack
The Case of the Mysterious Moll
The Case of the 16 Beans
The Case of the Transparent Nude (RH)
The Case of the Transposed Legs
The Case of the Two-Headed Idiot (RH)
The Case of the Two Strange Ladies
The Circus Stealers (RH)
Cleopatra's Tears
A Copy of Beowulf (RH)
The Crimson Cube (RH)
The Face of the Man From Saturn
Find the Clock
The Five Silver Buddhas
The 4th King
The Gallows Waits, My Lord! (RH)
The Green Jade Hand
Finger! Finger!
Hangman's Nights (RH)
I, Chameleon (RH)
I Killed Lincoln at 10:13! (RH)
The Iron Ring
The Man Who Changed His Skin (RH)
The Man with the Crimson Box
The Man with the Magic Eardrums
The Man with the Wooden Spectacles
The Marceau Case
The Matilda Hunter Murder

The Monocled Monster
The Murder of London Lew
The Murdered Mathematician
The Mysterious Card (RH)
The Mysterious Ivory Ball of Wong Shing Li (RH)
The Mystery of the Fiddling Cracksman
The Peacock Fan
The Photo of Lady X (RH)
The Portrait of Jirjohn Cobb
Report on Vanessa Hewstone (RH)
Riddle of the Travelling Skull
Riddle of the Wooden Parrakeet (RH)
The Scarlet Mummy (RH)
The Search for X-Y-Z
The Sharkskin Book
Sing Sing Nights
The Six From Nowhere (RH)
The Skull of the Waltzing Clown
The Spectacles of Mr. Cagliostro
Stand By—London Calling!
The Steeltown Strangler
The Stolen Gravestone (RH)
Strange Journey (RH)
The Strange Will
The Straw Hat Murders (RH)
The Street of 1000 Eyes (RH)
Thieves' Nights
Three Novellos (RH)
The Tiger Snake
The Trap (RH)
Vagabond Nights (Defrauded Yeggman)
Vagabond Nights 2 (10 Hours)
The Vanishing Gold Truck
The Voice of the Seven Sparrows
The Washington Square Enigma
When Thief Meets Thief
The White Circle (RH)
The Wonderful Scheme of Mr. Christopher Thorne
X. Jones—of Scotland Yard
Y. Cheung, Business Detective

Keeler Related Works

A To Izzard: A Harry Stephen Keeler Companion by Fender Tucker — Articles and stories about Harry, by Harry, and in his style. Included is a compleat bibliography.

Wild About Harry: Reviews of Keeler Novels — Edited by Richard Polt & Fender Tucker — 22 reviews of works by Harry Stephen Keeler from *Keeler News*. A perfect introduction to the author.

The Keeler Keyhole Collection: Annotated newsletter rants from Harry Stephen Keeler, edited by Francis M. Nevins. Over 400 pages of incredibly personal Keeleriana.

Fakealoo — Pastiches of the style of Harry Stephen Keeler by selected demented members of the HSK Society. Updated every year with the new winner.

Strands of the Web: Short Stories of Harry Stephen Keeler — 29 stories, just about all that Keeler wrote, are edited and introduced by Fred Cleaver.

RAMBLE HOUSE's LOON SANCTUARY

A Clear Path to Cross — Sharon Knowles short mystery stories by Ed Lynskey.

A Corpse Walks in Brooklyn and Other Stories — Volume 5 in the Day Keene in the Detective Pulps series.

A Jimmy Starr Omnibus — Three 40s novels by Jimmy Starr.

A Niche in Time and Other Stories — Classic SF by William F. Temple

A Roland Daniel Double: The Signal and The Return of Wu Fang — Classic thrillers from the 30s.

A Shot Rang Out — Three decades of reviews and articles by today's Anthony Boucher, Jon Breen. An essential book for any mystery lover's library.

A Smell of Smoke — A 1951 English countryside thriller by Miles Burton.

A Snark Selection — Lewis Carroll's *The Hunting of the Snark* with two Snarkian chapters by Harry Stephen Keeler — Illustrated by Gavin L. O'Keefe.

A Young Man's Heart — A forgotten early classic by Cornell Woolrich.

Alexander Laing Novels — *The Motives of Nicholas Holtz* and *Dr. Scarlett*, stories of medical mayhem and intrigue from the 30s.

An Angel in the Street — Modern hardboiled noir by Peter Genovese.

Automaton — Brilliant treatise on robotics: 1928-style! By H. Stafford Hatfield.

Away From the Here and Now — Clare Winger Harris stories, collected by Richard A. Lupoff

Beast or Man? — A 1930 novel of racism and horror by Sean M'Guire. Introduced by John Pelan.

Black Beadle — A 1939 thriller by E.C.R. Lorac.

Black Hogan Strikes Again — Australia's Peter Renwick pens a tale of the 30s outback.

Black River Falls — Suspense from the master, Ed Gorman.

Blondy's Boy Friend — A snappy 1930 story by Philip Wylie, writing as Leatrice Homesley.

Blood in a Snap — The *Finnegan's Wake* of the 21st century, by Jim Weiler.

Blood Moon — The first of the Robert Payne series by Ed Gorman.

Bogart '48 — Hollywood action with Bogie by John Stanley and Kenn Davis

Calling Lou Largo! — Two Lou Largo novels by William Ard.

Cornucopia of Crime — Francis M. Nevins assembled this huge collection of his writings about crime literature and the people who write it. Essential for any serious mystery library.

Corpse Without Flesh — Strange novel of forensics by George Bruce

Crimson Clown Novels — By Johnston McCulley, author of the Zorro novels, *The Crimson Clown* and *The Crimson Clown Again*.

Dago Red — 22 tales of dark suspense by Bill Pronzini.

Dark Sanctuary — Weird Menace story by H. B. Gregory

David Hume Novels — *Corpses Never Argue, Cemetery First Stop, Make Way for the Mourners, Eternity Here I Come*. 1930s British hardboiled fiction with an attitude.

Dead Man Talks Too Much — Hollywood boozer by Weed Dickenson.

Death Leaves No Card — One of the most unusual murdered-in-the-tub mysteries you'll ever read. By Miles Burton.

Death March of the Dancing Dolls and Other Stories — Volume Three in the Day Keene in the Detective Pulps series. Introduced by Bill Crider.

Deep Space and other Stories — A collection of SF gems by Richard A. Lupoff.

Detective Duff Unravels It — Episodic mysteries by Harvey O'Higgins.

Diabolic Candelabra — Classic 30s mystery by E.R. Punshon

Dictator's Way — Another D.S. Bobby Owen mystery from E.R. Punshon

Dime Novels: Ramble House's 10-Cent Books — *Knife in the Dark* by Robert Leslie Bellem, *Hot Lead* and *Song of Death* by Ed Earl Repp, *A Hashish House in New York* by H.H. Kane, and five more.

Doctor Arnoldi — Tiffany Thayer's story of the death of death.

Don Diablo: Book of a Lost Film — Two-volume treatment of a western by Paul Landres, with diagrams. Intro by Francis M. Nevins.

Dope and Swastikas — Two strange novels from 1922 by Edmund Snell

Dope Tales #1 — Two dope-riddled classics; *Dope Runners* by Gerald Grantham and *Death Takes the Joystick* by Phillip Condé.

Dope Tales #2 — Two more narco-classics; *The Invisible Hand* by Rex Dark and *The Smokers of Hashish* by Norman Berrow.

Dope Tales #3 — Two enchanting novels of opium by the master, Sax Rohmer. *Dope* and *The Yellow Claw.*

Double Hot — Two 60s softcore sex novels by Morris Hershman.

Double Sex — Yet two more panting thrillers from Morris Hershman.

Dr. Odin — Douglas Newton's 1933 racial potboiler comes back to life.

Evangelical Cockroach — Jack Woodford writes about writing.

Evidence in Blue — 1938 mystery by E. Charles Vivian.

Fatal Accident — Murder by automobile, a 1936 mystery by Cecil M. Wills.

Fighting Mad — Todd Robbins' 1922 novel about boxing and life

Finger-prints Never Lie — A 1939 classic detective novel by John G. Brandon.

Freaks and Fantasies — Eerie tales by Tod Robbins, collaborator of Tod Browning on the film FREAKS.

Gadsby — A lipogram (a novel without the letter E). Ernest Vincent Wright's last work, published in 1939 right before his death.

Gelett Burgess Novels — *The Master of Mysteries, The White Cat, Two O'Clock Courage, Ladies in Boxes, Find the Woman, The Heart Line, The Picaroons* and *Lady Mechante.* Recently added is A Gelett Burgess Sampler, edited by Alfred Jan. All are introduced by Richard A. Lupoff.

Geronimo — S. M. Barrett's 1905 autobiography of a noble American.

Hake Talbot Novels — *Rim of the Pit, The Hangman's Handyman.* Classic locked room mysteries, with mapback covers by Gavin O'Keefe.

Hands Out of Hell and Other Stories — John H. Knox's eerie hallucinations

Hell is a City — William Ard's masterpiece.

Hollywood Dreams — A novel of Tinsel Town and the Depression by Richard O'Brien.

Hostesses in Hell and Other Stories — Russell Gray's most graphic stories

House of the Restless Dead — Strange and ominous tales by Hugh B. Cave.

I Stole $16,000,000 — A true story by cracksman Herbert E. Wilson.

Inclination to Murder — 1966 thriller by New Zealand's Harriet Hunter.

Invaders from the Dark — Classic werewolf tale from Greye La Spina.

J. Poindexter, Colored — Classic satirical black novel by Irvin S. Cobb.

Jack Mann Novels — Strange murder in the English countryside. *Gees' First Case, Nightmare Farm, Grey Shapes, The Ninth Life, The Glass Too Many, Her Ways Are Death, The Kleinert Case* and *Maker of Shadows.*

Jake Hardy — A lusty western tale from Wesley Tallant.

Jim Harmon Double Novels — *Vixen Hollow/Celluloid Scandal, The Man Who Made Maniacs/Silent Siren, Ape Rape/Wanton Witch, Sex Burns Like Fire/Twist Session, Sudden Lust/Passion Strip, Sin Unlimited/Harlot Master, Twilight Girls/Sex Institution.* Written in the early 60s and never reprinted until now.

Joel Townsley Rogers Novels and Short Stories — By the author of *The Red Right Hand: Once In a Red Moon, Lady With the Dice, The Stopped Clock, Never Leave My Bed.* Also two short story collections: *Night of Horror* and *Killing Time.*

John Carstairs, Space Detective — Arboreal Sci-fi by Frank Belknap Long

Joseph Shallit Novels — *The Case of the Billion Dollar Body, Lady Don't Die on My Doorstep, Kiss the Killer, Yell Bloody Murder, Take Your Last Look.* One of America's best 50's authors and a favorite of author Bill Pronzini.

Keller Memento — 45 short stories of the amazing and weird by Dr. David Keller.

Killer's Caress — Cary Moran's 1936 hardboiled thriller.

Lady of the Yellow Death and Other Stories — More stories by Wyatt Blassingame.

League of the Grateful Dead and Other Stories — Volume One in the Day Keene in the Detective Pulps series.

Library of Death — Ghastly tale by Ronald S. L. Harding, introduced by John Pelan

Malcolm Jameson Novels and Short Stories — *Astonishing! Astounding!, Tarnished Bomb, The Alien Envoy and Other Stories* and *The Chariots of San Fernando and Other Stories.* All introduced and edited by John Pelan or Richard A. Lupoff.

Man Out of Hell and Other Stories — Volume II of the John H. Knox weird pulps collection.

Marblehead: A Novel of H.P. Lovecraft — A long-lost masterpiece from Richard A. Lupoff. This is the "director's cut", the long version that has never been published before.

Mark of the Laughing Death and Other Stories — Shockers from the pulps by Francis James, introduced by John Pelan.

Master of Souls — Mark Hansom's 1937 shocker is introduced by weirdologist John Pelan.

Max Afford Novels — *Owl of Darkness, Death's Mannikins, Blood on His Hands, The Dead Are Blind, The Sheep and the Wolves, Sinners in Paradise* and *Two Locked Room Mysteries and a Ripping Yarn* by one of Australia's finest mystery novelists.

Money Brawl — Two books about the writing business by Jack Woodford and H. Bedford-Jones. Introduced by Richard A. Lupoff.

More Secret Adventures of Sherlock Holmes — Gary Lovisi's second collection of tales about the unknown sides of the great detective.

Muddled Mind: Complete Works of Ed Wood, Jr. — David Hayes and Hayden Davis deconstruct the life and works of the mad, but canny, genius.

Murder among the Nudists — A mystery from 1934 by Peter Hunt, featuring a naked Detective-Inspector going undercover in a nudist colony.

Murder in Black and White — 1931 classic tennis whodunit by Evelyn Elder.

Murder in Shawnee — Two novels of the Alleghenies by John Douglas: *Shawnee Alley Fire* and *Haunts*.

Murder in Silk — A 1937 Yellow Peril novel of the silk trade by Ralph Trevor.

My Deadly Angel — 1955 Cold War drama by John Chelton.

My First Time: The One Experience You Never Forget — Michael Birchwood — 64 true first-person narratives of how they lost it.

Mysterious Martin, the Master of Murder — Two versions of a strange 1912 novel by Tod Robbins about a man who writes books that can kill.

Norman Berrow Novels — *The Bishop's Sword, Ghost House, Don't Go Out After Dark, Claws of the Cougar, The Smokers of Hashish, The Secret Dancer, Don't Jump Mr. Boland!, The Footprints of Satan, Fingers for Ransom, The Three Tiers of Fantasy, The Spaniard's Thumb, The Eleventh Plague, Words Have Wings, One Thrilling Night, The Lady's in Danger, It Howls at Night, The Terror in the Fog, Oil Under the Window, Murder in the Melody, The Singing Room.* This is the complete Norman Berrow library of locked-room mysteries, several of which are masterpieces.

Old Faithful and Other Stories — SF classic tales by Raymond Z. Gallun

Old Times' Sake — Short stories by James Reasoner from Mike Shayne Magazine.

One Dreadful Night — A classic mystery by Ronald S. L. Harding

Pair O' Jacks — A mystery novel and a diatribe about publishing by Jack Woodford

Perfect .38 — Two early Timothy Dane novels by William Ard. More to come.

Prince Pax — Devilish intrigue by George Sylvester Viereck and Philip Eldridge

Prose Bowl — Futuristic satire of a world where hack writing has replaced football as our national obsession, by Bill Pronzini and Barry N. Malzberg.

Red Light — The history of legal prostitution in Shreveport Louisiana by Eric Brock. Includes wonderful photos of the houses and the ladies.

Researching American-Made Toy Soldiers — A 276-page collection of a lifetime of articles by toy soldier expert Richard O'Brien.

Reunion in Hell — Volume One of the John H. Knox series of weird stories from the pulps. Introduced by horror expert John Pelan.

Ripped from the Headlines! — The Jack the Ripper story as told in the newspaper articles in the *New York* and *London Times.*

Rough Cut & New, Improved Murder — Ed Gorman's first two novels.

R.R. Ryan Novels — Freak Museum and The Subjugated Beast, two horror classics.

Ruby of a Thousand Dreams — The villain Wu Fang returns in this Roland Daniel novel.

Ruled By Radio — 1925 futuristic novel by Robert L. Hadfield & Frank E. Farncombe.

Rupert Penny Novels — *Policeman's Holiday, Policeman's Evidence, Lucky Policeman, Policeman in Armour, Sealed Room Murder, Sweet Poison, The Talkative Policeman, She had to Have Gas* and *Cut and Run* (by Martin Tanner.) Rupert Penny is the pseudonym of Australian Charles Thornett, a master of the locked room, impossible crime plot.

Sacred Locomotive Flies — Richard A. Lupoff's psychedelic SF story.

Sam — Early gay novel by Lonnie Coleman.

Sand's Game — Spectacular hard-boiled noir from Ennis Willie, edited by Lynn Myers and Stephen Mertz, with contributions from Max Allan Collins, Bill Crider, Wayne Dundee, Bill Pronzini, Gary Lovisi and James Reasoner.

Sand's War — More violent fiction from the typewriter of Ennis Willie

Satan's Den Exposed — True crime in Truth or Consequences New Mexico — Award-winning journalism by the *Desert Journal*.

Satans of Saturn — Novellas from the pulps by Otis Adelbert Kline and E. H. Price

Satan's Sin House and Other Stories — Horrific gore by Wayne Rogers

Secrets of a Teenage Superhero — Graphic lit by Jonathan Sweet

Sex Slave — Potboiler of lust in the days of Cleopatra by Dion Leclerq, 1966.

Sideslip — 1968 SF masterpiece by Ted White and Dave Van Arnam.

Slammer Days — Two full-length prison memoirs: *Men into Beasts* (1952) by George Sylvester Viereck and *Home Away From Home* (1962) by Jack Woodford.

Slippery Staircase — 1930s whodunit from E.C.R. Lorac

Sorcerer's Chessmen — John Pelan introduces this 1939 classic by Mark Hansom.

Star Griffin — Michael Kurland's 1987 masterpiece of SF drollery is back.

Stakeout on Millennium Drive — Award-winning Indianapolis Noir by Ian Woollen.

Strands of the Web: Short Stories of Harry Stephen Keeler — Edited and Introduced by Fred Cleaver.

Summer Camp for Corpses and Other Stories — Weird Menace tales from Arthur Leo Zagat; introduced by John Pelan.

Suzy — A collection of comic strips by Richard O'Brien and Bob Vojtko from 1970.

Tales of the Macabre and Ordinary — Modern twisted horror by Chris Mikul, author of the *Bizarrism* series.

Tales of Terror and Torment #1 — John Pelan selects and introduces this sampler of weird menace tales from the pulps.

Tenebrae — Ernest G. Henham's 1898 horror tale brought back.

The Amorous Intrigues & Adventures of Aaron Burr — by Anonymous. Hot historical action about the man who almost became Emperor of Mexico.

The Anthony Boucher Chronicles — edited by Francis M. Nevins. Book reviews by Anthony Boucher written for the *San Francisco Chronicle*, 1942 – 1947. Essential and fascinating reading by the best book reviewer there ever was.

The Barclay Catalogs — Two essential books about toy soldier collecting by Richard O'Brien

The Basil Wells Omnibus — A collection of Wells' stories by Richard A. Lupoff.

The Beautiful Dead and Other Stories — Dreadful tales from Donald Dale

The Best of 10-Story Book — edited by Chris Mikul, over 35 stories from the literary magazine Harry Stephen Keeler edited.

The Black Dark Murders — Vintage 50s college murder yarn by Milt Ozaki, writing as Robert O. Saber.

The Book of Time — The classic novel by H.G. Wells is joined by sequels by Wells himself and three stories by Richard A. Lupoff. Illustrated by Gavin L. O'Keefe.

The Case in the Clinic — One of E.C.R. Lorac's finest.

The Strange Case of the Antlered Man — A mystery of superstition by Edwy Searles Brooks.

The Case of the Bearded Bride — #4 in the Day Keene in the Detective Pulps series

The Case of the Little Green Men — Mack Reynolds wrote this love song to sci-fi fans back in 1951 and it's now back in print.

The Case of the Withered Hand — 1936 potboiler by John G. Brandon.

The Charlie Chaplin Murder Mystery — A 2004 tribute by noted film scholar, Wes D. Gehring.

The Chinese Jar Mystery — Murder in the manor by John Stephen Strange, 1934.

The Cloudbuilders and Other Stories — SF tales from Colin Kapp.

The Compleat Calhoon — All of Fender Tucker's works: Includes *Totah Six-Pack, Weed, Women and Song* and *Tales from the Tower*, plus a CD of all of his songs.

The Compleat Ova Hamlet — Parodies of SF authors by Richard A. Lupoff. This is a brand new edition with more stories and more illustrations by Trina Robbins.

The Contested Earth and Other SF Stories — A never-before published space opera and seven short stories by Jim Harmon.

The Singular Problem of the Stygian House-Boat — Two classic tales by John Kendrick Bangs about the denizens of Hades.

The Smiling Corpse — Philip Wylie and Bernard Bergman's odd 1935 novel.

The Spider: Satan's Murder Machines — A thesis about Iron Man

The Stench of Death: An Odoriferous Omnibus by Jack Moskovitz — Two complete novels and two novellas from 60's sleaze author, Jack Moskovitz.

The Story Writer and Other Stories — Classic SF from Richard Wilson

The Strange Case of the Antlered Man — 1935 dementia from Edwy Searles Brooks

The Strange Thirteen — Richard B. Gamon's odd stories about Raj India.

The Technique of the Mystery Story — Carolyn Wells' tips about writing.

The Threat of Nostalgia — A collection of his most obscure stories by Jon Breen

The Time Armada — Fox B. Holden's 1953 SF gem.

The Tongueless Horror and Other Stories — Volume One of the series of short stories from the weird pulps by Wyatt Blassingame.

The Town from Planet Five — From Richard Wilson, two SF classics, *And Then the Town Took Off* and *The Girls from Planet 5*

The Tracer of Lost Persons — From 1906, an episodic novel that became a hit radio series in the 30s. Introduced by Richard A. Lupoff.

The Trail of the Cloven Hoof — Diabolical horror from 1935 by Arlton Eadie. Introduced by John Pelan.

The Triune Man — Mindscrambling science fiction from Richard A. Lupoff.

The Unholy Goddess and Other Stories — Wyatt Blassingame's first DTP compilation

The Universal Holmes — Richard A. Lupoff's 2007 collection of five Holmesian pastiches and a recipe for giant rat stew.

The Werewolf vs the Vampire Woman — Hard to believe ultraviolence by either Arthur M. Scarm or Arthur M. Scram.

The Whistling Ancestors — A 1936 classic of weirdness by Richard E. Goddard and introduced by John Pelan.

The White Owl — A vintage thriller from Edmund Snell

The White Peril in the Far East — Sidney Lewis Gulick's 1905 indictment of the West and assurance that Japan would never attack the U.S.

The Wizard of Berner's Abbey — A 1935 horror gem written by Mark Hansom and introduced by John Pelan.

The Wonderful Wizard of Oz — by L. Frank Baum and illustrated by Gavin L. O'Keefe

Through the Looking Glass — Lewis Carroll wrote it; Gavin L. O'Keefe illustrated it.

Time Line — Ramble House artist Gavin O'Keefe selects his most evocative art inspired by the twisted literature he reads and designs.

Tiresias — Psychotic modern horror novel by Jonathan M. Sweet.

Tortures and Towers — Two novellas of terror by Dexter Dayle.

Totah Six-Pack — Fender Tucker's six tales about Farmington in one sleek volume.

Tree of Life, Book of Death — Grania Davis' book of her life.

Triple Quest — An arty mystery from the 30s by E.R. Punshon.

Trail of the Spirit Warrior — Roger Haley's saga of life in the Indian Territories.

Two Kinds of Bad — Two 50s novels by William Ard about Danny Fontaine

Two Suns of Morcali and Other Stories — Evelyn E. Smith's SF tour-de-force

Ultra-Boiled — 23 gut-wrenching tales by our Man in Brooklyn, Gary Lovisi.

Up Front From Behind — A 2011 satire of Wall Street by James B. Kobak.

Victims & Villains — Intriguing Sherlockiana from Derham Groves.

Wade Wright Novels — *Echo of Fear, Death At Nostalgia Street, It Leads to Murder* and *Shadows' Edge*, a double book featuring *Shadows Don't Bleed* and *The Sharp Edge*.

Walter S. Masterman Novels — *The Green Toad, The Flying Beast, The Yellow Mistletoe, The Wrong Verdict, The Perjured Alibi, The Border Line, The Bloodhounds Bay, The Curse of Cantire* and *The Baddington Horror*. Masterman wrote horror and mystery, some introduced by John Pelan.

We Are the Dead and Other Stories — Volume Two in the Day Keene in the Detective Pulps series, introduced by Ed Gorman. When done, there may be 11 in the series.

Welsh Rarebit Tales — Charming stories from 1902 by Harle Oren Cummins

West Texas War and Other Western Stories — by Gary Lovisi.

What If? Volume 1, 2 and 3 — Richard A. Lupoff introduces three decades worth of SF short stories that should have won a Hugo, but didn't.

When the Batman Thirsts and Other Stories — Weird tales from Frederick C. Davis.

Whip Dodge: Man Hunter — Wesley Tallant's saga of a bounty hunter of the old West.

Win, Place and Die! — The first new mystery by Milt Ozaki in decades. The ultimate novel of 70s Reno.

Writer 1 and 2 — A magnus opus from Richard A. Lupoff summing up his life as writer.

You'll Die Laughing — Bruce Elliott's 1945 novel of murder at a practical joker's English countryside manor.

RAMBLE HOUSE

Fender Tucker, Prop.   Gavin L. O'Keefe, Graphics

www.ramblehouse.com   fender@ramblehouse.com

228-826-1783   10329 Sheephead Drive, Vancleave MS 39565